The Betrothed

C000247149

Walter Scott

CHAPTER THE FIRST.

Now in these days were hotte wars upon the Marches of Wales.
LEWIS'S *History.*

The Chronicles, from which this narrative is extracted, assure us, that during the long period when the Welsh princes maintained their independence, the year 1187 was peculiarly marked as favourable to peace betwixt them and their warlike neighbours, the Lords Marchers, who inhabited those formidable castles on the frontiers of the ancient British, on the ruins of which the traveller gazes with wonder. This was the time when Baldwin, Archbishop of Canterbury, accompanied by the learned Giraldus de Barri, afterwards Bishop of Saint David's, preached the Crusade from castle to castle, from town to town; awakened the inmost valleys of his native Cambria with the call to arms for recovery of the Holy Sepulchre; and, while he deprecated the feuds and wars of Christian men against each other, held out to the martial spirit of the age a general object of ambition, and a scene of adventure, where the favour of Heaven, as well as earthy renown, was to reward the successful champions.

Yet the British chieftains, among the thousands whom this spirit- stirring summons called from their native land to a distant and perilous expedition, had perhaps the best excuse for declining the summons. The superior skill of the Anglo-Norman knights, who were engaged in constant inroads on the Welsh frontier, and who were frequently detaching from it large portions, which they fortified with castles, thus making good what they had won, was avenged, indeed, but not compensated, by the furious inroads of the British, who, like the billows of a retiring tide, rolled on successively, with noise, fury, and devastation; but, on each retreat, yielded ground insensibly to their invaders.

A union among the native princes might have opposed a strong and permanent barrier to the encroachments of the strangers; but they were, unhappily, as much at discord among themselves as they were with the Normans, and were constantly engaged in private war with each other, of which the common enemy had the sole advantage.

The invitation to the Crusade promised something at least of novelty to a nation peculiarly ardent in their temper; and it was accepted by many, regardless of the consequences which must ensue, to the country which they left defenceless. Even the most celebrated enemies of the Saxon and Norman race laid aside their enmity against the invaders of their country, to enrol themselves under the banners of the Crusade.

Amongst these was reckoned Gwenwyn, (or more properly Gwenwynwen, though we retain the briefer appellative,) a British prince who continued exercising a precarious sovereignty over such parts of Powys-Land as had not been subjugated by the Mortimers, Guarines, Latimers, FitzAlans, and other Norman nobles, who, under various pretexts, and sometimes contemning all other save the open avowal of superior force, had severed and appropriated large portions of that once extensive and independent principality, which, when Wales was unhappily divided into three parts on the death of Roderick Mawr, fell to the lot of his youngest son, Mervyn. The undaunted resolution and stubborn ferocity of Gwenwyn, descendant of that prince, had long made him beloved among the "Tall men" or Champions of Wales; and he was enabled, more by the number of those who served under him, attracted by his reputation, than by the natural strength of his dilapidated principality, to retaliate the encroachments of the English by the most wasteful inroads.

Yet even Gwenwyn on the present occasion seemed to forget his deeply sworn hatred against his dangerous neighbours. The Torch of Pengwern (for so Gwenwyn was called, from his frequently laying the province of Shrewsbury in conflagration) seemed at present to burn as calmly as a taper in the bower of a lady; and the Wolf of Plinlimmon, another name with which the bards had graced Gwenwyn, now slumbered as peacefully as the shepherd's dog on the domestic hearth.

But it was not alone the eloquence of Baldwin or of Girald which had lulled into peace a spirit so restless and fierce. It is true, their exhortations had done more towards it than Gwenwyn's followers had thought possible. The Archbishop had induced the British Chief to break bread, and to mingle in silvan sports, with his nearest, and hitherto one of his most determined enemies, the old Norman warrior Sir Raymond Berenger, who, sometimes beaten, sometimes victorious, but never subdued, had, in spite of Gwenwyn's hottest incursions, maintained his Castle of Garde Doloureuse, upon the marches of Wales; a place strong by nature, and well fortified by art, which the Welsh prince had found it impossible to conquer, either by open force or by stratagem, and which, remaining with a strong garrison in his rear, often checked his incursions, by rendering his retreat precarious. On this account, Gwenwyn of Powys-Land had an hundred times vowed the death of Raymond Berenger, and the demolition of his castle; but the policy of the sagacious old warrior, and his long experience in all warlike practice, were such as, with the aid of his more powerful countrymen, enabled him to defy the attempts of his fiery neighbour. If there was a man, therefore, throughout England, whom Gwenwyn hated more than another, it was Raymond Berenger; and yet the good Archbishop Baldwin could prevail on the Welsh prince to meet him as a friend and ally in the cause of the Cross. He even invited Raymond to the autumn festivities of his Welsh palace, where the old knight, in all honourable courtesy, feasted and hunted for more than a week in the dominions of his hereditary foe.

To requite this hospitality, Raymond invited the Prince of Powys, with a chosen but limited train, during the ensuing Christmas, to the Garde Doloureuse, which some antiquaries have endeavoured to identify with the Castle of Colune, on the river of the same name. But the length of time, and some geographical difficulties, throw doubts upon this ingenious conjecture.

As the Welshman crossed the drawbridge, he was observed by his faithful bard to shudder with involuntary emotion; nor did Cadwallon, experienced as he was in life, and well acquainted with the character of his master, make any doubt that he was at that moment strongly urged by the apparent opportunity, to seize upon the strong fortress which had been so long the object of his cupidity, even at the expense of violating his good faith.

Dreading lest the struggle of his master's conscience and his ambition should terminate unfavourably for his fame, the bard arrested his attention by whispering in their native language, that "the teeth which bite hardest are those which are out of sight;" and Gwenwyn looking around him, became aware that, though, only unarmed squires and pages appeared in the courtyard, yet the towers and battlements connecting them were garnished with archers and men-at-arms.

They proceeded to the banquet, at which Gwenwyn, for the first time, beheld Eveline Berenger, the sole child of the Norman castellane, the inheritor of his domains and of his supposed wealth, aged only sixteen, and the most beautiful damsel upon the Welsh marches. Many a spear had already been shivered in maintenance of her charms; and the gallant Hugo de Lacy, Constable of Chester, one of the most redoubted warriors of the time, had laid at Eveline's feet the prize which his chivalry had gained in a great tournament held near that ancient town. Gwenwyn considered these triumphs as so many additional recommendations to Eveline; her beauty was incontestable, and she was heiress of the fortress which he so much longed to possess, and which he began now to think might be acquired by means more smooth than those with which he was in the use of working out his will.

Again, the hatred which subsisted between the British and their Saxon and Norman invaders; his long and ill-extinguished feud with this very Raymond Berenger; a general recollection that alliances between the Welsh and English had rarely been happy; and a consciousness that the measure which he meditated would be unpopular among his followers, and appear a dereliction of the systematic principles on which he had hitherto acted, restrained him from speaking his wishes to Raymond or his daughter. The idea of the rejection of his suit did not for a moment occur to him; he was convinced he had but to speak his wishes, and that the daughter of a Norman, castellane, whose rank or power were not of the highest order among the nobles of the frontiers, must be delighted and honoured by a proposal for allying his family with that of the sovereign of a hundred mountains.

There was indeed another objection, which in later times would have been of considerable weight—Gwenwyn was already married. But Brengwain was a childless bride; sovereigns (and among sovereigns the Welsh prince ranked himself) marry for lineage, and the Pope was not likely to be scrupulous, where the question was to oblige a prince who had assumed the Cross with such ready zeal, even although, in fact, his thoughts had been much more on the Garde Doloureuse than on Jerusalem. In the meanwhile, if Raymond Berenger (as was suspected) was not liberal enough in his opinions to permit Eveline to hold the temporary rank of concubine, which the manners of Wales warranted Gwenwyn to offer as an interim, arrangement, he had only to wait for a few months, and sue for a divorce through the Bishop of Saint David's, or some other intercessor at the Court of Rome.

Agitating these thoughts in his mind, Gwenwyn prolonged his residence at the Castle of Berenger, from Christmas till Twelfthday; and endured the presence of the Norman cavaliers who resorted to Raymond's festal halls, although, regarding themselves, in virtue of their rank of knighthood, equal to the most potent sovereigns, they made small account of the long descent of the Welsh prince, who, in their eyes, was but the chief of a semibarbarous province; while he, on his part, considered them little better than a sort of privileged robbers, and with the utmost difficulty restrained himself from manifesting his open hatred, when he beheld them careering in the exercises of chivalry, the habitual use of which rendered them such formidable enemies to his country. At length, the term of feasting was ended, and knight and squire departed from the castle, which once more assumed the aspect of a solitary and guarded frontier fort.

But the Prince of Powys-Land, while pursuing his sports on his own mountains and valleys, found that even the abundance of the game, as well as his release from the society of the Norman chivalry, who affected to treat him as an equal, profited him nothing so long as the light and beautiful form of Eveline, on her white palfrey, was banished from the train of sportsmen. In short, he hesitated no longer, but took into his confidence his chaplain, an able and sagacious man, whose pride was flattered by his patron's communication, and who, besides, saw in the proposed scheme some contingent advantages for himself and his order. By his counsel, the proceedings for Gwenwyn's divorce were prosecuted under favourable auspices, and the unfortunate Brengwain was removed to a nunnery, which perhaps she found a more cheerful habitation than the lonely retreat in which she had led a neglected life, ever since Gwenwyn had despaired of her bed being blessed with issue. Father Einion also dealt with the chiefs and elders of the land, and represented to them the advantage which in future wars they were certain to obtain by the possession of the Garde Doloureuse, which had for more than a century covered and protected a considerable tract of country, rendered their advance difficult, and their retreat perilous, and, in a word, prevented their carrying their incursions as far as the gates of Shrewsbury. As for the union with the Saxon damsel, the fetters which it was to form might not (the good father hinted) be found more permanent than those which had bound Gwenwyn to her predecessor, Brengwain.

These arguments, mingled with others adapted to the views and wishes of different individuals, were so prevailing, that the chaplain in the course of a few weeks was able to report to his princely patron, that this proposed match would meet with no opposition from the elders and nobles of his dominions. A golden bracelet, six ounces in weight, was the instant reward of the priest's dexterity in negotiation, and he was appointed by Gwenwyn to commit to paper those proposals, which he doubted not were to throw the Castle of Garde Doloureuse, notwithstanding its melancholy name, into an ecstasy of joy. With some difficulty the chaplain prevailed on his patron to say nothing in this letter upon his temporary plan of concubinage, which he wisely judged might be considered as an affront both by Eveline and her father. The matter of the divorce he represented as almost entirely settled, and wound up his letter with a moral application, in which were many allusions to Vashti, Esther, and Ahasuerus.

Having despatched this letter by a swift and trusty messenger, the British prince opened in all solemnity the feast of Easter, which had come round during the course of these external and internal negotiations.

Upon the approaching Holy-tide, to propitiate the minds of his subjects and vassals, they were invited in large numbers to partake of a princely festivity at Castell-Coch, or the Red- Castle, as it was then called, since better known by the name of Powys-Castle, and in latter times the princely seat of the Duke of Beaufort. The architectural magnificence of this noble residence is of a much later period than that of Gwenwyn, whose palace, at the time we speak of, was a low, long-roofed edifice of red stone, whence the castle derived its name; while a ditch and palisade were, in addition to the commanding situation, its most important defences.

CHAPTER THE SECOND

In Madoc's tent the clarion sounds,
With rapid clangor hurried far;
Each hill and dale the note rebounds,
But when return the sons of war?
Thou, born of stern Necessity,
Dull Peace! the valley yields to thee,
And owns thy melancholy sway.
 WELSH POEM.

The feasts of the ancient British princes usually exhibited all the rude splendour and liberal indulgence of mountain hospitality, and Gwenwyn was, on the present occasion, anxious to purchase popularity by even an unusual display of profusion; for he was sensible that the alliance which he meditated might indeed be tolerated, but could not be approved, by his subjects and followers.

The following incident, trifling in itself, confirmed his apprehensions. Passing one evening, when it was become nearly dark, by the open window of a guard-room, usually occupied by some few of his most celebrated soldiers, who relieved each other in watching his palace, he heard Morgan, a man distinguished for strength, courage, and ferocity, say to the companion with whom he was sitting by the watch-fire, "Gwenwyn is turned to a priest, or a woman! When was it before these last months, that a follower of his was obliged to gnaw the meat from the bone so closely, as I am now peeling the morsel which I hold in my hand?"

"Wait but awhile," replied his comrade, "till the Norman match be accomplished; and so small will be the prey we shall then drive from the Saxon churls, that we may be glad to swallow, like hungry dogs, the very bones themselves."

Gwenwyn heard no more of their conversation; but this was enough to alarm his pride as a soldier, and his jealousy as a prince. He was sensible, that the people over whom he ruled were at once fickle in their disposition, impatient of long repose, and full of hatred against their neighbours; and he almost dreaded the consequences of the inactivity to which a long truce might reduce them. The risk was now incurred, however; and to display even more than his wonted splendour and liberality, seemed the best way of reconciling the wavering affections of his subjects.

A Norman would have despised the barbarous magnificence of an entertainment, consisting of kine and sheep roasted whole, of goat's flesh and deer's flesh seethed in the skins of the animals themselves; for the Normans piqued themselves on the quality rather than the quantity of their food, and, eating rather delicately than largely, ridiculed the coarser taste of the Britons, although the last were in their banquets much more moderate than were the Saxons; nor would the oceans of *Crw* and hydromel, which overwhelmed the guests like a deluge, have made up, in their opinion, for the absence of the more elegant and costly beverage which they had learnt to love in the south of Europe. Milk, prepared in various ways, was another material of the British entertainment, which would not have received their approbation, although a nutriment which, on ordinary occasions, often supplied the Avant of all others among the ancient inhabitants, whose country was rich in flocks and herds, but poor in agricultural produce.

The banquet was spread in a long low hall, built of rough wood lined with shingles, having a fire at each end, the smoke of which, unable to find its way through the imperfect chimneys in the roof, rolled in cloudy billows above the heads of the revellers, who sat on low seats, purposely to avoid its stifling fumes. The mien and appearance of the company assembled was wild, and, even in their social hours, almost terrific. Their prince himself had the gigantic port and fiery eye fitted to sway an unruly people, whose delight was in the field of battle; and the long mustaches which he and most of his champions wore, added to the formidable dignity of his presence. Like most of those present, Gwenwyn was clad in a simple tunic of white linen cloth, a remnant of the dress which the Romans had introduced into provincial Britain; and he was distinguished by the Eudorchawg, or chain of twisted gold links, with which the Celtic tribes always decorated their chiefs. The collar, indeed, representing in form the species of links made by children out of rushes, was common to chieftains of inferior rank, many of whom bore it in virtue of their birth, or had won it by military exploits; but a ring of gold, bent around the head, intermingled with Gwenwyn's hair—for he claimed the rank of one of three diademed princes of Wales, and his armlets and anklets, of the same metal, were peculiar to the Prince of Powys, as an independent sovereign. Two squires of his body, who dedicated their whole attention to his service, stood at the Prince's back; and at his feet sat a page, whose duty it was to keep them warm by chafing and by wrapping them in his mantle. The same right of sovereignty, which assigned to Gwenwyn his golden crownlet, gave him a title to the attendance of the foot-bearer, or youth, who lay on the rushes, and whose duty it was to cherish the Prince's feet in his lap or bosom.

Notwithstanding the military disposition of the guests, and the danger arising from the feuds into which they were divided, few of the feasters wore any defensive armour, except the light goat-skin buckler, which hung behind each man's seat. On the other hand, they were well provided with offensive weapons; for the broad, sharp, short, two-edged sword was another legacy of the Romans. Most added a wood-knife or poniard; and there were store of javelins, darts, bows, and arrows, pikes, halberds, Danish axes, and Welsh hooks and bills; so, in case of ill-blood arising during the banquet, there was no lack of weapons to work mischief.

But although the form of the feast was somewhat disorderly, and that the revellers were unrestrained by the stricter rules of good-breeding which the laws of chivalry imposed, the Easter banquet of Gwenwyn possessed, in the attendance of twelve eminent bards, one source of the most exalted pleasure, in a much higher degree than the proud Normans could themselves boast. The latter, it is true, had their minstrels, a race of men trained to the profession of poetry, song, and music; but although those arts were highly honoured, and the individual professors, when they attained to eminence, were often richly rewarded, and treated with distinction, the order of minstrels, as such, was held in low esteem, being composed chiefly of worthless and dissolute strollers, by whom the art was assumed, in order to escape from the necessity of labour, and to have the means of pursuing a wandering and dissipated course of life. Such, in all times, has been the censure upon the calling of those who dedicate themselves to the public amusement; among whom those distinguished by individual excellence are sometimes raised high in the social circle, while far the more numerous professors, who only reach mediocrity, are sunk into the lower scale. But such was not the case with the order of bards in Wales, who, succeeding to the dignity of the Druids, under whom they had originally formed a subordinate fraternity, had many immunities, were held in the highest reverence and esteem, and exercised much influence with their countrymen. Their power over the public mind even rivalled that of the priests themselves, to whom indeed they bore some resemblance; for they never wore arms, were initiated into their order by secret and mystic solemnities, and homage was rendered to their *Awen*, or flow of poetic inspiration, as if it had been indeed marked with a divine character. Thus possessed of power and consequence, the bards were not unwilling to exercise their privileges, and sometimes, in doing so, their manners frequently savoured of caprice.

This was perhaps the case with Cadwallon, the chief bard of Gwenwyn, and who, as such, was expected to have poured forth the tide of song in the banqueting-hall of his prince. But neither the anxious and breathless expectation of the assembled chiefs and champions—neither the dead silence which stilled the roaring hall, when his harp was reverently placed before him by his attendant—nor even the commands or entreaties of the Prince himself —could extract from Cadwallon more than a short and interrupted prelude upon the instrument, the notes of which arranged themselves into an air inexpressibly mournful, and died away in silence. The Prince frowned darkly on the bard, who was himself far too deeply lost in gloomy thought, to offer any apology, or even to observe his displeasure. Again he touched a few wild notes, and, raising his looks upward, seemed to be on the very point of bursting forth into a tide of song similar to those with which this master of his art was wont to enchant his hearers. But the effort was in vain—he declared that his right hand was withered, and pushed the instrument from him.

A murmur went round the company, and Gwenwyn read in their aspects that they received the unusual silence of Cadwallon on this high occasion as a bad omen. He called hastily on a young and ambitious bard, named Caradoc of Menwygent, whose rising fame was likely soon to vie with the established reputation of Cadwallon, and summoned him to sing something which might command the applause of his sovereign and the gratitude of the company. The young man was ambitious, and understood the arts of a courtier. He commenced a poem, in which, although under a feigned name, he drew such a poetic picture of Eveline Berenger, that Gwenwyn was enraptured; and while all who had seen the beautiful original at once recognized the resemblance, the eyes of the Prince confessed at once his passion for the subject, and his admiration of the poet. The figures of Celtic poetry, in themselves highly imaginative, were scarce sufficient for the enthusiasm of the ambitious bard, rising in his tone as he perceived the feelings which he was exciting. The praises of the Prince mingled with those of the Norman beauty; and "as a lion," said the poet, "can only be led by the hand of a chaste and beautiful maiden, so a chief can only acknowledge the empire of the most virtuous, the most lovely of her sex. Who asks of the noonday sun, in what quarter of the world he was born? and who shall ask of such charms as hers, to what country they owe their birth?"

Enthusiasts in pleasure as in war, and possessed of imaginations which answered readily to the summons of their poets, the Welsh chiefs and leaders united in acclamations of applause; and the song of the bard went farther to render popular the intended alliance of the Prince, than had all the graver arguments of his priestly precursor in the same topic.

Gwenwyn himself, in a transport of delight, tore off the golden bracelets which he wore, to bestow them upon a bard whose song had produced an effect so desirable; and said, as he looked at the silent and sullen Cadwallon, "The silent harp was never strung with golden wires."

"Prince," answered the bard, whose pride was at least equal to that of Gwenwyn himself, "you pervert the proverb of Taliessin—it is the flattering harp which never lacked golden strings."

Gwenwyn, turning sternly towards him, was about to make an angry answer, when the sudden appearance of Jorworth, the messenger whom he had despatched to Raymond Berenger, arrested his purpose. This rude envoy entered the hall bare-legged, excepting the sandals of goat-skin which he wore, and having on his shoulder a cloak of the same, and a short javelin in his hand. The dust on his garments, and the flush on his brow, showed with what hasty zeal his errand had been executed. Gwenwyn demanded of him eagerly, "What news from Garde Doloureuse, Jorworth ap Jevan?"

"I bear them in my bosom," said the son of Jevan; and, with much reverence, he delivered to the Prince a packet, bound with silk, and sealed with the impression of a swan, the ancient cognizance of the House of Berenger. Himself ignorant of writing or reading, Gwenwyn, in anxious haste, delivered the letter to Cadwallon, who usually acted as secretary when the chaplain was not in presence, as chanced then to be the case. Cadwallon, looking at the letter, said briefly, "I read no Latin. Ill betide the Norman, who writes to a Prince of Powys in other language than that of Britain! and well was the hour, when that noble tongue alone was spoken from Tintadgel to Cairleoil!"

Gwenwyn only replied to him with an angry glance.

"Where is Father Einion?" said the impatient Prince.

"He assists in the church," replied one of his attendants, "for it is the feast of Saint—"

"Were it the feast of Saint David," said Gwenwyn, "and were the pyx between his hands, he must come hither to me instantly!"

One of the chief henchmen sprung off, to command his attendance, and, in the meantime, Gwenwyn eyed the letter containing the secret of his fate, but which it required an interpreter to read, with such eagerness and anxiety, that Caradoc, elated by his former success, threw in a few notes to divert, if possible, the tenor of his patron's thoughts during the interval. A light and lively air, touched by a hand which seemed to hesitate, like the submissive voice of an inferior, fearing to interrupt his master's meditations, introduced a stanza or two applicable to the subject.

"And what though thou, O scroll," he said, apostrophizing the letter, which lay on the table before his master, "dost speak with the tongue of the stranger? Hath not the cuckoo a harsh note, and yet she tells us of green buds and springing flowers? What if thy language be that of the stoled priest, is it not the same which binds hearts and hands together at the altar? And what though thou delayest to render up thy treasures, are not all pleasures most sweet, when enhanced by expectation? What were the chase, if the deer dropped at our feet the instant he started from the cover—or what value were there in the love of the maiden, were it yielded without coy delay?"

The song of the bard was here broken short by the entrance of the priest, who, hasty in obeying the summons of his impatient master, had not tarried to lay aside even the stole, which he had worn in the holy service; and many of the elders thought it was no good omen, that, so habited, a priest should appear in a festive assembly, and amid profane minstrelsy.

The priest opened the letter of the Norman Baron, and, struck with surprise at the contents, lifted his eyes in silence.

"Read it!" exclaimed the fierce Gwenwyn.

"So please you," replied the more prudent chaplain, "a smaller company were a fitter audience."

"Read it aloud!" repeated the Prince, in a still higher tone; "there sit none here who respect not the honour of their prince, or who deserve not his confidence. Read it, I say, aloud! and by Saint David, if Raymond the Norman hath dared —"

He stopped short, and, reclining on his seat, composed himself to an attitude of attention; but it was easy for his followers to fill up the breach in his exclamation which prudence had recommended.

The voice of the chaplain was low and ill-assured as he read the following epistle:—

"Raymond Berenger, the noble Norman Knight, Seneschal of the Garde Doloureuse, to Gwenwyn, Prince of Powys, (may peace be between them!) sendeth health.

"Your letter, craving the hand of our daughter Eveline Berenger, was safely delivered to us by your servant, Jorworth ap Jevan, and we thank you heartily for the good meaning therein expressed to us and to ours. But, considering within ourselves the difference of blood and lineage, with the impediments and causes of offence which have often arisen in like cases, we hold it fitter to match our daughter among our own people; and this by no case in disparagement of you, but solely for the weal of you, of ourselves, and of our mutual dependants, who will be the more safe from the risk of quarrel betwixt us, that we essay not to draw the bonds of our intimacy more close than beseemeth. The sheep and the goats feed together in peace on the same pastures, but they mingle not in blood, or race, the one with the other. Moreover, our daughter Eveline hath been sought in marriage by a noble and potent Lord of the Marches, Hugo de Lacy, the Constable of Chester, to which most honourable suit we have returned a favourable answer. It is therefore impossible that we should in this matter grant to you the boon you seek; nevertheless, you shall at all times find us, in other matters, willing to pleasure you; and hereunto we call God, and Our Lady, and Saint Mary Magdalene of Quatford, to witness; to whose keeping we heartily recommend you.

"Written by our command, at our Castle of Garde Doloureuse, within the Marches of Wales, by a reverend priest, Father Aldrovand, a black monk of the house of Wenlock; and to which we have appended our seal, upon the eve of the blessed martyr Saint Alphegius, to whom be honour and glory!"

The voice of Father Einion faltered, and the scroll which he held in his hand trembled in his grasp, as he arrived at the conclusion of this epistle; for well he knew that insults more slight than Gwenwyn would hold the least word it contained, were sure to put every drop of his British blood into the most vehement commotion. Nor did it fail to do so. The Prince had gradually drawn himself up from the posture of repose in which he had prepared to listen to the epistle; and when it concluded, he sprung on his feet like a startled lion, spurning from him as he rose the foot-bearer, who rolled at some distance on the floor. "Priest," he said, "hast thou read that accursed scroll fairly? for if thou hast added, or diminished, one word, or one letter, I will have thine eyes so handled, that thou shalt never read letter more!"

The monk replied, trembling, (for he was well aware that the sacerdotal character was not uniformly respected among the irascible Welshmen,) "By the oath of my order, mighty prince, I have read word for word, and letter for letter."

There was a momentary pause, while the fury of Gwenwyn, at this unexpected affront, offered to him in the presence of all his Uckelwyr, (*i.e.* noble chiefs, literally men of high stature,) seemed too big for utterance, when the silence was broken by a few notes from the hitherto mute harp of Cadwallon. The Prince looked round at first with displeasure at the interruption, for he was himself about to speak; but when he beheld the bard bending over his harp with an air of inspiration, and blending together, with unexampled skill, the wildest and most exalted tones of his art, he himself became an auditor instead of a speaker, and Cadwallon, not the Prince, seemed to become the central point of the assembly, on whom all eyes were bent, and to whom each ear was turned with breathless eagerness, as if his strains were the responses of an oracle.

"We wed not with the stranger,"—thus burst the song from the lips of the poet. "Vortigern wedded with the stranger; thence came the first wo upon Britain, and a sword upon her nobles, and a thunderbolt upon her palace. We wed not with the enslaved Saxon— the free and princely stag seeks not for his bride the heifer whose neck the yoke hath worn. We wed not with the rapacious Norman—the noble hound scorns to seek a mate from the herd of ravening wolves. When was it heard that the Cymry, the descendants of Brute, the true children of the soil of fair Britain, were plundered, oppressed, bereft of their birthright, and insulted even in their last retreats?—when, but since they stretched their hand in friendship to the stranger, and clasped to their bosoms the daughter of the Saxon? Which of the two is feared?—the empty water-course of summer, or the channel of the headlong winter torrent?—A maiden smiles at the summer-shrunk brook while she crosses it, but a barbed horse and his rider will fear to stem the wintry flood. Men of Mathravel and Powys, be the dreaded flood of winter—Gwenwyn, son of Cyverliock!—may thy plume be the topmost of its waves!"

All thoughts of peace, thoughts which, in themselves, were foreign to the hearts of the warlike British, passed before the song of Cadwallon like dust before the whirlwind, and the unanimous shout of the assembly declared for instant war. The Prince himself spoke not, but, looking proudly around him, flung abroad his arm, as one who cheers his followers to the attack.

The priest, had he dared, might have reminded Gwenwyn, that the Cross which he had assumed on his shoulder, had consecrated his arm to the Holy War, and precluded his engaging in any civil strife. But the task was too dangerous for Father Einion's courage, and he shrunk from the hall to the seclusion of his own convent. Caradoc, whose brief hour of popularity was past, also retired, with humbled and dejected looks, and not without a glance of indignation at his triumphant rival, who had so judiciously reserved his display of art for the theme of war, that was ever most popular with the audience.

The chiefs resumed their seats no longer for the purpose of festivity, but to fix, in the hasty manner customary among these prompt warriors, where they were to assemble their forces, which, upon such occasions, comprehended almost all the able-bodied males of the country,—for all, excepting the priests and the bards, were soldiers,—and to settle the order of their descent upon the devoted marches, where they proposed to signalize, by general ravage, their sense of the insult which their Prince had received, by the rejection of his suit.

CHAPTER THE THIRD

The sands are number'd, that make up my life;
Here must I stay, and here my life must end.
  HENRY VI. ACT. I. SCENE IV.

When Raymond Berenger had despatched his mission to the Prince of Powys, he was not unsuspicious, though altogether fearless, of the result. He sent messengers to the several dependants who held their fiefs by the tenure of *cornage*, and warned them to be on the alert, that he might receive instant notice of the approach of the enemy. These vassals, as is well known, occupied the numerous towers, which, like so many falcon-nests, had been built on the points most convenient to defend the frontiers, and were bound to give signal of any incursion of the Welsh, by blowing their horns; which sounds, answered from tower to tower, and from station to station, gave the alarm for general defence. But although Raymond considered these precautions as necessary, from the fickle and precarious temper of his neighbours, and for maintaining his own credit as a soldier, he was far from believing the danger to be imminent; for the preparations of the Welsh; though on a much more extensive scale than had lately been usual, were as secret, as their resolution of war had been suddenly adopted.

It was upon the second morning after the memorable festival of Castell-Coch, that the tempest broke on the Norman frontier. At first a single, long, and keen bugle-blast, announced the approach of the enemy; presently the signals of alarm were echoed from every castle and tower on the borders of Shropshire, where every place of habitation was then a fortress. Beacons were lighted upon crags and eminences, the bells were rung backward in the churches and towns, while the general and earnest summons to arms announced an extremity of danger which even the inhabitants of that unsettled country had not hitherto experienced.

Amid this general alarm, Raymond Berenger, having busied himself in arranging his few but gallant followers and adherents, and taken such modes of procuring intelligence of the enemy's strength and motions as were in his power, at length ascended the watch- tower of the castle, to observe in person the country around, already obscured in several places by the clouds of smoke, which announced the progress and the ravages of the invaders. He was speedily joined by his favourite squire, to whom the unusual heaviness of his master's looks was cause of much surprise, for till now they had ever been blithest at the hour of battle. The squire held in his hand his master's helmet, for Sir Raymond was all armed, saving the head.

"Dennis Morolt," said the veteran soldier, "are our vassals and liegemen all mustered?"

"All, noble sir, but the Flemings, who are not yet come in."

"The lazy hounds, why tarry they?" said Raymond. "Ill policy it is to plant such sluggish natures in our borders. They are like their own steers, fitter to tug a plough than for aught that requires mettle."

"With your favour," said Dennis, "the knaves can do good service notwithstanding. That Wilkin Flammock of the Green can strike like the hammers of his own fulling-mill."

"He will fight, I believe, when he cannot help it," said Raymond; "but he has no stomach for such exercise, and is as slow and as stubborn as a mule."

"And therefore are his countrymen rightly matched against the Welsh," replied Dennis Morolt, "that their solid and unyielding temper may be a fit foil to the fiery and headlong dispositions of our dangerous neighbours, just as restless waves are best opposed by steadfast rocks.—Hark, sir, I hear Wilkin Flammock's step ascending the turret-stair, as deliberately as ever monk mounted to matins."

Step by step the heavy sound approached, until the form of the huge and substantial Fleming at length issued from the turret-door to the platform where they "were conversing. Wilkin Flammock was cased in bright armour, of unusual weight and thickness, and cleaned with exceeding care, which marked the neatness of his nation; but, contrary to the custom of the Normans, entirely plain, and void of carving, gilding, or any sort of ornament. The basenet, or steel-cap, had no visor, and left exposed a broad countenance, with heavy and unpliable features, which announced the character of his temper and understanding. He carried in his hand a heavy mace.

"So, Sir Fleming," said the Castellane, "you are in no hurry, methinks, to repair to the rendezvous."

"So please you," answered the Fleming, "we were compelled to tarry, that we might load our wains with our bales of cloth and other property."

"Ha! wains?—how many wains have you brought with you?"

"Six, noble sir," replied Wilkin.

"And how many men?" demanded Raymond Berenger.

"Twelve, valiant sir," answered Flammock.

"Only two men to each baggage-wain? I wonder you would thus encumber yourself," said Berenger.

"Under your favour, sir, once more," replied Wilkin, "it is only the value which I and my comrades set upon our goods, that inclines us to defend them with our bodies; and, had we been obliged to leave our cloth to the plundering clutches of yonder vagabonds, I should have seen small policy in stopping here to give them the opportunity of adding murder to robbery. Gloucester should have been my first halting-place."

The Norman knight gazed on the Flemish artisan, for such was Wilkin Flammock, with such a mixture of surprise and contempt, as excluded indignation. "I have heard much," he said, "but this is the first time that I have heard one with a beard on his lip avouch himself a coward."

"Nor do you hear it now," answered Flammock, with the utmost composure —"I am always ready to fight for life and property; and my coming to this country, where they are both in constant danger, shows that I care not much how often I do so. But a sound skin is better than a slashed one, for all that."

"Well," said Raymond Berenger, "fight after thine own fashion, so thou wilt but fight stoutly with that long body of thine. We are like to have need for all that we can do.—Saw you aught of these rascaille Welsh?—have they Gwenwyn's banner amongst them?"

"I saw it with the white dragon displayed," replied Wilkin; "I could not but know it, since it was broidered in my own loom."

Raymond looked so grave upon this intelligence, that Dennis Morolt, unwilling the Fleming should mark it, thought it necessary to withdraw his attention. "I can tell thee," he said to Flammock, "that when the Constable of Chester joins us with his lances, you shall see your handiwork, the dragon, fly faster homeward than ever flew the shuttle which wove it."

"It must fly before the Constable comes up, Dennis Morolt," said Berenger, "else it will fly triumphant over all our bodies."

"In the name of God and the Holy Virgin!" said Dennis, "what may you mean, Sir Knight?—not that we should fight with the Welsh before the Constable joins us?"—He paused, and then, well understanding the firm, yet melancholy glance, with which his master answered the question, he proceeded, with yet more vehement earnestness—"You cannot mean it—you cannot intend that we shall quit this castle, which we have so often made good against them, and contend in the field with two hundred men against thousands?— Think better of it, my beloved master, and let not the rashness of your old age blemish that character for wisdom and warlike skill, which your former life has so nobly won."

"I am not angry with you for blaming my purpose, Dennis," answered the Norman, "for I know you do it in love to me and mine. But, Dennis Morolt, this thing must be—we must fight the Welshmen within these three hours, or the name of Raymond Berenger must be blotted from the genealogy of his house."

"And so we will—we will fight them, my noble master," said the esquire; "fear not cold counsel from Dennis Morolt, where battle is the theme. But we will fight them under the walls of the castle, with honest Wilkin Flammock and his crossbows on the wall to protect our flanks, and afford us some balance against the numerous odds."

"Not so, Dennis," answered his master—"In the open field we must fight them, or thy master must rank but as a mansworn knight. Know, that when I feasted yonder wily savage in my halls at Christmas, and when the wine was flowing fastest around, Gwenwyn threw out some praises of the fastness and strength of my castle, in a manner which intimated it was these advantages alone that had secured me in former wars from defeat and captivity. I spoke in answer, when I had far better been silent; for what availed my idle boast, but as a fetter to bind me to a deed next to madness? If, I said, a prince of the Cymry shall come in hostile fashion before the Garde Doloureuse, let him pitch his standard down in yonder plain by the bridge, and, by the word of a good knight, and the faith of a Christian man, Raymond Berenger will meet him as willingly, be he many or be he few, as ever Welshman was met withal."

Dennis was struck speechless when he heard of a promise so rash, so fatal; but his was not the casuistry which could release his master from the fetters with which his unwary confidence had bound him. It was otherwise with Wilkin Flammock. He stared—he almost laughed, notwithstanding the reverence due to the Castellane, and his own insensibility to risible emotions. "And is this all?" he said. "If your honour had pledged yourself to pay one hundred florins to a Jew or to a Lombard, no doubt you must have kept the day, or forfeited your pledge; but surely one day is as good as another to keep a promise for fighting, and that day is best in which the promiser is strongest. But indeed, after all, what signifies any promise over a wine flagon?"

"It signifies as much as a promise can do that is given elsewhere. The promiser," said Berenger, "escapes not the sin of a word- breaker, because he hath been a drunken braggart."

"For the sin," said Dennis, "sure I am, that rather than you should do such a deed of dole, the Abbot of Glastonbury would absolve you for a florin."

"But what shall wipe out the shame?" demanded Berenger—"how shall I dare to show myself again among press of knights, who have broken my word of battle pledged, for fear of a Welshman and his naked savages? No! Dennis Morolt, speak on it no more. Be it for weal or wo, we fight them to-day, and upon yonder fair field."

"It may be," said Flammock, "that Gwenwyn may have forgotten the promise, and so fail to appear to claim it in the appointed space; for, as we heard, your wines of France flooded his Welsh brains deeply."

"He again alluded to it on the morning after it was made," said the Castellane —"trust me, he will not forget what will give him such a chance of removing me from his path for ever."

As he spoke, they observed that large clouds of dust, which had been seen at different points of the landscape, were drawing down towards the opposite side of the river, over which an ancient bridge extended itself to the appointed place of combat. They were at no loss to conjecture the cause. It was evident that Gwenwyn, recalling the parties who had been engaged in partial devastation, was bending with his whole forces towards the bridge and the plain beyond it.

"Let us rush down and secure the pass," said Dennis Morolt; "we may debate with them with some equality by the advantage of defending the bridge. Your word bound you to the plain as to a field of battle, but it did not oblige you to forego such advantages as the passage of the bridge would afford. Our men, our horses, are ready—let our bowmen secure the banks, and my life on the issue."

"When I promised to meet him in yonder field, I meant," replied Raymond Berenger, "to give the Welshman the full advantage of equality of ground. I so meant it—he so understood it; and what avails keeping my word in the letter, if I break it in the sense? We move not till the last Welshman has crossed the bridge; and then—"

"And then," said Dennis, "we move to our death!—May God forgive our sins! —But—"

"But what?" said Berenger; "something sticks in thy mind that should have vent."

"My young lady, your daughter the Lady Eveline—"

"I have told her what is to be. She shall remain in the castle, where I will leave a few chosen veterans, with you, Dennis, to command them. In twenty-four hours the siege will be relieved, and we have defended it longer with a slighter garrison. Then to her aunt, the Abbess of the Benedictine sisters—thou, Dennis, wilt see her placed there in honour and safety, and my sister will care for her future provision as her wisdom shall determine." "*I leave you at this pinch!*" said Dennis Morolt, bursting into tears —"*I shut myself up within walls, when my master rides to his last of battles!—I become esquire to a lady, even though it be to the Lady Eveline, when he lies dead under his shield!—*Raymond Berenger, is it for this that I have buckled thy armour so often?"

The tears gushed from the old warrior's eyes as fast as from those of a girl who weeps for her lover; and Raymond, taking him kindly by the hand, said, in a soothing tone, "Do not think, my good old servant, that, were honour to be won, I would drive thee from my side. But this is a wild and an inconsiderate deed, to which my fate or my folly has bound me. I die to save my name from dishonour; but, alas! I must leave on my memory the charge of imprudence."

"Let me share your imprudence, my dearest master," said Dennis Morolt, earnestly—"the poor esquire has no business to be thought wiser than his master. In many a battle my valour derived some little fame from partaking in thee deeds which won your renown— deny me not the right to share in that blame which your temerity may incur; let them not say, that so rash was his action, even his old esquire was not permitted to partake in it! I am part of yourself—it is murder to every man whom you take with you, if you leave me behind."

"Dennis," said Berenger, "you make me feel yet more bitterly the folly I have yielded to. I. would grant you the boon you ask, sad as it is—But my daughter —"

"Sir Knight," said the Fleming, who had listened to this dialogue with somewhat less than his usual apathy, "it is not my purpose this day to leave this castle; now, if you could trust my troth to do what a plain man may for the protection of my Lady Eveline—"

"How, sirrah!" said Raymond; "you do not propose to leave the castle? Who gives you right to propose or dispose in the case, until my pleasure is known?"

"I shall be sorry to have words with you, Sir Castellane," said the imperturbable Fleming;—"but I hold here, in this township, certain mills, tenements, cloth-yards, and so forth, for which I am to pay man-service in defending this Castle of the Garde Doloureuse, and in this I am ready. But if you call on me to march from hence, leaving the same castle defenceless, and to offer up my life in a battle which you acknowledge to be desperate, I must needs say my tenure binds me not to obey thee."

"Base mechanic!" said Morolt, laying his hand on his dagger, and menacing the Fleming.

But Raymond Berenger interfered with voice and hand—"Harm him not, Morolt, and blame him not. He hath a sense of duty, though not after our manner; and he and his knaves will fight best behind stone walls. They are taught also, these Flemings, by the practice of their own country, the attack and defence of walled cities and fortresses, and are especially skilful in working of mangonels and military engines. There are several of his countrymen in the castle, besides his own followers. These I propose to leave behind; and I think they will obey him more readily than any but thyself—how think'st thou? Thou wouldst not, I know, from a miscontrued point of honour, or a blind love to me, leave this important place, and the safety of Eveline, in doubtful hands?"

"Wilkin Flammock is but a Flemish clown, noble sir," answered Dennis, as much overjoyed as if he had obtained some important advantage; "but I must needs say he is as stout and true as any whom you might trust; and, besides, his own shrewdness will teach him there is more to be gained by defending such a castle as this, than by yielding it to strangers, who may not be likely to keep the terms of surrender, however fairly they may offer them."

"It is fixed then," said Raymond Berenger. "Then, Dennis, thou shalt go with me, and he shall remain behind.—Wilkin Flammock," he said, addressing the Fleming solemnly, "I speak not to thee the language of chivalry, of which thou knowest nothing; but, as thou art an honest man, and a true Christian, I conjure thee to stand to the defence of this castle. Let no promise of the enemy draw thee to any base composition—no threat to any surrender. Relief must speedily arrive, if you fulfil your trust to me and to my daughter, Hugo de Lacy will reward you richly—if you fail, he will punish you severely."

"Sir Knight," said Flammock, "I am pleased you have put your trust so far in a plain handicraftsman. For the Welsh, I am come from a land for which we were compelled—yearly compelled—to struggle with the sea; and they who can deal with the waves in a tempest, need not fear an undisciplined people in their fury. Your daughter shall be as dear to me as mine own; and in that faith you may prick forth—if, indeed, you will not still, like a wiser man, shut gate, down portcullis, up drawbridge, and let your archers and my crossbows man the wall, and tell the knaves you are not the fool that they take you for."

"Good fellow, that must not be," said the Knight. "I hear my daughter's voice," he added hastily; "I would not again meet her, again to part from her. To Heaven's keeping I commit thee, honest Fleming.—Follow me, Dennis Morolt."

The old Castellane descended the stair of the southern tower hastily, just as his daughter Eveline ascended that of the eastern turret, to throw herself at his feet once more. She was followed by the Father Aldrovand, chaplain of her father; by an old and almost invalid huntsman, whose more active services in the field and the chase had been for some time chiefly limited to the superintendence of the Knight's kennels, and the charge especially of his more favourite hounds; and by Rose Flammock, the daughter of Wilkin, a blue-eyed Flemish maiden, round, plump, and shy as a partridge, who had been for some time permitted to keep company with the high-born Norman damsel, in a doubtful station, betwixt that of an humble friend and a superior domestic. Eveline rushed upon the battlements, her hair dishevelled, and her eyes drowned in tears, and eagerly demanded of the Fleming where her father was.

Flammock made a clumsy reverence, and attempted some answer; but his voice seemed to fail him. He turned his back upon Eveline without ceremony, and totally disregarding the anxious inquiries of the huntsman and the chaplain, he said hastily to his daughter, in his own language, "Mad work! mad work! look to the poor maiden, Roschen—*Der alter Herr ist verruckt.*"

Without farther speech he descended the stairs, and never paused till he reached the buttery. Here he called like a lion for the controller of these regions, by the various names of Kammerer, Keller-master, and so forth, to which the old Reinold, an ancient Norman esquire, answered not, until the Netherlander fortunately recollected his Anglo-Norman title of butler. This, his regular name of office, was the key to the buttery-hatch, and the old man instantly appeared, with his gray cassock and high rolled hose, a ponderous bunch of keys suspended by a silver chain to his broad leathern girdle, which, in consideration of the emergency of the time, he had thought it right to balance on the left side with a huge falchion, which seemed much too weighty for his old arm to wield.

"What is your will," he said, "Master Flammock? or what are your commands, since it is my lord's pleasure that they shall be laws to me for a time?"

"Only a cup of wine, good Meister Keller-master—butler, I mean."

"I am glad you remember the name of mine office," said Reinold, with some of the petty resentment of a spoiled domestic, who thinks that a stranger has been irregularly put in command over him.

"A flagon of Rhenish, if you love me," answered the Fleming, "for my heart is low and poor within me, and I must needs drink of the best."

"And drink you shall," said Reinold, "if drink will give you the courage which perhaps you want."—He descended to the secret crypts, of which he was the guardian, and returned with a silver flagon, which might contain about a quart.

—"Here is such wine," said Reinold, "as thou hast seldom tasted," and was about to pour it out into a cup.

"Nay, the flagon—the flagon, friend Reinold; I love a deep and solemn draught when the business is weighty," said Wilkin. He seized on the flagon accordingly, and drinking a preparatory mouthful, paused as if to estimate the strength and flavour of the generous liquor. Apparently he was pleased with both, for he nodded in approbation to the butler; and, raising the flagon to his mouth once more, he slowly and gradually brought the bottom of the vessel parallel with the roof of the apartment, without suffering one drop of the contents to escape him.

"That hath savour, Herr Keller-master," said he, while he was recovering his breath by intervals, after so long a suspense of respiration; "but, may Heaven forgive you for thinking it the best I have ever tasted! You little know the cellars of Ghent and of Ypres."

"And I care not for them," said Reinold; "those of gentle Norman blood hold the wines of Gascony and France, generous, light, and cordial, worth all the acid potations of the Rhine and the Neckar."

"All is matter of taste," said the Fleming; "but hark ye—Is there much of this wine in the cellar?"

"Methought but now it pleased not your dainty palate?" said Reinold.

"Nay, nay, my friend," said Wilkin, "I said it had savour—I may have drunk better—but this is right good, where better may not be had.—Again, how much of it hast thou?"

"The whole butt, man," answered the butler; "I have broached a fresh piece for you."

"Good," replied Flammock; "get the quart-pot of Christian measure; heave the cask up into this same buttery, and let each soldier of this castle be served with such a cup as I have here swallowed. I feel it hath done me much good—my heart was sinking when I saw the black smoke arising from mine own fulling-mills yonder. Let each man, I say, have a full quart-pot—men defend not castles on thin liquors."

"I must do as you will, good Wilkin Flammock," said the butler; "but I pray you, remember all men are not alike. That which will but warm your Flemish hearts, will put wildfire into Norman brains; and what may only encourage your countrymen to man the walls, will make ours fly over the battlements."

"Well, you know the conditions of your own countrymen best; serve out to them what wines and measure you list—only let each Fleming have a solemn quart of Rhenish.—But what will you do for the English churls, of whom there are a right many left with us?"

The old butler paused, and rubbed his brow.—"There will be a strange waste of liquor," he said; "and yet I may not deny that the emergency may defend the expenditure. But for the English, they are, as you wot, a mixed breed, having much of your German sullenness, together with a plentiful touch of the hot blood of yonder Welsh furies. Light wines stir them not; strong heavy draughts would madden them. What think you of ale, an invigorating, strengthening liquor, that warms the heart without inflaming the brain?"

"Ale!" said the Fleming.—"Hum—ha—is your ale mighty, Sir Butler?—is it double ale?"

"Do you doubt my skill?" said the butler.—"March and October have witnessed me ever as they came round, for thirty years, deal with the best barley in Shropshire.—You shall judge."

He filled, from a large hogshead in the corner of the buttery, the flagon which the Fleming had just emptied, and which was no sooner replenished than Wilkin again drained it to the bottom.

"Good ware," he said, "Master Butler, strong stinging ware. The English churls will fight like devils upon it—let them be furnished with mighty ale along with their beef and brown bread. And now, having given you your charge, Master Reinold, it is time I should look after mine own."

Wilkin Flammock left the buttery, and with a mien and judgment alike undisturbed by the deep potations in which he had so recently indulged, undisturbed also by the various rumours concerning what was passing without doors, he made the round of the castle and its outworks, mustered the little garrison, and assigned to each their posts, reserving to his own countrymen the management of the arblasts, or crossbows, and of the military engines which were contrived by the proud Normans, and were incomprehensible to the ignorant English, or, more properly, Anglo-Saxons, of the period, but which his more adroit countrymen managed with great address. The jealousies entertained by both the Normans and English, at being placed under the temporary command of a Fleming, gradually yielded to the military and mechanical skill which he displayed, as well as to a sense of the emergency, which became greater with every moment.

CHAPTER THE FOURTH

Beside yon brigg out ower yon burn,
Where the water bickereth bright and sheen,
Shall many a falling courser spurn,
And knights shall die in battle keen.
    PROPHECY OF THOMAS THE RHYMER.

The daughter of Raymond Berenger, with the attendants whom we have mentioned, continued to remain upon the battlements of the Garde Doloureuse, in spite of the exhortations of the priest that she would rather await the issue of this terrible interval in the chapel, and amid the rites of religion. He perceived, at length, that she was incapable, from grief and fear, of attending to, or understanding his advice; and, sitting down beside her, while the huntsman and Rose Flammock stood by, endeavoured to suggest such comfort as perhaps he scarcely felt himself.

"This is but a sally of your noble father's," he said; "and though it may seem it is made on great hazard, yet who ever questioned Sir Raymond Berenger's policy of wars?—He is close and secret in his purposes. I guess right well he had not marched out as he proposes, unless he knew that the noble Earl of Arundel, or the mighty Constable of Chester, were close at hand."

"Think you this assuredly, good father?—Go, Raoul—go, my dearest Rose— look to the east—see if you cannot descry banners or clouds of dust.—Listen —listen—hear you no trumpets from that quarter?"

"Alas! my lady," said Raoul, "the thunder of heaven could scarce be heard amid the howling of yonder Welsh wolves." Eveline turned as he spoke, and looking towards the bridge, she beheld an appalling spectacle. The river, whose stream washes on three sides the base of the proud eminence on which the castle is situated, curves away from the fortress and its corresponding village on the west, and the hill sinks downward to an extensive plain, so extremely level as to indicate its alluvial origin. Lower down, at the extremity of this plain, where the banks again close on the river, were situated the manufacturing houses of the stout Flemings, which were now burning in a bright flame. The bridge, a high, narrow combination of arches of unequal size, was about half a mile distant from the castle, in the very centre of the plain. The river itself ran in a deep rocky channel, was often unfordable, and at all times difficult of passage, giving considerable advantage to the defenders of the castle, who had spent on other occasions many a dear drop of blood to defend the pass, which Raymond Berenger's fantastic scruples now induced him to abandon. The Welshmen, seizing the opportunity with the avidity with which men grasp an unexpected benefit, were fast crowding over the high and steep arches, while new bands, collecting from different points upon the farther bank, increased the continued stream of warriors, who, passing leisurely and uninterrupted, formed their line of battle on the plain opposite to the castle.

At first Father Aldrovand viewed their motions without anxiety, nay, with the scornful smile of one who observes an enemy in the act of falling into the snare spread for them by superior skill. Raymond Berenger, with his little body of infantry and cavalry, were drawn up on the easy hill which is betwixt the castle and the plain, ascending from the former towards the fortress; and it seemed clear to the Dominican, who had not entirely forgotten in the cloister his ancient military experience, that it was the Knight's purpose to attack the disordered enemy when a certain number had crossed the river, and the others were partly on the farther side, and partly engaged in the slow and perilous manoeuvre of effecting their passage. But when large bodies of the white-mantled Welshmen were permitted without interruption to take such order on the plain as their habits of fighting recommended, the monk's countenance, though he still endeavoured to speak encouragement to the terrified Eveline, assumed a different and an anxious expression; and his acquired habits of resignation contended strenuously with his ancient military ardour. "Be patient," he said, "my daughter, and be of good comfort; thine eyes shall behold the dismay of yonder barbarous enemy. Let but a minute elapse, and thou shalt see them scattered like dust.—Saint George! they will surely cry thy name now, or never!"

The monk's beads passed meanwhile rapidly through his hands, but many an expression of military impatience mingled itself with his orisons. He could not conceive the cause why each successive throng of mountaineers, led under their different banners, and headed by their respective chieftains, was permitted, without interruption, to pass the difficult defile, and extend themselves in battle array on the near side of the bridge, while the English, or rather Anglo-Norman cavalry, remained stationary, without so much as laying their lances in rest. There remained, as he thought, but one hope—one only rational explanation of this unaccountable inactivity—this voluntary surrender of every advantage of ground, when that of numbers was so tremendously on the side of the enemy. Father Aldrovand concluded, that the succours of the Constable of Chester, and other Lord Marchers, must be in the immediate vicinity, and that the Welsh were only permitted to pass the river without opposition, that their retreat might be the more effectually cut off, and their defeat, with a deep river in their rear, rendered the more signally calamitous. But even while he clung to this hope, the monk's heart sunk within him, as, looking in every direction from which the expected succours might arrive, he could neither see nor hear the slightest token which announced their approach. In a frame of mind approaching more nearly to despair than to hope, the old man continued alternately to tell his beads, to gaze anxiously around, and to address some words of consolation in broken phrases to the young lady, until the general shout of the Welsh, ringing from the bank of the river to the battlements of the castle, warned him, in a note of exultation, that the very last of the British had defiled through the pass, and that their whole formidable array stood prompt for action upon the hither side of the river.

This thrilling and astounding clamour, to which each Welshman lent his voice with all the energy of defiance, thirst of battle, and hope of conquest, was at length answered by the blast of the Norman trumpets,—the first sign of activity which had been exhibited on the part of Raymond Berenger. But cheerily as they rang, the trumpets, in comparison of the shout which they answered, sounded like the silver whistle of the stout boatswain amid the howling of the tempest.

At the same moment when the trumpets were blown, Berenger gave signal to the archers to discharge their arrows, and the men-at- arms to advance under a hail-storm of shafts, javelins, and stones, shot, darted, and slung by the Welsh against their steel- clad assailants.

The veterans of Raymond, on the other hand, stimulated by so many victorious recollections, confident in the talents of their accomplished leader, and undismayed even by the desperation of their circumstances, charged the mass of the Welshmen with their usual determined valour. It was a gallant sight to see this little body of cavalry advance to the onset, their plumes floating above their helmets, their lances in rest, and projecting six feet in length before the breasts of their coursers; their shields hanging from their necks, that their left hands might have freedom to guide their horses; and the whole body rushing on with an equal front, and a momentum of speed which increased with every second. Such an onset might have startled naked men, (for such were the Welsh, in respect of the mail-sheathed Normans,) but it brought no terrors to the ancient British, who had long made it their boast that they exposed their bare bosoms and white tunics to the lances and swords of the men-at-arms, with as much confidence as if they had been born invulnerable. It was not indeed in their power to withstand the weight of the first shock, which, breaking their ranks, densely as they were arranged, carried the barbed horses into the very centre of their host, and well-nigh up to the fatal standard, to which Raymond Berenger, bound by his fatal vow, had that day conceded so much vantage-ground. But they yielded like the billows, which give way, indeed, to the gallant ship, but only to assail her sides, and to unite in her wake. With wild and horrible clamours, they closed their tumultuous ranks around Berenger and his devoted followers, and a deadly scene of strife ensued.

The best warriors of Wales had on this occasion joined the standard of

Gwenwyn; the arrows of the men of Gwentland, whose skill in archery almost equalled that of the Normans themselves, rattled on the helmets of the men-at-arms; and the spears of the people of Deheubarth, renowned for the sharpness and temper of their steel heads, were employed against the cuirasses not without fatal effect, notwithstanding the protection, which these afforded to the rider.

It was in vain that the archery belonging to Raymond's little band, stout yeomen, who, for the most part, held possession by military tenure, exhausted their quivers on the broad mark afforded them by the Welsh army. It is probable, that every shaft carried a Welshman's life on its point; yet, to have afforded important relief to the cavalry, now closely and inextricably engaged, the slaughter ought to have been twenty-fold at least. Meantime, the Welsh, galled by this incessant discharge, answered it by volleys from their own archers, whose numbers made some amends for their inferiority, and who were supported by numerous bodies of darters and slingers. So that the Norman archers, who had more than once attempted to descend from their position to operate a diversion in favour of Raymond and his devoted band, were now so closely engaged in front, as obliged them to abandon all thoughts of such a movement.

Meanwhile, that chivalrous leader, who from the first had hoped for no more than an honourable death, laboured with all his power to render his fate signal, by involving in it that of the Welsh Prince, the author of the war. He cautiously avoided the expenditure of his strength by hewing among the British; but, with the shock of his managed horse, repelled the numbers who pressed on him, and leaving the plebeians to the swords of his companions, shouted his war-cry, and made his way towards the fatal standard of Gwenwyn, beside which, discharging at once the duties of a skilful leader and a brave soldier, the Prince had stationed himself. Raymond's experience of the Welsh disposition, subject equally to the highest flood, and most sudden ebb of passion, gave him some hope that a successful attack upon this point, followed by the death or capture of the Prince, and the downfall of his standard, might even yet strike such a panic, as should change the fortunes of the day, otherwise so nearly desperate. The veteran, therefore, animated his comrades to the charge by voice and example; and, in spite of all opposition, forced his way gradually onward. But Gwenwyn in person, surrounded by his best and noblest champions, offered a defence as obstinate as the assault was intrepid. In vain they were borne to the earth by the barbed horses, or hewed down by the invulnerable riders. Wounded and overthrown, the Britons continued their resistance, clung round the legs of the Norman steeds, and cumbered their advance while their brethren, thrusting with pikes, proved every joint and crevice of the plate and mail, or grappling with the men-at-arms, strove to pull them from their horses by main force, or beat them down with their bills and Welsh hooks. And wo betide those who were by these various means dismounted, for the long sharp knives worn by the Welsh, soon pierced them with a hundred wounds, and were then only merciful when the first inflicted was deadly.

The combat was at this point, and had raged for more than half an hour, when Berenger, having forced his horse within two spears' length of the British standard, he and Gwenwyn were so near to each other as to exchange tokens of mutual defiance.

"Turn thee, Wolf of Wales," said Berenger, "and abide, if thou darest, one blow of a good knight's sword! Raymond Berenger spits at thee and thy banner."

"False Norman churl!" said Gwenwyn, swinging around his head a mace of prodigious weight, and already clottered with blood, "thy iron headpiece shall ill protect thy lying tongue, with which I will this day feed the ravens."

Raymond made no farther answer, but pushed his horse towards the Prince, who advanced to meet him with equal readiness. But ere they came within reach of each other's weapons, a Welsh champion, devoted like the Romans who opposed the elephants of Pyrrhus, finding that the armour of Raymond's horse resisted the repeated thrusts of his spear, threw himself under the animal, and stabbed him in the belly with his long knife. The noble horse reared and fell, crushing with his weight the Briton who had wounded him; the helmet of the rider burst its clasps in the fall, and rolled away from his head, giving to view his noble features and gray hairs. He made more than one effort to extricate himself from the fallen horse, but ere he could succeed, received his death-wound from the hand of Gwenwyn, who hesitated not to strike him down with his mace while in the act of extricating himself.

During the whole of this bloody day, Dennis Morolt's horse had kept pace for pace, and his arm blow for blow, with his master's. It seemed as if two different bodies had been moving under one act of volition. He husbanded his strength, or put it forth, exactly as he observed his knight did, and was close by his side, when he made the last deadly effort. At that fatal moment, when Raymond Berenger rushed on the chief, the brave squire forced his way up to the standard, and, grasping it firmly, struggled for possession of it with a gigantic Briton, to whose care it had been confided, and who now exerted his utmost strength to defend it. But even while engaged in this mortal struggle, the eye of Morolt scarcely left his master; and when he saw him fall, his own force seemed by sympathy to abandon him, and the British champion had no longer any trouble in laying him prostrate among the slain.

The victory of the British was now complete. Upon the fall of their leader, the followers of Raymond Berenger would willingly have fled or surrendered. But the first was impossible, so closely had they been enveloped; and in the cruel wars maintained by the Welsh upon their frontiers, quarter to the vanquished was out of question. A few of the men-at-arms were lucky enough to disentangle themselves from the tumult, and, not even attempting to enter the castle, fled in various directions, to carry their own fears among the inhabitants of the marches, by announcing the loss of the battle, and the fate of the far-renowned Raymond Berenger.

The archers of the fallen leader, as they had never been so deeply involved in the combat, which had been chiefly maintained by the cavalry, became now, in their turn, the sole object of the enemy's attack. But when they saw the multitude come roaring towards them like a sea, with all its waves, they abandoned the bank which they had hitherto bravely defended, and began a regular retreat to the castle in the best order which they could, as the only remaining means of securing their lives. A few of their lightfooted enemies attempted to intercept them, during the execution of this prudent manoeuvre, by outstripping them in their march, and throwing themselves into the hollow way which led to the castle, to oppose their retreat. But the coolness of the English archers, accustomed to extremities of every kind, supported them on the present occasion. While a part of them, armed with glaives and bills, dislodged the Welsh from the hollow way, the others, facing in the opposite direction, and parted into divisions, which alternately halted and retreated, maintained such a countenance as to check pursuit, and exchange a severe discharge of missiles with the Welsh, by which both parties were considerable sufferers.

At length, having left more than two-thirds of their brave companions behind them, the yeomanry attained the point, which, being commanded by arrows and engines from the battlements, might be considered as that of comparative safety. A volley of large stones, and square-headed bolts of great size and thickness, effectually stopped the farther progress of the pursuit, and those who had led it drew back their desultory forces to the plain, where, with shouts of jubilee and exultation, their countrymen were employed in securing the plunder of the field; while some, impelled by hatred and revenge, mangled and mutilated the limbs of the dead Normans, in a manner unworthy of their national cause and their own courage. The fearful yells with which this dreadful work was consummated, while it struck horror into the minds of the slender garrison of the Garde Doloureuse, inspired them at the same time with the resolution rather to defend the fortress to the last extremity, than to submit to the mercy of so vengeful an enemy.

CHAPTER THE FIFTH

That baron he to his castle fled,
To Barnard Castle then fled he;
The uttermost walls were eathe to win,
The Earls have won them speedilie;-
The uttermost walls were stone and brick;
But though they won them soon anon,
Long ere they won the inmost walls,
For they were hewn in rock of stone.
  PERCY'S RELICS OF ANCIENT POETRY.

The unhappy fate of the battle was soon evident to the anxious spectators upon the watch-towers of the Garde Doloureuse, which name the castle that day too well deserved. With difficulty the confessor mastered his own emotions to control those of the females on whom he attended, and who were now joined in their lamentation by many others—women, children, and infirm old men, the relatives of those whom they saw engaged in this unavailing contest. These helpless beings had been admitted to the castle for security's sake, and they had now thronged to the battlements, from which Father Aldrovand found difficulty in making them descend, aware that the sight of them on the towers, that should have appeared lined with armed men, would be an additional encouragement to the exertions of the assailants. He urged the Lady Eveline to set an example to this group of helpless, yet intractable mourners.

Preserving, at least endeavouring to preserve, even in the extremity of grief, that composure which the manners of the times enjoined—for chivalry had its stoicism as well as philosophy— Eveline replied in a voice which she would fain have rendered firm, and which was tremulous in her despite—"Yes, father, you say well—here is no longer aught left for maidens to look upon. Warlike meed and honoured deed sunk when yonder white plume touched the bloody ground.—Come, maidens, there is no longer aught left us to see—To mass, to mass—the tourney is over!"

There was wildness in her tone, and when she rose, with the air of one who would lead out a procession, she staggered, and would have fallen, but for the support of the confessor. Hastily wrapping her head in her mantle, as if ashamed of the agony of grief which she could not restrain, and of which her sobs and the low moaning sounds that issued from under the folds enveloping her face, declared the excess, she suffered Father Aldrovand to conduct her whither he would.

"Our gold," he said, "has changed to brass, our silver to dross, our wisdom, to folly—it is His will, who confounds the counsels of the wise, and shortens the arm of the mighty. To the chapel—to the chapel, Lady Eveline; and instead of vain repining, let us pray to God and the saints to turn away their displeasure, and to save the feeble remnant from the jaws of the devouring wolf."

Thus speaking, he half led, half supported Eveline, who was at the moment almost incapable of thought and action, to the castle- chapel, where, sinking before the altar, she assumed the attitude at least of devotion, though her thoughts, despite the pious words which her tongue faltered out mechanically, were upon the field of battle, beside the body of her slaughtered parent. The rest of the mourners imitated their young lady in her devotional posture, and in the absence of her thoughts. The consciousness that so many of the garrison had been cut off in Raymond's incautious sally, added to their sorrows the sense of personal insecurity, which was exaggerated by the cruelties which were too often exercised by the enemy, who, in the heat of victory, were accustomed to spare neither sex nor age.

The monk, however, assumed among them the tone of authority which his character warranted, rebuked their wailing and ineffectual complaints, and having, as he thought, brought them to such a state of mind as better became their condition, he left them to their private devotions to indulge his own anxious curiosity by inquiring into the defences of the castle. Upon the outward walls he found Wilkin Flammock, who, having done the office of a good and skilful captain in the mode of managing his artillery, and beating back, as we have already seen, the advanced guard of the enemy, was now with his own hand measuring out to his little garrison no stinted allowance of wine.

"Have a care, good Wilkin," said the father, "that thou dost not exceed in this matter. Wine is, thou knowest, like fire and water, an excellent servant, but a very bad master."

"It will be long ere it overflow the deep and solid skulls of my countrymen," said Wilkin Flammock. "Our Flemish courage is like our Flanders horses—the one needs the spur, and the other must have a taste of the winepot; but, credit me, father, they are of an enduring generation, and will not shrink in the washing.—But indeed, if I were to give the knaves a cup more than enough, it were not altogether amiss, since they are like to have a platter the less."

"How do you mean!" cried the monk, starting; "I trust in the saints the provisions have been cared for?"

"Not so well as in your convent, good father," replied Wilkin, with the same immoveable stolidity of countenance. "We had kept, as you know, too jolly a Christmas to have a very fat Easter. Yon Welsh hounds, who helped to eat up our victuals, are now like to get into our hold for the lack of them."

"Thou talkest mere folly," answered the monk; "orders were last evening given by our lord (whose soul God assoilzie!) to fetch in the necessary supplies from the country around!

"Ay, but the Welsh were too sharp set to permit us to do that at our ease this morning, which should have been done weeks and months since. Our lord deceased, if deceased he be, was one of those who trusted to the edge of the sword, and even so hath come of it. Commend me to a crossbow and a well-victualled castle, if I must needs fight at all.—You look pale, my good father, a cup of wine will revive you."

The monk motioned away from him the untasted cup, which Wilkin pressed him to with clownish civility. "We have now, indeed," he said, "no refuge, save in prayer!"

"Most true, good father;" again replied the impassible Fleming; "pray therefore as much as you will. I will content myself with fasting, which will come whether I will or no."—At this moment a horn was heard before the gate.—"Look to the portcullis and the gate, ye knaves!—What news, Neil Hansen?"

"A messenger from the Welsh tarries at the Mill-hill, just within shot of the cross-bows; he has a white flag, and demands admittance."

"Admit him not, upon thy life, till we be prepared for him," said Wilkin. "Bend the bonny mangonel upon the place, and shoot him if he dare to stir from the spot where he stands till we get all prepared to receive him," said Flammock in his native language. "And, Neil, thou houndsfoot, bestir thyself —let every pike, lance, and pole in the castle be ranged along the battlements, and pointed through the shot-holes—cut up some tapestry into the shape of banners, and show them from the highest towers.—Be ready when I give a signal, to strike *naker*, and blow trumpets, if we have any; if not, some cow-horns—anything for a noise. And hark ye, Neil Hansen, do you, and four or five of your fellows, go to the armoury and slip on coats-of-mail; our Netherlandish corslets do not appal them so much. Then let the Welsh thief be blindfolded and brought in amongst us—Do you hold up your heads and keep silence—leave me to deal with him—only have a care there be no English among us."

The monk, who in his travels had acquired some slight knowledge of the Flemish language, had well-nigh started when he heard the last article in Wilkin's instructions to his countryman, but commanded himself, although a little surprised, both at this suspicious circumstance, and at the readiness and dexterity with which the rough-hewn Fleming seemed to adapt his preparations to the rules of war and of sound policy.

Wilkin, on his part, was not very certain whether the monk had not heard and understood more of what he said to his countryman, than what he had intended. As if to lull asleep any suspicion which Father Aldrovand might entertain, he repeated to him in English most of the directions which he had given, adding, "Well, good father, what think you of it?"

"Excellent well," answered the father, "and done as if you had practised war from the cradle, instead of weaving broad-cloth."

"Nay, spare not your jibes, father," answered Wilkin.—"I know full well that you English think that Flemings have nought in their brainpan but sodden beef and cabbage; yet you see there goes wisdom to weaving of webs."

"Right, Master Wilkin Flammock," answered the father; "but, good Fleming, wilt thou tell me what answer thou wilt make to the Welsh Prince's summons?"

"Reverend father, first tell me what the summons will be," replied the Fleming.

"To surrender this castle upon the instant," answered the monk. "What will be your reply?"

"My answer will be, Nay—unless upon good composition."

"How, Sir Fleming! dare you mention composition and the castle of the Garde Doloureuse in one sentence?" said the monk.

"Not if I may do better," answered the Fleming. "But would your reverence have me dally until the question amongst the garrison be, whether a plump priest or a fat Fleming will be the better flesh to furnish their shambles?"

"Pshaw!" replied Father Aldrovand, "thou canst not mean such folly. Relief must arrive within twenty-four hours at farthest. Raymond Berenger expected it for certain within such a space."

"Raymond Berenger has been deceived this morning in more matters than one," answered the Fleming.

"Hark thee, Flanderkin," answered the monk, whose retreat from the world had not altogether quenched his military habits and propensities, "I counsel thee to deal uprightly in this matter, as thou dost regard thine own life; for here are as many English left alive, notwithstanding the slaughter of to-day, as may well suffice to fling the Flemish bull-frogs into the castle-ditch, should they have cause to think thou meanest falsely, in the keeping of this castle, and the defence of the Lady Eveline."

"Let not your reverence be moved with unnecessary and idle fears," replied Wilkin Flammock—"I am castellane in this house, by command of its lord, and what I hold for the advantage of mine service, that will I do."

"But I," said the angry monk, "I am the servant of the Pope—the chaplain of this castle, with power to bind and unloose. I fear me thou art no true Christian, Wilkin Flammock, but dost lean to the heresy of the mountaineers. Thou hast refused to take the blessed cross—thou hast breakfasted, and drunk both ale and wine, ere thou hast heard mass. Thou art not to be trusted, man, and I will not trust thee—I demand to be present at the conference betwixt thee and the Welshman."

"It may not be, good father," said Wilkin, with the same smiling, heavy countenance, which he maintained on all occasions of life, however urgent. "It is true, as thou sayest, good father, that I have mine own reasons for not marching quite so far as the gates of Jericho at present; and lucky I have such reasons, since I had not else been here to defend the gate of the Garde Doloureuse. It is also true that I may have been sometimes obliged to visit my mills earlier than the chaplain was called by his zeal to the altar, and that my stomach brooks not working ere I break my fast. But for this, father, I have paid a mulet even to your worshipful reverence, and methinks since you are pleased to remember the confession so exactly, you should not forget the penance and the absolution."

The monk, in alluding to the secrets of the confessional, had gone a step beyond what the rules of his order and of the church permitted. He was baffled by the Fleming's reply, and finding him unmoved by the charge of heresy, he could only answer, in some confusion, "You refuse, then, to admit me to the conference with the Welshman?"

"Reverend father," said Wilkin, "it altogether respecteth secular matters. If aught of religious tenor should intervene, you shall be summoned without delay."

"I will be there in spite of thee, thou Flemish ox," muttered the monk to himself, but in a tone not to be heard by the by-standers; and so speaking he left the battlements.

Wilkin Flammock, a few minutes afterwards, having first seen that all was arranged on the battlements, so as to give an imposing idea of a strength which did not exist, descended to a small guard-room, betwixt the outer and inner gate, where he was attended by half-a-dozen of his own people, disguised in the Norman armour which they had found in the armoury of the castle,— their strong, tall, and bulky forms, and motionless postures, causing them to look rather like trophies of some past age, than living and existing soldiers. Surrounded by these huge and inanimate figures, in a little vaulted room which almost excluded daylight, Flammock received the Welsh envoy, who was led in blindfolded betwixt two Flemings, yet not so carefully watched but that they permitted him to have a glimpse of the preparations on the battlements, which had, in fact, been made chiefly for the purpose of imposing on him. For the same purpose an occasional clatter of arms was made without; voices were heard as if officers were going their rounds; and other sounds of active preparation seemed to announce that a numerous and regular garrison was preparing to receive an attack.

When the bandage was removed from Jorworth's eyes,—for the same individual who had formerly brought Gwenwyn's offer of alliance, now bare his summons of surrender,—he looked haughtily around him and demanded to whom he was to deliver the commands of his master, the Gwenwyn, son of Cyvelioc, Prince of Powys.

"His highness," answered Flammock, with his usual smiling indifference of manner, "must be contented to treat with Wilkin Flammock of the Fulling-mills, deputed governor of the Garde Douloureuse."

"Thou deputed governor!" exclaimed Jorworth; "thou?—a Low-country weaver!—it is impossible. Low as they are, the English Crogan cannot have sunk to a point so low, as to be commanded by *thee!*—these men seem English, to them I will deliver my message."

"You may if you will," replied Wilkin, "but if they return you any answer save by signs, you shall call me *schelm*."

"Is this true?" said the Welsh envoy, looking towards the men-at-arms, as they seemed, by whom Flammock was attended; "are you really come to this pass? I thought that the mere having been born on British earth, though the children of spoilers and invaders, had inspired you with too much pride to brook the yoke of a base mechanic. Or, if you are not courageous, should you not be cautious?—Well speaks the proverb, Wo to him that will trust a stranger! Still mute—still silent?—answer me by word or sign—Do you really call and acknowledge him as your leader?"

The men in armour with one accord nodded their casques in reply to Jorworth's question, and then remained motionless as before.

The Welshman, with the acute genius of his country, suspected there was something in this which he could not entirely comprehend, but, preparing himself to be upon his guard, he proceeded as follows: "Be it as it may, I care not who hears the message of my sovereign, since it brings pardon and mercy to the inhabitants of this Castell an Carrig, which you have called the Garde Douloureuse, to cover the usurpation of the territory by the change of the name. Upon surrender of the same to the Prince of Powys, with its dependencies, and with the arms which it contains, and with the maiden Eveline Berenger, all within the castle shall depart unmolested, and have safe-conduct wheresoever they will, to go beyond the marches of the Cymry."

"And how, if we obey not this summons?" said the imperturbable Wilkin Flammock.

"Then shall your portion be with Raymond Berenger, your late leader," replied Jorworth, his eyes, while he was speaking, glancing with the vindictive ferocity which dictated his answer. "So many strangers as be here amongst ye, so many bodies to the ravens, so many heads to the gibbet!—It is long since the kites have had such a banquet of lurdane Flemings and false Saxons."

"Friend Jorworth," said Wilkin, "if such be thy only message, bear mine answer back to thy master, That wise men trust not to the words of others that safety, which they can secure by their own deeds. We have walls high and strong enough, deep moats, and plenty of munition, both longbow and arblast. We will keep the castle, trusting the castle will keep us, till God shall send us succour."

"Do not peril your lives on such an issue," said the Welsh emissary, changing his language to the Flemish, which, from occasional communication with those of that nation in Pembrokeshire, he spoke fluently, and which he now adopted, as if to conceal the purport of his discourse from the supposed English in the apartment. "Hark thee hither," he proceeded, "good Fleming. Knowest thou not that he in whom is your trust, the Constable De Lacy, hath bound himself by his vow to engage in no quarrel till he crosses the sea, and cannot come to your aid without perjury? He and the other Lords Marchers have drawn their forces far northward to join the host of Crusaders. What will it avail you to put us to the toil and trouble of a long siege, when you can hope no rescue?"

"And what will it avail me more," said Wilkin, answering in his native language and looking at the Welshman fixedly, yet with a countenance from which all expression seemed studiously banished, and which exhibited, upon features otherwise tolerable, a remarkable compound of dulness and simplicity, "what will it avail me whether your trouble be great or small?"

"Come, friend Flammock," said the Welshman, "frame not thyself more unapprehensive than nature hath formed thee. The glen is dark, but a sunbeam can light the side of it. Thy utmost efforts cannot prevent the fall of this castle; but thou mayst hasten it, and the doing so shall avail thee much." Thus speaking, he drew close up to Wilkin, and sunk his voice to an insinuating whisper, as he said, "Never did the withdrawing of a bar, or the raising of a portcullis, bring such vantage to Fleming as they may to thee, if thou wilt."

"I only know," said Wilkin, "that the drawing the one, and the dropping the other, have cost me my whole worldly subsistence."

"Fleming, it shall be compensated to thee with an overflowing measure. The liberality of Gwenwyn is as the summer rain."

"My whole mills and buildings have been this morning burnt to the earth—"

"Thou shalt have a thousand marks of silver, man, in the place of thy goods," said the Welshman; but the Fleming continued, without seeming to hear him, to number up his losses.

"My lands are forayed, twenty kine driven off, and—"

"Threescore shall replace them," interrupted Jorworth, "chosen from the most bright-skinned of the spoil."

"But my daughter—but the Lady Eveline"—said the Fleming, with some slight change in his monotonous voice, which seemed to express doubt and perplexity—"You are cruel conquerors, and—"

"To those who resist us we are fearful," said Jorworth, "but not to such as shall deserve clemency by surrender. Gwenwyn will forget the contumelies of Raymond, and raise his daughter to high honour among the daughters of the Cymry. For thine own child, form but a wish for her advantage, and it shall be fulfilled to the uttermost. Now, Fleming, we understand each other."

"I understand thee, at least," said Flammock.

"And I thee, I trust?" said Jorworth, bending his keen, wild blue eye on the stolid and unexpressive face of the Netherlander, like an eager student who seeks to discover some hidden and mysterious meaning in a passage of a classic author, the direct import of which seems trite and trivial.

"You believe that you understand me," said Wilkin; "but here lies the difficulty,—which of us shall trust the other?"

"Darest thou ask?" answered Jorworth. "Is it for thee, or such as thee, to express doubt of the purposes of the Prince of Powys?"

"I know them not, good Jorworth, but through thee; and well I wot thou art not one who will let thy traffic miscarry for want of aid from the breath of thy mouth."

"As I am a Christian man," said Jorworth, hurrying asseveration on asseveration—"by the soul of my father—by the faith of my mother—by the black rood of—"

"Stop, good Jorworth—thou heapest thine oaths too thickly on each other, for me to value them to the right estimate," said Flammock; "that which is so lightly pledged, is sometimes not thought worth redeeming. Some part of the promised guerdon in hand the whilst, were worth an hundred oaths."

"Thou suspicious churl, darest thou doubt my word?"

"No—by no means," answered Wilkin;—"nevertheless, I will believe thy deed more readily."

"To the point, Fleming," said Jorworth—"What wouldst thou have of me?"

"Let me have some present sight of the money thou didst promise, and I will think of the rest of thy proposal."

"Base silver-broker!" answered Jorworth, "thinkest thou the Prince of Powys has as many money-bags, as the merchants of thy land of sale and barter? He gathers treasures by his conquests, as the waterspout sucks up water by its strength, but it is to disperse them among his followers, as the cloudy column restores its contents to earth and ocean. The silver that I promise thee has yet to be gathered out of the Saxon chests—nay, the casket of Berenger himself must be ransacked to make up the tale."

"Methinks I could do that myself, (having full power in the castle,) and so save you a labour," said the Fleming.

"True," answered Jorworth, "but it would be at the expense of a cord and a noose, whether the Welsh took the place or the Normans relieved it—the one would expect their booty entire—the other their countryman's treasures to be delivered undiminished."

"I may not gainsay that," said the Fleming. "Well, say I were content to trust you thus far, why not return my cattle, which are in your own hands, and at your disposal? If you do not pleasure me in something beforehand, what can I expect of you afterwards?"

"I would pleasure you in a greater matter," answered the equally suspicious Welshman. "But what would it avail thee to have thy cattle within the fortress? They can be better cared for on the plain beneath."

"In faith," replied the Fleming, "thou sayst truth—they will be but a trouble to us here, where we have so many already provided for the use of the garrison. —And yet, when I consider it more closely, we have enough of forage to maintain all we have, and more. Now, my cattle are of a peculiar stock, brought from the rich pastures of Flanders, and I desire to have them restored ere your axes and Welsh hooks be busy with their hides."

"You shall have them this night, hide and horn," said Jorworth; "it is but a small earnest of a great boon."

"Thanks to your munificence," said the Fleming; "I am a simple-minded man, and bound my wishes to the recovery of my own property."

"Thou wilt be ready, then, to deliver the castle?" said Jorworth.

"Of that we will talk farther to-morrow," said Wilkin Flammock; "if these English and Normans should suspect such a purpose, we should have wild work—they must be fully dispersed ere I can hold farther communication on the subject. Meanwhile, I pray thee, depart suddenly, and as if offended with the tenor of our discourse."

"Yet would I fain know something more fixed and absolute," said Jorworth.

"Impossible—impossible," said the Fleming: "see you not yonder tall fellow begins already to handle his dagger—Go hence in haste, and angrily—and forget not the cattle."

"I will not forget them," said Jorworth; "but if thou keep not faith with us—"

So speaking, he left the apartment with a gesture of menace, partly really directed to Wilkin himself, partly assumed in consequence of his advice. Flammock replied in English, as if that all around might understand, what he said,

"Do thy worst, Sir Welshman! I am a true man; I defy the proposals of rendition, and will hold out this castle to thy shame and thy master's!—Here—let him be blindfolded once more, and returned in safety to his attendants without; the next Welshman who appears before the gate of the Garde Doloureuse, shall be more sharply received."

The Welshman was blindfolded and withdrawn, when, as Wilkin Flammock himself left the guardroom, one of the seeming men-at-arms, who had been present at this interview, said in his ear, in English, "Thou art a false traitor, Flammock, and shalt die a traitor's death!"

Startled at this, the Fleming would have questioned the man farther, but he had disappeared so soon as the words were uttered. Flammock was disconcerted by this circumstance, which showed him that his interview with Jorworth had been observed, and its purpose known or conjectured, by some one who was a stranger to his confidence, and might thwart his intentions; and he quickly after learned that this was the case.

CHAPTER THE SIXTH

Blessed Mary, mother dear,

To a maiden bend thine ear,
Virgin undefiled, to thee
A wretched virgin bends the knee.
  HYMN TO THE VIRGIN.

The daughter of the slaughtered Raymond had descended from the elevated station whence she had beheld the field of battle, in the agony of grief natural to a child whose eyes have beheld the death of an honoured and beloved father. But her station, and the principles of chivalry in which she had been trained up, did not permit any prolonged or needless indulgence of inactive sorrow. In raising the young and beautiful of the female sex to the rank of princesses, or rather goddesses, the spirit of that singular system exacted from them, in requital, a tone of character, and a line of conduct, superior and something contradictory to that of natural or merely human feeling. Its heroines frequently resembled portraits shown by an artificial light—strong and luminous, and which placed in high relief the objects on which it was turned; but having still something of adventitious splendour, which, compared with that of the natural day, seemed glaring and exaggerated.

It was not permitted to the orphan of the Garde Doloureuse, the daughter of a line of heroes, whose stem was to be found in the race of Thor, Balder, Odin, and other deified warriors of the North, whose beauty was the theme of a hundred minstrels, and her eyes the leading star of half the chivalry of the warlike marches of Wales, to mourn her sire with the ineffectual tears of a village maiden. Young as she was, and horrible as was the incident which she had but that instant witnessed, it was not altogether so appalling to her as to a maiden whose eye had not been accustomed to the rough, and often fatal sports of chivalry, and whose residence had not been among scenes and men where war and death had been the unceasing theme of every tongue, whose imagination had not been familiarized with wild and bloody events, or, finally, who had not been trained up to consider an honourable "death under shield," as that of a field of battle was termed, as a more desirable termination to the life of a warrior, than that lingering and unhonoured fate which comes slowly on, to conclude the listless and helpless inactivity of prolonged old age. Eveline, while she wept for her father, felt her bosom glow when she recollected that he died in the blaze of his fame, and amidst heaps of his slaughtered enemies; and when she thought of the exigencies of her own situation, it was with the determination to defend her own liberty, and to avenge her father's death, by every means which Heaven had left within her power.

The aids of religion were not forgotten; and according to the custom of the times, and the doctrines of the Roman church, she endeavoured to propitiate the favour of Heaven by vows as well as prayers. In a small crypt, or oratory, adjoining to the chapel, was hung over an altar-piece, on which a lamp constantly burned, a small picture of the Virgin Mary, revered as a household and peculiar deity by the family of Berenger, one of whose ancestors had brought it from the Holy Land, whither he had gone upon pilgrimage. It was of the period of the Lower Empire, a Grecian painting, not unlike those which in Catholic countries are often imputed to the Evangelist Luke. The crypt in which it was placed was accounted a shrine of uncommon sanctity—nay, supposed to have displayed miraculous powers; and Eveline, by the daily garland of flowers which she offered before the painting, and by the constant prayers with which they were accompanied, had constituted herself the peculiar votaress of Our Lady of the Garde Doloureuse, for so the picture was named.

Now, apart from others, alone, and in secrecy, sinking in the extremity of her sorrow before the shrine of her patroness, she besought the protection of kindred purity for the defence of her freedom and honour, and invoked vengeance on the wild and treacherous chieftain who had slain her father, and was now beleaguering her place of strength. Not only did she vow a large donative in lands to the shrine of the protectress whose aid she implored; but the oath passed her lips, (even though they faltered, and though something within her remonstrated against the vow,) that whatsoever favoured knight Our Lady of the Garde Doloureuse might employ for her rescue, should obtain from her in guerdon whatever boon she might honourably grant, were it that of her virgin hand at the holy altar. Taught as she was to believe, by the assurances of many a knight, that such a surrender was the highest boon which Heaven could bestow, she felt as discharging a debt of gratitude when she placed herself entirely at the disposal of the pure and blessed patroness in whose aid she confided. Perhaps there lurked in this devotion some earthly hope of which she was herself scarce conscious, and which reconciled her to the indefinite sacrifice thus freely offered. The Virgin, (this flattering hope might insinuate,) kindest and most benevolent of patronesses, will use compassionately the power resigned to her, and *he* will be the favoured champion of Maria, upon whom her votaress would most willingly confer favour.

But if there was such a hope, as something selfish will often mingle with our noblest and purest emotions, it arose unconscious of Eveline herself, who, in the full assurance of implicit faith, and fixing on the representative of her adoration, eyes in which the most earnest supplication, the most humble confidence, struggled with unbidden tears, was perhaps more beautiful than when, young as she was, she was selected to bestow the prize of chivalry in the lists of Chester. It was no wonder that, in such a moment of high excitation, when prostrated in devotion before a being of whose power to protect her, and to make her protection assured by a visible sign, she doubted nothing, the Lady Eveline conceived she saw with her own eyes the acceptance of her vow. As she gazed on the picture with an over-strained eye, and an imagination heated with enthusiasm, the expression seemed to alter from the hard outline, fashioned by the Greek painter; the eyes appeared to become animated, and to return with looks of compassion the suppliant entreaties of the votaress, and the mouth visibly arranged itself into a smile of inexpressible sweetness. It even seemed to her that the head made a gentle inclination.

Overpowered by supernatural awe at appearances, of which her faith permitted her not to question the reality, the Lady Eveline folded her arms on her bosom, and prostrated her forehead on the pavement, as the posture most fitting to listen to divine communication.

But her vision went not so far; there was neither sound nor voice, and when, after stealing her eyes all around the crypt in which she knelt, she again raised them to the figure of Our Lady, the features seemed to be in the form in which the limner had sketched them, saving that, to Eveline's imagination, they still retained an august and yet gracious expression, which she had not before remarked upon the countenance. With awful reverence, almost amounting to fear, yet comforted, and even elated, with the visitation she had witnessed, the maiden repeated again and again the orisons which she thought most grateful to the ear of her benefactress; and rising at length, retired backwards, as from the presence of a sovereign, until she attained the outer chapel.

Here one or two females still knelt before the saints which the walls and niches presented for adoration; but the rest of the terrified suppliants, too anxious to prolong their devotions, had dispersed through the castle to learn tidings of their friends, and to obtain some refreshment, or at least some place of repose for themselves and their families.

Bowing her head, and muttering an ave to each saint as she passed his image, (for impending danger makes men observant of the rites of devotion,) the Lady Eveline had almost reached the door of the chapel, when a man-at-arms, as he seemed, entered hastily; and, with a louder voice than suited the holy place, unless when need was most urgent, demanded the Lady Eveline. Impressed with the feelings of veneration which the late scene had produced, she was about to rebuke his military rudeness, when he spoke again, and in anxious haste, "Daughter, we are betrayed!" and though the form, and the coat-of-mail which covered it, were those of a soldier, the voice was that of Father Aldrovand, who, eager and anxious at the same time, disengaged himself from the mail hood, and showed his countenance.

"Father," she said, "what means this? Have you forgotten the confidence in

Heaven which you are wont to recommend, that you bear other arms than your order assigns to you?"

"It may come to that ere long," said Father Aldrovand; "for I was a soldier ere I was a monk. But now I have donn'd this harness to discover treachery, not to resist force. Ah! my beloved daughter— we are dreadfully beset—foemen without—traitors within!—The false Fleming, Wilkin Flammock, is treating for the surrender of the castle!"

"Who dares say so?" said a veiled female, who had been kneeling unnoticed in a sequestered corner of the chapel, but who now started up and came boldly betwixt Lady Eveline and the monk.

"Go hence, thou saucy minion," said the monk, surprised at this bold interruption; "this concerns not thee."

"But it *doth* concern me," said the damsel, throwing back her veil, and discovering the juvenile countenance of Rose, the daughter of Wilkin Flammock, her eyes sparkling, and her cheeks blushing with anger, the vehemence of which made a singular contrast with the very fair complexion, and almost infantine features of the speaker, whose whole form and figure was that of a girl who has scarce emerged from childhood, and indeed whose general manners were as gentle and bashful as they now seemed bold, impassioned, and undaunted.—"Doth it not concern me," she said, "that my father's honest name should be tainted with treason? Doth it not concern the stream when the fountain is troubled? It *doth* concern me, and I will know the author of the calumny."

"Damsel," said Eveline, "restrain thy useless passion; the good father, though he cannot intentionally calumniate thy father, speaks, it may be, from false report."

"As I am an unworthy priest," said the father, "I speak from the report of my own ears. Upon the oath of my order, myself heard this Wilkin Flammock chaffering with the Welshman for the surrender of the Garde Doloureuse. By help of this hauberk and mail hood, I gained admittance to a conference where he thought there were no English ears. They spoke Flemish too, but I knew the jargon of old."

"The Flemish," said the angry maiden, whose headstrong passion led her to speak first in answer to the last insult offered, "is no jargon like your piebald English, half Norman, half Saxon, but a noble Gothic tongue, spoken by the brave warriors who fought against the Roman Kaisars, when Britain bent the neck to them—and as for this he has said of Wilkin Flammock," she continued, collecting her ideas into more order as she went on, "believe it not, my dearest lady; but, as you value the honour of your own noble father, confide, as in the Evangelists, in the honesty of mine!" This she spoke with an imploring tone of voice, mingled with sobs, as if her heart had been breaking.

Eveline endeavoured to soothe her attendant. "Rose," she said, "in this evil time suspicions will light on the best men, and misunderstandings will arise among the best friends.—Let us hear the good father state what he hath to charge upon your parent. Fear not but that Wilkin shall be heard in his defence. Thou wert wont to be quiet and reasonable."

"I am neither quiet nor reasonable on this matter," said Rose, with redoubled indignation; "and it is ill of you, lady, to listen to the falsehoods of that reverend mummer, who is neither true priest nor true soldier. But I will fetch one who shall confront him either in casque or cowl." So saying, she went hastily out of the chapel, while the monk, after some pedantic circumlocution, acquainted the Lady Eveline with what he had overheard betwixt Jorworth and Wilkin; and proposed to her to draw together the few English who were in the castle, and take possession of the innermost square tower; a keep which, as usual in Gothic fortresses of the Norman period, was situated so as to make considerable defence, even after the exterior works of the castle, which it commanded, were in the hand of the enemy.

"Father," said Eveline, still confident in the vision she had lately witnessed, "this were good counsel in extremity; but otherwise, it were to create the very evil we fear, by seating our garrison at odds amongst themselves. I have a strong, and not unwarranted confidence, good father, in our blessed Lady of the Garde Doloureuse, that we shall attain at once vengeance on our barbarous enemies, and escape from our present jeopardy; and I call you to witness the vow I have made, that to him whom Our Lady should employ to work us succour, I will refuse nothing, were it my father's inheritance, or the hand of his daughter."

"*Ave Maria! Ave Regina Coeli!*" said the priest; "on a rock more sure you could not have founded your trust.—But, daughter," he continued after the proper ejaculation had been made, "have you never heard, even by a hint, that there was a treaty for your hand betwixt our much honoured lord, of whom we are cruelly bereft, (may God assoilzie his soul!) and the great house of Lacy?"

"Something I may have heard," said Eveline, dropping her eyes, while a slight tinge suffused her cheek; "but I refer me to the disposal of our Lady of Succour and Consolation."

As she spoke, Rose entered the chapel with the same vivacity she had shown in leaving it, leading by the hand her father, whose sluggish though firm step, vacant countenance, and heavy demeanour, formed the strongest contrast to the rapidity of her motions, and the anxious animation of her address. Her task of dragging him forward might have reminded the spectator of some of those ancient monuments, on which a small cherub, singularly inadequate to the task, is often represented as hoisting upward towards the empyrean the fleshy bulk of some ponderous tenant of the tomb, whose disproportioned weight bids fair to render ineffectual the benevolent and spirited exertions of its fluttering guide and assistant.

"Roschen—my child—what grieves thee?" said the Netherlander, as he yielded to his daughter's violence with a smile, which, being on the countenance of a father, had more of expression and feeling than those which seemed to have made their constant dwelling upon his lips.

"Here stands my father," said the impatient maiden; "impeach him with treason, who can or dare! There stands Wilkin Flammock, son of Dieterick, the Cramer of Antwerp,—let those accuse him to his face who slandered him behind his back!"

"Speak, Father Aldrovand," said the Lady Eveline; "we are young in our lordship, and, alas! the duty hath descended upon us in an evil hour; yet we will, so may God and Our Lady help us, hear and judge of your accusation to the utmost of our power."

"This Wilkin Flammock," said the monk, "however bold he hath made himself in villany, dares not deny that I heard him with my own ears treat for the surrender of the castle."

"Strike him, father!" said the indignant Rose,—"strike the disguised mummer! The steel hauberk may be struck, though not the monk's frock—strike him, or tell him that he lies foully!"

"Peace, Roschen, thou art mad," said her father, angrily; "the monk hath more truth than sense about him, and I would his ears had been farther off when he thrust them into what concerned him not."

Rose's countenance fell when she heard her father bluntly avow the treasonable communication of which she had thought him incapable— she dropt the hand by which she had dragged him into the chapel, and stared on the Lady Eveline, with eyes which seemed starting from their sockets, and a countenance from which the blood, with which it was so lately highly coloured, had retreated to garrison the heart.

Eveline looked upon the culprit with a countenance in which sweetness and dignity were mingled with sorrow. "Wilkin," she said, "I could not have believed this. What! on the very day of thy confiding benefactor's death, canst thou have been tampering with his murderers, to deliver up the castle, and betray thy trust!—But I will not upbraid thee—I deprive thee of the trust reposed in so unworthy a person, and appoint thee to be kept in ward in the western tower, till God send us relief; when, it may be, thy daughter's merits shall atone for thy offences, and save farther punishment.—See that our commands be presently obeyed."

"Yes—yes—yes!" exclaimed Rose, hurrying one word on the other as fast and vehemently as she could articulate—"Let us go—let us go to the darkest dungeon—darkness befits us better than light."

The monk, on the other hand, perceiving that the Fleming made no motion to obey the mandate of arrest, came forward, in a manner more suiting his ancient profession, and present disguise, than his spiritual character; and with the words, "I attach thee, Wilkin Flammock, of acknowledged treason to your liege lady," would have laid hand upon him, had not the Fleming stepped back and warned him off, with a menacing and determined gesture, while he said, —"Ye are mad!—all of you English are mad when the moon is full, and my silly girl hath caught the malady.—Lady, your honoured father gave me a charge, which I propose to execute to the best for all parties, and you cannot, being a minor, deprive me of it at your idle pleasure.—Father Aldrovand, a monk makes no lawful arrests.—Daughter Roschen, hold your peace and dry your eyes—you are a fool."

"I am, I am," said Rose, drying her eyes and regaining her elasticity of manner —"I am indeed a fool, and worse than a fool, for a moment to doubt my father's probity.—Confide in him, dearest lady; he is wise though he is grave, and kind though he is plain and homely in his speech. Should he prove false he will fare the worse! for I will plunge myself from the pinnacle of the Warder's Tower to the bottom of the moat, and he shall lose his own daughter for betraying his master's."

"This is all frenzy," said the monk—"Who trusts avowed traitors? —Here, Normans, English, to the rescue of your liege lady—Bows and bills—bows and bills!"

"You may spare your throat for your next homily, good father," said the Netherlander, "or call in good Flemish, since you understand it, for to no other language will those within hearing reply."

He then approached the Lady Eveline with a real or affected air of clumsy kindness, and something as nearly approaching to courtesy as his manners and features could assume. He bade her good-night, and assuring her that he would act for the best, left the chapel. The monk was about to break forth into revilings, but Eveline, with more prudence, checked his zeal.

"I cannot," she said, "but hope that this man's intentions are honest—"

"Now, God's blessing on you, lady, for that very word!" said Rose, eagerly interrupting her, and kissing her hand.

"But if unhappily they are doubtful," continued Eveline, "it is not by reproach that we can bring him to a better purpose. Good father, give an eye to the preparations for resistance, and see nought omitted that our means furnish for the defence of the castle."

"Fear nothing, my dearest daughter," said Aldrovand; "there are still some English hearts amongst us, and we will rather kill and eat the Flemings themselves, than surrender the castle."

"That were food as dangerous to come by as bear's venison, father," answered Rose, bitterly, still on fire with the idea that the monk treated her nation with suspicion and contumely.

On these terms they separated—the women to indulge their fears and sorrows in private grief, or alleviate them by private devotion; the monk to try to discover what were the real purposes of Wilkin Flammock, and to counteract them if possible, should they seem to indicate treachery. His eye, however, though sharpened by strong suspicion, saw nothing to strengthen his fears, excepting that the Fleming had, with considerable military skill, placed the principal posts of the castle in the charge of his own countrymen which must make any attempt to dispossess him of his present authority both difficult and dangerous. The monk at length retired, summoned by the duties of the evening service, and with the determination to be stirring with the light the next morning.

CHAPTER THE SEVENTH

Oh, sadly shines the morning sun
On leaguer'd castle wall,
When bastion, tower, and battlement,
Seemed nodding to their fall.
  OLD BALLAD.

True to his resolution, and telling his beads as he went, that he might lose no time, Father Aldrovand began his rounds in the castle so soon as daylight had touched the top of the eastern horizon. A natural instinct led him first to those stalls which, had the fortress been properly victualled for a siege, ought to have been tenanted by cattle; and great was his delight to see more than a score of fat kine and bullocks in the place which had last night been empty! One of them had already been carried to the shambles, and a Fleming or two, who played butchers on the occasion, were dividing the carcass for the cook's use. The good father had well-nigh cried out, a miracle; but, not to be too precipitate, he limited his transport to a private exclamation in honour of Our Lady of the Garde Doloureuse.

"Who talks of lack of provender?—who speaks of surrender now?" he said. "Here is enough to maintain us till Hugo de Lacy arrives, were he to sail back from Cyprus to our relief. I did purpose to have fasted this morning, as well to save victuals as on a religious score; but the blessings of the saints must not be slighted.—Sir Cook, let me have half a yard or so of broiled beef presently; bid the pantler send me a manchet, and the butler a cup of wine. I will take a running breakfast on the western battlements."

At this place, which was rather the weakest point of the Garde Doloureuse, the good father found Wilkin Flammock anxiously superintending the necessary measures of defence. He greeted him courteously, congratulated him on the stock of provisions with which the castle had been supplied during the night, and was inquiring how they had been so happily introduced through the Welsh besiegers, when Wilkin took the first occasion to interrupt him.

"Of all this another time, good father; but I wish at present, and before other discourse, to consult thee on a matter which presses my conscience, and moreover deeply concerns my worldly estate."

"Speak on, my excellent son," said the father, conceiving that he should thus gain the key to Wilkin's real intentions. "Oh, a tender conscience is a jewel! and he that will not listen when it saith, 'Pour out thy doubts into the ear of the priest,' shall one day have his own dolorous outcries choked with fire and brimstone. Thou wert ever of a tender conscience, son Wilkin, though thou hast but a rough and borrel bearing."

"Well, then," said Wilkin, "you are to know, good father, that I have had some dealings with my neighbour, Jan Vanwelt, concerning my daughter Rose, and that he has paid me certain gilders on condition I will match her to him."

"Pshaw, pshaw! my good son," said the disappointed confessor, "this gear can lie over—this is no time for marrying or giving in marriage, when we are all like to be murdered."

"Nay, but hear me, good father," said the Fleming, "for this point of conscience concerns the present case more nearly than you wot of.—You must know I have no will to bestow Rose on this same Jan Vanwelt, who is old, and of ill conditions; and I would know of you whether I may, in conscience, refuse him my consent?"

"Truly," said Father Aldrovand, "Rose is a pretty lass, though somewhat hasty;

and I think you may honestly withdraw your consent, always on paying back the gilders you have received."

"But there lies the pinch, good father," said the Fleming—"the refunding this money will reduce me to utter poverty. The Welsh have destroyed my substance; and this handful of money is all, God help me! on which I must begin the world again."

"Nevertheless, son Wilkin," said Aldrovand, "thou must keep thy word, or pay the forfeit; for what saith the text? *Quis habitabit in tabernaculo, quis requiescet in monte sancta?*— Who shall ascend to the tabernacle, and dwell in the holy mountain? Is it not answered again, *Qui jurat proximo et non decipit?*—Go to, my son—break not thy plighted word for a little filthy lucre —better is an empty stomach and an hungry heart with a clear conscience, than a fatted ox with iniquity and wordbreaking.—Sawest thou not our late noble lord, who (may his soul be happy!) chose rather to die in unequal battle, like a true knight, than live a perjured man, though he had but spoken a rash word to a Welshman over a wine flask?"

"Alas! then," said the Fleming, "this is even what I feared! We must e'en render up the castle, or restore to the Welshman, Jorworth, the cattle, by means of which I had schemed to victual and defend it."

"How—wherefore—what dost thou mean?" said the monk, in astonishment. "I speak to thee of Rose Flammock, and Jan Van- devil, or whatever you call him, and you reply with talk about cattle and castles, and I wot not what!"

"So please you, holy father, I did but speak in parables. This castle was the daughter I had promised to deliver over—the Welshman is Jan Vanwelt, and the gilders were the cattle he has sent in, as a part-payment beforehand of my guerdon."

"Parables!" said the monk, colouring with anger at the trick put on him; "what has a boor like thee to do with parables?—But I forgive thee—I forgive thee."

"I am therefore to yield the castle to the Welshman, or restore him his cattle?" said the impenetrable Dutchman.

"Sooner yield thy soul to Satan!" replied the monk.

"I fear it must be the alternative," said the Fleming; "for the example of thy honourable lord—"

"The example of an honourable fool"—answered the monk; then presently subjoined, "Our Lady be with her servant!—This Belgic- brained boor makes me forget what I would say."

"Nay, but the holy text which your reverence cited to me even now," continued the Fleming.

"Go to," said the monk; "what hast thou to do to presume to think of texts?—knowest thou not the letter of the Scripture slayeth, and that it is the exposition which maketh to live?—Art thou not like one who, coming to a physician, conceals from him half the symptoms of the disease?—I tell thee, thou foolish Fleming, the text speaketh but of promises made unto Christians, and there is in the Rubric a special exception of such as are made to Welshmen." At this commentary the Fleming grinned so broadly as to show his whole case of broad strong white teeth. Father Aldrovand himself grinned in sympathy, and then proceeded to say,—"Come, come, I see how it is. Thou hast studied some small revenge on me for doubting of thy truth; and, in verity, I think thou hast taken it wittily enough. But wherefore didst thou not let me into the secret from the beginning? I promise thee I had foul suspicions of thee.

"What!" said the Fleming, "is it possible I could ever think of involving your reverence in a little matter of deceit? Surely Heaven hath sent me more grace and manners.—Hark, I hear Jorworth's horn at the gate."

"He blows like a town swineherd," said Aldrovand, in disdain.

"It is not your reverence's pleasure that I should restore the cattle unto them, then?" said Flammock.

"Yes, thus far. Prithee, deliver him straightway over the walls such a tub of boiling water as shall scald the hair from his goatskin cloak. And, hark thee, do thou, in the first place, try the temperature of the kettle with thy forefinger, and that shall be thy penance for the trick thou hast played me."

The Fleming answered this with another broad grin of intelligence, and they proceeded to the outer gate, to which Jorworth had come alone. Placing himself at the wicket, which, however, he kept carefully barred, and speaking through a small opening, contrived for such purpose, Wilkin Flammock demanded of the Welshman his business.

"To receive rendition of the castle, agreeable to promise," said Jorworth.

"Ay? and art thou come on such errand alone?" said Wilkin.

"No, truly," answered Jorworth; "I have some two score of men concealed among yonder bushes."

"Then thou hadst best lead them away quickly," answered Wilkin, "before our archers let fly a sheaf of arrows among them."

"How, villain! Dost thou not mean to keep thy promise?" said the Welshman.

"I gave thee none," said the Fleming; "I promised but to think on what thou didst say. I have done so, and have communicated with my ghostly father, who will in no respect hear of my listening to thy proposal."

"And wilt thou," said Jorworth, "keep the cattle, which I simply sent into the castle on the faith of our agreement?"

"I will excommunicate and deliver him over to Satan," said the monk, unable to wait the phlegmatic and lingering answer of the Fleming, "if he give horn, hoof, or hair of them, to such an uncircumcised Philistine as thou or thy master."

"It is well, shorn priest," answered Jorworth in great anger. "But mark me— reckon not on your frock for ransom. When Gwenwyn hath taken this castle, as it shall not longer shelter such a pair of faithless traitors, I will have you sewed up each into the carcass of one of these kine, for which your penitent has forsworn himself, and lay you where wolf and eagle shall be your only companions."

"Thou wilt work thy will when it is matched with thy power," said the sedate Netherlander.

"False Welshman, we defy thee to thy teeth!" answered, in the same breath, the more irascible monk. "I trust to see hounds gnaw thy joints ere that day come that ye talk of so proudly."

By way of answer to both, Jorworth drew back his arm with his levelled javelin, and shaking the shaft till it acquired a vibratory motion, he hurled it with equal strength and dexterity right against the aperture in the wicket. It whizzed through the opening at which it was aimed, and flew (harmlessly, however) between the heads of the monk and the Fleming; the former of whom started back, while the latter only said, as he looked at the javelin, which stood quivering in the door of the guard-room, "That was well aimed, and happily baulked."

Jorworth, the instant he had flung his dart, hastened to the ambush which he had prepared, and gave them at once the signal and the example of a rapid retreat down the hill. Father Aldrovand would willingly have followed them with a volley of arrows, but the Fleming observed that ammunition was too precious with them to be wasted on a few runaways. Perhaps the honest man remembered that they had come within the danger of such a salutation, in some measure, on his own assurance. When the noise of the hasty retreat of Jorworth and his followers had died away, there ensued a dead silence, well corresponding with the coolness and calmness of that early hour in the morning.

"This will not last long," said Wilkin to the monk, in a tone of foreboding seriousness, which found an echo in the good father's bosom.

"It will not, and it cannot," answered Aldrovand; "and we must expect a shrewd attack, which I should mind little, but that their numbers are great, ours few; the extent of the walls considerable, and the obstinacy of these Welsh fiends almost equal to their fury. But we will do the best. I will to the Lady Eveline—She must show herself upon the battlements—She is fairer in feature than becometh a man of my order to speak of; and she has withal a breathing of her father's lofty spirit. The look and the word of such a lady will give a man double strength in the hour of need."

"It may be," said the Fleming; "and I will go see that the good breakfast which I have appointed be presently served forth; it will give my Flemings more strength than the sight of the ten thousand virgins—may their help be with us! —were they all arranged on a fair field."

CHAPTER THE EIGHTH

'Twas when ye raised,' mid sap and siege,
The banner of your rightful liege
At your she captain's call,
Who, miracle of womankind,
Lent mettle to the meanest hind
That mann'd her castle wall.
   WILLIAM STEWART ROSE.

The morning light was scarce fully spread abroad, when Eveline Berenger, in compliance with her confessor's advice, commenced her progress around the walls and battlements of the beleaguered castle, to confirm, by her personal entreaties, the minds of the valiant, and to rouse the more timid to hope and to exertion. She wore a rich collar and bracelets, as ornaments which indicated her rank—and high descent; and her under tunic, in the manner of the times, was gathered around her slender waist by a girdle, embroidered with precious stones, and secured by a large buckle of gold. From one side of the girdle was suspended a pouch or purse, splendidly adorned with needle-work, and on the left side it sustained a small dagger of exquisite workmanship. A dark-coloured mantle, chosen as emblematic of her clouded fortunes, was flung loosely around her; and its hood was brought forward, so as to shadow, but not hide, her beautiful countenance. Her looks had lost the high and ecstatic expression which had been inspired by supposed revelation, but they retained a sorrowful and mild, yet determined character—and, in addressing the soldiers, she used a mixture of entreaty and command—now throwing herself upon their protection—now demanding in her aid the just tribute of their allegiance.

The garrison was divided, as military skill dictated, in groups, on the points most liable to attack, or from which an assailing enemy might be best annoyed; and it was this unavoidable separation of their force into small detachments, which showed to disadvantage the extent of walls, compared with the number of the defenders; and though Wilkin Flammock had contrived several means of concealing this deficiency of force from the enemy, he could not disguise it from the defenders of the castle, who cast mournful glances on the length of battlements which were unoccupied save by sentinels, and then looked out to the fatal field of battle, loaded with the bodies of those who ought to have been their comrades in this hour of peril.

The presence of Eveline did much to rouse the garrison from this state of discouragement. She glided from post to post, from tower to tower of the old gray fortress, as a gleam of light passes over a clouded landscape, and touching its various points in succession, calls them out to beauty and effect. Sorrow and fear sometimes make sufferers eloquent. She addressed the various nations who composed her little garrison, each in appropriate language. To the English, she spoke as children of the soil—to the Flemings, as men who had become denizens by the right of hospitality—to the Normans, as descendants of that victorious race, whose sword had made them the nobles and sovereigns of every land where its edge had been tried. To them she used the language of chivalry, by whose rules the meanest of that nation regulated, or affected to regulate, his actions. The English she reminded of their good faith and honesty of heart; and to the Flemings she spoke of the destruction of their property, the fruits of their honest industry. To all she proposed vengeance for the death of their leader and his followers—to all she recommended confidence in God and Our Lady of the Garde Doloureuse; and she ventured to assure all, of the strong and victorious bands that were already in march to their relief.

"Will the gallant champions of the cross," she said, "think of leaving their native land, while the wail of women and of orphans is in their ears?—it were to convert their pious purpose into mortal sin, and to derogate from the high fame they have so well won. Yes—fight but valiantly, and perhaps, before the very sun that is now slowly rising shall sink in the sea, you will see it shining on the ranks of Shrewsbury and Chester. When did the Welshmen wait to hear the clangour of their trumpets, or the rustling of their silken banners? Fight bravely—fight freely but awhile!—our castle is strong—our munition ample —your hearts are good—your arms are powerful—God is nigh to us, and our friends are not far distant. Fight, then, in the name of all that is good and holy —fight for yourselves, for your wives, for your children, and for your property

—and oh! fight for an orphan maiden, who hath no other defenders but what a sense of her sorrows, and the remembrance of her father, may raise up among you."

Such speeches as these made a powerful impression on the men to whom they were addressed, already hardened, by habits and sentiments, against a sense of danger. The chivalrous Normans swore, on the cross of their swords, they would die to a man ere they would surrender their posts—the blunter Anglo-Saxons cried, "Shame on him who would render up such a lamb as Eveline to a Welsh wolf, while he could make her a bulwark with his body!"— Even the cold Flemings caught a spark of the enthusiasm with which the others were animated, and muttered to each other praises of the young lady's beauty, and short but honest resolves to do the best they might in her defence.

Rose Flammock, who accompanied her lady with one or two attendants upon her circuit around the castle, seemed to have relapsed into her natural character of a shy and timid girl, out of the excited state into which she had been brought by the suspicions which in the evening before had attached to her father's character. She tripped closely but respectfully after Eveline, and listened to what she said from time to time, with the awe and admiration of a child listening to its tutor, while only her moistened eye expressed how far she felt or comprehended the extent of the danger, or the force of the exhortations. There was, however, a moment when the youthful maiden's eye became more bright, her step more confident, her looks more elevated. This was when they approached the spot where her father, having discharged the duties of commander of the garrison, was now exercising those of engineer, and displaying great skill, as well as wonderful personal strength, in directing and assisting the establishment of a large mangonel, (a military engine used for casting stones,) upon a station commanding an exposed postern gate, which led from the western side of the castle down to the plain; and where a severe assault was naturally to be expected. The greater part of his armour lay beside him, but covered with his cassock to screen it from morning dew; while in his leathern doublet, with arms bare to the shoulder, and a huge sledge-hammer in his hand, he set an example to the mechanics who worked under his direction.

In slow and solid natures there is usually a touch of shamefacedness, and a sensitiveness to the breach of petty observances. Wilkin Flammock had been unmoved even to insensibility at the imputation of treason so lately cast upon him; but he coloured high, and was confused, while, hastily throwing on his cassock, he endeavoured, to conceal the dishabille in which he had been surprised by the Lady Eveline. Not so his daughter. Proud of her father's zeal, her eye gleamed from him to her mistress with a look of triumph, which seemed to say, "And this faithful follower is he who was suspected of treachery!"

Eveline's own bosom made her the same reproach; and anxious to atone for her momentary doubt of his fidelity, she offered for his acceptance a ring of value; "in small amends," she said, "of a momentary misconstruction." "It needs not, lady," said Flammock, with his usual bluntness, "unless I have the freedom to bestow the gaud on Rose; for I think she was grieved enough at that which moved me little,—as why should it?"

"Dispose of it as thou wilt," said Eveline; "the stone it bears is as true as thine own faith."

Here Eveline paused, and looking on the broad expanded plain which extended between the site of the castle and the river, observed how silent and still the morning was rising over what had so lately been a scene of such extensive slaughter.

"It will not be so long," answered Flammock; "we shall have noise enough, and that nearer to our ears than yesterday."

"Which way lie the enemy?" said Eveline; "methinks I can spy neither tents nor pavilions."

"They use none, lady," answered Wilkin Flammock. "Heaven has denied them the grace and knowledge to weave linen enough for such a purpose—Yonder they lie on both sides of the river, covered with nought but their white mantles. Would one think that a host of thieves and cut-throats could look so like the finest object in nature—a well-spread bleaching-field!—Hark!—hark—the wasps are beginning to buzz; they will soon be plying their stings."

In fact, there was heard among the Welsh army a low and indistinct murmur, like that of

"Bees alarmed and arming in their hives."

Terrified at the hollow menacing sound, which grew louder every moment, Rose, who had all the irritability of a sensitive temperament, clung to her father's arm, saying, in a terrified whisper, "It is like the sound of the sea the night before the great inundation."

"And it betokens too rough weather for woman to be abroad in," said Flammock. "Go to your chamber, Lady Eveline, if it be your will—and go you too, Roschen—God bless you both—ye do but keep us idle here."

And, indeed, conscious that she had done all that was incumbent upon her, and fearful lest the chill which she felt creeping over her own heart should infect others, Eveline took her vassal's advice, and withdrew slowly to her own apartment, often casting back her eye to the place where the Welsh, now drawn out and under arms, were advancing their ridgy battalions, like the waves of an approaching tide.

The Prince of Powys had, with considerable military skill, adopted a plan of attack suitable to the fiery genius of his followers, and calculated to alarm on every point the feeble garrison.

The three sides of the castle which were defended by the river, were watched each by a numerous body of the British, with instructions to confine themselves to the discharge of arrows, unless they should observe that some favourable opportunity of close attack should occur. But far the greater part of Gwenwyn's forces, consisting of three columns of great strength, advanced along the plain on the western side of the castle, and menaced, with a desperate assault, the walls, which, in that direction, were deprived of the defence of the river. The first of these formidable bodies consisted entirely of archers, who dispersed themselves in front of the beleaguered place, and took advantage of every bush and rising ground which could afford them shelter; and then began to bend their bows and shower their arrows on the battlements and loop-holes, suffering, however, a great deal more damage than they were able to inflict, as the garrison returned their shot in comparative safety, and with more secure and deliberate aim. Under cover, however, of their discharge of arrows, two very strong bodies of Welsh attempted to carry the outer defences of the castle by storm. They had axes to destroy the palisades, then called barriers; faggots to fill up the external ditches; torches to set fire to aught combustible which they might find; and, above all, ladders to scale the walls.

These detachments rushed with incredible fury towards the point of attack, despite a most obstinate defence, and the great loss which they sustained by missiles of every kind, and continued the assault for nearly an hour, supplied by reinforcements which more than recruited their diminished numbers. When they were at last compelled to retreat, they seemed to adopt a new and yet more harassing species of attack. A large body assaulted one exposed point of the fortress with such fury as to draw thither as many of the besieged as could possibly be spared from other defended posts, and when there appeared a point less strongly manned than was adequate to defence, that, in its turn, was furiously assailed by a separate body of the enemy.

Thus the defenders of the Garde Doloureuse resembled the embarrassed traveller, engaged in repelling a swarm of hornets, which, while he brushes them, from one part, fix in swarms upon another, and drive him to despair by their numbers, and the boldness and multiplicity of their attacks. The postern being of course a principal point of attack, Father Aldrovand, whose anxiety would not permit him to be absent from the walls, and who, indeed, where decency would permit, took an occasional share in the active defence of the place, hasted thither, as the point chiefly in danger.

Here he found the Fleming, like a second Ajax, grim with dust and blood, working with his own hands the great engine which he had lately helped to erect, and at the same time giving heedful eye to all the exigencies around.

"How thinkest thou of this day's work?" said the monk in a whisper.

"What skills it talking of it, father?" replied Flammock; "thou art no soldier, and I have no time for words."

"Nay, take thy breath," said the monk, tucking up the sleeves of his frock; "I will try to help thee the whilst—although, our Lady pity me, I know nothing of these strange devices—not even the names. But our rule commands us to labour; there can be no harm therefore, in turning this winch—or in placing this steel-headed piece of wood opposite to the chord, (suiting his actions to his words,) nor see I aught uncanonical in adjusting the lever thus, or in touching the spring."

The large bolt whizzed through the air as he spoke, and was so successfully aimed, that it struck down a Welsh chief of eminence, to which Gwenwyn himself was in the act of giving some important charge.

"Well driven, *trebuchet*—well flown, *quarrel!*" cried the monk, unable to contain his delight, and giving in his triumph, the true technical names to the engine, and the javelin which it discharged.

"And well aimed, monk," added Wilkin Flammock; "I think thou knowest more than is in thy breviary."

"Care not thou for that," said the father; "and now that thou seest I can work an engine, and that the Welsh knaves seem something low in stomach, what think'st thou of our estate?"

"Well enough—for a bad one—if we may hope for speedy succour; but men's bodies are of flesh, not of iron, and we may be at last wearied out by numbers. Only one soldier to four yards of wall, is a fearful odds; and the villains are aware of it, and keep us to sharp work."

The renewal of the assault here broke off their conversation, nor did the active enemy permit them to enjoy much repose until sunset; for, alarming them with repeated menaces of attack upon different points, besides making two or three formidable and furious assaults, they left them scarce time to breathe, or to take a moment's refreshment. Yet the Welsh paid a severe price for their temerity; for, while nothing could exceed the bravery with which their men repeatedly advanced to the attack, those which were made latest in the day had less of animated desperation than their first onset; and it is probable, that the sense of having sustained great loss, and apprehension of its effects on the spirits of his people, made nightfall, and the interruption of the contest, as acceptable to Gwenwyn as to the exhausted garrison of the Garde Doloureuse.

But in the camp or leaguer of the Welsh there was glee and triumph, for the loss of the past day was forgotten in recollection of the signal victory which had preceded this siege; and the dispirited garrison could hear from their walls the laugh and the song, the sound of harping and gaiety, which triumphed by anticipation over their surrender.

The sun was for some time sunk, the twilight deepened, and night closed with a blue and cloudless sky, in which the thousand spangles that deck the firmament received double brilliancy from some slight touch of frost, although the paler planet, their mistress, was but in her first quarter. The necessities of the garrison were considerably aggravated by that of keeping a very strong and watchful guard, ill according with the weakness of their numbers, at a time which appeared favourable to any sudden nocturnal alarm; and, so urgent was this duty, that those who had been more slightly wounded on the preceding day, were obliged to take their share in it, notwithstanding their hurts. The monk and Fleming, who now perfectly understood each other, went in company around the walls at midnight, exhorting the warders to be watchful, and examining with their own eyes the state of the fortress. It was in the course of these rounds, and as they were ascending an elevated platform by a range of narrow and uneven steps, something galling to the monk's tread, that they perceived on the summit to which they were ascending, instead of the black corslet of the Flemish sentinel who had been placed there, two white forms, the appearance of which struck Wilkin Flammock with more dismay than he had shown during any of the doubtful events of the preceding day's fight.

"Father," he said, "betake yourself to your tools—*es spuckt*—there are hobgoblins here."

The good father had not learned as a priest to defy the spiritual host, whom, as a soldier, he had dreaded more than any mortal enemy; but he began to recite, with chattering teeth, the exorcism of the church, *"Conjuro vos omnes, spiritus maligni, magni, atque parvi,"*—when he was interrupted by the voice of Eveline, who called out, "Is it you, Father Aldrovand?"

Much lightened at heart by finding they had no ghost to deal with, Wilkin Flammock and the priest advanced hastily to the platform, where they found the lady with her faithful Rose, the former with a half-pike in her hand, like a sentinel on duty.

"How is this, daughter?" said the monk; "how came you here, and thus armed?

and where is the sentinel,—the lazy Flemish hound, that should have kept the post?"

"May he not be a lazy hound, yet not a Flemish one, father?" said Rose, who was ever awakened by anything which seemed a reflection upon her country; "methinks I have heard of such curs of English breed."

"Go to, Rose, you are too malapert for a young maiden," said her father. "Once more, where is Peterkin Vorst, who should have kept this post?"

"Let him not be blamed for my fault," said Eveline, pointing to a place where the Flemish sentinel lay in the shade of the battlement fast asleep—"He was overcome with toil—had fought hard through the day, and when I saw him asleep as I came hither, like a wandering spirit that cannot take slumber or repose, I would not disturb the rest which I envied. As he had fought for me, I might, I thought, watch an hour for him; so I took his weapon with the purpose of remaining here till some one should come to relieve him."

"I will relieve the schelm, with a vengeance!" said Wilkin Flammock, and saluted the slumbering and prostrate warder with two kicks, which made his corslet clatter. The man started to his feet in no small alarm, which he would have communicated to the next sentinels and to the whole garrison, by crying out that the Welsh were upon the walls, had not the monk covered his broad mouth with his hand just as the roar was issuing forth.—"Peace, and get thee down to the under bayley," said he;—"thou deservest death, by all the policies of war—but, look ye, varlet, and see who has saved your worthless neck, by watching while you were dreaming of swine's flesh and beer-pots."

The Fleming, although as yet but half awake, was sufficiently conscious of his situation, to sneak off without reply, after two or three awkward congees, as well to Eveline as to those by whom his repose had been so unceremoniously interrupted.

"He deserves to be tied neck and heel, the houndsfoot," said Wilkin. "But what would you have, lady? My countrymen cannot live without rest or sleep." So saying, he gave a yawn so wide, as if he had proposed to swallow one of the turrets at an angle of the platform on which he stood, as if it had only garnished a Christmas pasty.

"True, good Wilkin," said Eveline; "and do you therefore take some rest, and trust to my watchfulness, at least till the guards are relieved. I cannot sleep if I would, and I would not if I could."

"Thanks, lady," said Flammock; "and in truth, as this is a centrical place, and the rounds must pass in an hour at farthest, I will e'en close my eyes for such a space, for the lids feel as heavy as flood-gates."

"Oh, father, father!" exclaimed Rose, alive to her sire's unceremonious neglect of decorum—"think where you are, and in whose presence!"

"Ay, ay, good Flammock," said the monk, "remember the presence of a noble Norman maiden is no place for folding of cloaks and donning of night-caps."

"Let him alone, father," said Eveline, who in another moment might have smiled at the readiness with which Wilkin Flammock folded himself in his huge cloak, extended his substantial form on the stone bench, and gave the most decided tokens of profound repose, long ere the monk had done speaking.—"Forms and fashions of respect," she continued, "are for times of ease and nicety;—when in danger, the soldier's bedchamber is wherever he can find leisure for an hour's sleep—his eating-hall, wherever he can obtain food. Sit thou down by Rose and me, good father, and tell us of some holy lesson which may pass away these hours of weariness and calamity."

The father obeyed; but however willing to afford consolation, his ingenuity and theological skill suggested nothing better than a recitation of the penitentiary psalms, in which task he continued until fatigue became too powerful for him also, when he committed the same breach of decorum for which he had upbraided Wilkin Flammock, and fell fast asleep in the midst of his devotions.

CHAPTER THE NINTH

"Oh, night of wo," she said, and wept,
"Oh, night foreboding sorrow!
"Oh, night of wo," she said and wept,
"But more I dread the morrow!"
  SIR GILBERT ELLIOT.

The fatigue which had exhausted Flammock and the monk, was unfelt by the two anxious maidens, who remained with their eyes bent, now upon the dim landscape, now on the stars by which it was lighted, as if they could have read there the events which the morrow was to bring forth. It was a placid and melancholy scene. Tree and field, and hill and plain, lay before them in doubtful light, while at greater distance, their eye could with difficulty trace one or two places where the river, hidden in general by banks and trees, spread its more expanded bosom to the stars, and the pale crescent. All was still, excepting the solemn rush of the waters, and now and then the shrill tinkle of a harp, which, heard from more than a mile's distance through the midnight silence, announced that some of the Welshmen still protracted their most beloved amusement. The wild notes, partially heard, seemed like the voice of some passing spirit; and, connected as they were with ideas of fierce and unrelenting hostility, thrilled on Eveline's ear, as if prophetic of war and wo, captivity and death. The only other sounds which disturbed the extreme stillness of the night, were the occasional step of a sentinel upon his post, or the hooting of the owls, which seemed to wail the approaching downfall of the moonlight turrets, in which they had established their ancient habitations.

The calmness of all around seemed to press like a weight on the bosom of the unhappy Eveline, and brought to her mind a deeper sense of present grief, and keener apprehension of future horrors, than had reigned there during the bustle, blood, and confusion of the preceding day. She rose up—she sat down —she moved to and fro on the platform—she remained fixed like a statue to a single spot, as if she were trying by variety of posture to divert her internal sense of fear and sorrow.

At length, looking at the monk and the Fleming as they slept soundly under the shade of the battlement, she could no longer forbear breaking silence. "Men are happy," she said, "my beloved Rose; their anxious thoughts are either diverted by toilsome exertion, or drowned in the insensibility which follows it. They may encounter wounds and death, but it is we who feel in the spirit a more keen anguish than the body knows, and in the gnawing sense of present ill and fear of future misery, suffer a living death, more cruel than that which ends our woes at once."

"Do not be thus downcast, my noble lady," said Rose; "be rather what you were yesterday, caring for the wounded, for the aged, for every one but yourself—exposing even your dear life among the showers of the Welsh arrows, when doing so could give courage to others; while I—shame on me— could but tremble, sob, and weep, and needed all the little wit I have to prevent my shouting with the wild cries of the Welsh, or screaming and groaning with those of our friends who fell around me."

"Alas! Rose," answered her mistress, "you may at pleasure indulge your fears to the verge of distraction itself—you have a father to fight and watch for you. Mine—my kind, noble, and honoured parent, lies dead on yonder field, and all which remains for me is to act as may best become his memory. But this moment is at least mine, to think upon and to mourn for him."

So saying, and overpowered by the long-repressed burst of filial sorrow, she sunk down on the banquette which ran along the inside of the embattled parapet of the platform, and murmuring to herself, "He is gone for ever!" abandoned herself to the extremity of grief. One hand grasped unconsciously the weapon which she held, and served, at the same time, to prop her forehead, while the tears, by which she was now for the first time relieved, flowed in torrents from her eyes, and her sobs seemed so convulsive, that Rose almost feared her heart was bursting. Her affection and sympathy dictated at once the kindest course which Eveline's condition permitted. Without attempting to control the torrent of grief in its full current, she gently sat her down beside the mourner, and possessing herself of the hand which had sunk motionless by her side, she alternately pressed it to her lips, her bosom, and her brow—now covered it with kisses, now bedewed it with tears, and amid these tokens of the most devoted and humble sympathy, waited a more composed moment to offer her little stock of consolation in such deep silence and stillness, that, as the pale light fell upon the two beautiful young women, it seemed rather to show a group of statuary, the work of some eminent sculptor, than beings whose eyes still wept, and whose hearts still throbbed. At a little distance, the gleaming corslet of the Fleming, and the dark garments of Father Aldrovand, as they lay prostrate on the stone steps, might represent the bodies of those for whom the principal figures were mourning.

After a deep agony of many minutes, it seemed that the sorrows of Eveline were assuming a more composed character; her convulsive sobs were changed for long, low, profound sighs, and the course of her tears, though they still flowed, was milder and less violent. Her kind attendant, availing herself of these gentler symptoms, tried softly to win the spear from her lady's grasp. "Let me be sentinel for a while." she said, "my sweet lady—I will at least scream louder than you, if any danger should approach." She ventured to kiss her cheek, and throw her arms around Eveline's neck while she spoke; but a mute caress, which expressed her sense of the faithful girl's kind intentions to minister if possible to her repose, was the only answer returned. They remained for many minutes silent in the same posture,—Eveline, like an upright and tender poplar,—Rose, who encircled her lady in her arms, like the woodbine which twines around it.

At length Rose suddenly felt her young mistress shiver in her embrace, and then Eveline's hand grasped her arm rigidly as she whispered, "Do you hear nothing?"

"No—nothing but the hooting of the owl," answered Rose, timorously.

"I heard a distant sound," said Eveline,—"I thought I heard it— hark, it comes again!—Look from the battlements, Rose, while I awaken the priest and thy father."

"Dearest lady," said Rose, "I dare not—what can this sound be that is heard by one only?—You are deceived by the rush of the river."

"I would not alarm the castle unnecessarily," said Eveline, pausing, "or even break your father's needful slumbers, by a fancy of mine—But hark—I hear it again—distinct amidst the intermitting sounds of the rushing water—a low tremulous sound, mingled with a tinkling like smiths or armourers at work upon their anvils."

Rose had by this time sprung up on the banquette, and flinging back her rich tresses of fair hair, had applied her hand behind her ear to collect the distant sound. "I hear it," she cried, "and it increases—Awake them, for Heaven's sake, and without a moment's delay!"

Eveline accordingly stirred the sleepers with the reversed end of the lance, and as they started to their feet in haste, she whispered in a hasty but cautious voice, "To arms—the Welsh are upon us!" "What—where?" said Wilkin Flammock,—"where be they?"

"Listen, and you will hear them arming," she replied.

"The noise is but in thine own fancy, lady," said the Fleming, whose organs were of the same heavy character with his form and his disposition. "I would I had not gone to sleep at all, since I was to be awakened so soon."

"Nay, but listen, good Flammock-the sound of armour comes from the north-east."

"The Welsh lie not in that quarter, lady," said Wilkin; "and besides, they wear no armour."

"I hear it—I hear it!" said Father Aldrovand, who had been listening for some time. "All praise to St. Benedict!—Our Lady of the Garde Doloureuse has been gracious to her servants as ever!— It is the tramp of horses—it is the clash of armour—the chivalry of the Marches are coming to our relief-Kyrie Eleison!"

"I hear something too," said Flammock,—"something like the hollow sound of the great sea, when it burst into my neighbour Klinkerman's warehouse, and rolled his pots and pans against each other. But it were an evil mistake, father, to take foes for friends—we were best rouse the people."

"Tush!" said the priest, "talk to me of pots and kettles?—Was I, squire of the body to Count Stephen Mauleverer for twenty years, and do I not know the tramp of a war-horse, or the clash of a mail-coat?—But call the men to the walls at any rate, and have me the best drawn up at the base-court—we may help them by a sally."

"That will not be rashly undertaken with my consent," murmured the Fleming; "but to the wall if you will, and 111 good time. But keep your Normans and English silent, Sir Priest, else their unruly and noisy joy will awaken the Welsh camp, and prepare them for their unwelcome visitors."

The monk laid his finger on his lip in sign of obedience, and they parted in opposite directions, each to rouse the defenders of the castle, who were soon heard drawing from all quarters to their posts upon the walls, with hearts in a very different mood from that in which they had descended from them. The utmost caution being used to prevent noise, the manning of the walls was accomplished in silence, and the garrison awaited in, breathless expectation the success of the forces who were rapidly advancing to their relief.

The character of the sounds which now loudly awakened the silence of this eventful night, could no longer be mistaken. They were distinguishable from the rushing of a mighty river, or from the muttering sound of distant thunder, by the sharp and angry notes which the clashing of the rider's arms mingled with the deep bass of the horses' rapid tread. From the long continuance of the sounds, their loudness, and the extent of horizon from which they seemed to come, all in the castle were satisfied that the approaching relief consisted of several very strong bodies of horse. At once this mighty sound ceased, as if the earth on which they trod had either devoured the armed squadrons or had become incapable of resounding to their tramp. The defenders of the Garde Doloureuse concluded that their friends had made a sudden halt, to give their horses breath, examine the leaguer of the enemy, and settle the order of attack upon them. The pause, however was but momentary.

The British, so alert at surprising their enemies, were themselves, on many occasions, liable to surprise. Their men were undisciplined, and sometimes negligent of the patient duties of the sentinel; and, besides, their foragers and flying parties, who scoured the country during the preceding day, had brought back tidings which had lulled them into fatal security. Their camp had been therefore carelessly guarded, and confident in the smallness of the garrison, they had altogether neglected the important military duty of establishing patrols and outposts at a proper distance from their main body. Thus the cavalry of the Lords Marchers, notwithstanding the noise which accompanied their advance, had approached very near the British camp without exciting the least alarm. But while they were arranging their forces into separate columns, in order to commence the assault, a loud and increasing clamour among the Welsh announced that they were at length aware of their danger. The shrill and discordant cries by which they endeavoured to assemble their men, each under the banner of his chief, resounded from their leaguer. But these rallying shouts were soon converted into screams, and clamours of horror and dismay, when the thundering charge of the barbed horses and heavily armed cavalry of the Anglo-Normans surprised their undefended camp.

Yet not even under circumstances so adverse did the descendants of the ancient Britons renounce their defence, or forfeit their old hereditary privilege, to be called the bravest of mankind. Their cries of defiance and resistance were heard resounding above the groans of the wounded, the shouts of the triumphant assailants, and the universal tumult of the night-battle. It was not until the morning light began to peep forth, that the slaughter or dispersion of Gwenwyn's forces was complete, and that the "earthquake voice of victory" arose in uncontrolled and unmingled energy of exultation.

Then the besieged, if they could be still so termed, looking from their towers over the expanded country beneath, witnessed nothing but one widespread scene of desultory flight and unrelaxed pursuit. That the Welsh had been permitted to encamp in fancied security upon the hither side of the river, now rendered their discomfiture more dreadfully fatal. The single pass by which they could cross to the other side was soon completely choked by fugitives, on whose rear raged the swords of the victorious Normans. Many threw themselves into the river, upon the precarious chance of gaining the farther side, and, except a few, who were uncommonly strong, skilful, and active, perished among the rocks and in the currents; others, more fortunate, escaped by fords, with which they had accidentally been made acquainted; many dispersed, or, in small bands, fled in reckless despair towards the castle, as if the fortress, which had beat them off when victorious, could be a place of refuge to them in their present forlorn condition; while others roamed wildly over the plain, seeking only escape from immediate and instant danger, without knowing whither they ran.

The Normans, meanwhile, divided into small parties, followed and slaughtered them at pleasure; while, as a rallying point for the victors, the banner of Hugo de Lacy streamed from a small mount, on which Gwenwyn had lately pitched his own, and surrounded by a competent force, both of infantry and horsemen, which the experienced Baron permitted on no account to wander far from it.

The rest, as we have already said, followed the chase with shouts of exultation and of vengeance, ringing around the battlements, which resounded with the cries, "Ha, Saint Edward!—Ha, Saint Dennis!—Strike—slay—no quarter to the Welsh wolves—think on Raymond Berenger!"

The soldiers on the walls joined in these vengeful and victorious clamours, and discharged several sheaves of arrows upon such fugitives, as, in their extremity, approached too near the castle. They would fain have sallied to give more active assistance in the work of destruction; but the communication being now open with the Constable of Chester's forces, Wilkin Flammock considered himself and the garrison to be under the orders of that renowned chief, and refused to listen to the eager admonitions of Father Aldrovand, who would, notwithstanding his sacerdotal character, have willingly himself taken charge of the sally which he proposed.

At length, the scene of slaughter seemed at an end. The retreat was blown on many a bugle, and knights halted on the plain to collect their personal followers, muster them under their proper pennon, and then march them slowly back to the great standard of their leader, around which the main body were again to be assembled, like the clouds which gather around the evening sun—a fanciful simile, which might yet be drawn farther, in respect of the level rays of strong lurid light which shot from those dark battalions, as the beams were flung back from their polished armour.

The plain was in this manner soon cleared of the horsemen, and remained occupied only by the dead bodies of the slaughtered Welshmen. The bands who had followed the pursuit to a greater distance were also now seen returning, driving before them, or dragging after them, dejected and unhappy captives, to whom they had given quarter when their thirst of blood was satiated.

It was then that, desirous to attract the attention of his liberators, Wilkin Flammock commanded all the banners of the castle to be displayed, under a general shout of acclamation from those who had fought under them. It was answered by a universal cry of joy from De Lacy's army, which rung so wide, as might even yet have startled such of the Welsh fugitives, as, far distant from this disastrous field of flight, might have ventured to halt for a moment's repose.

Presently after this greeting had been exchanged, a single rider advanced from the Constable's army towards the castle, showing, even at a distance, an unusual dexterity of horsemanship and grace of deportment. He arrived at the drawbridge, which was instantly lowered to receive him, whilst Flammock and the monk (for the latter, as far as he could, associated himself with the former in all acts of authority) hastened to receive the envoy of their liberator. They found him just alighted from the raven-coloured horse, which was slightly flecked with blood as well as foam, and still panted with the exertions of the evening; though, answering to the caressing hand of its youthful rider, he arched his neck, shook his steel caparison, and snorted to announce his unabated mettle and unwearied love of combat. The young man's eagle look bore the same token of unabated vigour, mingled with the signs of recent exertion. His helmet hanging at his saddle-bow, showed a gallant countenance, coloured highly, but not inflamed, which looked out from a rich profusion of short chestnut-curls; and although his armour was of a massive and simple form, he moved under it with such elasticity and ease, that it seemed a graceful attire, not a burden or encumbrance. A furred mantle had not sat on him with more easy grace than the heavy hauberk, which complied with every gesture of his noble form. Yet his countenance was so juvenile, that only the down on the upper lip announced decisively the approach to manhood. The females, who thronged into the court to see the first envoy of their deliverers, could not forbear mixing praises of his beauty with blessings on his valour; and one comely middle-aged dame, in particular, distinguished by the tightness with which her scarlet hose sat on a well-shaped leg and ankle, and by the cleanness of her coif, pressed close up to the young squire, and, more forward than, the rest, doubled the crimson hue of his cheek, by crying aloud, that Our Lady of the Garde Doloureuse had sent them news of their redemption by an angel from the sanctuary;—a speech which, although Father Aldrovand shook his head, was received by her companions with such general acclamation, as greatly embarrassed the young man's modesty.

"Peace, all of ye!" said Wilkin Flammock—"Know you no respects, you women, or have you never seen a young gentleman before, that you hang on him like flies on a honeycomb? Stand back, I say, and let us hear in peace what are the commands of the noble Lord of Lacy."

"These," said the young man, "I can only deliver in the presence of the right noble demoiselle, Eveline Berenger, if I may be thought worthy of such honour."

"That thou art, noble sir," said the same forward dame, who had before expressed her admiration so energetically; "I will uphold thee worthy of her presence, and whatever other grace a lady can do thee."

"Now, hold thy tongue, with a wanion!" said the monk; while in the same breath the Fleming exclaimed, "Beware the cucking-stool, Dame Scant-o'-Grace!" while he conducted the noble youth across the court. "Let my good horse be cared for," said the cavalier, as he put the bridle into the hand of a menial; and in doing so got rid of some part of his female retinue, who began to pat and praise the steed as much as they had done the rider; and some, in the enthusiasm of their joy, hardly abstained from kissing the stirrups and horse furniture.

But Dame Gillian was not so easily diverted from her own point as were some of her companions. She continued to repeat the word *cucking-stool*, till the Fleming was out of hearing, and then became more specific in her objurgation. —"And why *cucking-stool*, I pray, Sir Wilkin Butterfirkin? You are the man would stop an English mouth with a Flemish damask napkin, I trow! Marry quep, my cousin the weaver! And why the cucking-stool, I pray?—because my young lady is comely, and the young squire is a man of mettle, reverence to his beard that is to come yet! Have we not eyes to see, and have we not a mouth and a tongue?"

"In troth, Dame Gillian, they do you wrong who doubt it," said Eveline's nurse, who stood by; "but I prithee, keep it shut now, were it but for womanhood."

"How now, mannerly Mrs. Margery?" replied the incorrigible Gillian; "is your heart so high, because you dandled our young lady on your knee fifteen years since?—Let me tell you, the cat will find its way to the cream, though it was brought up on an abbess's lap."

"Home, housewife—home!" exclaimed her husband, the old huntsman, who was weary of this public exhibition of his domestic termagant —"home, or I will give you a taste of my dog lash—Here are both the confessor and Wilkin Flammock wondering at your impudence."

"Indeed!" replied Gillian; "and are not two fools enough for wonderment, that you must come with your grave pate to make up the number three?"

There was a general laugh at the huntsman's expense, under cover of which he prudently withdrew his spouse, without attempting to continue the war of tongues, in which she had shown such a decided superiority. This controversy, so light is the change in human spirits, especially among the lower class, awakened bursts of idle mirth among beings, who had so lately been in the jaws of danger, if not of absolute despair.

CHAPTER THE TENTH

They bore him barefaced on his bier,
  Six proper youths and tall,
And many a tear bedew'd his grave
  Within yon kirkyard wall.
  THE FRIAR OF ORDERS GRAY.

While these matters took place in the castle-yard, the young squire, Damian Lacy, obtained the audience which he had requested of Eveline Berenger, who received him in the great hall of the castle, seated beneath the dais, or canopy, and waited upon by Rose and other female attendants; of whom the first alone was permitted to use a tabouret or small stool in her presence, so strict were the Norman maidens of quality in maintaining their claims to high rank and observance.

The youth was introduced by the confessor and Flammock, as the spiritual character of the one, and the trust reposed by her late father in the other, authorized them to be present upon the occasion. Eveline naturally blushed, as she advanced two steps to receive the handsome youthful envoy; and her bashfulness seemed infectious, for it was with some confusion that Damian went through the ceremony of saluting the hand which she extended towards him in token of welcome. Eveline was under the necessity of speaking first.

"We advance as far as our limits will permit us," she said, "to greet with our thanks the messenger who brings us tidings of safety. We speak—unless we err—to the noble Damian of Lacy?"

"To the humblest of your servants," answered Damian, falling with some difficulty into the tone of courtesy which his errand and character required, "who approaches you on behalf of his noble uncle, Hugo de Lacy, Constable of Chester."

"Will not our noble deliverer in person honour with his presence the poor dwelling which he has saved?"

"My noble kinsman," answered Damian, "is now God's soldier, and bound by a vow not to come beneath a roof until he embark for the Holy Land. But by my voice he congratulates you on the defeat of your savage enemies, and sends you these tokens that the comrade and friend of your noble father hath not left his lamentable death many hours unavenged." So saying, he drew forth and laid before Eveline the gold bracelets, the coronet, and the eudorchawg, or chain of linked gold, which had distinguished the rank of the Welsh Prince.

"Gwenwyn hath then fallen?" said Eveline, a natural shudder combating with the feelings of gratified vengeance, as she beheld that the trophies were speckled with blood,—"The slayer of my father is no more!"

"My kinsman's lance transfixed the Briton as he endeavoured to rally his flying people—he died grimly on the weapon which had passed more than a fathom through his body, and exerted his last strength in a furious but ineffectual blow with his mace." "Heaven is just," said Eveline; "may his sins be forgiven to the man of blood, since he hath fallen by a death so bloody!— One question I would ask you, noble sir. My father's remains——" She paused unable to proceed. "An hour will place them at your disposal, most honoured lady," replied the squire, in the tone of sympathy which the sorrows of so young and so fair an orphan called irresistibly forth. "Such preparations as time admitted were making even when I left the host, to transport what was mortal of the noble Berenger from the field on which we found him amid a monument of slain which his own sword had raised. My kinsman's vow will not allow him to pass your portcullis; but, with your permission, I will represent him, if such be your pleasure, at these honoured obsequies, having charge to that effect."

"My brave and noble father," said Eveline, making an effort to restrain her tears, "will be best mourned by the noble and the brave." She would have continued, but her voice failed her, and she was obliged to withdraw abruptly, in order to give vent to her sorrow, and prepare for the funeral rites with such ceremony as circumstances should permit. Damian bowed to the departing mourner as reverently as he would have done to a divinity, and taking his horse, returned to his uncle's host, which had encamped hastily on the recent field of battle.

The sun was now high, and the whole plain presented the appearance of a bustle, equally different from the solitude of the early morning, and from the roar and fury of the subsequent engagement. The news of Hugo de Lacy's victory every where spread abroad with all alacrity of triumph, and had induced many of the inhabitants of the country, who had fled before the fury of the Wolf of Plinlimmon, to return to their desolate habitations. Numbers also of the loose and profligate characters which abound in a country subject to the frequent changes of war, had flocked thither in quest of spoil, or to gratify a spirit of restless curiosity. The Jew and the Lombard, despising danger where there was a chance of gain, might be already seen bartering liquors and wares with the victorious men-at-arms, for the blood-stained ornaments of gold lately worn by the defeated British. Others acted as brokers betwixt the Welsh captives and their captors; and where they could trust the means and good faith of the former, sometimes became bound for, or even advanced in ready money, the sums necessary for their ransom; whilst a more numerous class became themselves the purchasers of those prisoners who had no immediate means of settling with their conquerors.

That the spoil thus acquired might not long encumber the soldier, or blunt his ardour for farther enterprise, the usual means of dissipating military spoils were already at hand. Courtezans, mimes, jugglers, minstrels, and tale-tellers of every description, had accompanied the night-march; and, secure in the military reputation of the celebrated De Lacy, had rested fearlessly at some little distance until the battle was fought and won. These now approached, in many a joyous group, to congratulate the victors. Close to the parties which they formed for the dance, the song, or the tale, upon the yet bloody field, the countrymen, summoned in for the purpose, were opening large trenches for depositing the dead—leeches were seen tending the wounded— priests and monks confessing those in extremity—soldiers transporting from the field the bodies of the more honoured among the slain—peasants mourning over their trampled crops and plundered habitations—and widows and orphans searching for the bodies of husbands and parents, amid the promiscuous carnage of two combats. Thus wo mingled her wildest notes with those of jubilee and bacchanal triumph, and the plain of the Garde Doloureuse formed a singular parallel to the varied maze of human life, where joy and grief are so strangely mixed, and where the confines of mirth and pleasure often border on those of sorrow and of death.

About noon these various noises were at once silenced, and the attention alike of those who rejoiced or grieved was arrested by the loud and mournful sound of six trumpets, which, uplifting and uniting their thrilling tones in a wild and melancholy death-note, apprised all, that the obsequies of the valiant Raymond Berenger were about to commence. From a tent, which had been hastily pitched for the immediate reception of the body, twelve black monks, the inhabitants of a neighbouring convent, began to file out in pairs, headed by their abbot, who bore a large cross, and thundered forth the sublime notes of the Catholic *Miserere me, Domine*. Then came a chosen body of men-at-arms, trailing their lances, with their points reversed and pointed to the earth; and after them the body of the valiant Berenger, wrapped in his own knightly banner, which, regained from the hands of the Welsh, now served its noble owner instead of a funeral pall. The most gallant Knights of the Constable's household (for, like other great nobles of that period, he had formed it upon a scale which approached to that of royalty) walked as mourners and supporters of the corpse, which was borne upon lances; and the Constable of Chester himself, alone and fully armed, excepting the head, followed as chief mourner. A chosen body of squires, men-at-arms, and pages of noble descent, brought up the rear of the procession; while their nakers and trumpets echoed back, from time to time, the melancholy song of the monks, by replying in a note as lugubrious as their own.

The course of pleasure was arrested, and even that of sorrow was for a moment turned from her own griefs, to witness the last honours bestowed on him, who had been in life the father and guardian of his people.

The mournful procession traversed slowly the plain which had been within a few hours the scene of such varied events; and, pausing before the outer gate of the barricades of the castle, invited, by a prolonged and solemn flourish, the fortress to receive the remains of its late gallant defender. The melancholy summons was answered by the warder's horn—the drawbridge sunk—the portcullis rose—and Father Aldrovand appeared in the middle of the gateway, arrayed in his sacerdotal habit, whilst a little way behind him stood the orphaned damsel, in such weeds of mourning as time admitted, supported by her attendant Rose, and followed by the females of the household.

The Constable of Chester paused upon the threshold of the outer gate, and, pointing to the cross signed in white cloth upon his left shoulder, with a lowly reverence resigned to his nephew, Damian, the task of attending the remains of Raymond Berenger to the chapel within the castle. The soldiers of Hugo de Lacy, most of whom were bound by the same vow with himself, also halted without the castle gate, and remained under arms, while the death- peal of the chapel bell announced from within the progress of the procession.

It winded on through those narrow entrances, which were skilfully contrived to interrupt the progress of an enemy, even should he succeed in forcing the outer gate, and arrived at length in the great court-yard, where most of the inhabitants of the fortress, and those who, under recent circumstances, had taken refuge there, were drawn up, in order to look, for the last time, on their departed lord. Among these were mingled a few of the motley crowd from without, whom curiosity, or the expectation of a dole, had brought to the castle gate, and who, by one argument or another, had obtained from the warder permission to enter the interior.

The body was here set down before the door of the chapel, the ancient Gothic front of which formed one side of the court-yard, until certain prayers were recited by the priests, in which the crowd around were supposed to join with becoming reverence.

It was during this interval, that a man, whose peaked beard, embroidered girdle, and high-crowned hat of gray felt, gave him the air of a Lombard merchant, addressed Margery, the nurse of Eveline, in a whispering tone, and with a foreign accent.—"I am a travelling merchant, good sister, and am come hither in quest of gain—can you tell me whether I can have any custom in this castle?"

"You are come at an evil time, Sir Stranger—you may yourself see that this is a place for mourning and not for merchandise."

"Yet mourning times have their own commerce," said the stranger, approaching still closer to the side of Margery, and lowering his voice to a tone yet more confidential. "I have sable scarfs of Persian silk—black bugles, in which a princess might mourn for a deceased monarch—cyprus, such as the East hath seldom sent forth —black cloth for mourning hangings—all that may express sorrow and reverence in fashion and attire; and I know how to be grateful to those who help me to custom. Come, bethink you, good dame— such things must be had—I will sell as good ware and as cheap as another; and a kirtle to yourself, or, at your pleasure, a purse with five florins, shall be the meed of your kindness."

"I prithee peace, friend," said Margery, "and choose a better time for vaunting your wares—you neglect both place and season; and if you be farther importunate, I must speak to those who will show you the outward side of the castle gate. I marvel the warders would admit pedlars upon a day such as this —they would drive a gainful bargain by the bedside of their mother, were she dying, I trow." So saying, she turned scornfully from him.

While thus angrily rejected on the one side, the merchant felt his cloak receive an intelligent twitch upon the other, and, looking round upon the signal, he saw a dame, whose black kerchief was affectedly disposed, so as to give an appearance of solemnity to a set of light laughing features, which must have been captivating when young, since they retained so many good points when at least forty years had passed over them. She winked to the merchant, touching at the same time her under lip with her forefinger, to announce the propriety of silence and secrecy; then gliding from the crowd, retreated to a small recess formed by a projecting buttress of the chapel, as if to avoid the pressure likely to take place at the moment when the bier should be lifted. The merchant failed not to follow her example, and was soon by her side, when she did not give him the trouble of opening his affairs, but commenced the conversation herself.

"I have heard what you said to our Dame Margery—Mannerly Margery, as I call her—heard as much, at least, as led me to guess the rest, for I have got an eye in my head, I promise you."

"A pair of them, my pretty dame, and as bright as drops of dew in a May morning."

"Oh, you say so, because I have been weeping," said the scarlet- hosed Gillian, for it was even herself who spoke; "and to be sure, I have good cause, for our lord was always my very good lord, and would sometimes chuck me under the chin, and call me buxom Gillian of Croydon—not that the good gentleman was ever uncivil, for he would thrust a silver twopennies into my hand at the same time.— Oh! the friend that I have lost!—And I have had anger on his account too—I have seen old Raoul as sour as vinegar, and fit for no place but the kennel for a whole day about it; but, as I said to him, it was not for the like of me, to be affronting our master, and a great baron, about a chuck under the chin, or a kiss, or such like."

"No wonder you are so sorry for so kind a master, dame," said the merchant.

"No wonder, indeed," replied the dame, with a sigh; "and then what is to become of us?—It is like my young mistress will go to her aunt—or she will marry one of these Lacys that they talk so much of—or, at any rate, she will leave the castle; and it's like old Raoul and I will be turned to grass with the lord's old chargers. The Lord knows, they may as well hang him up with the old hounds, for he is both footless and fangless, and fit for nothing on earth that I know of."

"Your young mistress is that lady in the mourning mantle," said the merchant, "who so nearly sunk down upon the body just now?"

"In good troth is she, sir—and much cause she has to sink down. I am sure she will be to seek for such another father."

"I see you are a most discerning woman, gossip Gillian," answered the merchant; "and yonder youth that supported her is her bridegroom?"

"Much need she has for some one to support her," said Gillian; "and so have I for that matter, for what can poor old rusty Raoul do?"

"But as to your young lady's marriage?" said the merchant.

"No one knows more, than that such a thing was in treaty between our late lord and the great Constable of Chester, that came to-day but just in time to prevent the Welsh from cutting all our throats, and doing the Lord knoweth what mischief beside. But there is a marriage talked of, that is certain—and most folk think it must be for this smooth-cheeked boy, Damian, as they call him; for though the Constable has gotten a beard, which his nephew hath not, it is something too grizzled for a bridegroom's chin— Besides, he goes to the Holy Wars—fittest place for all elderly warriors—I wish he would take Raoul with him.—But what is all this to what you were saying about your mourning wares even now?— It is a sad truth, that my poor lord is gone—But what then?— Well-a-day, you know the good old saw,—

'Cloth must be wear,
Eat beef and drink beer,
Though the dead go to bier.'

And for your merchandising, I am as like to help you with my good word as Mannerly Margery, provided you bid fair for it; since, if the lady loves me not so much, I can turn the steward round my finger."

"Take this in part of your bargain, pretty Mistress Gillian," said the merchant; "and when my wains come up, I will consider you amply, if I get good sale by your favourable report.—But how shall I get into the castle again? for I would wish to consult you, being a sensible woman, before I come in with my luggage."

"Why," answered the complaisant dame, "if our English be on guard, you have only to ask for Gillian, and they will open the wicket to any single man at once; for we English stick all together, were it but to spite the Normans;—but if a Norman be on duty, you must ask for old Raoul, and say you come to speak of dogs and hawks for sale, and I warrant you come to speech of me that way. If the sentinel be a Fleming, you have but to say you are a merchant, and he will let you in for the love of trade."

The merchant repeated his thankful acknowledgment, glided from her side, and mixed among the spectators, leaving her to congratulate herself on having gained a brace of florins by the indulgence of her natural talkative humour; for which, on other occasions, she had sometimes dearly paid.

The ceasing of the heavy toll of the castle bell now gave intimation that the noble Raymond Berenger had been laid in the vault with his fathers. That part of the funeral attendants who had come from the host of De Lacy, now proceeded to the castle hall, where they partook, but with temperance, of some refreshments which were offered as a death-meal; and presently after left the castle, headed by young Damian, in the same slow and melancholy form in which they had entered. The monks remained within the castle to sing repeated services for the soul of the deceased, and for those of his faithful men-at-arms who had fallen around him, and who had been so much mangled during, and after, the contest with the Welsh, that it was scarce possible to know one individual from another; otherwise the body of Dennis Morolt would have obtained, as his faith well deserved, the honours of a separate funeral.

CHAPTER THE ELEVENTH.

——The funeral baked meats
Did coldly furnish forth the marriage table.
  HAMLET.

The religious rites which followed the funeral of Raymond Berenger, endured without interruption for the period of six days; during which, alms were distributed to the poor, and relief administered, at the expense of the Lady Eveline, to all those who had suffered by the late inroad. Death-meals, as they were termed, were also spread in honour of the deceased; but the lady herself, and most of her attendants, observed a stern course of vigil, discipline, and fasts, which appeared to the Normans a more decorous manner of testifying their respect for the dead, than the Saxon and Flemish custom of banqueting and drinking inordinately upon such occasions.

Meanwhile, the Constable De Lacy retained a large body of his men encamped under the walls of the Garde Doloureuse, for protection against some new irruption of the Welsh, while with the rest he took advantage of his victory, and struck terror into the British by many well-conducted forays, marked with ravages scarcely less hurtful than their own. Among the enemy, the evils of discord were added to those of defeat and invasion; for two distant relations of Gwenwyn contended for the throne he had lately occupied, and on this, as on many other occasions, the Britons suffered as much from internal dissension as from the sword of the Normans. A worse politician, and a less celebrated soldier, than the sagacious and successful De Lacy, could not have failed, under such circumstances, to negotiate as he did an advantageous peace, which, while it deprived Powys of a part of its frontier, and the command of some important passes, in which it was the Constable's purpose to build castles, rendered the Garde Doloureuse more secure than formerly, from any sudden attack on the part of their fiery and restless neighbours. De Lacy's care also went to re-establishing those settlers who had fled from their possessions, and putting the whole lordship, which now descended upon an unprotected female, into a state of defence as perfect as its situation on a hostile frontier could possibly permit.

Whilst thus anxiously provident in the affairs of the orphan of the Garde Doloureuse, De Lacy during the space we have mentioned, sought not to disturb her filial grief by any personal intercourse. His nephew, indeed, was despatched by times every morning to lay before her his uncle's *devoirs,* in the high- flown language of the day, and acquaint her with the steps which he had taken in her affairs. As a meed due to his relative's high services, Damian was always admitted to see Eveline on such occasions, and returned charged with her grateful thanks, and her implicit acquiescence in whatever the Constable proposed for her consideration.

But when the days of rigid mourning were elapsed, the young de Lacy stated, on the part of his kinsman, that his treaty with the Welsh being concluded, and all things in the district arranged as well as circumstances would permit, the Constable of Chester now proposed to return into his own territory, in order to resume his instant preparations for the Holy Land, which the duty of chastising her enemies had for some days interrupted.

"And will not the noble Constable, before he departs from this place," said Eveline, with a burst of gratitude which the occasion well merited, "receive the personal thanks of her that was ready to perish, when he so valiantly came to her aid?"

"It was even on that point that I was commissioned to speak," replied Damian; "but my noble kinsman feels diffident to propose to you that which he most earnestly desires—the privilege of speaking to your own ear certain matters of high import, and with which he judges it fit to intrust no third party."

"Surely," said the maiden, blushing, "there can be nought beyond the bounds of maidenhood, in my seeing the noble Constable whenever such is his pleasure."

"But his vow," replied Damian, "binds my kinsman not to come beneath a roof until he sets sail for Palestine; and in order to meet him, you must grace him so far as to visit his pavilion;—a condescension which, as a knight and Norman noble, he can scarcely ask of a damsel of high degree."

"And is that all?" said Eveline, who, educated in a remote situation, was a stranger to some of the nice points of etiquette which the damsels of the time observed in keeping their state towards the other sex. "Shall I not," she said, "go to render my thanks to my deliverer, since he cannot come hither to receive them? Tell the noble Hugo de Lacy, that, next to my gratitude to Heaven, it is due to him, and to his brave companions in arms. I will come to his tent as to a holy shrine; and, could such homage please him, I would come barefooted, were the road strewed with flints and with thorns."

"My uncle will be equally honoured and delighted with your resolve," said Damian; "but it will be his study to save you all unnecessary trouble, and with that view a pavilion shall be instantly planted before your castle gate, which, if it please you to grace it with your presence, may be the place for the desired interview."

Eveline readily acquiesced in what was proposed, as the expedient agreeable to the Constable, and recommended by Damian; but, in the simplicity of her heart, she saw no good reason why, under the guardianship of the latter, she should not instantly, and without farther form, have traversed the little familiar plain on which, when a child, she used to chase butterflies and gather king's-cups, and where of later years she was wont to exercise her palfrey on this well-known plain, being the only space, and that of small extent, which separated her from the camp of the Constable.

The youthful emissary, with whose presence she had now become familiar, retired to acquaint his kinsman and lord with the success of his commission; and Eveline experienced the first sensation of anxiety upon her own account which had agitated her bosom, since the defeat and death of Gwenwyn gave her permission to dedicate her thoughts exclusively to grief, for the loss which she had sustained in the person of her noble father. But now, when that grief, though not satiated, was blunted by solitary indulgence—now that she was to appear before the person of whose fame she had heard so much, of whose powerful protection she had received such recent proofs, her mind insensibly turned upon the nature and consequences of that important interview. She had seen Hugo de Lacy, indeed, at the great tournament at Chester, where his valour and skill were the theme of every tongue, and she had received the homage which he rendered her beauty when he assigned to her the prize, with all the gay flutterings of youthful vanity; but of his person and figure she had no distinct idea, excepting that he was a middle-sized man, dressed in peculiarly rich armour, and that the countenance, which looked out from under the shade of his raised visor, seemed to her juvenile estimate very nearly as old as that of her father. This person, of whom she had such slight recollection, had been the chosen instrument employed by her tutelar protectress in rescuing her from captivity, and in avenging the loss of a father, and she was bound by her vow to consider him as the arbiter of her fate, if indeed he should deem it worth his while to become so. She wearied her memory with vain efforts to recollect so much of his features as might give her some means of guessing at his disposition, and her judgment toiled in conjecturing what line of conduct he was likely to pursue towards her.

The great Baron himself seemed to attach to their meeting a degree of consequence, which was intimated by the formal preparations which he made for it. Eveline had imagined that he might have ridden to the gate of the castle in five minutes, and that, if a pavilion were actually necessary to the decorum of their interview, a tent could have been transferred from his leaguer to the castle gate, and pitched there in ten minutes more. But it was plain that the Constable considered much more form and ceremony as essential to their meeting; for in about half an hour after Damian de Lacy had left the castle, not fewer than twenty soldiers and artificers, under the direction of a pursuivant, whose tabard was decorated with the armorial bearings of the house of Lacy, were employed in erecting before the gate of the Garde Doloureuse one of those splendid pavilions, which were employed at tournaments and other occasions of public state. It was of purple silk, valanced with gold embroidery, having the chords of the same rich materials. The door-way was formed by six lances, the staves of which were plaited with silver, and the blades composed of the same precious metal. These were pitched into the ground by couples, and crossed at the top, so as to form a sort of succession of arches, which were covered by drapery of sea-green silk, forming a pleasing contrast with the purple and gold.

The interior of the tent was declared by Dame Gillian and others, whose curiosity induced them to visit it, to be of a splendour agreeing with the outside. There were Oriental carpets, and there were tapestries of Ghent and Bruges mingled in gay profusion, while the top of the pavilion, covered with sky-blue silk, was arranged so as to resemble the firmament, and richly studded with a sun, moon, and stars, composed of solid silver. This gorgeous pavilion had been made for the use of the celebrated William of Ypres, who acquired such great wealth as general of the mercenaries of King Stephen, and was by him created Earl of Albemarle; but the chance of War had assigned it to De Lacy, after one of the dreadful engagements, so many of which occurred during the civil wars betwixt Stephen and the Empress Maude, or Matilda. The Constable had never before been known to use it; for although wealthy and powerful, Hugo de Lacy was, on most occasions, plain and unostentatious; which, to those who knew him, made his present conduct seem the more remarkable. At the hour of noon he arrived, nobly mounted, at the gate of the castle, and drawing up a small body of servants, pages, and equerries, who attended him in their richest liveries, placed himself at their head, and directed his nephew to intimate to the Lady of the Garde Doloureuse, that the humblest of her servants awaited the honour of her presence at the castle gate.

Among the spectators who witnessed his arrival, there were many who thought that some part of the state and splendour attached to his pavilion and his retinue, had been better applied to set forth the person of the Constable himself, as his attire was simple even to meanness, and his person by no means of such distinguished bearing as might altogether dispense with the advantages of dress and ornament. The opinion became yet more prevalent, when he descended from horseback, until which time his masterly management of the noble animal he bestrode, gave a dignity to his person and figure, which he lost upon dismounting from his steel saddle. In height, the celebrated Constable scarce attained the middle size, and his limbs, though strongly built and well knit, were deficient in grace and ease of movement. His legs were slightly curved outwards, which gave him advantage as a horseman, but showed unfavourably when he was upon foot. He halted, though very slightly, in consequence of one of his legs having been broken by the fall of a charger, and inartificially set by an inexperienced surgeon. This, also, was a blemish in his deportment; and though his broad shoulders, sinewy arms, and expanded chest, betokened the strength which he often displayed, it was strength of a clumsy and ungraceful character. His language and gestures were those of one seldom used to converse with equals, more seldom still with superiors; short, abrupt, and decisive, almost to the verge of sternness. In the judgment of those who were habitually acquainted with the Constable, there was both dignity and kindness in his keen eye and expanded brow; but such as saw him for the first time judged less favourably, and pretended to discover a harsh and passionate expression, although they allowed his countenance to have, on the whole, a bold and martial character. His age was in reality not more than five-and-forty, but the fatigues of war and of climate had added in appearance ten years to that period of time. By far the plainest dressed man of his train, he wore only a short Norman mantle, over the close dress of shamois-leather, which, almost always covered by his armour, was in some places slightly soiled by its pressure. A brown hat, in which he wore a sprig of rosemary in memory of his vow, served for his head-gear— his good sword and dagger hung at a belt made of seal-skin.

Thus accoutred, and at the head of a glittering and gilded band of retainers, who watched his lightest glance, the Constable of Chester awaited the arrival of the Lady Eveline Berenger, at the gate of her castle of Garde Doloureuse.

The trumpets from within announced her presence—the bridge fell, and, led by Damian de Lacy in his gayest habit, and followed by her train of females, and menial or vassal attendants, she came forth in her loveliness from under the massive and antique portal of her paternal fortress. She was dressed without ornaments of any kind, and in deep mourning weeds, as best befitted her recent loss; forming, in this respect, a strong contrast with the rich attire of her conductor, whose costly dress gleamed with jewels and embroidery, while their age and personal beauty made them in every other respect the fair counterpart of each other; a circumstance which probably gave rise to the delighted murmur and buzz which passed through the bystanders on their appearance, and which only respect for the deep mourning of Eveline prevented from breaking out into shouts of applause.

The instant that the fair foot of Eveline had made a step beyond the palisades which formed the outward barrier of the castle, the Constable de Lacy stepped forward to meet her, and, bending his right knee to the earth, craved pardon for the discourtesy which his vow had imposed on him, while he expressed his sense of the honour with which she now graced him, as one for which his life, devoted to her service, would be an inadequate acknowledgment.

The action and speech, though both in consistence with the romantic gallantry of the times, embarrassed Eveline; and the rather that this homage was so publicly rendered. She entreated the Constable to stand up, and not to add to the confusion of one who was already sufficiently at a loss how to acquit herself of the heavy debt of gratitude which she owed him. The Constable arose accordingly, after saluting her hand, which she extended to him, and prayed her, since she was so far condescending, to deign to enter the poor hut he had prepared for her shelter, and to grant him the honour of the audience he had solicited. Eveline, without farther answer than a bow, yielded him her hand, and desiring the rest of her train to remain where they were, commanded the attendance of Rose Flammock.

"Lady," said the Constable, "the matters of which I am compelled thus hastily to speak, are of a nature the most private."

"This maiden," replied Eveline, "is my bower-woman, and acquainted with my most inward thoughts; I beseech you to permit her presence at our conference."

"It were better otherwise," said Hugo de Lacy, with some embarrassment; "but your pleasure shall be obeyed."

He led the Lady Eveline into the tent, and entreated her to be seated on a large pile of cushions, covered with rich Venetian silk. Rose placed herself behind her mistress, half kneeling upon the same cushions, and watched the motions of the all-accomplished soldier and statesman, whom the voice of fame lauded so loudly; enjoying his embarrassment as a triumph of her sex, and scarcely of opinion that his shamois doublet and square form accorded with the splendour of the scene, or the almost angelic beauty of Eveline, the other actor therein.

"Lady," said the Constable, after some hesitation, "I would willingly say what it is my lot to tell you, in such terms as ladies love to listen to, and which surely your excellent beauty more especially deserves; but I have been too long trained in camps and councils to express my meaning otherwise than simply and plainly."

"I shall the more easily understand you, my lord," said Eveline, trembling, though she scarce knew why.

"My story, then, must be a blunt one. Something there passed between your honourable father and myself, touching a union of our houses."—He paused, as if he wished or expected Eveline to say something, but, as she was silent, he proceeded. "I would to God, that, as he was at the beginning of this treaty, it had pleased Heaven he should have conducted and concluded it with his usual wisdom; but what remedy?—he has gone the path which we must all tread."

"Your lordship," said Eveline, "has nobly avenged the death of your noble friend."

"I have but done my devoir, lady, as a good knight, in defence of an endangered maiden—a Lord Marcher in protection of the frontier—and a friend in avenging his friend. But to the point.— Our long and noble line draws near to a close. Of my remote kinsman, Randal Lacy, I will not speak; for in him I see nothing that is good or hopeful, nor have we been at one for many years. My nephew, Damian, gives hopeful promise to be a worthy branch of our ancient tree—but he is scarce twenty years old, and hath a long career of adventure and peril to encounter, ere he can honourably propose to himself the duties of domestic privacy or matrimonial engagements. His mother also is English, some abatentent perhaps in the escutcheon of his arms; yet, had ten years more passed over him with the honours of chivalry, I should have proposed Damian de Lacy for the happiness to which I at present myself aspire."

"You—you, my lord!—it is impossible!" said Eveline, endeavouring at the same time to suppress all that could be offensive in the surprise which she could not help exhibiting.

"I do not wonder," replied the Constable, calmly,—for the ice being now broken, he resumed the natural steadiness of his manner and character,—"that you express surprise at this daring proposal. I have not perhaps the form that pleases a lady's eye, and I have forgotten,—that is, if I ever knew them,—the terms and phrases which please a lady's ear; but, noble Eveline, the Lady of Hugh de Lacy will be one of the foremost among the matronage of England."

"It will the better become the individual to whom so high a dignity is offered," said Eveline, "to consider how far she is capable of discharging its duties."

"Of that I fear nothing," said De Lacy. "She who hath been so excellent a daughter, cannot be less estimable in every other relation in life."

"I do not find that confidence in myself my lord," replied the embarrassed maiden, "with which you are so willing to load me—And I—forgive me—must crave time for other inquiries, as well as those which respect myself."

"Your father, noble lady, had this union warmly at heart. This scroll, signed with his own hand, will show it." He bent his knee as he gave the paper. "The wife of De Lacy will have, as the daughter of Raymond Berenger merits, the rank of a princess; his widow, the dowry of a queen."

"Mock me not with your knee, my lord, while you plead to me the paternal commands, which, joined to other circumstances"—she paused, and sighed deeply—"leave me, perhaps, but little room for free will!"

Imboldened by this answer, De Lacy, who had hitherto remained on his knee, rose gently, and assuming a seat beside the Lady Eveline, continued to press his suit,—not, indeed, in the language of passion, but of a plain-spoken man, eagerly urging a proposal on which his happiness depended. The vision of the miraculous image was, it may be supposed, uppermost in the mind of Eveline, who, tied down by the solemn vow she had made on that occasion, felt herself constrained to return evasive answers, where she might perhaps have given a direct negative, had her own wishes alone been to decide her reply.

"You cannot," she said, "expect from me, my lord, in this my so recent orphan state, that I should come to a speedy determination upon an affair of such deep importance. Give me leisure of your nobleness for consideration with myself —for consultation with my friends."

"Alas! fair Eveline," said the Baron, "do not be offended at my urgency. I cannot long delay setting forward on a distant and perilous expedition; and the short time left me for soliciting your favour, must be an apology for my importunity."

"And is it in these circumstances, noble De Lacy, that you would encumber yourself with family ties?" asked the maiden, timidly.

"I am God's soldier," said the Constable, "and He, in whose cause I fight in Palestine, will defend my wife in England."

"Hear then my present answer, my lord," said Eveline Berenger, rising from her seat. "To-morrow I proceed to the Benedictine nunnery at Gloucester, where resides my honoured father's sister, who is Abbess of that reverend house. To her guidance I will commit myself in this matter."

"A fair and maidenly resolution," answered De Lacy, who seemed, on his part, rather glad that the conference was abridged, "and, as I trust, not altogether unfavourable to the suit of your humble suppliant, since the good Lady Abbess hath been long my honoured friend." He then turned to Rose, who was about to attend her lady:—"Pretty maiden," he said, offering a chain of gold, "let this carcanet encircle thy neck, and buy thy good will."

"My good will cannot be purchased, my lord," said Rose, putting back the gift which he proffered.

"Your fair word, then," said the Constable, again pressing it upon her.

"Fair words are easily bought," said Rose, still rejecting the chain, "but they are seldom worth the purchase-money."

"Do you scorn my proffer, damsel?" said De Lacy: "it has graced the neck of a Norman count."

"Give it to a Norman countess then, my lord," said the damsel; "I am plain Rose Flammock, the weaver's daughter. I keep my good word to go with my good will, and a latten chain will become me as well as beaten gold."

"Peace, Rose," said her lady; "you are over malapert to talk thus to the Lord Constable.—And you, my lord," she continued, "permit me now to depart, since you are possessed of my answer to your present proposal. I regret it had not been of some less delicate nature, that by granting it at once, and without delay, I might have shown my sense of your services."

The lady was handed forth by the Constable of Chester, with the same ceremony which had been observed at their entrance, and she returned to her own castle, sad and anxious in mind for the event of this important conference. She gathered closely round her the great mourning veil, that the alteration of her countenance might not be observed; and, without pausing to speak even to Father Aldrovand, she instantly withdrew to the privacy of her own bower.

CHAPTER THE TWELFTH.

Now all ye ladies of fair Scotland,
   And ladies of England that happy would prove,
Marry never for houses, nor marry for land,
   Nor marry for nothing but only love.
   FAMILY QUARRELS.

When the Lady Eveline had retired into her own private chamber, Rose Flammock followed her unbidden, and proffered her assistance in removing the large veil which she had worn while she was abroad; but the lady refused her permission, saying, "You are forward with service, maiden, when it is not required of you."

"You are displeased with me, lady!" said Rose.

"And if I am, I have cause," replied Eveline. "You know my difficulties—you know what my duty demands; yet, instead of aiding me to make the sacrifice, you render it more difficult."

"Would I had influence to guide your path!" said Rose; "you should find it a smooth one—ay, an honest and straight one, to boot."

"How mean you, maiden?" said Eveline.

"I would have you," answered Rose, "recall the encouragement—the consent, I may almost call it, you have yielded to this proud baron. He is too great to be loved himself—too haughty to love you as you deserve. If you wed him, you wed gilded misery, and, it may be, dishonour as well as discontent."

"Remember, damsel," answered Eveline Berenger, "his services towards us."

"His services?" answered Rose. "He ventured his life for us; indeed, but so did every soldier in his host. And am I bound to wed any ruffling blade among them, because he fought when the trumpet sounded? I wonder what, is the meaning of their *devoir*, as they call it, when it shames them not to claim the highest reward woman can bestow, merely for discharging the duty of a gentleman, by a distressed creature. A gentleman, said I?—The coarsest boor in Flanders would hardly expect thanks for doing the duty of a man by women in such a case."

"But my father's wishes?" said the young lady.

"They had reference, without doubt, to the inclination of your father's daughter," answered the attendant. "I will not do my late noble lord—(may God assoilzie him!)—the injustice to suppose he would have urged aught in this matter which squared not with your free choice."

"Then my vow—my fatal vow, as I had well nigh called it?" said Eveline. "May Heaven forgive me my ingratitude to my patroness!"

"Even this shakes me not," said Rose; "I will never believe our Lady of Mercy would exact such a penalty for her protection, as to desire me to wed the man I could not love. She smiled, you say, upon your prayer. Go—lay at her feet these difficulties which oppress you, and see if she will not smile again. Or seek a dispensation from your vow—seek it at the expense of the half of your estate,—seek it at the expense of your whole property. Go a pilgrimage barefooted to Rome—do any thing but give your hand where you cannot give your heart."

"You speak warmly, Rose," said Eveline, still sighing as she spoke.

"Alas! my sweet lady, I have cause. Have I not seen a household where love was not—where, although there was worth and good will, and enough of the means of life, all was imbittered by regrets, which were not only vain, but criminal?"

"Yet, methinks, Rose, a sense of what is due to ourselves and to others may, if listened to, guide and comfort us under such feelings even as thou hast described."

"It will save us from sin, lady, but not from sorrow," answered Rose; "and wherefore should we, with our eyes open, rush into circumstances where duty must war with inclination?" Why row against wind and tide, when you may as easily take advantage of the breeze?"

"Because the voyage of my life lies where winds and currents oppose me," answered Eveline. "It is my fate, Rose."

"Not unless you make it such by choice," answered Rose. "Oh, could you but have seen the pale cheek, sunken eye, and dejected bearing of my poor mother!—I have said too much."

"It was then your mother," said her young lady, "of whose unhappy wedlock you have spoken?"

"It was—it was," said Rose, bursting into tears. "I have exposed my own shame to save you from sorrow. Unhappy she was, though most guiltless—so unhappy, that the breach of the dike, and the inundation in which she perished, were, but for my sake, to her welcome as night to the weary labourer. She had a heart like yours, formed to love and be loved; and it would be doing honour to yonder proud Baron, to say he had such worth as my father's.— Yet was she most unhappy. Oh! my sweet lady, be warned, and break off this ill-omened match!"

Eveline returned the pressure with which the affectionate girl, as she clung to her hand, enforced her well-meant advice, and then muttered with a profound sigh,—"Rose, it is too late."

"Never—never," said Rose, looking eagerly round the room. "Where are those writing materials?—Let me bring Father Aldrovand, and instruct him of your pleasure—or, stay, the good father hath himself an eye on the splendours of the world which he thinks he has abandoned—he will be no safe secretary.—I will go myself to the Lord Constable—*me* his rank cannot dazzle, or his wealth bribe, or his power overawe. I will tell him he doth no knightly part towards you, to press his contract with your father in such an hour of helpless sorrow—no pious part, in delaying the execution of his vows for the purpose of marrying or giving in marriage—no honest part, to press himself on a maiden whose heart has not decided in his favour—no wise part, to marry one whom he must presently abandon, either to solitude, or to the dangers of a profligate court."

"You have not courage for such an embassy, Rose," said her mistress, sadly smiling through her tears at her youthful attendant's zeal.

"Not courage for it!—and wherefore not?—Try me," answered the Flemish maiden, in return. "I am neither Saracen nor Welshman—his lance and sword scare me not. I follow not his banner—his voice of command concerns me not. I could, with your leave, boldly tell him he is a selfish man, veiling with fair and honourable pretexts his pursuit of objects which concern his own pride and gratification, and founding high claims on having rendered the services which common humanity demanded. And all for what?— Forsooth the great De Lacy must have an heir to his noble house, and his fair nephew is not good enough to be his representative, because his mother was of Anglo-Saxon strain, and the real heir must be pure unmixed Norman; and for this, Lady Eveline Berenger, in the first bloom of youth, must be wedded to a man who might be her father, and who, after leaving her unprotected for years, will return in such guise as might beseem her grandfather!"

"Since he is thus scrupulous concerning purity of lineage," said Eveline, "perhaps he may call to mind, what so good a herald as he is cannot fail to know—that I am of Saxon strain by my father's mother."

"Oh," replied Rose, "he will forgive that blot in the heiress of the Garde Doloureuse."

"Fie, Rose," answered her mistress, "thou dost him wrong in taxing him with avarice."

"Perhaps so," answered Rose; "but he is undeniably ambitious; and Avarice, I have heard, is Ambition's bastard brother, though Ambition be sometimes ashamed of the relationship."

"You speak too boldly, damsel," said Eveline; "and, while I acknowledge your affection, it becomes me to check your mode of expression."

"Nay, take that tone, and I have done," said Rose.—"To Eveline, whom I love, and who loves me, I can speak freely—but to the Lady of the Garde Doloureuse, the proud Norman damsel, (which when you choose to be you can be,) I can curtsy as low as my station demands, and speak as little truth as she cares to hear."

"Thou art a wild but a kind girl," said Eveline; "no one who did not know thee would think that soft and childish exterior covered such a soul of fire. Thy mother must indeed have been the being of feeling and passion you paint her;

for thy father—nay, nay, never arm in his defence until he be attacked—I only meant to say, that his solid sense and sound judgment are his most distinguished qualities."

"And I would you would avail yourself of them, lady," said Rose.

"In fitting things I will; but he were rather an unmeet counsellor in that which we now treat of," said Eveline.

"You mistake him," answered Rose Flammock, "and underrate his value. Sound judgment is like to the graduated measuring-wand, which, though usually applied only to coarser cloths, will give with equal truth the dimensions of Indian silk, or of cloth of gold."

"Well—well—this affair presses not instantly at least," said the young lady. "Leave me now, Rose, and send Gillian the tirewoman hither—I have directions to give about the packing and removal of my wardrobe."

"That Gillian the tirewoman hath been a mighty favourite of late," said Rose; "time was when it was otherwise."

"I like her manners as little as thou dost," said Eveline; "but she is old Raoul's wife—she was a sort of half favourite with my dear father—who, like other men, was perhaps taken by that very freedom which we think unseemly in persons of our sex; and then there is no other woman in the Castle that hath such skill in empacketing clothes without the risk of their being injured."

"That last reason alone," said Rose, smiling, "is, I admit, an irresistible pretension to favour, and Dame Gillian shall presently attend you.—But take my advice, lady—keep her to her bales and her mails, and let her not prate to you on what concerns her not."

So saying, Rose left the apartment, and her young lady looked after her in silence—then murmured to herself—"Rose loves me truly; but she would willingly be more of the mistress than the maiden; and then she is somewhat jealous of every other person that approaches me.—It is strange, that I have not seen Damian de Lacy since my interview with the Constable. He anticipates, I suppose, the chance of his finding in me a severe aunt!"

But the domestics, who crowded for orders with reference to her removal early on the morrow, began now to divert the current of their lady's thoughts from the consideration of her own particular situation, which, as the prospect presented nothing pleasant, with the elastic spirit of youth, she willingly postponed till farther leisure.

CHAPTER THE THIRTEENTH

Too much rest is rust,
  There's ever cheer in changing;
We tyne by too much trust,
So we'll be up and ranging.
  OLD SONG.

Early on the subsequent morning, a gallant company, saddened indeed by the deep mourning which their principals wore, left the well-defended Castle of the Garde Doloureuse, which had been so lately the scene of such remarkable events.

The sun was just beginning to exhale the heavy dews which had fallen during the night, and to disperse the thin gray mist which eddied around towers and battlements, when Wilkin Flammock, with six crossbowmen on horseback, and as many spearmen on foot, sallied forth from under the Gothic gate-way, and crossed the sounding drawbridge. After this advanced guard, came four household servants well mounted, and after them, as many inferior female attendants, all in mourning. Then rode forth the young Lady Eveline herself, occupying the centre of the little procession, and her long black robes formed a striking contrast to the colour of her milk-white palfrey. Beside her, on a Spanish jennet, the gift of her affectionate father,—who had procured it at a high rate, and who would have given half his substance to gratify his daughter, —sat the girlish form of Rose Flammock, who had so much of juvenile shyness in her manner, so much of feeling and of judgment in her thoughts and actions. Dame Margery followed, mixed in the party escorted by Father Aldrovand, whose company she chiefly frequented; for Margery affected a little the character of the devotee, and her influence in the family, as having been Eveline's nurse, was so great as to render her no improper companion for the chaplain, when her lady did not require her attendance on her own person. Then came old Raoul the huntsman, his wife, and two or three other officers of Raymond Berenger's household; the steward, with his golden chain, velvet cassock, and white wand, bringing up the rear, which was closed by a small band of archers, and four men-at-arms. The guards, and indeed the greater part of the attendants, were only designed to give the necessary degree of honour to the young lady's movements, by accompanying her a short space from the castle, where they were met by the Constable of Chester, who, with a retinue of thirty lances, proposed himself to escort Eveline as far as Gloucester, the place of her destination. Under his protection no danger was to be apprehended, even if the severe defeat so lately sustained by the Welsh had not of itself been likely to prevent any attempt, on the part of those hostile mountaineers, to disturb the safety of the marches for some time to come. In pursuance of this arrangement, which permitted the armed part of Eveline's retinue to return for the protection of the castle, and the restoration of order in the district around, the Constable awaited her at the fatal bridge, at the head of the gallant band of selected horsemen whom he had ordered to attend upon him. The parties halted, as if to salute each other; but the Constable, observing that Eveline drew her veil more closely around her, and recollecting the loss she had so lately sustained on that luckless spot, had the judgment to confine his greeting to a mute reverence, so low that the lofty plume which he wore, (for he was now in complete armour,) mingled with the flowing mane of his gallant horse. Wilkin Flammock next halted, to ask the lady if she had any farther commands.

"None, good Wilkin," said Eveline; "but to be, as ever, true and watchful."

"The properties of a good mastiff," said Flammock. "Some rude sagacity, and a stout hand instead of a sharp case of teeth, are all that I can claim to be added to them—I will do my best.—Fare thee well, Roschen! Thou art going among strangers—forget not the qualities which made thee loved at home. The saints bless thee— farewell!"

The steward next approached to take his leave, but in doing so, had nearly met with a fatal accident. It had been the pleasure of Raoul, who was in his own disposition cross-grained, and in person rheumatic, to accommodate himself with an old Arab horse, which had been kept for the sake of the breed, as lean, and almost as lame as himself, and with a temper as vicious as that of a fiend. Betwixt the rider and the horse was a constant misunderstanding, testified on Raoul's part by oaths, rough checks with the curb, and severe digging with the spurs, which Mahound (so paganishly was the horse named) answered by plunging, bounding, and endeavouring by all expedients to unseat his rider, as well as striking and lashing out furiously at whatever else approached him. It was thought by many of the household, that Raoul preferred this vicious cross-tempered animal upon all occasions when he travelled in company with his wife, in order to take advantage by the chance, that amongst the various kicks, plunges, gambades, lashings out, and other eccentricities of Mahound, his heels might come in contact with Dame Gillian's ribs. And now, when as the important steward spurred up his palfrey to kiss his young lady's hand, and to take his leave, it seemed to the bystanders as if Raoul so managed his bridle and spur, that Mahound jerked out his hoofs at the same moment, one of which coming in contact with the steward's thigh, would have splintered it like a rotten reed, had the parties been a couple of inches nearer to each other. As it was, the steward sustained considerable damage; and they that observed the grin upon Raoul's vinegar countenance entertained little doubt, that Mahound's heels then and there avenged certain nods, and winks, and wreathed smiles, which had passed betwixt the gold-chained functionary and the coquettish tirewoman, since the party left the castle.

This incident abridged the painful solemnity of parting betwixt the Lady Eveline and her dependents, and lessened, at the same time, the formality of her meeting with the Constable, and, as it were, resigning herself to his protection.

Hugo de Lacy, having commanded six of his men-at-arms to proceed as an advanced-guard, remained himself to see the steward properly deposited on a litter, and then, with the rest of his followers, marched in military fashion about one hundred yards in the rear of Lady Eveline and her retinue, judiciously forbearing to present himself to her society while she was engaged in the orisons which the place where they met naturally suggested, and waiting patiently until the elasticity of youthful temper should require some diversion of the gloomy thoughts which the scene inspired.

Guided by this policy, the Constable did not approach the ladies until the advance of the morning rendered it politeness to remind them, that a pleasant spot for breaking their fast occurred in the neighbourhood, where he had ventured to make some preparations for rest and refreshment. Immediately after the Lady Eveline had intimated her acceptance of this courtesy, they came in sight of the spot he alluded to, marked by an ancient oak, which, spreading its broad branches far and wide, reminded the traveller of that of Mamre, under which celestial beings accepted the hospitality of the patriarch. Across two of these huge projecting arms was flung a piece of rose-coloured sarsanet, as a canopy to keep off the morning beams, which were already rising high. Cushions of silk, interchanged with others covered with the furs of animals of the chase, were arranged round a repast, which a Norman cook had done his utmost to distinguish, by the superior delicacy of his art, from the gross meals of the Saxons, and the penurious simplicity of the Welsh tables. A fountain, which bubbled from under a large mossy stone at some distance, refreshed the air with its sound, and the taste with its liquid crystal; while, at the same time, it formed a cistern for cooling two or three flasks of Gascon wine and hippocras, which were at that time the necessary accompaniments of the morning meal.

When Eveline, with Rose, the Confessor, and at some farther distance her faithful nurse, was seated at this silvan banquet, the leaves rustling to a gentle breeze, the water bubbling in the background, the birds twittering around, while the half-heard sounds of conversation and laughter at a distance announced that their guard was in the vicinity, she could not avoid making the Constable some natural compliment on his happy selection of a place of repose.

"You do me more than justice," replied the Baron; "the spot was selected by my nephew, who hath a fancy like a minstrel. Myself am but slow in imagining such devices."

Rose looked full at her mistress, as if she endeavoured to look into her very inmost soul; but Eveline answered with the utmost simplicity,—"And wherefore hath not the noble Damian waited to join us at the entertainment which he hath directed?"

"He prefers riding onward," said the Baron, "with some light-horsemen; for, notwithstanding there are now no Welsh knaves stirring, yet the marches are never free from robbers and outlaws; and though there is nothing to fear for a band like ours, yet you should not be alarmed even by the approach of danger."

"I have indeed seen but too much of it lately," said Eveline; and relapsed into the melancholy mood from which the novelty of the scene had for a moment awakened her.

Meanwhile, the Constable, removing, with the assistance of his squire, his mailed hood and its steel crest, as well as his gauntlets, remained in his flexible coat of mail, composed entirely of rings of steel curiously interwoven, his hands bare, and his brows covered with a velvet bonnet of a peculiar fashion, appropriated to the use of knights, and called a *mortier*, which permitted him both to converse and to eat more easily than when he wore the full defensive armour. His discourse was plain, sensible, and manly; and, turning upon the state of the country, and the precautions to be observed for governing and defending so disorderly a frontier, it became gradually interesting to Eveline, one of whose warmest wishes was to be the protectress of her father's vassals. De Lacy, on his part, seemed much pleased; for, young as Eveline was, her questions showed intelligence, and her mode of answering, both apprehension and docility. In short, familiarity was so far established betwixt them, that in the nest stage of their journey, the Constable seemed to think his appropriate place was at the Lady Eveline's bridle-rein; and although she certainly did not countenance his attendance, yet neither did she seem willing to discourage it. Himself no ardent lover, although captivated both by the beauty and the amiable qualities of the fair orphan, De Lacy was satisfied with being endured as a companion, and made no efforts to improve the opportunity which this familiarity afforded him, by recurring to any of the topics of the preceding day.

A halt was made at noon in a small village, where the same purveyor had made preparations for their accommodation, and particularly for that of the Lady Eveline; but, something to her surprise, he himself remained invisible. The conversation of the Constable of Chester was, doubtless, in the highest degree instructive; but at Eveline's years, a maiden might be excused for wishing some addition to the society in the person of a younger and less serious attendant; and when she recollected the regularity with which Damian Lacy had hitherto made his respects to her, she rather wondered at his continued absence. But her reflection went no deeper than the passing thought of one who was not quite so much delighted with her present company, as not to believe it capable of an agreeable addition. She was lending a patient ear to the account which the Constable gave her of the descent and pedigree of a gallant knight of the distinguished family of Herbert, at whose castle he proposed to repose during the night, when one of the retinue announced a messenger from the Lady of Baldringham.

"My honoured father's aunt," said Eveline, arising to testify that respect for age and relationship which the manners of the time required.

"I knew not," said the Constable, "that my gallant friend had such a relative."

"She was my grandmother's sister," answered Eveline, "a noble Saxon lady; but she disliked the match formed with a Norman house, and never saw her sister after the period of her marriage."

She broke off, as the messenger, who had the appearance of the steward of a person of consequence, entered the presence, and, bending his knee reverently, delivered a letter, which, being examined by Father Aldrovand, was found to contain the following invitation, expressed, not in French, then the general language of communication amongst the gentry, but in the old Saxon language, modified as it now was by some intermixture of French.

"If the grand-daughter of Aelfried of Baldringham hath so much of the old Saxon strain as to desire to see an ancient relation, who still dwells in the house of her forefathers, and lives after their manner, she is thus invited to repose for the night in the dwelling of Ermengarde of Baldringham."

"Your pleasure will be, doubtless, to decline the present hospitality?" said the Constable De Lacy; "the noble Herbert expects us, and has made great preparation."

"Your presence, my lord," said Eveline, "will more than console him for my absence. It is fitting and proper that I should meet my aunt's advances to reconciliation, since she has condescended to make them."

De Lacy's brow was slightly clouded, for seldom had he met with anything approaching to contradiction of his pleasure. "I pray you to reflect, Lady Eveline," he said, "that your aunt's house is probably defenceless, or at least very imperfectly guarded.—Would it not be your pleasure that I should continue my dutiful attendance?"

"Of that, my lord, mine aunt can, in her own house, be the sole judge; and methinks, as she has not deemed it necessary to request the honour of your lordship's company, it were unbecoming in me to permit you to take the trouble of attendance;—you have already had but too much on my account."

"But for the sake of your own safety, madam," said De Lacy, unwilling to leave his charge.

"My safety, my lord, cannot be endangered in the house of so near a relative; whatever precautions she may take on her own behalf, will doubtless be amply sufficient for mine."

"I hope it will be found so," said De Lacy; "and I will at least add to them the security of a patrol around the castle during your abode in it." He stopped, and then proceeded with some hesitation to express his hope, that Eveline, now about to visit a kinswoman whose prejudices against the Norman race were generally known, would be on her guard against what she might hear upon that subject.

Eveline answered with dignity, that the daughter of Raymond Berenger was unlikely to listen to any opinions which would affect the dignity of that good knight's nation and descent; and with this assurance, the Constable, finding it impossible to obtain any which had more special reference to himself and his suit, was compelled to remain satisfied. He recollected also that the castle of Herbert was within two miles of the habitation of the Lady of Baldringham, and that his separation from Eveline was but for one night; yet a sense of the difference betwixt their years, and perhaps of his own deficiency in those lighter qualifications by which the female heart is supposed to be most frequently won, rendered even this temporary absence matter of anxious thought and apprehension; so that, during their afternoon journey, he rode in silence by Eveline's side, rather meditating what might chance to- morrow, than endeavouring to avail himself of present opportunity. In this unsocial manner they travelled on until the point was reached where they were to separate for the evening.

This was an elevated spot, from which they could see, on the right hand, the castle of Amelot Herbert, rising high upon an eminence, with all its Gothic pinnacles and turrets; and on the left, low- embowered amongst oaken woods, the rude and lonely dwelling in which the Lady of Baldringham still maintained the customs of the Anglo-Saxons, and looked with contempt and hatred on all innovations that had been introduced since the battle of Hastings.

Here the Constable De Lacy, having charged a part of his men to attend the Lady Eveline to the house of her relation, and to keep watch around it with the utmost vigilance, but at such a distance as might not give offence or inconvenience to the family, kissed her hand, and took a reluctant leave.

Eveline proceeded onwards by a path so little trodden, as to show the solitary condition of the mansion to which it led. Large kine, of an uncommon and valuable breed, were feeding in the rich pastures around; and now and then fallow deer, which appeared to have lost the shyness of their nature, tripped across the glades of the woodland, or stood and lay in small groups under some great oak. The transient pleasure which such a scene of rural quiet was calculated to afford, changed to more serious feelings, when a sudden turn brought her at once in front of the mansion-house, of which she had seen nothing since she first beheld it from the point where she parted with the Constable, and which she had more than one reason for regarding with some apprehension.

The house, for it could not be termed a castle, was only two stories high, low and massively built, with doors and windows forming the heavy round arch which is usually called Saxon;—the walls were mantled with various creeping plants, which had crept along them undisturbed—grass grew up to the very threshold, at which hung a buffalo's horn, suspended by a brass chain. A massive door of black oak closed a gate, which much resembled the ancient entrance to a ruined sepulchre, and not a soul appeared to acknowledge or greet their arrival.

"Were I you, my Lady Eveline," said the officious dame Gillian, "I would turn bridle yet; for this old dungeon seems little likely to afford food or shelter to Christian folk."

Eveline imposed silence on her indiscreet attendant, though herself exchanging a look with Rose which confessed something like timidity, as she commanded Raoul to blow the horn at the gate. "I have heard," she said, "that my aunt loves the ancient customs so well, that she is loath to admit into her halls any thing younger than the time of Edward the Confessor."

Raoul, in the meantime, cursing the rude instrument which baffled his skill in sounding a regular call, and gave voice only to a tremulous and discordant roar, which seemed to shake the old walls, thick as they were, repeated his summons three times before they obtained admittance. On the third sounding, the gate opened, and a numerous retinue of servants of both sexes appeared in the dark and narrow hall, at the upper end of which a great fire of wood was sending its furnace-blast up an antique chimney, whose front, as extensive as that of a modern kitchen, was carved over with ornaments of massive stone, and garnished on the top with a long range of niches, from each of which frowned the image of some Saxon Saint, whose barbarous name was scarce to be found in the Romish calendar.

The same officer who had brought the invitation from his lady to Eveline, now stepped forward, as she supposed, to assist her from her palfrey; but it was in reality to lead it by the bridle-rein into the paved hall itself, and up to a raised platform, or dais, at the upper end of which she was at length permitted to dismount. Two matrons of advanced years, and four young women of gentle birth, educated by the bounty of Ermengarde, attended with reverence the arrival of her kinswoman. Eveline would have inquired of them for her grand-aunt, but the matrons with much respect laid their fingers on their mouths, as if to enjoin her silence; a gesture which, united to the singularity of her reception in other respects, still farther excited her curiosity to see her venerable relative.

It was soon gratified; for, through a pair of folding doors, which opened not far from the platform on which she stood, she was ushered into a large low apartment hung with arras; at the upper end of which, under a species of canopy, was seated the ancient Lady of Baldringham. Fourscore years had not quenched the brightness of her eyes, or bent an inch of her stately height; her gray hair was still so profuse as to form a tier, combined as it was with a chaplet of ivy leaves; her long dark-coloured gown fell in ample folds, and the broidered girdle, which gathered it around her, was fastened by a buckle of gold, studded with precious stones, which were worth an Earl's ransom; her features, which had once been beautiful, or rather majestic, bore still, though faded and wrinkled, an air of melancholy and stern grandeur, that assorted well with her garb and deportment. She had a staff of ebony in her hand; at her feet rested a large aged wolf-dog, who pricked his ears and bristled up his neck, as the step of a stranger, a sound so seldom heard in those halls, approached the chair in which his aged mistress sat motionless.

"Peace, Thryme," said the venerable dame; "and thou, daughter of the house of Baldringham, approach, and fear not their ancient servant."

The hound sunk down to his couchant posture when she spoke, and, excepting the red glare of his eyes, might have seemed a hieroglyphical emblem, lying at the feet of some ancient priestess of Woden or Freya; so strongly did the appearance of Ermengarde, with her rod and her chaplet, correspond with the ideas of the days of Paganism. Yet he who had thus deemed of her would have done therein much injustice to a venerable Christian matron, who had given many a hide of land to holy church, in honour of God and Saint Dunstan.

Ermengarde's reception of Eveline was of the same antiquated and formal cast with her mansion and her exterior. She did not at first arise from her seat when the noble maiden approached her, nor did she even admit her to the salute which she advanced to offer; but, laying her hand on Eveline's arm, stopped her as she advanced, and perused her countenance with an earnest and unsparing eye of minute observation.

"Berwine," she said to the most favoured of the two attendants, "our niece hath the skin and eyes of the Saxon hue; but the hue of her eye-brows and hair is from the foreigner and alien.—Thou art, nevertheless,—welcome to my house, maiden," she added, addressing Eveline, "especially if thou canst bear to hear that thou art not absolutely a perfect creature, as doubtless these flatterers around thee have taught thee to believe."

So saying, she at length arose, and saluted her niece with a kiss on the forehead. She released her not, however, from her grasp, but proceeded to give the attention to her garments which she had hitherto bestowed upon her features.

"Saint Dunstan keep us from vanity!" she said; "and so this is the new guise— and modest maidens wear such tunics as these, showing the shape of their persons as plain as if (Saint Mary defend us!) they were altogether without garments? And see, Berwine, these gauds on the neck, and that neck itself uncovered as low as the shoulder—these be the guises which strangers have brought into merry England! and this pouch, like a player's placket, hath but little to do with housewifery, I wot; and that dagger, too, like a glee-man's wife, that rides a mumming in masculine apparel—dost thou ever go to the wars, maiden, that thou wearest steel at thy girdle?"

Eveline, equally surprised and disobliged by the depreciating catalogue of her apparel, replied to the last question with some spirit,—"The mode may have altered, madam; but I only wear such garments as are now worn by those of my age and condition. For the poniard, may it please you, it is not many days since I regarded it as the last resource betwixt me and dishonour."

"The maiden speaks well and boldly, Berwine," said Dame Ermengarde; "and, in truth, pass we but over some of these vain fripperies, is attired in a comely fashion. Thy father, I hear, fell knight-like in the field of battle."

"He did so," answered Eveline, her eyes filling with tears at the recollection of her recent loss.

"I never saw him," continued Dame Ermengarde; "he carried the old Norman scorn towards the Saxon stock, whom they wed but for what they can make by them, as the bramble clings to the elm;—nay, never seek to vindicate him," she continued, observing that Eveline was about to speak, "I have known the Norman spirit for many a year ere thou wert born."

At this moment the steward appeared in the chamber, and, after a long genuflection, asked his lady's pleasure concerning the guard of Norman soldiers who remained without the mansion.

"Norman soldiers so near the house of Baldringham!" said the old lady, fiercely; "who brings them hither, and for what purpose?"

"They came, as I think," said the sewer, "to wait on and guard this gracious young lady."

"What, my daughter," said Ermengarde, in a tone of melancholy reproach, "darest thou not trust thyself unguarded for one night in the castle of thy forefathers?"

"God forbid else!" said Eveline. "But these men are not mine, nor under my authority. They are part of the train of the Constable de Lacy, who left them to watch around the castle, thinking there might be danger from robbers."

"Robbers," said Ermengarde, "have never harmed the house of Baldringham, since a Norman robber stole from it its best treasure in the person of thy grandmother—And so, poor bird, thou art already captive—unhappy flutterer! But it is thy lot, and wherefore should I wonder or repine? When was there fair maiden, with a wealthy dower, but she was ere maturity destined to be the slave of some of those petty kings, who allow us to call nothing ours that their passions can covet? Well—I cannot aid thee—I am but a poor and neglected woman, feeble both from sex and age.—And to which of these De Lacys art thou the destined household drudge?"

A question so asked, and by one whose prejudices were of such a determined character, was not likely to draw from Eveline any confession of the real circumstances in which she was placed, since it was but too plain her Saxon relation could have afforded her neither sound counsel nor useful assistance. She replied therefore briefly, that as the Lacys, and the Normans in general, were unwelcome to her kinswoman, she would entreat of the commander of the patrol to withdraw it from the neighbourhood of Baldringham.

"Not so, my niece," said the old lady; "as we cannot escape the Norman neighbourhood, or get beyond the sound of their curfew, it signifies not whether they be near our walls or more far off, so that they enter them, not. And, Berwine, bid Hundwolf drench the Normans with liquor, and gorge them with food—the food of the best, and liquor of the strongest. Let them not say the old Saxon hag is churlish of her hospitality. Broach a piece of wine, for I warrant their gentle stomachs brook no ale."

Berwine, her huge bunch of keys jangling at her girdle, withdrew to give the necessary directions, and presently returned. Meanwhile Ermengarde proceeded to question her niece more closely. "Is it that thou wilt not, or canst not, tell me to which of the De Lacys thou art to be bondswoman?—to the overweening Constable, who, sheathed in impenetrable armour, and mounted on a swift and strong horse as invulnerable as himself, takes pride that he rides down and stabs at his ease, and with perfect safety, the naked Welshmen?—or is it to his nephew, the beardless Damian?—or must thy possessions go to mend a breach in the fortunes of that other cousin, Randal Lacy, the decayed reveller, who, they say, can no longer ruffle it among the debauched crusaders for want of means?"

"My honoured aunt," replied Eveline, naturally displeased with this discourse, "to none of the Lacy's, and I trust to none other, Saxon or Norman, will your kinswoman become a household drudge.

"There was, before the death of my honoured father, some treaty betwixt him and the Constable, on which account I cannot at present decline his attendance; but what may be the issue of it, fate must determine."

"But I can show thee, niece, how the balance of fate inclines," said Ermengarde, in a low and mysterious voice. "Those united with us by blood have, in some sort, the privilege of looking forward beyond the points of present time, and seeing in their very bud the thorns or flowers which are one day to encircle their head."

"For my own sake, noble kinswoman," answered Eveline, "I would decline such foreknowledge, even were it possible to acquire it without transgressing the rules of the Church. Could I have foreseen what has befallen me within these last unhappy days, I had lost the enjoyment of every happy moment before that time."

"Nevertheless, daughter," said the Lady of Baldringham, "thou, like others of thy race, must within this house conform to the rule, of passing one night within the chamber of the Red-Finger.— Berwine, see that it be prepared for my niece's reception."

"I—I—have heard speak of that chamber, gracious aunt," said Eveline, timidly, "and if it may consist with your good pleasure, I would not now choose to pass the night there. My health has suffered by my late perils and fatigues, and with your good-will I will delay to another time the usage, which I have heard is peculiar to the daughters of the house of Baldringham."

"And which, notwithstanding, you would willingly avoid," said the old Saxon lady, bending her brows angrily. "Has not such disobedience cost your house enough already?"

"Indeed, honoured and gracious lady," said Berwine, unable to forbear interference, though well knowing the obstinacy of her patroness, "that chamber is in disrepair, and cannot easily on a sudden be made fit for the Lady Eveline; and the noble damsel looks so pale, and hath lately suffered so much, that, might I have the permission to advise, this were better delayed."

"Thou art a fool, Berwine," said the old lady, sternly; "thinkest thou I will bring anger and misfortune on my house, by suffering this girl to leave it without rendering the usual homage to the Red-Finger? Go to—let the room be made ready—small preparation may serve, if she cherish not the Norman nicety about bed and lodging. Do not reply; but do as I command thee.—And you, Eveline—are you so far degenerated from the brave spirit of your ancestry, that you dare not pass a few hours in an ancient apartment?"

"You are my hostess, gracious madam," said Eveline, "and must assign my apartment where you judge proper—my courage is such as innocence and some pride of blood and birth have given me. It has been, of late, severely tried; but, since such is your pleasure, and the custom of your house, my heart is yet strong enough to encounter what you propose to subject me to."

She paused here in displeasure; for she resented, in some measure, her aunt's conduct, as unkind and inhospitable. And yet when she reflected upon the foundation of the legend of the chamber to which she was consigned, she could not but regard the Lady of Baldringham as having considerable reason for her conduct, according to the traditions of the family, and the belief of the times, in which Eveline herself was devout.

CHAPTER THE FOURTEENTH

Sometimes, methinks, I hear the groans of ghosts,
Then hollow sounds and lamentable screams;
Then, like a dying echo from afar,
My mother's voice, that cries, "Wed not, Almeyda—
Forewanvd, Almeyda, marriage is thy crime."
DON SEBASTIAN.

The evening at Baldringham would have seemed of portentous and unendurable length, had it not been that apprehended danger makes times pass quickly betwixt us and the dreaded hour, and that if Eveline felt little interested or amused by the conversation of her aunt and Berwine, which turned upon the long deduction of their ancestors from the warlike Horsa, and the feats of Saxon champions, and the miracles of Saxon monks, she was still better pleased to listen to these legends, than to anticipate her retreat to the destined and dreaded apartment where she was to pass the night. There lacked not, however, such amusement as the house of Baldringham could afford, to pass away the evening. Blessed by a grave old Saxon monk, the chaplain of the house, a sumptuous entertainment, which might have sufficed twenty hungry men, was served up before Ermengarde and her niece, whose sole assistants, beside the reverend man, were Berwine and Rose Flammock. Eveline was the less inclined to do justice to this excess of hospitality, that the dishes were all of the gross and substantial nature which the Saxons admired, but which contrasted disadvantageously with the refined and delicate cookery of the Normans, as did the moderate cup of light and high-flavoured Gascon wine, tempered with more than half its quantity of the purest water, with the mighty ale, the high-spiced pigment and hippocras, and the other potent liquors, which, one after another, were in vain proffered for her acceptance by the steward Hundwolf, in honour of the hospitality of Baldringham.

Neither were the stated amusements of evening more congenial to Eveline's taste, than the profusion of her aunt's solid refection. When the boards and tresses, on which the viands had been served, were withdrawn from the apartment, the menials, under direction of the steward, proceeded to light several long waxen torches, one of which was graduated for the purpose of marking the passing time, and dividing it into portions. These were announced by means of brazen balls, suspended by threads from the torch, the spaces betwixt them being calculated to occupy a certain time in burning; so that, when the flame reached the thread, and the balls fell, each in succession, into a brazen basin placed for its reception, the office of a modern clock was in some degree discharged. By this light the party was arranged for the evening.

The ancient Ermengarde's lofty and ample chair was removed, according to ancient custom, from the middle of the apartment to the warmest side of a large grate, filled with charcoal, and her guest was placed on her right, as the seat of honour. Berwine then arranged in due order the females of the household, and, having seen that each was engaged with her own proper task, sat herself down to ply the spindle and distaff. The men, in a more remote circle, betook themselves to the repairing of their implements of husbandry, or new furbishing weapons of the chase, under the direction of the steward Hundwolf. For the amusement of the family thus assembled, an old glee-man sung to a harp, which had but four strings, a long and apparently interminable legend, upon some religious subject, which was rendered almost unintelligible to Eveline, by the extreme and complicated affectation of the poet, who, in order to indulge in the alliteration which was accounted one great ornament of Saxon poetry, had sacrificed sense to sound, and used words in the most forced and remote sense, provided they could be compelled into his service. There was also all the obscurity arising from elision, and from the most extravagant and hyperbolical epithets.

Eveline, though well acquainted with the Saxon language, soon left off listening to the singer, to reflect for a moment on the gay fabliaux and imaginative *lais* of the Norman minstrels, and then to anticipate, with anxious apprehension, what nature of visitation she might be exposed to in the mysterious chamber in which she was doomed to pass the night.

The hour of parting at length approached. At half an hour before mid-night, a period ascertained by the consumption of the huge waxen torch, the ball which was secured to it fell clanging into the brazen basin placed beneath, and announced to all the hour of rest. The old glee-man paused in his song, instantaneously, and in the middle of a stanza, and the household were all on foot at the signal, some retiring to their own apartments, others lighting torches or bearing lamps to conduct the visitors to their places of repose. Among these last was a bevy of bower-women, to whom the duty was assigned of conveying the Lady Eveline to her chamber for the night. Her aunt took a solemn leave of her, crossed her forehead, kissed it, and whispered in her ear, "Be courageous, and be fortunate."

"May not my bower-maiden, Rose Flammock, or my tire-woman, Dame Gillian, Raoul's wife, remain in the apartment with me for this night?" said Eveline.

"Flammock-Raoul!" repeated Ermengarde, angrily; "is thy household thus made up? The Flemings are the cold palsy to Britain, the Normans the burning fever."

"And the poor Welsh will add," said Rose, whose resentment began to surpass her awe for the ancient Saxon dame, "that the Anglo- Saxons were the original disease, and resemble a wasting pestilence."

"Thou art too bold, sweetheart," said the Lady Ermengarde, looking at the Flemish maiden from under her dark brows; "and yet there is wit in thy words. Saxon, Dane, and Norman, have rolled like successive billows over the land, each having strength to subdue what they lacked wisdom to keep. When shall it be otherwise?"

"When, Saxon, and Briton, and Norman, and Fleming," answered Rose, boldly, "shall learn to call themselves by one name, and think themselves alike children of the land they were born in."

"Ha!" exclaimed the Lady of Baldringham, in the tone of one half surprised, half-pleased. Then turning to her relation, she said, "There are words and wit in this maiden; see that she use but do not abuse them."

"She is as kind and faithful, as she is prompt and ready-witted." said Eveline. "I pray you, dearest aunt, let me use her company for this night."

"It may not be—it were dangerous to both. Alone you must learn your destiny, as have all the females of our race, excepting your grandmother, and what have been the consequences of her neglecting the rules of our house? Lo! her descendant stands before me an orphan in the very bloom of youth."

"I will go, then," said Eveline with a sigh of resignation; "and it shall never be said I incurred future wo, to shun present terror."

"Your attendants," said the Lady Ermengarde, "may occupy the anteroom, and be almost within your call. Berwine will show you the apartment—I cannot; for we, thou knowest, who have once entered it, return not thither again. Farewell, my child, and may heaven bless thee!"

With more of human emotion and sympathy than she had yet shown, the Lady again saluted Eveline, and signed to her to follow Berwine, who, attended by two damsels bearing torches, waited to conduct her to the dreaded apartment.

Their torches glared along the rudely built walls and dark arched roofs of one or two long winding passages; these by their light enabled them to descend the steps of a winding stair, whose inequality and ruggedness showed its antiquity; and finally led into a tolerably large chamber on the lower story of the edifice, to which some old hangings, a lively fire on the hearth, the moonbeams stealing through a latticed window, and the boughs of a myrtle plant which grew around the casement, gave no uncomfortable appearance. "This," said Berwine, "is the resting-place of your attendants," and she pointed to the couches which had been prepared for Rose and Dame Gillian; "we," she added, "proceed farther."

She then took a torch from the attendant maidens, both of whom seemed to shrink back with fear, which was readily caught by Dame Gillian, although she was not probably aware of the cause. But Rose Flammock, unbidden, followed her mistress without hesitation, as Berwine conducted her through a small wicket at the upper end of the apartment, clenched with many an iron nail, into a second but smaller anteroom or wardrobe, at the end of which was a similar door. This wardrobe had also its casement mantled with evergreens, and, like the former, it was faintly enlightened by the moonbeams.

Berwine paused here, and, pointing to Rose, demanded of Eveline, "Why does she follow?"

"To share my mistress's danger, be it what it may," answered Rose, with her characteristic readiness of speech and resolution.

"Speak," she said, "my dearest lady," grasping Eveline's hand, while she addressed her; "you will not drive your Rose from you? If I am less high-minded than one of your boasted race, I am bold and quick-witted in all honest service.—You tremble like the aspen! Do not go into this apartment—do not be gulled by all this pomp and mystery of terrible preparation; bid defiance to this antiquated, and, I think, half-pagan superstition."

"The Lady Eveline must go, minion," replied Berwine, sternly; "and she must go without any malapert adviser or companion."

"Must go—-*must go*!" repeated Rose. "Is this language to a free and noble maiden?—Sweet lady, give me once but the least hint that you wish it, and their '*must go*' shall be put to the trial. I will call from the casement on the Norman cavaliers, and tell them we have fallen, into a den of witches, instead of a house of hospitality."

"Silence, madwoman," said Berwine, her voice quivering with anger and fear; "you know not who dwells in the next chamber."

"I will call those who will soon see to that," said Rose, flying to the casement, when Eveline, seizing her arm in her turn, compelled her to stop.

"I thank thy kindness, Rose," she said, "but it cannot help me in this matter. She who enters yonder door, must do so alone."

"Then I will enter it in your stead, my dearest lady," said Rose. "You are pale—you are cold—you will die with terror if you go on. There may be as much of trick as of supernatural agency in this matter—me they shall not deceive—or if some stern spirit craves a victim,—better Rose than her lady."

"Forbear, forbear," said Eveline, rousing up her own spirits; "you make me ashamed of myself. This is an ancient ordeal, which regards the females descended from the house of Baldringham as far as in the third degree, and them only. I did not indeed expect, in my present circumstances, to have been called upon to undergo it; but, since the hour summons me, I will meet it as freely as any of my ancestors."

So saying, she took the torch from the hand of Berwine, and wishing good-night to her and Rose, gently disengaged herself from the hold of the latter, and advanced into the mysterious chamber. Rose pressed after her so far as to see that it was an apartment of moderate dimensions, resembling that through which they had last passed, and lighted by the moonbeams, which came through a window lying on the same range with those of the anterooms. More she could not see, for Eveline turned on the threshold, and kissing her at the same time, thrust her gently back into the smaller apartment which she had just left, shut the door of communication, and barred and bolted it, as if in security against her well-meant intrusion.

Berwine now exhorted Rose, as she valued her life, to retire into the first anteroom, where the beds were prepared, and betake herself, if not to rest, at least to silence and devotion; but the faithful Flemish girl stoutly refused her entreaties, and resisted her commands.

"Talk not to me of danger," she said; "here I remain, that I may be at least within hearing of my mistress's danger, and wo betide those who shall offer her injury!—Take notice, that twenty Norman spears surround this inhospitable dwelling, prompt to avenge whatsoever injury shall be offered to the daughter of Raymond Berenger."

"Reserve your threats for those who are mortal," said Berwine, in a low, but piercing whisper; "the owner of yonder chamber fears them not. Farewell—thy danger be on thine own head!"

She departed, leaving Rose strangely agitated by what had passed, and somewhat appalled at her last words. "These Saxons," said the maiden, within herself, "are but half converted after all, and hold many of their old hellish rites in the worship of elementary spirits. Their very saints are unlike to the saints of any Christian country, and have, as it were, a look of something savage and fiendish—their very names sound pagan and diabolical. It is fearful being alone here—and all is silent as death in the apartment into which my lady has been thus strangely compelled. Shall I call up Gillian?—but no—she has neither sense, nor courage, nor principle, to aid me on such an occasion—better alone than have a false friend for company. I will see if the Normans are on their post, since it is to them I must trust, if a moment of need should arrive."

Thus reflecting, Rose Flammock went to the window of the little apartment, in order to satisfy herself of the vigilance of the sentinels, and to ascertain the exact situation of the corps de garde. The moon was at the full, and enabled her to see with accuracy the nature of the ground without. In the first place, she was rather disappointed to find, that instead of being so near the earth as she supposed, the range of windows which gave light as well to the two anterooms as to the mysterious chamber itself, looked down upon an ancient moat, by which they were divided from the level ground on the farther side. The defence which this fosse afforded seemed to have been long neglected, and the bottom, entirely dry, was choked in many places with bushes and low trees, which rose up against the wall of the castle, and by means of which it seemed to Rose the windows might be easily scaled, and the mansion entered. From the level plain beyond, the space adjoining to the castle was in a considerable degree clear, and the moonbeams slumbered on its close and beautiful turf, mixed with long shadows of the towers and trees. Beyond this esplanade lay the forest ground, with a few gigantic oaks scattered individually along the skirt of its dark and ample domain, like champions, who take their ground of defiance in front of a line of arrayed battle.

The calm beauty and repose of a scene so lovely, the stillness of all around, and the more matured reflections which the whole suggested, quieted, in some measure, the apprehensions which the events of the evening had inspired. "After all," she reflected, "why should I be so anxious on account of the Lady Eveline? There is among the proud Normans and the dogged Saxons scarce a single family of note, but must needs be held distinguished from others by some superstitious observance peculiar to their race, as if they thought it scorn to go to Heaven like a poor simple Fleming, such as I am.—Could I but see the Norman sentinel, I would hold myself satisfied with my mistress's security.—And yonder one stalks along the gloom, wrapt in his long white mantle, and the moon tipping the point of his lance with silver.—What ho, Sir Cavalier!"

The Norman turned his steps, and approached the ditch as she spoke. "What is your pleasure, damsel?" he demanded.

"The window next to mine is that of the Lady Eveline Berenger, whom you are appointed to guard. Please to give heedful watch upon this side of the castle."

"Doubt it not, lady," answered the cavalier; and enveloping himself in his long *chappe*, or military watch-cloak, he withdrew to a large oak tree at some distance, and stood there with folded arms, and leaning on his lance, more like a trophy of armour than a living warrior.

Imboldened by the consciousness, that in case of need succour was close at hand, Rose drew back into her little chamber, and having ascertained, by listening, that there was no noise or stirring in that of Eveline, she began to make some preparations for her own repose. For this purpose she went into the outward ante-room, where Dame Gillian, whose fears had given way to the soporiferous effects of a copious draught of *lithe-alos*, (mild ale, of the first strength and quality,) slept as sound a sleep as that generous Saxon beverage could procure.

Muttering an indignant censure on her sloth and indifference, Rose caught, from the empty couch which had been destined for her own use, the upper covering, and dragging it with her into the inner ante-room, disposed it so as, with the assistance of the rushes which strewed that apartment, to form a sort of couch, upon which, half seated, half reclined, she resolved to pass the night in as close attendance upon her mistress as circumstances permitted. Thus seated, her eye on the pale planet which sailed in full glory through the blue sky of midnight, she proposed to herself that sleep should not visit her eyelids till the dawn of morning should assure her of Eveline's safety.

Her thoughts, meanwhile, rested on the boundless and shadowy world beyond the grave, and on the great and perhaps yet undecided question, whether the separation of its inhabitants from those of this temporal sphere is absolute and decided, or whether, influenced by motives which we cannot appreciate, they continue to hold shadowy communication with those yet existing in earthly reality of flesh and blood? To have denied this, would, in the age of crusades and of miracles, have incurred the guilt of heresy; but Rose's firm good sense led her to doubt at least the frequency of supernatural interference, and she comforted herself with an opinion, contradicted, however, by her own involuntary starts and shudderings at every leaf which moved, that, in submitting to the performance of the rite imposed on her, Eveline incurred no real danger, and only sacrificed to an obsolete family superstition.

As this conviction strengthened on Rose's mind, her purpose of vigilance began to decline—her thoughts wandered to objects towards which they were not directed, like sheep which stray beyond the charge of their shepherd—her eyes no longer brought back to her a distinct apprehension of the broad, round, silvery orb on which they continued to gaze. At length they closed, and seated on the folded mantle, her back resting against the wall of the apartment, and her white arms folded on her bosom, Rose Flammock fell fast asleep.

Her repose was fearfully broken by a shrill and piercing shriek from the apartment where her lady reposed. To start up and fly to the door was the work of a moment with the generous girl, who never permitted fear to struggle with love or duty. The door was secured with both bar and bolt; and another fainter scream, or rather groan, seemed to say, aid must be instant, or in vain. Rose next rushed to the window, and screamed rather than called to the Norman soldier, who, distinguished by the white folds of his watch-cloak, still retained his position under the old oak-tree.

At the cry of "Help, help!—the Lady Eveline is murdered!" the seeming statue, starting at once into active exertion, sped with the swiftness of a race-horse to the brink of the moat, and was about to cross it, opposite to the spot where Rose stood at the open casement, urging him to speed by voice and gesture.

"Not here—not here!" she exclaimed, with breathless precipitation, as she saw him make towards her—"the window to the right—scale it, for God's sake, and undo the door of communication."

The soldier seemed to comprehend her—he dashed into the moat without hesitation, securing himself by catching at the boughs of trees as he descended. In one moment he vanished among the underwood; and in another, availing himself of the branches of a dwarf oak, Rose saw him upon her right, and close to the window of the fatal apartment. One fear remained—the casement might be secured against entrance from without—but no! at the thrust of the Norman it yielded, and its clasps or fastenings being worn with time, fell inward with a crash which even Dame Gillian's slumbers were unable to resist.

Echoing scream upon scream, in the usual fashion of fools and cowards, she entered the cabinet from the ante-room, just as the door of Eveline's chamber opened, and the soldier appeared, bearing in his arms the half-undressed and lifeless form of the Norman maiden herself. Without speaking a word, he placed her in Rose's arms, and with the same precipitation with which he had entered, threw himself out of the opened window from which Rose had summoned him.

Gillian, half distracted with fear and wonder, heaped exclamations on questions, and mingled questions with cries for help, till Rose sternly rebuked her in a tone which seemed to recall her scattered senses. She became then composed enough to fetch a lamp which remained lighted in the room she had left, and to render herself at least partly useful in suggesting and applying the usual modes for recalling the suspended sense. In this they at length succeeded, for Eveline fetched a fuller sigh, and opened her eyes; but presently shut them again, and letting her head drop on Rose's bosom, fell into a strong shuddering fit; while her faithful damsel, chafing her hands and her temples alternately with affectionate assiduity, and mingling caresses with these efforts, exclaimed aloud, "She lives!—She is recovering!—Praised be God!"

"Praised be God!" was echoed in a solemn tone from the window of the apartment; and turning towards it in terror, Rose beheld the armed and plumed head of the soldier who had come so opportunely to their assistance, and who, supported by his arms, had raised himself so high as to be able to look into the interior of the cabinet.

Rose immediately ran towards him. "Go—go—good friend," she said; "the lady recovers—your reward shall await you another time. Go— begone!—yet stay—keep on your post, and I will call you if there is farther need. Begone— be faithful, and be secret."

The soldier obeyed without answering a word, and she presently saw him descend into the moat. Rose then returned back to her mistress, whom she found supported by Gillian, moaning feebly, and muttering hurried and unintelligible ejaculations, all intimating that she had laboured under a violent shock sustained from some alarming cause.

Dame Gillian had no sooner recovered some degree of self- possession, than her curiosity became active in proportion. "What means all this?" she said to Rose; "what has been doing among you?"

"I do not know," replied Rose.

"If you do not," said Gillian, "who should?—Shall I call the other women, and raise the house?"

"Not for your life," said Rose, "till my lady is able to give her own orders; and for this apartment, so help me Heaven, as I will do my best to discover the secrets it contains!—Support my mistress the whilst."

So saying, she took the lamp in her hand, and, crossing her brow, stepped boldly across the mysterious threshold, and, holding up the light, surveyed the apartment.

It was merely an old vaulted chamber, of very moderate dimensions. In one corner was an image of the Virgin, rudely cut, and placed above a Saxon font of curious workmanship. There were two seats and a couch, covered with coarse tapestry, on which it seemed that Eveline had been reposing. The fragments of the shattered casement lay on the floor; but that opening had been only made when the soldier forced it in, and she saw no other access by which a stranger could have entered an apartment, the ordinary access to which was barred and bolted.

Rose felt the influence of those terrors which she had hitherto surmounted; she cast her mantle hastily around her head, as if to shroud her sight from some blighting vision, and tripping back to the cabinet, with more speed and a less firm step than when she left it, she directed Gillian to lend her assistance in conveying Eveline to the next room; and having done so, carefully secured the door of communication, as if to put a barrier betwixt them, and the suspected danger.

The Lady Eveline was now so far recovered that she could sit up, and was trying to speak, though but faintly. "Rose," she said at length, "I have seen her —my doom is sealed."

Rose immediately recollected the imprudence of suffering Gillian to hear what her mistress might say at such an awful moment, and hastily adopting the proposal she had before declined, desired her to go and call other two maidens of their mistress's household.

"And where am I to find them in this house," said Dame Gillian, "where strange men run about one chamber at midnight, and devils, for aught I know, frequent the rest of the habitation?"

"Find them where you can," said Rose, sharply; "but begone presently."

Gillian withdrew lingeringly, and muttering at the same time something which could not distinctly be understood. No sooner was she gone, than Rose, giving way to the enthusiastic affection which she felt for her mistress, implored her, in the most tender terms, to open her eyes, (for she had again closed them,) and speak to Rose, her own Rose, who was ready, if necessary, to die by her mistress's side.

"To-morrow—to-morrow, Rose," murmured Eveline—"I cannot speak at present."

"Only disburden your mind with one word—tell what has thus alarmed you—

what danger you apprehend."

"I have seen her," answered Eveline—"I have seen the tenant of yonder chamber—the vision fatal to my race!—Urge me no more—to- morrow you shall know all."

As Gillian entered with two of the maidens of her mistress's household, they removed the Lady Eveline, by Rose's directions, into a chamber at some distance which the latter had occupied, and placed her in one of their beds, where Rose, dismissing the others (Gillian excepted) to seek repose where they could find it, continued to watch her mistress. For some time she continued very much disturbed, but, gradually, fatigue, and the influence of some narcotic which Gillian had sense enough to recommend and prepare, seemed to compose her spirits. She fell into a deep slumber, from which she did not awaken until the sun was high over the distant hills.

CHAPTER THE FIFTEENTH.

I see a hand you cannot see,
  Which beckons me away;
I hear a voice you cannot hear,
  Which says I must not stay.
  MALLET.

When Eveline first opened her eyes, it seemed to be without any recollection of what had passed on the night preceding. She looked round the apartment, which was coarsely and scantily furnished, as one destined for the use of domestics and menials, and said to Rose, with a smile, "Our good kinswoman maintains the ancient Saxon hospitality at a homely rate, so far as lodging is concerned. I could have willingly parted with last night's profuse supper, to have obtained a bed of a softer texture. Methinks my limbs feel as if I had been under all the flails of a Franklin's barn-yard."

"I am glad to see you so pleasant, madam," answered Rose, discreetly avoiding any reference to the events of the night before.

Dame Gillian was not so scrupulous. "Your ladyship last night lay down on a better bed than this," she said, "unless I am much mistaken; and Rose Flammock and yourself know best why you left it."

If a look could have killed, Dame Gillian would have been in deadly peril from that which Rose shot at her, by way of rebuke for this ill-advised communication. It had instantly the effect which was to be apprehended, for

Lady Eveline seemed at first surprised and confused; then, as recollections of the past arranged themselves in her memory, she folded her hands, looked on the ground, and wept bitterly, with much agitation.

Rose entreated her to be comforted, and offered to fetch the old Saxon chaplain of the house to administer spiritual consolation, if her grief rejected temporal comfort.

"No—call him not," said Eveline, raising her head and drying her eyes—"I have had enough of Saxon kindness. What a fool was I to expect, in that hard and unfeeling woman, any commiseration for my youth—my late sufferings—my orphan condition! I will not permit her a poor triumph over the Norman blood of Berenger, by letting her see how much I have suffered under her inhuman infliction. But first, Rose, answer me truly, was any inmate of Baldringham witness to my distress last night?"

Rose assured her that she had been tended exclusively by her own retinue, herself and Gillian, Blanche and Ternotte. She seemed to receive satisfaction from this assurance. "Hear me, both of you," she said, "and observe my words, as you love and as you fear me. Let no syllable be breathed from your lips of what has happened this night. Carry the same charge to my maidens. Lend me thine instant aid, Gillian, and thine, my dearest Rose, to change these disordered garments, and arrange this dishevelled hair. It was a poor vengeance she sought, and all because of my country. I am resolved she shall not see the slightest trace of the sufferings she has inflicted."

As she spoke thus, her eyes flashed with indignation, which seemed to dry up the tears that had before filled them. Rose saw the change of her manner with a mixture of pleasure and concern, being aware that her mistress's predominant failing was incident to her, as a spoiled child, who, accustomed to be treated with kindness, deference, and indulgence, by all around her, was apt to resent warmly whatever resembled neglect or contradiction.

"God knows," said the faithful bower-maiden, "I would hold my hand out to catch drops of molten lead, rather than endure your tears; and yet, my sweet mistress, I would rather at present see you grieved than angry. This ancient lady hath, it would seem, but acted according to some old superstitious rite of her family, which is in part yours. Her name is respectable, both from her conduct and possessions; and hard pressed as you are by the Normans, with whom your kinswoman, the Prioress, is sure to take part. I was in hope you might have had some shelter and countenance from the Lady of Baldringham."

"Never, Rose, never," answered Eveline; "you know not—you cannot fuess what she has made me suffer—exposing me to witchcraft and fiends. Thyself said it, and said it truly—the Saxons are still half Pagans, void of Christianity, as of nurture and kindliness."

"Ay, but," replied Rose, "I spoke then to dissuade you from a danger now that the danger is passed and over, I may judge of it otherwise."

"Speak not for them, Rose," replied Eveline, angrily; "no innocent victim was ever offered up at the altar of a fiend with more indifference than my father's kinswoman delivered up me—me, an orphan, bereaved of my natural and powerful support. I hate her cruelty—I hate her house—I hate the thought of all that has happened here—of all, Rose, except thy matchless faith and fearless attachment. Go, bid our train saddle directly—I will be gone instantly —I will not attire myself" she added, rejecting the assistance she had at first required—"I will have no ceremony— tarry for no leave-taking."

In the hurried and agitated manner of her mistress, Rose recognized with anxiety another mood of the same irritable and excited temperament, which had before discharged itself in tears and fits. But perceiving, at the same time, that remonstrance was in vain, she gave the necessary orders for collecting their company, saddling, and preparing for departure; hoping, that as her mistress removed to a farther distance from the scene where her mind had received so severe a shock, her equanimity might, by degrees, be restored.

Dame Gillian, accordingly, was busied with arranging the packages of her lady, and all the rest of Lady Eveline's retinue in preparing for instant departure, when, preceded by her steward, who acted also as a sort of gentleman-usher, leaning upon her confidential Berwine, and followed by two or three more of the most distinguished of her household, with looks of displeasure on her ancient yet lofty brow, the Lady Ermengarde entered the apartment.

Eveline, with a trembling and hurried hand, a burning cheek, and other signs of agitation, was herself busied about the arrangement of some baggage, when her relation made her appearance. At once, to Rose's great surprise, she exerted a strong command over herself, and, repressing every external appearance of disorder, she advanced to meet her relation, with a calm and haughty stateliness equal to her own.

"I come to give you good morning, our niece," said Ermengarde, haughtily indeed, yet with more deference than she seemed at first to have intended, so much did the bearing of Eveline impose respect upon her;—"I find that you have been pleased to shift that chamber which was assigned you, in conformity with the ancient custom of this household, and betake yourself to the apartment of a menial."

"Are you surprised at that, lady?" demanded Eveline in her turn; "or are you disappointed that you find me not a corpse, within the limits of the chamber which your hospitality and affection allotted to me?"

"Your sleep, then, has been broken?" said Ermengarde, looking fixedly at the Lady Eveline, as she spoke.

"If I complain not, madam, the evil must be deemed of little consequence. What has happened is over and passed, and it is not my intention to trouble you with the recital."

"She of the ruddy finger," replied Ermengarde, triumphantly, "loves not the blood of the stranger."

"She had less reason, while she walked the earth, to love that of the Saxon," said Eveline, "unless her legend speaks false in that matter; and unless, as I well suspect, your house is haunted, not by the soul of the dead who suffered within its walls, but by evil spirits, such as the descendants of Hengist and Horsa are said still in secret to worship."

"You are pleasant, maiden," replied the old lady, scornfully, "or, if your words are meant in earnest, the shaft of your censure has glanced aside. A house, blessed by the holy Saint Dunstan, and by the royal and holy Confessor, is no abode for evil spirits."

"The house of Baldringham," replied Eveline, "is no abode for those who fear such spirits; and as I will, with all humility, avow myself of the number, I shall presently leave it to the custody of Saint Dunstan."

"Not till you have broken your fast, I trust?" said the Lady of Baldringham; "you will not, I hope, do my years and our relationship such foul disgrace?"

"Pardon me, madam," replied the Lady Eveline; "those who have experienced your hospitality at night, have little occasion for breakfast in the morning.— Rose, are not those loitering knaves assembled in the court-yard, or are they yet on their couches, making up for the slumber they have lost by midnight disturbances?"

Rose announced that her train was in the court, and mounted; when, with a low reverence, Eveline endeavoured to pass her relation, and leave the apartment without farther ceremony. Ermengarde at first confronted her with a grim and furious glance, which seemed to show a soul fraught with more rage than the thin blood and rigid features of extreme old age had the power of expressing, and raised her ebony staff as if about even to proceed to some act of personal violence. But she changed her purpose, and suddenly made way for Eveline, who passed without farther parley; and as she descended the staircase, which conducted from the apartment to the gateway, she heard the voice of her aunt behind her, like that of an aged and offended sibyl, denouncing wrath and wo upon her insolence and presumption.

"Pride," she exclaimed, "goeth before destruction, and a haughty spirit before a fall. She who scorneth the house of her forefathers, a stone from its battlements shall crush her! She who mocks the gray hairs of a parent, never shall one of her own locks be silvered with age! She who weds with a man of war and of blood, her end shall neither be peaceful nor bloodless!"

Hurrying to escape from these and other ominous denunciations, Eveline rushed from the house, mounted her palfrey with the precipitation of a fugitive, and, surrounded by her attendants, who had caught a part of her alarm, though without conjecturing the cause, rode hastily into the forest; old Raoul, who was well acquainted with the country, acting as their guide.

Agitated more than she was willing to confess to herself, by thus leaving the habitation of so near a relation, loaded with maledictions, instead of the blessings which are usually bestowed on a departing kinswoman, Eveline hastened forward, until the huge oak-trees with intervening arms had hidden from her view the fatal mansion.

The trampling and galloping of horse was soon after heard, announcing the approach of the patrol left by the Constable for the protection of the mansion, and who now, collecting from their different stations, came prepared to attend the Lady Eveline on her farther road to Gloucester, great part of which lay through the extensive forest of Deane, then a silvan region of large extent, though now much denuded of trees for the service of the iron mines. The Cavaliers came up to join the retinue of Lady Eveline, with armour glittering in the morning rays, trumpets sounding, horses prancing, neighing, and thrown, each by his chivalrous rider, into the attitude best qualified to exhibit the beauty of the steed and dexterity of the horseman; while their lances, streaming with long penoncelles, were brandished in every manner which could display elation of heart and readiness of hand. The sense of the military character of her countrymen of Normandy gave to Eveline a feeling at once of security and of triumph, which operated towards the dispelling of her gloomy thoughts, and of the feverish disorder which affected her nerves. The rising sun also—the song of the birds among the bowers—the lowing of the cattle as they were driven to pasture—the sight of the hind, who, with her fawn trotting by her side, often crossed some forest glade within view of the travellers,—all contributed to dispel the terror of Eveline's nocturnal visions, and soothe to rest the more angry passions which had agitated her bosom at her departure from Baldringham. She suffered her palfrey to slacken his pace, and, with female attention to propriety, began to adjust her riding robes, and compose her head-dress, disordered in her hasty departure. Rose saw her cheek assume a paler but more settled hue, instead of the angry hectic which had coloured it —saw her eye become more steady as she looked with a sort of triumph upon her military attendants, and pardoned (what on other occasions she would probably have made some reply to) her enthusiastic exclamations in praise of her countrymen.

"We journey safe," said Eveline, "under the care of the princely and victorious Normans. Theirs is the noble wrath of the lion, which destroys or is appeased at once—there is no guile in their romantic affection, no sullenness mixed with their generous indignation—they know the duties of the hall as well as those of battle; and were they to be surpassed in the arts of war, (which will only be when Plinlimmon is removed from its base,) they would still remain superior to every other people in generosity and courtesy."

"If I do not feel all their merits so strongly as if I shared their blood." said Rose, "I am at least glad to see them around us, in woods which are said to abound with dangers of various kinds. And I confess, my heart is the lighter, that I can now no longer observe the least vestige of that ancient mansion, in which we passed so unpleasant a night, and the recollection of which will always be odious to me."

Eveline looked sharply at her. "Confess the truth, Rose; thou wouldst give thy best kirtle to know all of my horrible adventure."

"It is but confessing that I am a woman," answered Rose; "and did I say a man, I dare say the difference of sex would imply but a small abatement of curiosity."

"Thou makest no parade of other feelings, which prompt thee to inquire into my fortunes," said Eveline; "but, sweet Rose, I give thee not the less credit for them. Believe me, thou shalt know all—but, I think, not now."

"At your pleasure," said Rose; "and yet, methinks, the bearing in your solitary bosom such a fearful secret will only render the weight more intolerable. On my silence you may rely as on that of the Holy Image, which hears us confess what it never reveals. Besides, such things become familiar to the imagination when they have been spoken of, and that which is familiar gradually becomes stripped of its terrors."

"Thou speakest with reason, my prudent Rose; and surely in this gallant troop, borne like a flower on a bush by my good palfrey Yseulte—fresh gales blowing round us, flowers opening and birds singing, and having thee by my bridle-rein, I ought to feel this a fitting time to communicate what thou hast so good a title to know. And—yes!—thou shalt know all!—Thou art not, I presume, ignorant of the qualities of what the Saxons of this land call a *Bahrgeist*?"

"Pardon me, lady," answered Rose, "my father discouraged my listening to such discourses. I might see evil spirits enough, he said, without my imagination being taught to form, such as were fantastical. The word Bahr-geist, I have heard used by Gillian and other Saxons; but to me it only conveys some idea of indefinite terror, of which I never asked nor received an explanation."

"Know then," said Eveline, "it is a spectre, usually the image of a departed person, who, either for wrong sustained in some particular place during life, or through treasure hidden there, or from some such other cause, haunts the spot from time to time, becomes familiar to those who dwell there, takes an interest in their fate, occasionally for good, in other instances or times for evil. The Bahr-geist is, therefore, sometimes regarded as the good genius, sometimes as the avenging fiend, attached to particular families and classes of men. It is the lot of the family of Baldringham (of no mean note in other respects) to be subject to the visits of such a being."

"May I ask the cause (if it be known) of such visitation?" said Rose, desirous to avail herself to the uttermost of the communicative mood of her young lady, which might not perhaps last very long.

"I know the legend but imperfectly," replied Eveline, proceeding with a degree of calmness, the result of strong exertion over her mental anxiety, "but in general it runs thus:—Baldrick, the Saxon hero who first possessed yonder dwelling, became enamoured of a fair Briton, said to have been descended from those Druids of whom the Welsh speak so much, and deemed not unacquainted with the arts of sorcery which they practised, when they offered up human sacrifices amid those circles of unhewn and living rock, of which thou hast seen so many. After more than two years' wedlock, Baldrick became weary of his wife to such a point, that he formed the cruel resolution of putting her to death. Some say he doubted her fidelity—some that the matter was pressed on him by the church, as she was suspected of heresy—some that he removed her to make way for a more wealthy marriage—but all agree in the result. He sent two of his Cnichts to the house of Baldringham, to put to death the unfortunate Vanda, and commanded them to bring him the ring which had circled her finger on the day of wedlock, in token that his orders were accomplished. The men were ruthless in their office; they strangled Vanda in yonder apartment, and as the hand was so swollen that no effort could draw off the ring, they obtained possession of it by severing the finger. But long before the return of those cruel perpetrators of her death, the shadow of Vanda had appeared before her appalled husband, and holding up to him her bloody hand, made him fearfully sensible how well his savage commands had been obeyed. After haunting him in peace and war, in desert, court, and camp, until he died despairingly on a pilgrimage to the Holy Land, the Bahr-geist, or ghost of the murdered Vanda, became so terrible in the House of Baldringham, that the succour of Saint Dunstan was itself scarcely sufficient to put bounds to her visitation. Yea, the blessed saint, when he had succeeded in his exorcism, did, in requital of Baldrick's crime, impose a strong and enduring penalty upon every female descendant of the house in the third degree; namely, that once in their lives, and before their twenty-first year, they should each spend a solitary night in the chamber of the murdered Vanda, saying therein certain prayers, as well for her repose, as for the suffering soul of her murderer. During that awful space, it is generally believed that the spirit of the murdered person appears to the female who observes the vigil, and shows some sign of her future good or bad fortune. If favourable, she appears with a smiling aspect, and crosses them with her unbloodied hand; but she announces evil fortune by showing the hand from which the finger was severed, with a stern countenance, as if resenting upon the descendant of her husband his inhuman cruelty. Sometimes she is said to speak. These particulars I learned long since from an old Saxon dame, the mother of our Margery, who had been an attendant on my grandmother, and left the House of Baldringham when she made her escape from it with my father's father."

"Did your grandmother ever render this homage," said Rose, "which seems to me—under favour of St. Dunstan—to bring humanity into too close intercourse with a being of a doubtful nature?"

"My grandfather thought so, and never permitted my grandmother to revisit the house of Baldringham after her marriage; hence disunion betwixt him and his son on the one part, and the members of that family on the other. They laid sundry misfortunes, and particularly the loss of male heirs which at that time befell them, to my parent's not having done the hereditary homage to the bloody-fingered Bahr-geist."

"And how could you, my dearest lady," said Rose, "knowing that they held among them a usage so hideous, think of accepting the invitation of Lady Ermengarde?"

"I can hardly answer you the question," answered Eveline. "Partly I feared my father's recent calamity, to be slain (as I have heard him say his aunt once prophesied of him) by the enemy he most despised, might be the result of this rite having been neglected; and partly I hoped, that if my mind should be appalled at the danger, when it presented itself closer to my eye, it could not be urged on me in courtesy and humanity. You saw how soon my cruel-hearted relative pounced upon the opportunity, and how impossible it became for me, bearing the name, and, I trust, the spirit of Berenger, to escape from the net in which I had involved myself."

"No regard for name or rank should have engaged me," replied Rose, "to place myself where apprehension alone, even without the terrors of a real visitation, might have punished my presumption with insanity. But what, in the name of

Heaven, did you see at this horrible rendezvous?"

"Ay, there is the question," said Eveline, raising her hand to her brow—"how I could witness that which I distinctly saw, yet be able to retain command of thought and intellect!—I had recited the prescribed devotions for the murderer and his victim, and sitting down on the couch which was assigned me, had laid aside such of my clothes as might impede my rest—I had surmounted, in short, the first shock which I experienced in committing myself to this mysterious chamber, and I hoped to pass the night in slumber as sound as my thoughts were innocent. But I was fearfully disappointed. I cannot judge how long I had slept, when my bosom was oppressed by an unusual weight, which seemed at once to stifle my voice, stop the beating of my heart, and prevent me from drawing my breath; and when I looked up to discover the cause of this horrible suffocation, the form of the murdered British matron stood over my couch taller than life, shadowy, and with a countenance where traits of dignity and beauty were mingled with a fierce expression of vengeful exultation. She held over me the hand which bore the bloody marks of her husband's cruelty, and seemed as if she signed the cross, devoting me to destruction; while, with an unearthly tone, she uttered these words:—

`Widow'd wife, and married maid,
  Betrothed, betrayer, and betray'd!'

The phantom stooped over me as she spoke, and lowered her gory fingers, as if to touch my face, when, terror giving me the power of which it at first deprived me, I screamed aloud—the casement of the apartment was thrown open with a loud noise,—and—But what signifies my telling all this to thee, Rose, who show so plainly, by the movement of eye and lip, that you consider me as a silly and childish dreamer?"

"Be not angry, my dear lady," said Rose; "I do indeed believe that the witch we call Mara has been dealing with you; but she, you know, is by leeches considered as no real phantom, but solely the creation of our own imagination, disordered by causes which arise from bodily indisposition."

"Thou art learned, maiden," said Eveline, rather peevishly; "but when I assure thee that my better angel came to my assistance in a human form.—that at his appearance the fiend vanished—and that he transported me in his arms out of the chamber of terror, I think thou wilt, as a good Christian, put more faith in that which I tell you."

"Indeed, indeed, my sweetest mistress, I cannot," replied Rose. "It is even that circumstance of the guardian angel which makes me consider the whole as a dream. A Norman sentinel, whom I myself called from his post on purpose, did indeed come to your assistance, and, breaking into your apartment, transported you to that where I myself received you from his arms in a lifeless condition."

"A Norman soldier, ha!" said Eveline, colouring extremely; "and to whom, maiden, did you dare give commission to break into my sleeping chamber?"

"Your eyes flash anger, madam, but is it reasonable they should?— Did I not hear your screams of agony, and was I to stand fettered by ceremony at such a moment?—no more than if the castle had been on fire."

"I ask you again, Rose," said her mistress, still with discomposure, though less angrily than at first, "whom you directed to break into my apartment?"

"Indeed, I know not, lady," said Rose; "for beside that he was muffled in his mantle, little chance was there of my knowing his features, even had I seen them fully. But I can soon discover the cavalier; and I will set about it, that I may give him the reward I promised, and warn him to be silent and discreet in this matter."

"Do so," said Eveline; "and if you find him among those soldiers who attend us, I will indeed lean to thine opinion, and think that fantasy had the chief share in the evils I have endured the last night."

Rose struck her palfrey with the rod, and, accompanied by her mistress, rode up to Philip Guarine, the Constable's squire, who for the present commanded their little escort. "Good Guarine," she said, "I had talk with one of these sentinels last night from my window, and he did me some service, for which I promised him recompense—Will you inquire for the man, that I may pay him his guerdon?"

"Truly, I will owe him a guerdon, also, pretty maiden," answered the squire; "for if a lance of them approached near enough the house to hold speech from the windows, he transgressed the precise orders of his watch."

"Tush! you must forgive that for my sake," said Rose. "I warrant, had I called on yourself, stout Guarine, I should have had influence to bring you under my chamber window."

Guarine laughed, and shrugged his shoulders. "True it is," he said, "when women are in place, discipline is in danger."

He then went to make the necessary inquiries among his band, and returned with the assurance, that his soldiers, generally and severally, denied having approached the mansion of the Lady Ermengarde on the preceding night.

"Thou seest, Rose," said Eveline, with a significant look to her attendant.

"The poor rogues are afraid of Guarine's severity," said Rose, "and dare not tell the truth—I shall have some one in private claiming the reward of me."

"I would I had the privilege myself, damsel," said Guarine; "but for these fellows, they are not so timorous as you suppose them, being even too ready to avouch their roguery when it hath less excuse—Besides, I promised them impunity.—Have you any thing farther to order?"

"Nothing, good Guarine," said Eveline; "only this small donative to procure wine for thy soldiers, that they may spend the next night more merrily than the last.—And now he is gone,—Maiden, thou must, I think, be now well aware, that what thou sawest was no earthly being?"

"I must believe mine own ears and eyes, madam," replied Rose.

"Do—but allow me the same privilege," answered Eveline. "Believe me that my deliverer (for so I must call him) bore the features of one who neither was, nor could be, in the neighbourhood of Baldringham. Tell me but one thing— What dost thou think of this extraordinary prediction—

'Widow'd wife, and wedded maid,
Betrothed, betrayer, and betray'd'

Thou wilt say it is an idle invention of my brain—but think it for a moment the speech of a true diviner, and what wouldst thou say of it?"

"That you may be betrayed, my dearest lady, but never can be a betrayer," answered Rose, with animation.

Eveline reached her hand out to her friend, and as she pressed affectionately that which Rose gave in return, she whispered to her with energy, "I thank thee for the judgment, which my own heart confirms."

A cloud of dust now announced the approach of the Constable of Chester and his retinue, augmented by the attendance of his host Sir William Herbert, and some of his neighbours and kinsmen, who came to pay their respects to the orphan of the Garde Doloureuse, by which appellation Eveline was known upon her passage through their territory.

Eveline remarked, that, at their greeting, De Lacy looked with displeased surprise at the disarrangement of her dress and equipage, which her hasty departure from Baldringham had necessarily occasioned; and she was, on her part, struck with an expression of countenance which seemed to say, "I am not to be treated as an ordinary person, who may be received with negligence, and treated slightly with impunity." For the first time, she thought that, though always deficient in grace and beauty, the Constable's countenance was formed to express the more angry passions with force and vivacity, and that she who shared his rank and name must lay her account with the implicit surrender of her will and wishes to those of an arbitrary lord and master.

But the cloud soon passed from the Constable's brow; and in the conversation which he afterwards maintained with Herbert and the other knights and gentlemen, who from time to time came to greet and accompany them for a little way on their journey, Eveline had occasion to admire his superiority, both of sense and expression, and to remark the attention and deference with which his words were listened to by men too high in rank, and too proud, readily to admit any pre-eminence that was not founded on acknowledged merit. The regard of women is generally much influenced by the estimation which an individual maintains in the opinion of men; and Eveline, when she concluded her journey in the Benedictine nunnery in Gloucester, could not think without respect upon the renowned warrior, and celebrated politician, whose acknowledged abilities appeared to place him above every one whom she had seen approach him. His wife, Eveline thought, (and she was not without ambition,) if relinquishing some of those qualities in a husband which are in youth most captivating to the female imagination, must be still generally honoured and respected, and have contentment, if not romantic felicity, within her reach.

CHAPTER THE SIXTEENTH

The Lady Eveline remained nearly four months with her aunt, the Abbess of the Benedictine nunnery, under whose auspices the Constable of Chester saw his suit advance and prosper as it would probably have done under that of the deceased Raymond Berenger, her brother. It is probable, however, that, but for the supposed vision of the Virgin, and the vow of gratitude which that supposed vision had called forth, the natural dislike of so young a person to a match so unequal in years, might have effectually opposed his success. Indeed Eveline, while honouring the Constable's virtues, doing justice to his high character, and admiring his talents, could never altogether divest herself of a secret fear of him, which, while it prevented her from expressing any direct disapprobation of his addresses, caused her sometimes to shudder, she scarce knew why, at the idea of their becoming successful.

The ominous words, "betraying and betrayed," would then occur to her memory; and when her aunt (the period of the deepest mourning being elapsed) had fixed a period for her betrothal, she looked forward to it with a feeling of terror, for which she was unable to account to herself, and which, as well as the particulars of her dream, she concealed even from Father Aldrovand in the hours of confession. It was not aversion to the Constable—it was far less preference to any other suitor—it was one of those instinctive movements and emotions by which Nature seems to warn us of approaching danger, though furnishing no information respecting its nature, and suggesting no means of escaping from it.

So strong were these intervals of apprehension, that if they had been seconded by the remonstrances of Rose Flammock, as formerly, they might perhaps have led to Eveline's yet forming some resolution unfavourable to the suit of the Constable. But, still more zealous for her lady's honour than even for her happiness, Rose had strictly forborne every effort which could affect Eveline's purpose, when she had once expressed her approbation of De Lacy's addresses; and whatever she thought or anticipated concerning the proposed marriage, she seemed from that moment to consider it as an event which must necessarily take place.

De Lacy himself, as he learned more intimately to know the merit of the prize which he was desirous of possessing, looked forward with different feelings towards the union, than those with which he had first proposed the measure to Raymond Berenger. It was then a mere match of interest and convenience, which had occurred to the mind of a proud and politic feudal lord, as the best mode of consolidating the power and perpetuating the line of his family. Nor did even the splendour of Eveline's beauty make that impression upon De Lacy, which it was calculated to do on the fiery and impassioned chivalry of the age. He was past that period of life when the wise are captivated by outward form, and might have said with truth, as well as with discretion, that he could have wished his beautiful bride several years older, and possessed of a more moderate portion of personal charms, in order to have rendered the match more fitted for his own age and disposition. This stoicism, however, vanished, when, on repeated interviews with his destined bride, he found that she was indeed inexperienced in life, but desirous to be guided by superior wisdom; and that, although gifted with high spirit, and a disposition which began to recover its natural elastic gaiety, she was gentle, docile, and, above all, endowed with a firmness of principle, which seemed to give assurance that she would tread uprightly, and without spot, the slippery paths in which youth, rank, and beauty, are doomed to move.

As feelings of a warmer and more impassioned kind towards Eveline began to glow in De Lacy's bosom, his engagements as a crusader became more and more burdensome to him. The Benedictine Abbess, the natural guardian of Eveline's happiness, added to these feelings by her reasoning and remonstrances. Although a nun and a devotee, she held in reverence the holy state of matrimony, and comprehended so much of it as to be aware, that its important purposes could not be accomplished while the whole continent of Europe was interposed betwixt the married pair; for as to a hint from the

Constable, that his young spouse might accompany him into the dangerous and dissolute precincts of the Crusader's camp, the good lady crossed herself with horror at the proposal, and never permitted it to be a second time mentioned in her presence.

It was not, however, uncommon for kings, princes, and other persons of high consequence, who had taken upon them the vow to rescue Jerusalem, to obtain delays, and even a total remission of their engagement, by proper application to the Church of Rome. The Constable was sure to possess the full advantage of his sovereign's interest and countenance, in seeking permission to remain in England, for he was the noble to whose valour and policy Henry had chiefly intrusted the defence of the disorderly Welsh marches; and it was by no means with his good-will that so useful a subject had ever assumed the cross.

It was settled, therefore, in private betwixt the Abbess and the Constable, that the latter should solicit at Rome, and with the Pope's Legate in England, a remission of his vow for at least two years; a favour which it was thought could scarce be refused to one of his wealth and influence, backed as it was with the most liberal offers of assistance towards the redemption of the Holy Land. His offers were indeed munificent; for he proposed, if his own personal attendance were dispensed with, to send an hundred lances at his own cost, each lance accompanied by two squires, three archers, and a varlet or horse-boy; being double the retinue by which his own person was to have been accompanied. He offered besides to deposit the sum of two thousand bezants to the general expenses of the expedition, to surrender to the use of the Christian armament those equipped vessels which he had provided, and which even now awaited the embarkation of himself and his followers.

Yet, while making these magnificent proffers, the Constable could not help feeling they would be inadequate to the expectations of the rigid prelate Baldwin, who, as he had himself preached the crusade, and brought the Constable and many others into that holy engagement, must needs see with displeasure the work of his eloquence endangered, by the retreat of so important an associate from his favourite enterprise. To soften, therefore, his disappointment as much as possible, the Constable offered to the Archbishop, that, in the event of his obtaining license to remain in Britain, his forces should be led by his nephew, Danxian Lacy, already renowned for his early feats of chivalry, the present hope of his house, and, failing heirs of his own body, its future head and support.

The Constable took the most prudent method of communicating this proposal to the Archbishop Baldwin, through a mutual friend, on whose good offices he could depend, and whose interest with the Prelate was regarded as great. But notwithstanding the splendour of the proposal, the Prelate heard it with sullen and obstinate silence, and referred for answer to a personal conference with the Constable at an appointed day, when concerns of the church would call the Archbishop to the city of Gloucester. The report of the mediator was such as induced the Constable to expect a severe struggle with the proud and powerful churchman; but, himself proud and powerful, and backed by the favour of his sovereign, he did not expect to be foiled in the contest.

The necessity that this point should be previously adjusted, as well as the recent loss of Eveline's father, gave an air of privacy to De Lacy's courtship, and prevented its being signalized by tournaments and feats of military skill, in which he would have been otherwise desirous to display his address in the eyes of his mistress. The rules of the convent prevented his giving entertainments of dancing, music, or other more pacific revels; and although the Constable displayed his affection by the most splendid gifts to his future bride and her attendants, the whole affair, in the opinion of the experienced Dame Gillian, proceeded more with the solemnity of a funeral, than the light pace of an approaching bridal.

The bride herself felt something of this, and thought occasionally it might have been lightened by the visits of young Damian, in whose age, so nearly corresponding to her own, she might have expected some relief from the formal courtship of his graver uncle. But he came not; and from what the Constable said concerning him, she was led to imagine that the relations had, for a time at least, exchanged occupations and character. The elder De Lacy continued, indeed, in nominal observance of his vow, to dwell in a pavilion by the gates of Gloucester; but he seldom donned his armour, substituted costly damask and silk for his war-worn shamois doublet, and affected at his advanced time of life more gaiety of attire than his contemporaries remembered as distinguishing his early youth. His nephew, on the contrary, resided almost constantly on the marches of Wales, occupied in settling by prudence, or subduing by main force, the various disturbances by which these provinces were continually agitated; and Eveline learned with surprise, that it was with difficulty his uncle had prevailed on him to be present at the ceremony of their being betrothed to each other, or, as the Normans entitled the ceremony, their *fiancailles*. This engagement, which preceded the actual marriage for a space more or less, according to circumstances, was usually celebrated with a solemnity corresponding to the rank of the contracting parties.

The Constable added, with expressions of regret, that Damian gave himself too little rest, considering his early youth, slept too little, and indulged in too restless a disposition—that his health was suffering—and that a learned Jewish leech, whose opinion had been taken, had given his advice that the warmth of a more genial climate was necessary to restore his constitution to its general and natural vigour.

Eveline heard this with much regret, for she remembered Damian as the angel of good tidings, who first brought her news of deliverance from the forces of the Welsh; and the occasions on which they had met, though mournful, brought a sort of pleasure in recollection, so gentle had been the youth's deportment, and so consoling his expressions of sympathy. She wished she could see him, that she might herself judge of the nature of his illness; for, like other damsels of that age, she was not entirely ignorant of the art of healing, and had been taught by Father Aldrovand, himself no mean physician, how to extract healing essences from plants and herbs gathered under planetary hours. She thought it possible that her talents in this art, slight as they were, might perhaps be of service to one already her friend and liberator, and soon about to become her very near relation.

It was therefore with a sensation of pleasure mingled with some confusion, (at the idea, doubtless, of assuming the part of medical adviser to so young a patient,) that one evening, while the convent was assembled about some business of their chapter, she heard Gillian announce that the kinsman of the Lord Constable desired to speak with her. She snatched up the veil, which she wore in compliance with the customs of the house, and hastily descended to the parlour, commanding the attendance of Gillian, who, nevertheless, did not think proper to obey the signal.

When she entered the apartment, a man whom she had never seen before advanced, kneeling on one knee, and taking up the hem of her veil, saluted it with an air of the most profound respect. She stepped back, surprised and alarmed, although there was nothing in the appearance of the stranger to justify her apprehension. He seemed to be about thirty years of age, tall of stature, and bearing a noble though wasted form, and a countenance on which disease, or perhaps youthful indulgence, had anticipated the traces of age. His demeanour seemed courteous and respectful, even in a degree which approached to excess. He observed Eveline's surprise, and said, in a tone of pride, mingled with emotion, "I fear that I have been mistaken, and that my visit is regarded as an unwelcome intrusion."

"Arise, sir," answered Eveline, "and let me know your name and business I was summoned to a kinsman of the Constable of Chester."

"And you expected the stripling Damian," answered the stranger. "But the match with which England rings will connect you with others of the house besides that young person; and amongst these, with the luckless Randal de Lacy. Perhaps," continued he, "the fair Eveline Berenger may not even have heard his name breathed by his more fortunate kinsman—more fortunate in every respect, but *most* fortunate in his present prospects."

This compliment was accompanied by a deep reverence, and Eveline stood much embarrassed how to reply to his civilities; for although she now remembered to have heard this Randal slightly mentioned by the Constable when speaking of his family, it was in terms which implied there was no good understanding betwixt them. She therefore only returned his courtesy by general thanks for the honour of his visit, trusting he would then retire; but such was not his purpose.

"I comprehend," he said, "from the coldness with which the Lady Eveline Berenger receives me, that what she has heard of me from my kinsman (if indeed he thought me worthy of being mentioned to her at all) has been, to say the least, unfavourable. And yet my name once stood as high in fields and courts, as that of the Constable; nor is it aught more disgraceful than what is indeed often esteemed the worst of disgraces—poverty, which prevents my still aspiring to places of honour and fame. If my youthful follies have been numerous, I have paid for them by the loss of my fortune, and the degradation of my condition; and therein, my happy kinsman might, if he pleased, do me some aid—I mean not with his purse or estate; for, poor as I am, I would not live on alms extorted from the reluctant hand of an estranged friend; but his countenance would put him to no cost, and, in so far, I might expect some favour."

"In that my Lord Constable," said Eveline, "must judge for himself. I have—as yet, at least—no right to interfere in his family affairs; and if I should ever have such right, it will well become me to be cautious how I use it."

"It is prudently answered," replied Randal; "but what I ask of you is merely, that you, in your gentleness, would please to convey to my cousin a suit, which I find it hard to bring my ruder tongue to utter with sufficient submission. The usurers, whose claims have eaten like a canker into my means, now menace me with a dungeon—a threat which they dared not mutter, far less attempt to execute, were it not that they see me an outcast, unprotected by the natural head of my family, and regard me rather as they would some unfriended vagrant, than as a descendant of the powerful house of Lacy."

"It is a sad necessity," replied Eveline; "but I see not how I can help you in such extremity."

"Easily," replied Randal de Lacy. "The day of your betrothal is fixed, as I hear reported; and it is your right to select what witnesses you please to the solemnity, which may the saints bless! To every one but myself, presence or absence upon that occasion is a matter of mere ceremony—to me it is almost life or death. So an I situated, that the marked instance of slight or contempt, implied by my exclusion from this meeting of our family, will be held for the signal of my final expulsion from the House of the De Lacy's, and for a thousand bloodhounds to assail me without mercy or forbearance, whom, cowards as they are, even the slightest show of countenance from my powerful kinsman would compel to stand at bay. But why should I occupy your time in talking thus?—Farewell, madam—be happy—and do not think of me the more harshly, that for a few minutes I have broken the tenor of your happy thoughts, by forcing my misfortunes on your notice."

"Stay, sir," said Eveline, affected by the tone and manner of the noble suppliant; "you shall not have it to say that you have told your distress to Eveline Berenger, without receiving such aid as is in her power to give. I will mention your request to the Constable of Chester."

"You must do more, if you really mean to assist me," said Randal de Lacy, "you must make that request your own. You do not know," said he, continuing to bend on her a fixed and expressive look, "how hard it is to change the fixed purpose of a De Lacy—a twelvemonth hence you will probably be better acquainted with the firm texture of our resolutions. But, at present, what can withstand your wish should you deign to express it?"

"Your suit, sir, shall not be lost for want of my advancing it with my good word and good wishes," replied Eveline; "but you must be well aware that its success or failure must rest with the Constable himself."

Randal de Lacy took his leave with the same air of deep reverence which had marked his entrance; only that, as he then saluted the skirt of Eveline's robe, he now rendered the same homage by touching her hand with his lip. She saw him depart with a mixture of emotions, in which compassion was predominant; although in his complaints of the Constable's unkindness to him there was something offensive, and his avowal of follies and excess seemed uttered rather in the spirit of wounded pride, than in that of contrition.

When Eveline next saw the Constable, she told him of the visit of Randal and of his request; and strictly observing his countenance while she spoke, she saw, that at the first mention of his kinsman's name, a gleam of anger shot along his features. He soon subdued it, however, and, fixing his eyes on the ground, listened to Eveline's detailed account of the visit, and her request "that Randal might be one of the invited witnesses to their *fiancailles*."

The Constable paused for a moment, as if he were considering how to elude the solicitation. At length he replied, "You do not know for whom you ask this, or you would perhaps have forborne your request; neither are you apprized of its full import, though my crafty cousin well knows, that when I do him this grace which he asks, I bind myself, as it were, in the eye of the world once more—and it will be for the third time—to interfere in his affairs, and place them on such a footing as may afford him the means of re-establishing his fallen consequence, and repairing his numerous errors."

"And wherefore not, my lord?" said the generous Eveline. "If he has been ruined only through follies, he is now of an age when these are no longer tempting snares; and if his heart and hand be good, he may yet be an honour to the House of De Lacy."

The Constable shook his head. "He hath indeed," he said, "a heart and hand fit for service, God knoweth, whether in good or evil. But never shall it be said that you, my fair Eveline, made request of Hugh de Lacy, which he was not to his uttermost willing to comply with. Randal shall attend at our *fiancailles*; there is indeed the more cause for his attendance, as I somewhat fear we may lack that of our valued nephew Damian, whose malady rather increases than declines, and, as I hear, with strange symptoms of unwonted disturbance of mind and starts of temper, to which the youth had not hitherto been subject."

CHAPTER THE SEVENTEENTH.

Ring out the merry bell, the bride approaches,
The blush upon her cheek has shamed the morning,
For that is dawning palely. Grant, good saints,
These clouds betoken nought of evil omen!
  OLD PLAY.

The day of the _fiancailles, or espousals, was now approaching; and it seems that neither the profession of the Abbess, nor her practice at least, were so rigid as to prevent her selecting the great parlour of the convent for that holy rite, although necessarily introducing many male guests within those vestal precincts, and notwithstanding that the rite itself was the preliminary to a state which the inmates of the cloister had renounced for ever.

The Abbess's Norman pride of birth, and the real interest which she took in her niece's advancement, overcame all scruples; and the venerable mother might be seen in unwonted bustle, now giving orders to the gardener for decking the apartment with flowers—now to her cellaress, her precentrix, and the lay-sisters of the kitchen, for preparing a splendid banquet, mingling her commands on these worldly subjects with an occasional ejaculation on their vanity and worthlessness, and every now and then converting the busy and anxious looks which she threw upon her preparations into a solemn turning upward of eyes and folding of hands, as one who sighed over the mere earthly pomp which she took such trouble in superintending. At another time the good lady might have been seen in close consultation with Father Aldrovand, upon the ceremonial, civil and religious, which was to accompany a solemnity of such consequence to her family.

Meanwhile the reins of discipline, although relaxed for a season, were not entirely thrown loose. The outer court of the convent was indeed for the time opened for the reception of the male sex; but the younger sisters and novices of the house being carefully secluded in the more inner apartments of the extensive building, under the immediate eye of a grim old nun, or, as the conventual rule designed her, an ancient, sad, and virtuous person, termed Mistress of the Novices, were not permitted to pollute their eyes by looking on waving plumes and rustling mantles. A few sisters, indeed, of the Abbess's own standing, were left at liberty, being such goods as it was thought could not, in shopman's phrase, take harm from the air, and which are therefore left lying on the counter. These antiquated dames went mumping about with much affected indifference, and a great deal of real curiosity, endeavouring indirectly to get information concerning names, and dresses, and decorations, without daring to show such interest in these vanities as actual questions on the subject might have implied.

A stout band of the Constable's spearmen guarded the gate of the nunnery, admitting within the hallowed precinct the few only who were to be present at the solemnity, with their principal attendants, and while the former were ushered with all due ceremony into the apartments dressed out for the occasion, the attendants, although detained in the outer court, were liberally supplied with refreshments of the most substantial kind; and had the amusement, so dear to the menial classes, of examining and criticising their masters and mistresses, as they passed into the interior apartments prepared for their reception.

Amongst the domestics who were thus employed were old Raoul the huntsman and his jolly dame—he gay and glorious, in a new cassock of green velvet, she gracious and comely, in a kirtle of yellow silk, fringed with minivair, and that at no mean cost, were equally busied in beholding the gay spectacle. The most inveterate wars have their occasional terms of truce; the most bitter and boisterous weather its hours of warmth and of calmness; and so was it with the matrimonial horizon of this amiable pair, which, usually cloudy, had now for brief space cleared up. The splendour of their new apparel, the mirth of the spectacle around them, with the aid, perhaps, of a bowl of muscadine quaffed by Raoul, and a cup of hippocras sipped by his wife, had rendered them rather more agreeable in each other's eyes than was their wont; good cheer being in such cases, as oil is to a rusty lock, the means of making those valves move smoothly and glibly, which otherwise work not together at all, or by shrieks and groans express their reluctance to move in union. The pair had stuck themselves into a kind of niche, three or four steps from the ground, which contained a small stone bench, whence their curious eyes could scrutinize with advantage every guest who entered the court.

Thus placed, and in their present state of temporary concord, Raoul with his frosty visage formed no unapt representative of January, the bitter father of the year; and though Gillian was past the delicate bloom of youthful May, yet the melting fire of a full black eye, and the genial glow of a ripe and crimson cheek, made her a lively type of the fruitful and jovial August. Dame Gillian used to make it her boast, that she could please every body with her gossip, when she chose it, from Raymond Berenger down to Robin the horse-boy; and like a good housewife, who, to keep her hand in use, will sometimes even condescend to dress a dish for her husband's sole eating, she now thought proper to practise her powers of pleasing on old Raoul, fairly conquering, in her successful sallies of mirth and satire, not only his cynical temperament towards all human kind, but his peculiar and special disposition to be testy with his spouse. Her jokes, such as they were, and the coquetry with which they were enforced, had such an effect on this Timon of the woods, that he curled up his cynical nose, displayed his few straggling teeth like a cur about to bite, broke out into a barking laugh, which was more like the cry of one of his own hounds—stopped short in the explosion, as if he had suddenly recollected that it was out of character; yet, ere he resumed his acrimonious gravity, shot such a glance at Gillian as made his nut-cracker jaws, pinched eyes, and convolved nose, bear no small resemblance to one of those fantastic faces which decorate the upper end of old bass viols.

"Is not this better than laying your dog-leash on your loving wife, as if she were a brach of the kennel?" said August to January.

"In troth is it," answered January, in a frost-bitten tone;—"and so it is also better than doing the brach-tricks which bring the leash into exercise."

"Humph!" said Gillian, in the tone of one who thought her husband's proposition might bear being disputed; but instantly changing the note to that of tender complaint, "Ah! Raoul," she said, "do you not remember how you once beat me because our late lord—Our Lady assoilzie him!—took my crimson breast-knot for a peony rose?"

"Ay, ay," said the huntsman; "I remember our old master would make such mistakes—Our Lady assoilzie him! as you say—The best hound will hunt counter."

"And how could you think, dearest Raoul, to let the wife of thy bosom go so long without a new kirtle?" said his helpmate.

"Why, thou hast got one from our young lady that might serve a countess," said Raoul, his concord jarred by her touching this chord—"how many kirtles wouldst thou have?"

"Only two, kind Raoul; just that folk may not count their children's age by the date of Dame Gillian's last new gown."

"Well, well—it is hard that a man cannot be in good-humour once and away without being made to pay for it. But thou shalt have a new kirtle at Michaelmas, when I sell the buck's hides for the season. The very antlers should bring a good penny this year."

"Ay, ay," said Gillian; "I ever tell thee, husband, the horns would be worth the hide in a fair market."

Raoul turned briskly round as if a wasp had stung him, and there is no guessing what his reply might have been to this seemingly innocent observation, had not a gallant horseman at that instant entered the court, and, dismounting like the others, gave his horse to the charge of a squire, or equerry, whose attire blazed with embroidery.

"By Saint Hubert, a proper horseman, and a *destrier* for an earl," said Raoul; "and my Lord Constable's liveries withal—yet I know not the gallant."

"But I do," said Gillian; "it is Randal de Lacy, the Constable's kinsman, and as good a man as ever came of the name!"

"Oh! by Saint Hubert, I have heard of him—men say he is a reveller, and a jangler, and a waster of his goods."

"Men lie now and then," said Gillian dryly.

"And women also," replied Raoul;—"why, methinks he winked on thee just now."

"That right eye of thine saw never true since our good lord-Saint Mary rest him!—flung a cup of wine in thy face, for pressing over boldly into his withdrawing-room."

"I marvel," said Raoul, as if he heard her not, "that yonder ruffler comes hither. I have heard that he is suspected to have attempted the Constable's life, and that they have not spoken together for five years."

"He comes on my young lady's invitation, and that I know full well," said Dame Gillian; "and he is less like to do the Constable wrong than to have wrong at his hand, poor gentleman, as indeed he has had enough of that already."

"And who told thee so?" said Raoul, bitterly.

"No matter, it was one who knew all about it very well," said the dame, who began to fear that, in displaying her triumph of superior information, she had been rather over-communicative.

"It must have been the devil, or Randal himself" said Raoul, "for no other mouth is large enough for such a lie.—But hark ye, Dame Gillian, who is he that presses forward next, like a man that scarce sees how he goes?"

"Even your angel of grace, my young Squire Damian" said Dame Gillian.

"It is impossible!" answered Raoul—"call me blind if thou wilt;— but I have never seen man so changed in a few weeks—and his attire is flung on him so wildly as if he wore a horse-cloth round him instead of a mantle—What can ail the youth?—he has made a dead pause at the door, as if he saw something on the threshold that debarred his entrance—Saint Hubert, but he looks as if he were elf-stricken!"

"You ever thought him such a treasure!" said Gillian; "and now look at him as he stands by the side of a real gentleman, how he stares and trembles as if he were distraught."

"I will speak to him," said Raoul, forgetting his lameness, and springing from his elevated station—"I will speak to him; and if he be unwell, I have my lancets and fleams to bleed man as well as brute."

"And a fit physician for such a patient," muttered Gillian,—"a dog-leech for a dreamy madman, that neither knows his own disease nor the way to cure it."

Meanwhile the old huntsman made his way towards the entrance, before which Damian remained standing, in apparent uncertainty whether he should enter or not, regardless of the crowd around, and at the same time attracting their attention by the singularity of his deportment.

Raoul had a private regard for Damiah; for which, perhaps, it was a chief reason, that of late his wife had been in the habit of speaking of him in a tone more disrespectful than she usually applied to handsome young men. Besides, he understood the youth was a second Sir Tristrem in silvan sports by wood and river, and there needed no more to fetter Raoul's soul to him with bands of steel. He saw with great concern his conduct attract general notice, mixed with some ridicule.

"He stands," said the town-jester, who had crowded into the gay throng, "before the gate, like Balaam's ass in the Mystery, when the animal sees so much more than can be seen by any one else."

A cut from Raoul's ready leash rewarded the felicity of this application, and sent the fool howling off to seek a more favourable audience, for his pleasantry. At the same time Raoul pressed up to Damian, and with an earnestness very different from his usual dry causticity of manner, begged him for God's sake not to make himself the general spectacle, by standing there as if the devil sat on the doorway, but either to enter, or, what might be as becoming, to retire, and make himself more fit in apparel for attending on a solemnity so nearly concerning his house.

"And what ails my apparel, old man?" said Damian, turning sternly on the huntsman, as one who has been hastily and uncivilly roused from a reverie.

"Only, with respect to your valour," answered the huntsman, "men do not usually put old mantles over new doublets; and methinks, with submission, that of yours neither accords with your dress, nor is fitted for this noble presence."

"Thou art a fool!" answered Damian, "and as green in wit as gray in years. Know you not that in these days the young and old consort together—contract together—wed together? and should we take more care to make our apparel consistent than our actions?"

"For God's sake, my lord," said Raoul, "forbear these wild and dangerous words! they may be heard by other ears than mine, and construed by worse interpreters. There may be here those who will pretend to track mischief from light words, as I would find a buck from his frayings. Your cheek is pale, my lord, your eye is blood-shot; for Heaven's sake, retire!"

"I will not retire," said Damian, with yet more distemperature of manner, "till I have seen the Lady Eveline."

"For the sake of all the saints," ejaculated Raoul, "not now!—You will do my lady incredible injury by forcing yourself into her presence in this condition."

"Do you think so!" said Damian, the remark seeming to operate as a sedative which enabled him to collect his scattered thoughts.—"Do you really think so? —I thought that to have looked upon her once more—but no—you are in the right, old man."

He turned from the door as if to withdraw, but ere he could accomplish his purpose, he turned yet more pale than before, staggered, and fell on the pavement ere Raoul could afford him his support, useless as that might have proved. Those who raised him were surprised to observe that his garments were soiled with blood, and that the stains upon his cloak, which had been criticised by Raoul, were of the same complexion. A grave-looking personage, wrapped in a sad-coloured mantle, came forth from the crowd.

"I knew how it would be," he said; "I made venesection this morning, and commanded repose and sleep according to the aphorisms of Hippocrates; but if young gentlemen will neglect the ordinance of their physician, medicine will avenge herself. It is impossible that my bandage or ligature, knit by these fingers, should have started, but to avenge the neglect of the precepts of art."

"What means this prate?" said the voice of the Constable, before which all others were silent. He had been summoned forth just as the rite of espousal or betrothing was concluded, on the confusion occasioned by Damian's situation, and now sternly commanded the physician to replace the bandages which had slipped from his nephew's arm, himself assisting in the task of supporting the patient, with the anxious and deeply agitated feelings of one who saw a near and justly valued relative—as yet, the heir of his fame and family—stretched before him in a condition so dangerous.

But the griefs of the powerful and the fortunate are often mingled with impatience of interrupted prosperity. "What means this?" he demanded sternly of the leech. "I sent you this morning to attend my nephew on the first tidings of his illness, and commanded that he should make no attempt to be present on this day's solemnity, yet I find him in this state, and in this place."

"So please your lordship," replied the leech, with a conscious self-importance, which even the presence of the Constable could not subdue—*"Curatio est canonica, non coacta;* which signifieth, my lord, that the physician acteth his cure by rules of art and science—by advice and prescription, but not by force or violence upon the patient, who cannot be at all benefited unless he be voluntarily amenable to the orders of his medicum."

"Tell me not of your jargon," said De Lacy; "if my nephew was lightheaded enough to attempt to come hither in the heat of a delirious distemper, you should have had sense to prevent him, had it been by actual force."

"It may be," said, Randal de Lacy, joining the crowd, who, forgetting the cause which had brought them together, were now assembled about Damian, "that more powerful was the magnet which drew our kinsman hither, than aught the leech could do to withhold him."

The Constable, still busied about his nephew, looked up as Randal spoke, and, when he was done, asked, with formal coldness of manner, "Ha, fair kinsman, of what magnet do you speak?"

"Surely of your nephew's love and regard to your lordship," answered Randal, "which, not to mention his respect for the lady Eveline, must have compelled him hither, if his limbs were able to bear him.—And here the bride comes, I think, in charity, to thank him for his zeal."

"What unhappy case is this?" said the Lady Eveline, pressing forward, much disordered with the intelligence of Damian's danger, which had been suddenly conveyed to her. "Is there nothing in which my poor service may avail?"

"Nothing, lady," said the Constable, rising from beside his nephew, and taking her hand; "your kindness is here mistimed. This motley assembly, this unseeming confusion, become not your presence."

"Unless it could be helpful, my lord," said Eveline, eagerly. "It is your nephew who is in danger—my deliverer—one of my deliverers, I would say."

"He is fitly attended by his chirurgeon," said the Constable, leading back his reluctant bride to the convent, while the medical attendant triumphantly exclaimed,

"Well judgeth my Lord Constable, to withdraw his noble Lady from the host of petticoated empirics, who, like so many Amazons, break in upon and derange the regular course of physical practice, with their petulant prognostics, their rash recipes, their mithridate, their febrifuges, their amulets, and their charms. Well speaketh the Ethnic poet,

'Non audet, nisi qua didicit, dare quod medicorum est;
Promittunt medici—tractant fabrilia fabri,'"

As he repeated these lines with much emphasis, the doctor permitted his patient's arm to drop from his hand, that he might aid the cadence with a flourish of his own. "There," said he to the spectators, "is what none of you understand—no, by Saint Luke, nor the Constable himself."

"But he knows how to whip in a hound that babbles when he should be busy," said Raoul; and, silenced by this hint, the chirurgeon betook himself to his proper duty, of superintending the removal of young Damian to an apartment in the neighbouring street, where the symptoms of his disorder seemed rather to increase than diminish, and speedily required all the skill and attention which the leech could bestow.

The subscription of the contract of marriage had, as already noticed, been just concluded, when the company assembled on the occasion were interrupted by the news of Damian's illness. When the Constable led his bride from the court-yard into the apartment where the company was assembled, there was discomposure and uneasiness on the countenance of both; and it was not a little increased by the bride pulling her hand hastily from the hold of the bridegroom, on observing that the latter was stained with recent blood, and had in truth left the same stamp upon her own. With a faint exclamation she showed the marks to Rose, saying at the same time, "What bodes this?—Is this the revenge of the Bloody-finger already commencing?"

"It bodes nothing, my dearest lady," said Rose—"it is our fears that are prophets, not those trifles which we take for augury. For God's sake, speak to my lord! He is surprised at your agitation."

"Let him ask me the cause himself," said Eveline; "fitter it should be told at his bidding, than be offered by me unasked."

The Constable, while his bride stood thus conversing with her maiden, had also observed, that in his anxiety to assist his nephew, he had transferred part of his blood from his own hands to Eveline's dress. He came forward to apologize for what at such a moment seemed almost ominous. "Fair lady," said he, "the blood of a true De Lacy can never bode aught but peace and happiness to you."

Eveline seemed as if she would have answered, but could not immediately find words. The faithful Rose, at the risk of incurring the censure of being over forward, hastened to reply to the compliment. "Every damsel is bound to believe what you say, my noble lord," was her answer, "knowing how readily that blood hath ever flowed for protecting the distressed, and so lately for our own relief."

"It is well spoken, little one," answered the Constable; "and the Lady Eveline is happy in a maiden who so well knows how to speak when it is her own pleasure to be silent.—Come, lady," he added, "let us hope this mishap of my kinsman is but like a sacrifice to fortune, which permits not the brightest hour to pass without some intervening shadow. Damian, I trust, will speedily recover; and be we mindful that the blood-drops which alarm you have been drawn by a friendly steel, and are symptoms rather of recovery than of illness. —Come, dearest lady, your silence discourages our friends, and wakes in them doubts whether we be sincere in the welcome due to them. Let me be your sewer," he said; and, taking a silver ewer and napkin from the standing cupboard, which was loaded with plate, he presented them on his knee to his bride.

Exerting herself to shake off the alarm into which she had been thrown by some supposed coincidence of the present accident with the apparition at Baldringham, Eveline, entering into her betrothed husband's humour, was about to raise him from the ground, when she was interrupted by the arrival of a hasty messenger, who, coming into the room without ceremony, informed the Constable that his nephew was so extremely ill, that if he hoped to see him alive, it would be necessary he should come to his lodgings instantly.

The Constable started up, made a brief adieu to Eveline and to the guests, who, dismayed at this new and disastrous intelligence, were preparing to disperse themselves, when, as he advanced towards the door, he was met by a Paritor, or Summoner of the Ecclesiastical Court, whose official dress had procured him unobstructed entrance into the precincts of the abbey.

"Deus vobiscum," said the paritor; "I would know which of this fair company is the Constable of Chester?"

"I am he," answered the elder De Lacy; "but if thy business be not the more hasty, I cannot now speak with thee—I am bound on matters of life and death."

"I take all Christian people to witness that I have discharged my duty," said the paritor, putting into the hand of the Constable a slip of parchment.

"How is this, fellow?" said the Constable, in great indignation— "for whom or what does your master the Archbishop take me, that he deals with me in this uncourteous fashion, citing me to compear before him more like a delinquent than a friend or a nobleman?"

"My gracious lord," answered the paritor, haughtily, "is accountable to no one but our Holy Father the Pope, for the exercise of the power which is intrusted to him by the canons of the Church. Your lordship's answer to my citation?"

"Is the Archbishop present in this city?" said the Constable, after a moment's reflection—"I knew not of his purpose to travel hither, still less of his purpose to exercise authority within these bounds."

"My gracious lord the Archbishop," said the paritor, "is but now arrived in this city, of which he is metropolitan; and, besides, by his apostolical commission, a legate *a latere* hath plenary jurisdiction throughout all England, as those may find (whatsoever be their degree) who may dare to disobey his summons."

"Hark thee, fellow," said the Constable, regarding the paritor with a grim and angry countenance, "were it not for certain respects, which I promise thee thy tawny hood hath little to do with, thou wert better have swallowed thy citation, seal and all, than delivered it to me with the addition of such saucy terms. Go hence, and tell your master I will see him within the space of an hour, during which time I am delayed by the necessity of attending a sick relation."

The paritor left the apartment with more humility in his manner than when he had entered, and left the assembled guests to look upon each other in silence and dismay.

The reader cannot fail to remember how severely the yoke of the Roman supremacy pressed both on the clergy and laity of England during the reign of Henry II. Even the attempt of that wise and courageous monarch to make a stand for the independence of his throne in the memorable case of Thomas a Becket, had such an unhappy issue, that, like a suppressed rebellion, it was found to add new strength to the domination of the Church. Since the submission of the king in that ill-fated struggle, the voice of Rome had double potency whenever it was heard, and the boldest peers of England held it more wise to submit to her imperious dictates, than to provoke a spiritual censure which had so many secular consequences. Hence the slight and scornful manner in which the Constable was treated by the prelate Baldwin struck a chill of astonishment into the assembly of friends whom he had collected to witness his espousals; and as he glanced his haughty eye around, he saw that many who would have stood by him through life and death in any other quarrel, had it even been with his sovereign, were turning pale at the very thought of a collision with the Church. Embarrassed, and at the same time incensed at their timidity, the Constable hasted to dismiss them, with the general assurance that all would be well—that his nephew's indisposition was a trifling complaint, exaggerated by a conceited physician, and by his own want of care—and that the message of the Archbishop, so unceremoniously delivered, was but the consequence of their mutual and friendly familiarity, which induced them sometimes, for the jest's sake, to reverse or neglect the ordinary forms of intercourse.—"If I wanted to speak with the prelate Baldwin on express business and in haste, such is the humility and indifference to form of that worthy pillar of the Church, that I should not fear offence," said the Constable, "did I send the meanest horseboy in my troop to ask an audience of him."

So he spoke—but there was something in his countenance which contradicted his words; and his friends and relations retired from the splendid and joyful ceremony of his espousals as from a funeral feast, with anxious thoughts and with downcast eyes.

Randal was the only person, who, having attentively watched the whole progress of the affair during the evening, ventured to approach his cousin as he left the house, and asked him, "in the name of their reunited friendship, whether he had nothing to command him?" assuring him, with a look more expressive than his words, that he would not find him cold in his service.

"I have nought which can exercise your zeal, fair cousin," replied the Constable, with the air of one who partly questioned the speaker's sincerity; and the parting reverence with which he accompanied his words, left Randal no pretext for continuing his attendance, as he seemed to have designed.

CHAPTER THE EIGHTEENTH.

Oh, were I seated high as my ambition,
I'd place this naked foot on necks of monarchs!
    MYSTERIOUS MOTHER.

The most anxious and unhappy moment of Hugo de Lacy's life, was unquestionably that in which, by espousing Eveline with all civil and religious solemnity, he seemed to approach to what for some time he had considered as the prime object of his wishes. He was assured of the early possession of a beautiful and amiable wife, endowed with such advantage of worldly goods, as gratified his ambition as well as his affections—Yet, even in this fortunate moment, the horizon darkened around him, in a manner which presaged nought but storm and calamity. At his nephew's lodging he learned that the pulse of the patient had risen, and his delirium had augmented, and all around him spoke very doubtfully of his chance of recovery, or surviving a crisis which seemed speedily approaching. The Constable stole towards the door of the apartment which his feelings permitted him not to enter, and listened to the raving which the fever gave rise to. Nothing can be more melancholy than to hear the mind at work concerning its ordinary occupations, when the body is stretched in pain and danger upon the couch of severe sickness; the contrast betwixt the ordinary state of health, its joys or its labours, renders doubly affecting the actual helplessness of the patient before whom these visions are rising, and we feel a corresponding degree of compassion for the sufferer whose thoughts are wandering so far from his real condition.

The Constable felt this acutely, as he heard his nephew shout the war-cry of the family repeatedly, appearing, by the words of command and direction, which he uttered from time to time, to be actively engaged in leading his men-at-arms against the Welsh. At another time he uttered various terms of the *manege*, of falconry, and of the chase—he mentioned his uncle's name repeatedly on these occasions, as if the idea of his kinsman had been connected alike with his martial encounters, and with his sports by wood and river. Other sounds there were, which he muttered so low as to be altogether undistinguishable.

With a heart even still more softened towards his kinsman's sufferings from hearing the points on which his mind wandered, the Constable twice applied his hand to the latch of the door, in order to enter the bedroom, and twice forebore, his eyes running faster with tears than he chose should be witnessed by the attendants. At length, relinquishing his purpose, he hastily left the house, mounted his horse, and followed only by four of his personal attendants, rode towards the palace of the Bishop, where, as he learned from public rumour, the Archprelate Baldwin had taken up his temporary residence.

The train of riders and of led-horses, of sumpter mules, and of menials and attendants, both lay and ecclesiastical, which thronged around the gate of the Episcopal mansion, together with the gaping crowd of inhabitants who had gathered around, some to gaze upon the splendid show, some to have the chance of receiving the benediction of the Holy Prelate, was so great as to impede the Constable's approach to the palace-door; and when this obstacle was surmounted, he found another in the obstinacy of the Archbishop's attendants, who permitted him not, though announced by name and title, to cross the threshold of the mansion, until they should receive the express command of their master to that effect.

The Constable felt the full effect of this slighting reception. He had dismounted from his horse in full confidence of being instantly admitted into the palace at least, if not into the Prelate's presence; and as he now stood on foot among the squires, grooms, and horseboys of the spiritual lord, he was so much disgusted, that his first impulse was to remount his horse, and return to his pavilion, pitched for the time before the city walls, leaving it to the Bishop to seek him there, if he really desired an interview. But the necessity of conciliation almost immediately rushed on his mind, and subdued the first haughty impulse of his offended pride. "If our wise King," he said to himself, "hath held the stirrup of one Prelate of Canterbury when living, and submitted to the most degrading observances before his shrine when dead, surely I need not be more scrupulous towards his priestly successor in the same overgrown authority." Another thought, which he dared hardly to acknowledge, recommended the same humble and submissive course. He could not but feel that, in endeavouring to evade his vows as a crusader, he was incurring some just censure from the Church; and he was not unwilling to hope, that his present cold and scornful reception on Baldwin's part, might be meant as a part of the penance which his conscience informed him his conduct was about to receive.

After a short interval, De Lacy was at length invited to enter the palace of the Bishop of Gloucester, in which he was to meet the Primate of England; but there was more than one brief pause, in hall and anteroom, ere he at length was admitted to Baldwin's presence.

The successor of the celebrated Becket had neither the extensive views, nor the aspiring spirit, of that redoubted personage; but, on the other hand, saint as the latter had become, it may be questioned, whether, in his professions for the weal of Christendom, he was half so sincere as was the present Archbishop. Baldwin was, in truth, a man well qualified to defend the powers which the Church had gained, though perhaps of a character too sincere and candid to be active in extending them. The advancement of the Crusade was the chief business of his life, his success the principal cause of his pride; and, if the sense of possessing the powers of eloquent persuasion, and skill to bend the minds of men to his purpose, was blended with his religious zeal, still the tenor of his life, and afterwards his death before Ptolemais, showed that the liberation of the Holy Sepulchre from the infidels was the unfeigned object of all his exertions. Hugo de Lacy well knew this; and the difficulty of managing such a temper appeared much greater to him on the eve of the interview in which the attempt was to be made, than he had suffered himself to suppose when the crisis was yet distant.

The Prelate, a man of a handsome and stately form, with features rather too severe to be pleasing, received the Constable in all the pomp of ecclesiastical dignity. He was seated on a chair of oak, richly carved with Gothic ornaments, and placed above the rest of the floor under a niche of the same workmanship. His dress was the rich episcopal robe, ornamented with costly embroidery, and fringed around the neck and cuffs; it opened from the throat and in the middle, and showed an under vestment of embroidery, betwixt the folds of which, as if imperfectly concealed, peeped the close shirt of hair-cloth which the Prelate constantly wore under all his pompous attire. His mitre was placed beside him on an oaken table of the same workmanship with his throne, against which also rested his pastoral staff, representing a shepherd's crook of the simplest form, yet which had proved more powerful and fearful than lance or scimetar, when wielded by the hand of Thomas a Becket. A chaplain in a white surplice kneeled at a little distance before a desk, and read forth from an illuminated volume some portion of a theological treatise, in which Baldwin appeared so deeply interested, that he did not appear to notice the entrance of the Constable, who, highly displeased at this additional slight, stood on the floor of the hall, undetermined whether to interrupt the reader, and address the Prelate at once, or to withdraw without saluting him at all. Ere he had formed a resolution, the chaplain had arrived at some convenient pause in the lecture, where the Archbishop stopped him with, "*Satis est, mi fili.*"

It was in vain that the proud secular Baron strove to conceal the embarrassment with which he approached the Prelate, whose attitude was plainly assumed for the purpose of impressing him with awe and solicitude. He tried, indeed, to exhibit a demeanour of such ease as might characterize their old friendship, or at least of such indifference as might infer the possession of perfect tranquillity; but he failed in both, and his address expressed mortified pride, mixed with no ordinary degree of embarrassment. The genius of the Catholic Church was on such occasions sure to predominate over the haughtiest of the laity.

"I perceive," said De Lacy, collecting his thoughts, and ashamed to find he had difficulty in doing so,—"I perceive that an old friendship is here dissolved. Methinks Hugo de Lacy might have expected another messenger to summon him to this reverend presence, and that another welcome should wait him on his arrival."

The Archbishop raised himself slowly in his seat, and made a half- inclination towards the Constable, who, by an instinctive desire of conciliation, returned it lower than he had intended, or than the scanty courtesy merited. The Prelate at the same time signing to his chaplain, the latter rose to withdraw, and receiving permission in the phrase "*Do veniam*," retreated reverentially, without either turning his back or looking upwards, his eyes fixed on the ground, his hands still folded in his habit, and crossed over his bosom.

When this mute attendant had disappeared, the Prelate's brow became more open, yet retained a dark shade of grave displeasure, and he replied to the address of De Lacy, but still without rising from his seat. "It skills not now, my lord, to say what the brave Constable of Chester has been to the poor priest Baldwin, or with what love and pride we beheld him assume the holy sign of salvation, and, to honour Him by whom he has himself been raised to honour, vow himself to the deliverance of the Holy Land. If I still see that noble lord before me, in the same holy resolution, let me know the joyful truth, and I will lay aside rochet and mitre, and tend his horse like a groom, if it be necessary by such menial service to show the cordial respect I bear to him."

"Reverend father," answered De Lacy, with hesitation, "I had hoped that the propositions which were made to you on my part by the Dean of Hereford, might have seemed more satisfactory in your eyes." Then, regaining his native confidence, he proceeded with more assurance in speech and manner; for the cold inflexible looks of the Archbishop irritated him. "If these proposals can be amended, my lord, let me know in what points, and, if possible, your pleasure shall be done, even if it should prove somewhat unreasonable. I would have peace, my lord, with Holy Church, and am the last who would despise her mandates. This has been known by my deeds in field, and counsels in the state; nor can I think my services have merited cold looks and cold language from the Primate of England."

"Do you upbraid the Church with your services, vain man?" said Baldwin. "I tell thee, Hugo de Lacy, that what Heaven hath wrought for the Church by thy hand, could, had it been the divine pleasure, have been achieved with as much ease by the meanest horseboy in thy host. It is *thou* that art honoured, in being the chosen instrument by which great things have been wrought in Israel.— Nay, interrupt me not—I tell thee, proud baron, that, in the sight of Heaven, thy wisdom is but as folly— thy courage, which thou dost boast, but the cowardice of a village maiden—thy strength weakness—thy spear an osier, and thy sword a bulrush."

"All this I know, good father," said the Constable, "and have ever heard it repeated when such poor services as I may have rendered are gone and past. Marry, when there was need for my helping hand, I was the very good lord of priest and prelate, and one who should be honoured and prayed for with patrons and founders who sleep in the choir and under the high altar. There was no thought, I trow, of osier or of bulrush, when I have been prayed to couch my lance or draw my weapon; it is only when they are needless that they and their owner are undervalued. Well, my reverend father, be it so,— if the Church can cast the Saracens from the Holy Land by grooms and horseboys, wherefore do you preach knights and nobles from the homes and the countries which they are born to protect and defend?"

The Archbishop looked steadily on him as he replied, "Not for the sake of their fleshly arm do we disturb your knights and barons in their prosecution of barbarous festivities, and murderous feuds, which you call enjoying their homes and protecting their domains, —not that Omnipotence requires their arm of flesh to execute the great predestined work of liberation—but for the weal of their immortal souls." These last words he pronounced with great emphasis.

The Constable paced the floor impatiently, and muttered to himself, "Such is the airy guerdon for which hosts on hosts have been drawn from Europe to drench the sands of Palestine with their gore—such the vain promises for which we are called upon to barter our country, our lands, and our lives!"

"Is it Hugo de Lacy speaks thus?" said the Archbishop, arising from his seat, and qualifying his tone of censure with the appearance of shame and of regret —"Is it he who underprizes the renown of a knight—the virtue of a Christian —the advancement of his earthly honour—the more incalculable profit of his immortal soul?—Is it he who desires a solid and substantial recompense in lands or treasures, to be won by warring on his less powerful neighbours at home, while knightly honour and religious faith, his vow as a knight and his baptism as a Christian, call him to a more glorious and more dangerous strife? —Can it be indeed Hugo de Lacy, the mirror of the Anglo-Norman chivalry, whose thoughts can conceive such sentiments, whose words can utter them?"

"Flattery and fair speech, suitably mixed with taunts and reproaches, my lord," answered the Constable, colouring and biting his lip, "may carry your point with others; but I am of a temper too solid to be either wheedled or goaded into measures of importance. Forbear, therefore, this strain of affected amazement; and believe me, that whether he goes to the Crusade or abides at home, the character of Hugo de Lacy will remain as unimpeached in point of courage as that of the Archbishop Baldwin in point of sanctitude."

"May it stand much higher," said the Archbishop, "than the reputation with which you vouchsafe to compare it! but a blaze may be extinguished as well as a spark; and I tell the Constable of Chester, that the fame which has set on his basnet for so many years, may flit from it in one moment, never to be recalled."

"Who dares to say so?" said the Constable, tremblingly alive to the honour for which he had encountered so many dangers.

"A friend," said the Prelate, "whose stripes should be received as benefits. You think of pay, Sir Constable, and of guerdon, as if you still stood in the market, free to chaffer on the terms of your service. I tell you, you are no longer your own master—you are, by the blessed badge you have voluntarily assumed, the soldier of God himself; nor can you fly from your standard without such infamy as even coistrels or grooms are unwilling to incur."

"You deal all too hardly with us, my lord," said Hugo de Lacy, stopping short in his troubled walk. "You of the spirituality make us laymen the pack-horses of your own concerns, and climb to ambitious heights by the help of our over-burdened shoulders; but all hath its limits—Becket transgressed it, and——"

A gloomy and expressive look corresponded with the tone in which he spoke this broken sentence; and the Prelate, at no loss to comprehend his meaning, replied, in a firm and determined voice, "And he was *murdered!*—that is what you dare to hint to me— even to me, the successor of that glorified saint—as a motive for complying with your fickle and selfish wish to withdraw your hand from the plough. You know not to whom you address such a threat. True, Becket, from a saint militant on earth, arrived, by the bloody path of martyrdom, to the dignity of a saint in Heaven; and no less true is it, that, to attain a seat a thousand degrees beneath that of his blessed predecessor, the unworthy Baldwin were willing to submit, under Our Lady's protection, to whatever the worst of wicked men can inflict on his earthly frame."

"There needs not this show of courage, reverend father," said Lacy, recollecting himself, "where there neither is, nor can be, danger. I pray you, let us debate this matter more deliberately. I have never meant to break off my purpose for the Holy Land, but only to postpone it. Methinks the offers that I have made are fair, and ought to obtain for me what has been granted to others in the like case—a slight delay in the time of my departure."

"A slight delay on the part of such a leader as you, noble De Lacy," answered the Prelate, "were a death-blow to our holy and most gallant enterprise. To meaner men we might have granted the privilege of marrying and giving in marriage, even although they care not for the sorrows of Jacob; but you, my lord, are a main prop of our enterprise, and, being withdrawn, the whole fabric may fall to the ground. Who in England will deem himself obliged to press forward, when Hugo de Lacy falls back? Think, my lord, less upon your plighted bride, and more on your plighted word; and believe not that a union can ever come to good, which shakes your purpose towards our blessed undertaking for the honour of Christendom."

The Constable was embarrassed by the pertinacity of the Prelate, and began to give way to his arguments, though most reluctantly, and only because the habits and opinions of the time left him no means of combating his arguments, otherwise than by solicitation. "I admit," he said, "my engagements for the Crusade, nor have I—I repeat it—farther desire than that brief interval which may be necessary to place my important affairs in order. Meanwhile, my vassals, led by my nephew——"

"Promise that which is within thy power," said the Prelate. "Who knows whether, in resentment of thy seeking after other things than HIS most holy cause, thy nephew may not be called hence, even while we speak together?"

"God forbid!" said the Baron, starting up, as if about to fly to his nephew's assistance; then suddenly pausing, he turned on the Prelate a keen and investigating glance. "It is not well," he said, "that your reverence should thus trifle with the dangers which threaten my house. Damian is dear to me for his own good qualities—dear for the sake of my only brother.—May God forgive us both! he died when we were in unkindness with each other.—My lord, your words import that my beloved nephew suffers pain and incurs danger on account of my offences?" The Archbishop perceived he had at length touched the chord to which his refractory penitent's heart-strings must needs vibrate. He replied with circumspection, as well knowing with whom he had to deal, —"Far be it from me to presume to interpret the counsels of Heaven! but we read in Scripture, that when the fathers eat sour grapes, the teeth of the children are set on edge. What so reasonable as that we should be punished for our pride and contumacy, by a judgment specially calculated to abate and bend that spirit of surquedry? You yourself best know if this disease clung to thy nephew before you had meditated defection from the banner of the Cross."

Hugo de Lacy hastily recollected himself, and found that it was indeed true, that, until he thought of his union with Eveline, there had appeared no change in his nephew's health. His silence and confusion did not escape the artful Prelate. He took the hand of the warrior as he stood before him overwhelmed in doubt, lest his preference of the continuance of his own house to the rescue of the Holy Sepulchre should have been punished by the disease which threatened his nephew's life. "Come," he said, "noble De Lacy—the judgment provoked by a moment's presumption may be even yet averted by prayer and penitence. The dial went back at the prayer of the good King Hezekiah—down, down upon thy knees, and doubt not that, with confession, and penance, and absolution, thou mayst yet atone for thy falling away from the cause of Heaven."

Borne down by the dictates of the religion in which he had been educated, and by the fears lest his delay was punished by his nephew's indisposition and danger, the Constable sunk on his knees before the Prelate, whom he had shortly before well-nigh braved, confessed, as a sin to be deeply repented of, his purpose of delaying his departure for Palestine, and received, with patience at least, if not with willing acquiescence, the penance inflicted by the Archbishop; which consisted in a prohibition to proceed farther in his proposed wedlock with the Lady Eveline, until he was returned from Palestine, where he was bound by his vow to abide for the term of three years.

"And now, noble De Lacy," said the Prelate, "once more my best beloved and most honoured friend—is not thy bosom lighter since thou hast thus nobly acquitted thee of thy debt to Heaven, and cleansed thy gallant spirit from those selfish and earthly stains which dimmed its brightness?"

The Constable sighed. "My happiest thoughts at this moment," he said, "would arise from knowledge that my nephew's health is amended."

"Be not discomforted on the score of the noble Damian, your hopeful and valorous kinsman," said the Archbishop, "for well I trust shortly ye shall hear of his recovery; or that, if it shall please God to remove him to a better world, the passage shall be so easy, and his arrival in yonder haven of bliss so speedy, that it were better for him to have died than to have lived."

The Constable looked at him, as if to gather from his countenance more certainty of his nephew's fate than his words seemed to imply; and the Prelate, to escape being farther pressed on the subject on which he was perhaps conscious he had ventured too far, rung a silver bell which stood before him on the table, and commanded the chaplain who entered at the summons, that he should despatch a careful messenger to the lodging of Damian Lacy to bring particular accounts of his health.

"A stranger," answered the chaplain, "just come from the sick chamber of the noble Damian Lacy, waits here even now to have speech of my Lord Constable."

"Admit him instantly," said the Archbishop—"my mind tells me he brings us joyful tidings.—Never knew I such humble penitence,— such willing resignation of natural affections and desires to the doing of Heaven's service, but it was rewarded with a guerdon either temporal or spiritual."

As he spoke, a man singularly dressed entered the apartment. His garments, of various colours, and showily disposed, were none of the newest or cleanest, neither were they altogether fitting for the presence in which he now stood.

"How now, sirrah!" said the Prelate; "when was it that jugglers and minstrels pressed into the company of such as we without permission?"

"So please you," said the man, "my instant business was not with your reverend lordship, but with my lord the Constable, to whom I will hope that my good news may atone for my evil apparel."

"Speak, sirrah, does my kinsman live?" said the Constable eagerly.

"And is like to live, my lord," answered the man—"a favourable crisis (so the leeches call it) hath taken place in his disorder, and they are no longer under any apprehensions for his life."

"Now, God be praised, that hath granted me so much mercy!" said the Constable.

"Amen, amen!" replied the Archbishop solemnly.—"About what period did this blessed change take place?"

"Scarcely a quarter of an hour since," said the messenger, "a soft sleep fell on the sick youth, like dew upon a parched field in summer—he breathed freely —the burning heat abated—and, as I said, the leeches no longer fear for his life."

"Marked you the hour, my Lord Constable?" said the Bishop, with exultation —"Even then you stooped to those counsels which Heaven suggested through the meanest of its servants! But two words avouching penitence—but one brief prayer—and some kind saint has interceded for an instant hearing, and a liberal granting of thy petition. Noble Hugo," he continued, grasping his hand in a species of enthusiasm, "surely Heaven designs to work high things by the hand of him whose faults are thus readily forgiven—whose prayer is thus instantly heard. For this shall *Te Deum Laudamus* be said in each church, and each convent in Gloucester, ere the world be a day older."

The Constable, no less joyful, though perhaps less able to perceive an especial providence in his nephew's recovery, expressed his gratitude to the messenger of the good tidings, by throwing him his purse.

"I thank you, noble lord," said the man; "but if I stoop to pick up this taste of your bounty, it is only to restore it again to the donor."

"How now, sir?" said the Constable, "methinks thy coat seems not so well lined as needs make thee spurn at such a guerdon."

"He that designs to catch larks, my lord," replied the messenger, "must not close his net upon sparrows—I have a greater boon to ask of your lordship, and therefore I decline your present gratuity."

"A greater boon, ha!" said the Constable,—"I am no knight-errant, to bind myself by promise to grant it ere I know its import; but do thou come to my pavilion to-morrow, and thou wilt not find me unwilling to do what is reason."

So saying, he took leave of the Prelate, and returned homeward, failing not to visit his nephew's lodging as he passed, where he received the same pleasant assurances which had been communicated by the messenger of the particoloured mantle.

CHAPTER THE NINETEENTH.

He was a minstrel—in his mood
  Was wisdom mix'd with folly;
A tame companion to the good,
But wild and fierce among the rude,
  And jovial with the jolly.
  ARCHIBALD ARMSTRONG.

The events of the preceding day had been of a nature so interesting, and latterly so harassing, that the Constable felt weary as after a severely contested battle-field, and slept soundly until the earliest beams of dawn saluted him through the opening of the tent. It was then that, with a mingled feeling of pain and satisfaction, he began to review the change which had taken place in his condition since the preceding morning. He had then risen an ardent bridegroom, anxious to find favour in the eyes of his fair bride, and scrupulous about his dress and appointments, as if he had been as young in years as in hopes and wishes. This was over, and he had now before him the painful task of leaving his betrothed for a term of years, even before wedlock had united them indissolubly, and of reflecting that she was exposed to all the dangers which assail female constancy in a situation thus critical. When the immediate anxiety for his nephew was removed, he was tempted to think that he had been something hasty in listening to the arguments of the Archbishop, and in believing that Damian's death or recovery depended upon his own accomplishing, to the letter, and without delay, his vow for the Holy Land. "How many princes and kings," he thought to himself, "have assumed the Cross, and delayed or renounced it, yet lived and died in wealth and honour, without sustaining such a visitation as that with which Baldwin threatened me; and in what case or particular did such men deserve more indulgence than I? But the die is now cast, and it signifies little to inquire whether my obedience to the mandates of the Church has saved the life of my nephew, or whether I have not fallen, as laymen are wont to fall, whenever there is an encounter of wits betwixt them and those of the spirituality. I would to God it may prove otherwise, since, girding on my sword as Heaven's champion, I might the better expect Heaven's protection for her whom I must unhappily leave behind me."

As these reflections passed through his mind, he heard the warders at the entrance of his tent challenge some one whose footsteps were heard approaching it. The person stopped on their challenge, and presently after was heard the sound of a rote, (a small species of lute,) the strings of which were managed by means of a small wheel. After a short prelude, a manly voice, of good compass, sung verses, which, translated into modern language, might run nearly thus:

I.

"Soldier, wake—the day is peeping:,
Honour ne'er was won in sleeping,
Never when the sunbeams still
Lay unreflected on the hill:
'Tis when they are glinted back
From axe and armour, spear and jack,
That they promise future story
Many a page of deathless glory.
Shields that are the foe man's terror,
Ever are the morning's mirror.

II.

"Arm and up—the morning beam
Hath call'd the rustic to his team,
Hath call'd the falc'ner to the lake,
Hath call'd the huntsman to the brake;
The early student ponders o'er
His dusty tomes of ancient lore.
Soldier, wake—thy harvest, fame;
Thy study, conquest; war, thy game.
Shield, that would be foeman's terror,
Still should gleam the morning's mirror.

III.

"Poor hire repays the rustic's pain;
More paltry still the sportsman's gain;
Vainest of all, the student's theme
End in gome metaphysic dream.
Yet each is up, and each has toil'd
Since first the peep of dawn has smiled;
And each is eagerer in his aim
Than he who barters life for fame.
Up, up, and arm thee, son of terror!

Be thy bright shield the morning's mirror."

When the song was finished, the Constable heard some talking without, and presently Philip Guarine entered the pavilion to tell that a person, come hither as he said by the Constable's appointment, waited permission to speak with him.

"By my appointment?" said De Lacy; "admit him immediately."

The messenger of the preceding evening entered the tent, holding in one hand his small cap and feather, in the other the rote on which he had been just playing. His attire was fantastic, consisting of more than one inner dress of various colours, all of the brightest and richest dyes, and disposed so as to contrast with each other—the upper garment was a very short Norman cloak, in bright green. An embroidered girdle sustained, in lieu of offensive weapons, an inkhorn with its appurtenances on the one side, on the other a knife for the purposes of the table. His hair was cut in imitation of the clerical tonsure, which was designed to intimate that he had arrived to a certain rank in his profession; for the Joyous Science, as the profession of minstrelsy was termed, had its various ranks, like the degrees in the church and in chivalry. The features and the manners of the man seemed to be at variance with his profession and habit; for, as the latter was gay and fantastic, the former had a cast of gravity, and almost of sternness, which, unless when kindled by the enthusiasm of his poetical and musical exertions, seemed rather to indicate deep reflection, than the thoughtless vivacity of observation which characterized most of his brethren. His countenance, though not handsome, had therefore something in it striking and impressive, even from its very contrast with the particoloured hues and fluttering shape of his vestments; and the Constable felt something inclined to patronize him, as he said, "Good-morrow, friend, and I thank thee for thy morning greeting; it was well sung and well meant, for when we call forth any one to bethink him how time passes, we do him the credit of supposing that he can employ to advantage that flitting treasure."

The man, who had listened in silence, seemed to pause and make an effort ere he replied, "My intentions, at least, were good, when I ventured to disturb my lord thus early; and I am glad to learn that my boldness hath not been evil received at his hand."

"True," said the Constable, "you had a boon to ask of me. Be speedy, and say thy request—my leisure is short."

"It is for permission to follow you to the Holy Land, my lord," said the man.

"Thou hast asked what I can hardly grant, my friend," answered De Lacy —"Thou art a minstrel, art thou not?"

"An unworthy graduate of the Gay Science, my lord," said the musician; "yet let me say for myself, that I will not yield to the king of minstrels, Geoffrey Rudel, though the King of England hath given him four manors for one song. I would be willing to contend with him in romance, lay, or fable, were the judge to be King Henry himself."

"You have your own good word, doubtless," said De Lacy; "nevertheless, Sir Minstrel, thou goest not with me. The Crusade has been already too much encumbered by men of thy idle profession; and if thou dost add to the number, it shall not be under my protection. I am too old to be charmed by thy art, charm thou never so wisely."

"He that is young enough to seek for, and to win, the love of beauty," said the minstrel, but in a submissive tone, as if fearing his freedom might give offence, "should not term himself too old to feel the charms of minstrelsy."

The Constable smiled, not insensible to the flattery which assigned to him the character of a younger gallant. "Thou art a jester," he said, "I warrant me, in addition to thy other qualities."

"No," replied the minstrel, "it is a branch of our profession which I have for some time renounced—my fortunes have put me out of tune for jesting."

"Nay, comrade," said the Constable, "if thou hast been hardly dealt within the world, and canst comply with the rules of a family so strictly ordered as mine, it is possible we may agree together better than I thought. What is thy name and country? thy speech, methinks, sounds somewhat foreign."

"I am an Armorican, my lord, from the merry shores of Morbihan; and hence my tongue hath some touch of my country speech. My name is Renault Vidal."

"Such being the case, Renault," said the Constable, "thou shalt follow me, and I will give orders to the master of my household to have thee attired something according to thy function, but in more orderly guise than thou now appearest in. Dost thou understand the use of a weapon?"

"Indifferently, my lord," said the Armorican; at the same time taking a sword from the wall, he drew, and made a pass with it so close to the Constable's body as he sat on the couch, that he started up, crying, "Villain, forbear!"

"La you! noble sir," replied Vidal, lowering with all submission the point of his weapon—"I have already given you a proof of sleight which has alarmed even your experience—I have an hundred other besides."

"It may be so," said De Lacy, somewhat ashamed at having shown himself moved by the sudden and lively action of the juggler; "but I love not jesting with edge-tools, and have too much to do with sword and sword-blows in earnest, to toy with them; so I pray you let us have no more of this, but call me my squire and my chamberlain, for I am about to array me and go to mass."

The religious duties of the morning performed, it was the Constable's intention to visit the Lady Abbess, and communicate, with the necessary precautions and qualifications, the altered relations in which he was placed towards her niece, by the resolution he had been compelled to adopt, of departing for the Crusade before accomplishing his marriage, in the terms of the precontract already entered into. He was conscious that it would be difficult to reconcile the good lady to this change of measures, and he delayed some time ere he could think of the best mode of communicating and softening the unpleasant intelligence. An interval was also spent in a visit to his nephew, whose state of convalescence continued to be as favourable, as if in truth it had been a miraculous consequence of the Constable's having complied with the advice of the Archbishop.

From the lodging of Damian, the Constable proceeded to the convent of the Benedictine Abbess. But she had been already made acquainted with the circumstances which he came to communicate, by a still earlier visit from the Archbishop Baldwin himself. The Primate had undertaken the office of mediator on this occasion, conscious that his success of the evening before must have placed the Constable in a delicate situation with the relations of his betrothed bride, and willing, by his countenance and authority, to reconcile the disputes which might ensue. Perhaps he had better have left Hugo de Lacy to plead his own cause; for the Abbess, though she listened to the communication with all the respect due to the highest dignitary of the English Church, drew consequences from the Constable's change of resolution which the Primate had not expected. She ventured to oppose no obstacle to De Lacy's accomplishment of his vows, but strongly argued that the contract with her niece should be entirely set aside, and each, party left at liberty to form a new choice.

It was in vain that the Archbishop endeavoured to dazzle the Abbess with the future honours to be won by the Constable in the Holy Land; the splendour of which would attach not to his lady alone, but to all in the remotest degree allied to or connected with her. All his eloquence was to no purpose, though upon so favourite a topic he exerted it to the utmost. The Abbess, it is true, remained silent for a moment after his arguments had been exhausted, but it was only to consider how she should intimate in a suitable and reverent manner, that children, the usual attendants of a happy union, and the existence of which she looked to for the continuation of the house of her father and brother, could not be hoped for with any probability, unless the precontract was followed by marriage, and the residence of the married parties in the same country. She therefore insisted, that the Constable having altered his intentions in this most important particular, the *fiancailles* should be entirely abrogated and set aside; and she demanded of the Primate, as an act of justice, that, as he had interfered to prevent the bridegroom's execution of his original purpose, he should now assist with his influence wholly to dissolve an engagement which had been thus materially innovated upon.

The Primate, who was sensible he had himself occasioned De Lacy's breach of contract, felt himself bound in honour and reputation to prevent consequences so disagreeable to his friend, as the dissolution of an engagement in which his interest and inclinations were alike concerned. He reproved the Lady Abbess for the carnal and secular views which she, a dignitary of the church, entertained upon the subject of matrimony, and concerning the interest of her house. He even upbraided her with selfishly preferring the continuation of the line of Berenger to the recovery of the Holy Sepulchre, and denounced to her that Heaven would be avenged of the shortsighted and merely human policy, which postponed the interests of Christendom to those of an individual family.

After this severe homily, the Prelate took his departure, leaving the Abbess highly incensed, though she prudently forbore returning any irreverent answer to his paternal admonition.

In this humour the venerable lady was found by the Constable himself, when with some embarrassment, he proceeded to explain to her the necessity of his present departure for Palestine.

She received the communication with sullen dignity; her ample black robe and scapular seeming, as it were, to swell out in yet prouder folds as she listened to the reasons and the emergencies which compelled the Constable of Chester to defer the marriage which he avowed was the dearest wish of his heart, until after his return from the Crusade, for which he was about to set forth.

"Methinks," replied the Abbess, with much coldness, "if this communication is meant for earnest,—and it were no fit business— I myself no fit person,—for jesting with—methinks the Constable's resolution should have been proclaimed to us yesterday before the *fiancailles* had united his troth with that of Eveline Berenger, under expectations very different from those which he now announces."

"On the word of a knight and a gentleman, reverend lady," said the Constable, "I had not then the slightest thought that I should be called upon to take a step no less distressing to me, than, as I see with pain, it is unpleasing to you."

"I can scarcely conceive," replied the Abbess, "the cogent reasons, which, existing as they must have done yesterday, have nevertheless delayed their operation until to-day."

"I own," said De Lacy, reluctantly, "that I entertained too ready hopes of obtaining a remission from my vow, which my Lord of Canterbury hath, in his zeal for Heaven's service, deemed it necessary to refuse me."

"At least, then," said the Abbess, veiling her resentment under the appearance of extreme coldness, "your lordship will do us the justice to place us in the same situation in which we stood yesterday morning; and, by joining with my niece and her friends in desiring the abrogation of a marriage contract, entered into with very different views from those which you now entertain, put a young person in that state of liberty of which she is at present deprived by her contract with you."

"Ah, madam!" said the Constable, "what do you ask of me? and in a tone how cold and indifferent do you demand me to resign hopes, the dearest which my bosom ever entertained since the life-blood warmed it!"

"I am unacquainted with language belonging to such feelings, my lord," replied the Abbess; "but methinks the prospects which could be so easily adjourned for years, might, by a little, and a very little, farther self-control, be altogether abandoned."

Hugo de Lacy paced the room in agitation, nor did he answer until after a considerable pause. "If your niece, madam, shares the sentiments which you have expressed, I could not, indeed, with justice to her, or perhaps to myself, desire to retain that interest in her, which our solemn espousals have given me. But I must know my doom from her own lips; and if it is as severe as that which your expressions lead me to fear, I will go to Palestine the better soldier of Heaven, that I shall have little left on earth that can interest me."

The Abbess, without farther answer, called on her Praecentrix, and desired her to command her niece's attendance immediately. The Praecentrix bowed reverently, and withdrew.

"May I presume to inquire," said De Lacy, "whether the Lady Eveline hath been possessed of the circumstances which have occasioned this unhappy alteration in my purpose?"

"I have communicated the whole to her from point to point," said the Abbess, "even as it was explained to me this morning by my Lord of Canterbury, (for with him I have already spoken upon the subject,) and confirmed but now by your lordship's own mouth."

"I am little obliged to the Archbishop," said the Constable, "for having forestalled my excuses in the quarter where it was most important for me that they should be accurately stated, and favourably received."

"That," said the Abbess, "is but an item of the account betwixt you and the

Prelate,—it concerns not us."

"Dare I venture to hope," continued De Lacy, without taking offence at the dryness of the Abbess's manner, "that Lady Eveline has heard this most unhappy change of circumstances without emotion,—I would say, without displeasure?"

"She is the daughter of a Berenger, my lord," answered the Abbess, "and it is our custom to punish a breach of faith or to contemn it—never to grieve over it. What my niece may do in this case, I know not. I am a woman of religion, sequestered from the world, and would advise peace and Christian forgiveness, with a proper sense of contempt for the unworthy treatment which she has received. She has followers and vassals, and friends, doubtless, and advisers, who may not, in blinded zeal for worldly honour, recommend to her to sit down slightly with this injury, but desire she should rather appeal to the King, or to the arms of her father's followers, unless her liberty is restored to her by the surrender of the contract into which she has been enticed.—But she comes, to answer for herself."

Eveline entered at the moment, leaning on Rose's arm. She had laid aside mourning since the ceremony of the *fiancailles*, and was dressed in a kirtle of white, with an upper robe of pale blue. Her head was covered with a veil of white gauze, so thin, as to float about her like the misty cloud usually painted around the countenance of a seraph. But the face of Eveline, though in beauty not unworthy one of that angelic order, was at present far from resembling that of a seraph in tranquillity of expression. Her limbs trembled, her cheeks were pale, the tinge of red around the eyelids expressed recent tears; yet amidst these natural signs of distress and uncertainty, there was an air of profound resignation—a resolution to discharge her duty in every emergence reigning in the solemn expression of her eye and eyebrow, and showing her prepared to govern the agitation which she could not entirely subdue. And so well were these opposing qualities of timidity and resolution mingled on her cheek, that Eveline, in the utmost pride of her beauty, never looked more fascinating than at that instant; and Hugo de Lacy, hitherto rather an unimpassioned lover, stood in her presence with feelings as if all the exaggerations of romance were realized, and his mistress were a being of a higher sphere, from whose doom he was to receive happiness or misery, life or death.

It was under the influence of such a feeling, that the warrior dropped on one knee before Eveline, took the hand which she rather resigned than gave to him, pressed it to his lips fervently, and, ere he parted with it, moistened it with one of the few tears which he was ever known to shed. But, although surprised, and carried out of his character by a sudden impulse, he regained his composure on observing that the Abbess regarded his humiliation, if it can be so termed, with an air of triumph; and he entered on his defence before Eveline with a manly earnestness, not devoid of fervour, nor free from agitation, yet made in a tone of firmness and pride, which seemed assumed to meet and control that of the offended Abbess.

"Lady," he said, addressing Eveline, "you have heard from the venerable Abbess in what unhappy position I have been placed since yesterday by the rigour of the Archbishop—perhaps I should rather say by his just though severe interpretation of my engagement in the Crusade. I cannot doubt that all this has been stated with accurate truth by the venerable lady; but as I must no longer call her my friend, let me fear whether she has done me justice in her commentary upon the unhappy necessity which must presently compel me to leave my country, and with my country to forego—at best to postpone—the fairest hopes which man ever entertained. The venerable lady hath upbraided me, that being myself the cause that the execution of yesterday's contract is postponed, I would fain keep it suspended over your head for an indefinite term of years. No one resigns willingly such rights as yesterday gave me; and, let me speak a boastful word, sooner than yield them up to man of woman born, I would hold a fair field against all comers, with grinded sword and sharp spear, from sunrise to sunset, for three days' space. But what I would retain at the price of a thousand lives, I am willing to renounce if it would cost you a single sigh. If, therefore, you think you cannot remain happy as the betrothed of De Lacy, you may command my assistance to have the contract annulled, and make some more fortunate man happy."

He would have gone on, but felt the danger of being overpowered again by those feelings of tenderness so new to his steady nature, that he blushed to give way to them.

Eveline remained silent. The Abbess took the word. "Kinswoman," she said, "you hear that the generosity—or the justice—of the Constable of Chester, proposes, in consequence of his departure upon a distant and perilous expedition, to cancel a contract entered into upon the specific and precise understanding that he was to remain in England for its fulfilment. You cannot, methinks, hesitate to accept of the freedom which he offers you, with thanks for his bounty. For my part, I will reserve mine own, until I shall see that your joint application is sufficient to win to your purpose his Grace of Canterbury, who may again interfere with the actions of his friend the Lord Constable, over whom he has already exerted so much influence—for the weal, doubtless, of his spiritual concerns."

"If it is meant by your words, venerable lady," said the Constable, "that I have any purpose of sheltering myself behind the Prelate's authority, to avoid doing that which I proclaim my readiness, though not my willingness, to do, I can only say, that you are the first who has doubted the faith of Hugo de Lacy."— And while the proud Baron thus addressed a female and a recluse, he could not prevent his eye from sparkling, and his cheek from flushing.

"My gracious and venerable kinswoman," said Eveline, summoning together her resolution, "and you, my kind lord, be not offended if I pray you not to increase by groundless suspicions and hasty resentments your difficulties and mine. My lord, the obligations which I lie under to you are such as I can never discharge, since they comprehend fortune, life, and honour. Know that, in my anguish of mind, when besieged by the Welsh in my castle of the Garde Doloureuse, I vowed to the Virgin, that (my honour safe) I would place myself at the disposal of him whom our Lady should employ as her instrument to relieve me from yonder hour of agony. In giving me a deliverer, she gave me a master; nor could I desire a more noble one than Hugo de Lacy."

"God forbid, lady," said the Constable, speaking eagerly, as if he was afraid his resolution should fail ere he could get the renunciation uttered, "that I should, by such a tie, to which you subjected yourself in the extremity of your distress, bind you to any resolution in my favour which can put force on your own inclinations!"

The Abbess herself could not help expressing her applause of this sentiment, declaring it was spoken like a Norman gentleman; but at the same time, her eyes, turned towards her niece, seemed to exhort her to beware how she declined to profit by the candour of De Lacy.

But Eveline proceeded, with her eyes fixed on the ground, and a slight colour overspreading her face, to state her own sentiments, without listening to the suggestions of any one. "I will own, noble sir," she said, "that when your valour had rescued me from approaching destruction, I could have wished— honouring and respecting you, as I had done your late friend, my excellent father—that you could have accepted a daughter's service from me. I do not pretend entirely to have surmounted these sentiments, although I have combated them, as being unworthy of me, and ungrateful to you. But, from the moment you were pleased to honour me by a claim on this poor hand, I have studiously examined my sentiments towards you, and taught myself so far to make them coincide with my duty, that I may call myself assured that De Lacy would not find in Eveline Berenger an indifferent, far less an unworthy bride. In this, sir, you may boldly confide, whether the union you have sought for takes place instantly, or is delayed till a longer season. Still farther, I must acknowledge that the postponement of these nuptials will be more agreeable to me than their immediate accomplishment. I am at present very young, and totally inexperienced. Two or three years will, I trust, render me yet more worthy the regard of a man of honour."

At this declaration in his favour, however cold and qualified, De Lacy had as much difficulty to restrain his transports as formerly to moderate his agitation.

"Angel of bounty and of kindness!" he said, kneeling once more, and again possessing himself of her hand, "perhaps I ought in honour to resign voluntarily those hopes which you decline to ravish from me forcibly. But who could be capable of such unrelenting magnanimity?—Let me hope that my devoted attachment— that which you shall hear of me when at a distance— that which you shall know of me when near you—may give to your sentiments a more tender warmth than they now express; and, in the meanwhile, blame me not that I accept your plighted faith anew, under the conditions which you attach to it. I am conscious my wooing has been too late in life to expect the animated returns proper to youthful passion—Blame me not if I remain satisfied with those calmer sentiments which make life happy, though they cannot make possession rapturous. Your hand remains In my grasp, but it acknowledges not my pressure—Can it be that it refuses to ratify what your lips have said?"

"Never, noble De Lacy!" said Eveline, with more animation than she had yet expressed; and it appeared that the tone was at length sufficiently encouraging, since her lover was emboldened to take the lips themselves for guarantee.

It was with an air of pride, mingled with respect, that, after having received this pledge of fidelity, he turned to conciliate and to appease the offended Abbess. "I trust, venerable mother," he said, "that you will resume your former kind thoughts of me, which I am aware were only interrupted by your tender anxiety for the interest of her who should be dearest to us both. Let me hope that I may leave this fair flower under protection of the honoured lady who is her nest in blood, happy and secure as she must ever be, while listening to your counsels, and residing within these sacred walls."

But the Abbess was too deeply displeased to be propitiated by a compliment, which perhaps it had been better policy to have delayed till a calmer season. "My lord," she said, "and you, fair kinswoman, you ought needs to be aware how little my counsels—not frequently given where they are unwillingly listened to—can be of avail to those embarked in worldly affairs. I am a woman dedicated to religion, to solitude, and seclusion—to the service, in brief, of Our Lady and Saint Benedict. I have been already censured by my superior because I have, for love of you, fair niece, mixed more deeply in secular affairs than became the head of a convent of recluses—I will merit no farther blame on such an account; nor can you expect it of me. My brother's daughter, unfettered by worldly ties, had been the welcome sharer of my poor solitude. But this house is too mean for the residence of the vowed bride of a mighty baron; nor do I, in my lowliness and inexperience, feel fitness to exercise over such an one that authority, which must belong to me over every one whom this roof protects. The grave tenor of our devotions, and the serener contemplation to which the females of this house are devoted," continued the Abbess, with increasing heat and vehemence, "shall not, for the sake of my worldly connections, be disturbed by the intrusion of one whose thoughts must needs be on the worldly toys of love and marriage."

"I do indeed believe, reverend mother," said the Constable, in his turn giving way to displeasure, "that a richly-dowered maiden, unwedded, and unlikely to wed, were a fitter and more welcome inmate to the convent, than one who cannot be separated from the world, and whose wealth is not likely to increase the House's revenues."

The Constable did the Abbess great injury in this hasty insinuation, and it only went to confirm her purpose of rejecting all charge of her niece during his absence. She was in truth as disinterested as haughty; and her only reason for anger against her niece was, that her advice had not been adopted without hesitation, although the matter regarded Eveline's happiness exclusively.

The ill-timed reflection of the Constable confirmed her in the resolution which she had already, and hastily adopted. "May Heaven forgive you, Sir Knight," she replied, "your injurious thoughts of His servants! It is indeed time, for your soul's sake, that you do penance in the Holy Land, having such rash judgments to repent of.—For you, my niece, you cannot want that hospitality, which, without verifying, or seeming to verify, unjust suspicions, I cannot now grant to you, while you have, in your kinswoman of Baldringham, a secular relation, whose nearness of blood approaches mine, and who may open her gates to you without incurring the unworthy censure, that she means to enrich herself at your cost."

The Constable saw the deadly paleness which, came over Eveline's cheek at this proposal, and, without knowing the cause of her repugnance, he hastened to relieve her from the apprehensions which she seemed evidently to entertain. "No, reverend mother," he said, "since *you* so harshly reject the care of your kinswoman, she shall not be a burden to any of her other relatives. While Hugo de Lacy hath six gallant castles, and many a manor besides, to maintain fire upon their hearths, his betrothed bride shall burden no one with her society, who may regard it as otherwise than a great honour; and methinks I were much poorer than Heaven hath made me, could I not furnish friends and followers sufficient to serve, obey, and protect her."

"No, my lord," said Eveline, recovering from the dejection into which she had been thrown by the unkindness of her relative; "since some unhappy destiny separates me from the protection of my father's sister, to whom I could so securely have resigned myself, I will neither apply for shelter to any more distant relation, nor accept of that which you, my lord, so generously offer; since my doing so might excite harsh, and, I am sure, undeserved reproaches, against her by whom I was driven to choose a less advisable dwelling-place. I have made my resolution. I have, it is true, only one friend left, but she is a powerful one, and is able to protect me against the particular evil fate which seems to follow me, as well as against the ordinary evils of human life."

"The Queen, I suppose?" said the Abbess, interrupting her impatiently.

"The Queen of Heaven! venerable kinswoman," answered Eveline; "our Lady of the Garde Doloureuse, ever gracious to our house, and so lately my especial guardian and protectress. Methinks, since the vowed votaress of the Virgin rejects me, it is to her holy patroness whom I ought to apply for succour."

The venerable dame, taken somewhat at unawares by this answer, pronounced the interjection "Umph!" in a tone better befitting a Lollard or an Iconoclast, than a Catholic Abbess, and a daughter of the House of Berenger. Truth is, the Lady Abbess's hereditary devotion to the Lady of the Garde Doloureuse was much decayed since she had known the full merits of another gifted image, the property of her own convent.

Recollecting herself, however, she remained silent, while the Constable alleged the vicinity of the Welsh, as what might possibly again render the abode of his betrothed bride at the Garde Doloureuse as perilous as she had on a former occasion found it. To this Eveline replied, by reminding him of the great strength of her native fortress—the various sieges which it had withstood—and the important circumstance, that, upon the late occasion, it was only endangered, because, in compliance with a point of honour, her father Raymond had sallied out with the garrison, and fought at disadvantage a battle under the walls. She farther suggested, that it was easy for the Constable to name, from among his own vassals or hers, a seneschal of such approved prudence and valour, as might ensure the safety of the place, and of its lady.

Ere De Lacy could reply to her arguments the Abbess rose, and, pleading her total inability to give counsel in secular affairs, and the rules of her order, which called her, as she said, with a heightened colour and raised voice, "to the simple and peaceful discharge of her conventual duties," she left the betrothed parties in the locutory, or parlour, without any company, save Rose, who prudently remained at some distance.

The issue of their private conference seemed agreeable to both; and when Eveline told Rose that they were to return presently to the Garde Doloureuse, under a sufficient escort, and were to remain there during the period of the Crusade, it was in a tone of heartfelt satisfaction, which her follower had not heard her make use of for many days. She spoke also highly in praise of the kind acquiescence of the Constable in her wishes, and of his whole conduct, with a warmth of gratitude approaching to a more tender feeling.

"And yet, my dearest lady," said Rose, "if you will speak unfeignedly, you must, I am convinced, allow that you look upon this interval of years, interposed betwixt your contract and your marriage, rather as a respite than in any other light."

"I confess it," said Eveline, "nor have I concealed from, my future lord that such are my feelings, ungracious as they may seem. But it is my youth, Rose, my extreme youth, which makes me fear the duties of De Lacy's wife. Then those evil auguries hang strangely about me. Devoted to evil by one kinswoman, expelled almost from the roof of another, I seem to myself, at present, a creature who must carry distress with her, pass where she will. This evil hour, and, what is more, the apprehensions of it, will give way to time. When I shall have attained the age of twenty, Rose, I shall be a full-grown woman, with all the soul of a Berenger strong within me, to overcome those doubts and tremors which agitate the girl of seventeen."

"Ah! my sweet mistress," answered Rose, "may God and our Lady of the Garde Doloureuse guide all for the best!—But I would that this contract had not taken place, or, having taken place, that it could have been fulfilled by your immediate union."

CHAPTER THE TWENTIETH

The Kiugr call'd down his merry men all,
By one, and by two, and three;
Earl Marshal was wont to be the foremost man,
But the hindmost man was he.
OLD BALLAD.

If the Lady Eveline retired satisfied and pleased from her private interview with De Lacy, the joy on the part of the Constable rose to a higher pitch of rapture than he was in the habit of feeling or expressing; and it was augmented by a visit of the leeches who attended his nephew, from whom he received a minute and particular account of his present disorder, with every assurance of a speedy recovery.

The Constable caused alms to be distributed to the convents and to the poor, masses to be said, and tapers to be lighted. He visited the Archbishop, and received from him his full approbation of the course which he proposed to pursue, with the promise, that out of the plenary power which he held from the

Pope, the Prelate was willing, in consideration of his instant obedience, to limit his stay in the Holy Land to the term of three years, to become current from his leaving Britain, and to include the space necessary for his return to his native country. Indeed, having succeeded in the main point, the Archbishop judged it wise to concede every inferior consideration to a person of the Constable's rank and character, whose good-will to the proposed expedition was perhaps as essential to its success as his bodily presence.

In short, the Constable returned to his pavilion highly satisfied with the manner in which he had extricated himself from those difficulties which in the morning seemed almost insuperable; and when his officers assembled to disrobe him, (for great feudal lords had their levees and couchees, in imitation of sovereign princes,) he distributed gratuities amongst them, and jested and laughed in a much gayer humour than they had ever before witnessed.

"For thee," he said, turning to Vidal the minstrel, who, sumptuously dressed, stood to pay his respects among the other attendants, "I will give thee nought at present; but do thou remain by my bedside until I am asleep, and I will next morning reward thy minstrelsy as I like it."

"My lord," said Vidal, "I am already rewarded, both by the honour, and by the liveries, which better befit a royal minstrel than one of my mean fame; but assign me a subject, and I will do my best, not out of greed of future largess, but gratitude for past favours."

"Gramercy, good fellow," said the Constable. "Guarine," he added, addressing his squire, "let the watch be posted, and do thou remain within the tent— stretch thyself on the bear-hide, and sleep, or listen to the minstrelsy, as thou likest best. Thou thinkest thyself a judge, I have heard, of such gear."

It was usual, in those insecure times, for some faithful domestic to sleep at night within the tent of every great baron, that, if danger arose, he might not be unsupported or unprotected. Guarine accordingly drew his sword, and, taking it in his hand, stretched himself on the ground in such a manner, that, on the slightest alarm, he could spring up, sword in hand. His broad black eyes, in which sleep contended with a desire to listen to the music, were fixed on Vidal, who saw them glittering in the reflection of the silver lamp, like those of a dragon or a basilisk.

After a few preliminary touches on the chords of his rote, the minstrel requested of the Constable to name the subject on which he desired the exercise of his powers.

"The truth of woman," answered Hugo de Lacy, as he laid his head upon his pillow.

After a short prelude, the minstrel obeyed, by singing nearly as follows:—

"Woman's faith, and woman's trust—
Write the characters in dust;
Stamp them on the running stream,
Print them on the moon's pale best,
And each evanescent letter,
Shall be clearer, firmer, better,
And more permanent, I ween,
Than the thing those letters mean.

I have strain'd the spider's thread
'Gainst the promise of a maid;
I have weigh'd a grain of sand
'Gainst her plight of heart and hand;
I told my true love of the token,
How her faith proved light, and her word was broken
Again her word and truth she plight,
And I believed them again ere night."

"How now, sir knave," said the Constable, raising himself on his elbow, from what drunken rhymer did you learn that half-witted satire?"

"From an old, ragged, crossgrained friend of mine, called Experience," answered Vidal. "I pray Heaven, he may never take your lordship, or any other worthy man, under his tuition."

"Go to, fellow," said the Constable, in reply; "thou art one of those wiseacres, I warrant me, that would fain be thought witty, because thou canst make a jest of those things which wiser men hold worthy of most worship-the honour of men, and the truth of women. Dost thou call thyself a minstrel, and hast no tale of female fidelity?"

"I had right many a one, noble sir, but I laid them aside when I disused my practice of the jesting part of the Joyous Science. Nevertheless, if it pleases your nobleness to listen, I can sing you an established lay upon such a subject."

De Lacy made a sign of acquiescence, and laid himself as if to slumber; while Vidal began one of those interminable and almost innumerable adventures concerning that paragon of true lovers, fair Ysolte; and of the constant and uninterrupted faith and affection which she displayed in numerous situations of difficulty and peril, to her paramour, the gallant Sir Tristrem, at the expense of her less favoured husband, the luckless King Mark of Cornwall; to whom, as all the world knows, Sir Tristrem was nephew.

This was not the lay of love and fidelity which De Lacy would have chosen; but a feeling like shame prevented his interrupting it, perhaps because he was unwilling to yield to or acknowledge the unpleasing sensations excited by the tenor of the tale. He soon fell asleep, or feigned to do so; and the harper, continuing for a time his monotonous chant, began at length himself to feel the influence of slumber; his words, and the notes which he continued to touch upon the harp, were broken and interrupted, and seemed to escape drowsily from his fingers and voice. At length the sounds ceased entirely, and the minstrel seemed to have sunk into profound repose, with his head reclining on his breast, and one arm dropped down by his side, while the other rested on his harp. His slumber, however, was not very long, and when he awoke from it, and cast his eyes around him, reconnoitering, by the light of the night-lamp, whatever was in the tent, he felt a heavy hand, which pressed his shoulder as if gently to solicit his attention. At the same time the voice of the vigilant Philip Guarine whispered in his ear, "Thine office for the night is ended—depart to thine own quarters with all the silence thou mayst."

The minstrel wrapt himself in his cloak without reply, though perhaps not without feeling some resentment at a dismissal so unceremonious.

CHAPTER THE TWENTY-FIRST.

Oh! then I see Queen Mab has been with you.
  ROMEO AND JULIET.

The subject on which the mind has last been engaged at night is apt to occupy our thoughts even during slumber, when Imagination, uncorrected by the organs of sense, weaves her own fantastic web out of whatever ideas rise at random in the sleeper. It is not surprising, therefore, that De Lacy in his dreams had some confused idea of being identified with the unlucky Mark of Cornwall; and that he awakened from such unpleasant visions with a brow more clouded than when he was preparing for his couch on the evening before. He was silent, and seemed lost in thought, while his squire assisted at his levee with the respect now only paid to sovereigns. "Guarine," at length he said, "know you the stout Fleming, who was said to have borne him so well at the siege of the Garde Doloureuse?—a tall, big, brawny man."

"Surely, my lord," answered his squire; "I know Wilkin Flammock—I saw him but yesterday."

"Indeed!" replied the Constable—"Here, meanest thou?—In this city of Gloucester?"

"Assuredly, my good lord. He came hither partly about his merchandise, partly, I think, to see his daughter Rose, who is in attendance on the gracious young Lady Eveline."

"He is a stout soldier, is he not?"

"Like most of his kind—a rampart to a castle, but rubbish in the field," said the Norman squire.

"Faithful, also, is he not?" continued the Constable.

"Faithful as most Flemings, while you can pay for their faith," replied Guarine, wondering a little at the unusual interest taken in one whom he esteemed a being of an inferior order; when, after some farther inquiries, the Constable ordered the Fleming's attendance to be presently commanded.

Other business of the morning now occurred, (for his speedy departure required many arrangements to be hastily adopted,) when, as the Constable was giving audience to several officers of his troops, the bulky figure of Wilkin Flammock was seen at the entrance of the pavilion, in jerkin of white cloth, and having only a knife by his side.

"Leave the tent, my masters," said De Lacy, "but continue in attendance in the neighbourhood; for here comes one I must speak to in private." The officers withdrew, and the Constable and Fleming were left alone. "You are Wilkin Mammock, who fought well against the Welsh at the Garde Doloureuse?"

"I did my best, my lord," answered Wilkin—"I was bound to it by my bargain; and I hope ever to act like a man of credit."

"Methinks" said the Constable, "that you, so stout of limb, and, as I hear, so bold in spirit, might look a little higher than this weaving trade of thine."

"No one is reluctant to mend his station, my lord," said Wilkin; "yet I am so far from complaining of mine, that I would willingly consent it should never be better, on condition I could be assured it were never worse."

"Nay, but, Flammock," said the Constable, "I mean higher things for you than your modesty apprehends—I mean to leave thee in a charge of great trust."

"Let it concern bales of drapery, my lord, and no one will perform it better," said the Fleming.

"Away! thou art too lowly minded," said the Constable. "What think'st thou of being dubbed knight, as thy valour well deserves, and left as Chattelain of the Garde Doloureuse?"

"For the knighthood, my lord, I should crave your forgiveness; for it would sit on me like a gilded helmet on a hog. For any charge, whether of castle or cottage, I trust I might discharge it as well as another."

"I fear me thy rank must be in some way mended," said the Constable, surveying the unmilitary dress of the figure before him; "it is at present too mean to befit the protector and guardian of a young lady of high birth and rank."

"I the guardian of a young lady of birth and rank!" said Flammock, his light large eyes turning larger, lighter, and rounder as he spoke.

"Even thou," said the Constable. "The Lady Eveline proposes to take up her residence in her castle of the Garde Doloureuse. I have been casting about to whom I may intrust the keeping of her person as well as of the stronghold. Were I to choose some knight of name, as I have many in my household, he would be setting about to do deeds of vassalage upon the Welsh, and engaging himself in turmoils, which would render the safety of the castle precarious; or he would be absent on feats of chivalry, tournaments, and hunting parties; or he would, perchance, have shows of that light nature under the walls, or even within the courts of the castle, turning the secluded and quiet abode, which becomes the situation of the Lady Eveline, into the misrule of a dissolute revel.—Thee I can confide in—thou wilt fight when it is requisite, yet wilt not provoke danger for the sake of danger itself—thy birth, thy habits, will lead thee to avoid those gaieties, which, however fascinating to others, cannot but be distasteful to thee—thy management will be as regular, as I will take care that it shall be honourable; and thy relation to her favourite, Rose, will render thy guardianship more agreeable to the Lady Eveline, than, perchance, one of her own rank—And, to speak to thee a language which, thy nation readily comprehends, the reward, Fleming, for the regular discharge of this most weighty trust, shall be beyond thy most flattering hope."

The Fleming had listened to the first part of this discourse with an expression of surprise, which gradually gave way to one of deep and anxious reflection. He gazed fixedly on the earth for a minute after the Constable had ceased speaking, and then raising up his eyes suddenly, said, "It is needless to seek for round-about excuses. This cannot be your earnest, my lord—but if it is, the scheme is naught."

"How and wherefore?" asked the Constable, with displeased surprise.

"Another man may grasp at your bounty," continued Wilkin, "and leave you to take chance of the value you were to receive for it; but I am a downright dealer, I will not take payment for service I cannot render."

"But I demand, once more, wherefore thou canst not, or rather wilt not, accept this trust?" said the Constable. "Surely, if I am willing to confer such confidence, it is well thy part to answer it."

"True, my lord," said the Fleming; "but methinks the noble Lord de Lacy should feel, and the wise Lord de Lacy should foresee, that a Flemish weaver is no fitting guardian for his plighted bride. Think her shut up in yonder solitary castle, under such respectable protection, and reflect how long the place will be solitary in this land of love and of adventure! We shall have minstrels singing ballads by the threave under our windows, and such twangling of harps as would be enough to frighten our walls from their foundations, as clerks say happened to those of Jericho—We shall have as many knights-errant around us as ever had Charlemagne, or King Arthur. Mercy on me! A less matter than a fine and noble recluse immured—so will they term it—in a tower, under the guardianship of an old Flemish weaver, would bring half the chivalry in England round us, to break lances, vow vows, display love-liveries, and I know not what follies besides.—Think you such gallants, with the blood flying through their veins like quicksilver, would much mind *my* bidding them begone?"

"Draw bolts, up with the drawbridge, drop portcullis," said the Constable, with a constrained smile.

"And thinks your lordship such gallants would mind these impediments? such are the very essence of the adventures which they come to seek.—The Knight of the Swan would swim through the moat—he of the Eagle would fly over the wails—he of the Thunderbolt would burst open the gates."

"Ply crossbow and mangonel," said de Lacy.

"And be besieged in form," said the Fleming, "like the Castle of Tintadgel in the old hangings, all for the love of fair lady?—And then those gay dames and demoiselles, who go upon adventure from castle to castle, from tournament to tournament, with bare bosoms, flaunting plumes, poniards at their sides, and javelins in their hands, chattering like magpies, and fluttering like jays, and, ever and anon, cooing like doves—how am I to exclude such from the Lady Eveline's privacy?"

"By keeping doors shut, I tell thee," answered the Constable, still in the same tone of forced jocularity; "a wooden bar will be thy warrant."

"Ay, but," answered Flammock, "if the Flemish weaver say *shut*, when the Norman young lady says *open*, think which has best chance of being obeyed. At a word, my lord, for the matter of guardianship, and such like, I wash my hands of it—I would not undertake to be guardian to the chaste Susannah, though she lived in an enchanted castle, which no living thing could approach."

"Thou holdest the language and thoughts," said De Lacy, "of a vulgar debauchee, who laughs at female constancy, because he has lived only with the most worthless of the sex. Yet thou shouldst know the contrary, having, as I know, a most virtuous daughter—"

"Whose mother was not less so," said Wilkin, breaking in upon the Constable's speech with somewhat more emotion than he usually displayed, "But law, my lord, gave me authority to govern and direct my wife, as both law and nature give me power and charge over my daughter. That which I can govern, I can be answerable for; but how to discharge me so well of a delegated trust, is another question.—Stay at home, my good lord," continued the honest Fleming, observing that his speech made some impression upon De Lacy; "let a fool's advice for once be of avail to change a wise man's purpose, taken, let me say, in no wise hour. Remain in your own land, rule your own vassals, and protect your own bride. You only can claim her cheerful love and ready obedience; and sure I am, that, without pretending to guess what she may do if separated from you, she will, under your own eye, do the duty of a faithful and a loving spouse."

"And the Holy Sepulchre?" said the Constable, with a sigh, his heart confessing the wisdom of the advice, which circumstances prevented him from following.

"Let those who lost the Holy Sepulchre regain it, my lord," replied Flammock. "If those Latins and Greeks, as they call them, are no better men than I have heard, it signifies very little whether they or the heathen have the country that has cost Europe so much blood and treasure." "In good faith," said the Constable, "there is sense in what thou say'st; but I caution thee to repeat it not, lest thou be taken for a heretic or a Jew. For me, my word and oath are pledged beyond retreat, and I have only to consider whom I may best name for that important station, which thy caution has—not without some shadow of reason—induced thee to decline."

"There is no man to whom your lordship can so naturally or honourably transfer such a charge," said Wilkin Flammock, "as to the kinsman near to you, and possessed of your trust; yet much better would it be were there no such trust to be reposed in any one."

"If," said the Constable, "by my near kinsman, you mean Randal de Lacy, I care not if I tell you, that I consider him as totally worthless, and undeserving of honourable confidence."

"Nay, I mean another," said Flammock, "nearer to you by blood, and, unless I greatly mistake, much nigher also in affection—I had in mind your lordship's nephew, Damian de Lacy."

The Constable started as if a wasp had stung him; but instantly replied, with forced composure, "Damian was to have gone in my stead to Palestine—it now seems I must go in his; for, since this last illness, the leeches have totally changed their minds, and consider that warmth of the climate as dangerous, which they formerly decided to be salutary. But our learned doctors, like our learned priests, must ever be in the right, change their counsels as they may; and we poor laymen still in the wrong. I can, it is true, rely on Damian with the utmost confidence; but he is young, Flammock—very young—and in that particular, resembles but too nearly the party who might be otherwise committed to his charge."

"Then once more, my lord," said the plain-spoken Fleming, "remain at home, and be yourself the protector of what is naturally so dear to you."

"Once more, I repeat, that I cannot," answered the Constable. "The step which I have adopted as a great duty, may perhaps be a great error—I only know that it is irretrievable."

"Trust your nephew, then, my lord," replied Wilkin—"he is honest and true; and it is better trusting young lions than old wolves. He may err, perhaps, but it will not be from premeditated treachery."

"Thou art right, Flammock," said the Constable; "and perhaps I ought to wish I had sooner asked thy counsel, blunt as it is. But let what has passed be a secret betwixt us; and bethink thee of something that may advantage thee more than the privilege of speaking about my affairs."

"That account will be easily settled, my lord," replied Flammock; "for my object was to ask your lordship's favour to obtain certain extensions of our privileges, in yonder wild corner where we Flemings have made our retreat."

"Thou shalt have them, so they be not exorbitant," said the Constable. And the honest Fleming, among whose good qualities scrupulous delicacy was not the foremost, hastened to detail, with great minuteness, the particulars of his request or petition, long pursued in vain, but to which this interview was the means of insuring success.

The Constable, eager to execute the resolution which he had formed, hastened to the lodging of Damian de Lacy, and to the no small astonishment of his nephew, intimated to him his change of destination; alleging his own hurried departure, Damian's late and present illness, together with the necessary protection to be afforded to the Lady Eveline, as reasons why his nephew must needs remain behind him—to represent him during his absence—to protect the family rights, and assert the family honour of the house of De Lacy—above all, to act as the guardian of the young and beautiful bride, whom his uncle and patron had been in some measure compelled to abandon for a time.

Damian yet occupied his bed while the Constable communicated this change of purpose. Perhaps he might think the circumstance fortunate, that in this position he could conceal from his uncle's observation the various emotions which he could not help feeling; while the Constable, with the eagerness of one who is desirous of hastily finishing what he has to say on an unpleasant subject, hurried over an account of the arrangements which he had made, in order that his nephew might have the means of discharging, with sufficient effect, the important trust committed to him.

The youth listened as to a voice in a dream, which he had not the power of interrupting, though there was something within him which whispered there would be both prudence and integrity in remonstrating against his uncle's alteration of plan. Something he accordingly attempted to say, when the Constable at length paused; but it was too feebly spoken to shake a resolution fully though hastily adopted and explicitly announced, by one not in the use to speak before his purpose was fixed, or to alter it when it was declared.

The remonstrance of Damian, besides, if it could be termed such, was spoken in terms too contradictory to be intelligible. In one moment he professed his regret for the laurels which he had hoped to gather in Palestine, and implored his uncle not to alter his purpose, but permit him to attend his banner thither; and in the next sentence, he professed his readiness to defend the safety of Lady Eveline with the last drop of his blood. De Lacy saw nothing inconsistent in these feelings, though they were for the moment contradictory to each other. It was natural, he thought, that a young knight should be desirous to win honour—natural also that he should willingly assume a charge so honourable and important as that with which he proposed to invest him; and therefore he thought that it was no wonder that, assuming his new office willingly, the young man should yet feel regret at losing the prospect of honourable adventure, which he must abandon. He therefore only smiled in reply to the broken expostulations of his nephew; and, having confirmed his former arrangement, left the young man to reflect at leisure on his change of destination, while he himself, in a second visit to the Benedictine Abbey, communicated the purpose which he had adopted, to the Abbess, and to his bride-elect.

The displeasure of the former lady was in no measure abated by this communication; in which, indeed, she affected to take very little interest. She pleaded her religious duties, and her want of knowledge of secular affairs, if she should chance to mistake the usages of the world; yet she had always, she said, understood, that the guardians of the young and beautiful of her own sex were chosen from the more mature of the other.

"Your own unkindness, lady," answered the Constable, "leaves me no better choice than I have made. Since the Lady Eveline's nearest friends deny her the privilege of their roof, on account of the claim with which she has honoured me, I, on my side, were worse than ungrateful did I not secure for her the protection of my nearest male heir. Damian is young, but he is true and honourable; nor does the chivalry of England afford me a better choice."

Eveline seemed surprised, and even struck with consternation, at the resolution which her bridegroom thus suddenly announced; and perhaps it was fortunate that the remark of the Lady Abbess made the answer of the Constable necessary, and prevented him from observing that her colour shifted more than once from pale to deep red. Rose, who was not excluded from the conference, drew close up to her mistress; and, by affecting to adjust her veil, while in secret she strongly pressed her hand, gave her time and encouragement to compose her mind for a reply. It was brief and decisive, and announced with a firmness which showed that the uncertainty of the moment had passed away or been suppressed. "In case of danger," she said, "she would not fail to apply to Damian de Lacy to come to her aid, as he had once done before; but she did not apprehend any danger at present, within her own secure castle of the Garde Doloureuse, where it was her purpose to dwell, attended only by her own household. She was resolved," she continued, "in consideration of her peculiar condition, to observe the strictest retirement, which she expected would not be violated even by the noble young knight who was to act as her guardian, unless some apprehension for her safety made his visit unavoidable."

The Abbess acquiesced, though coldly, in a proposal, which her ideas of decorum recommended; and preparations were hastily made for the Lady Eveline's return to the castle of her father. Two interviews which intervened before her leaving the convent, were in their nature painful. The first was when Damian was formally presented to her by his uncle, as the delegate to whom he had committed the charge of his own property, and, which was much dearer to him, as he affirmed, the protection of her person and interest.

Eveline scarce trusted herself with one glance; but that single look comprehended and reported to her the ravage which disease, aided by secret grief, had made on the manly form and handsome countenance of the youth before her. She received his salutation in a manner as embarrassed as that in which it was made; and, to his hesitating proffer of service, answered, that she trusted only to be obliged to him for his good-will during the interval of his uncle's absence.

Her parting with the Constable was the next trial which she was to undergo. It was not without emotion, although she preserved her modest composure, and De Lacy his calm gravity of deportment. His voice faltered, however, when he came to announce, "that it were unjust she should be bound by the engagement which she had been graciously contented to abide under. Three years he had assigned for its term; to which space the Arch-bishop Baldwin had consented to shorten the period of his absence. If I appear not when these are elapsed," he said, "let the Lady Eveline conclude that the grave holds De Lacy, and seek out for her mate some happier man. She cannot find one more grateful, though there are many who better deserve her."

On these terms they parted; and the Constable, speedily afterwards embarking, ploughed the narrow seas for the shores of Flanders, where he proposed to unite his forces with the Count of that rich and warlike country, who had lately taken the Cross, and to proceed by the route which should be found most practicable on their destination for the Holy Land. The broad pennon, with the arms of the Lacys, streamed forward with a favourable wind from the prow of the vessel, as if pointing to the quarter of the horizon where its renown was to be augmented; and, considering the fame of the leader, and the excellence of the soldiers who followed him, a more gallant band, in proportion to their numbers, never went to avenge on the Saracens the evils endured by the Latins of Palestine.

Meanwhile Eveline, after a cold parting with the Abbess, whose offended dignity had not yet forgiven the slight regard which she had paid to her opinion, resumed her journey homeward to her paternal castle, where her household was to be arranged in a manner suggested by the Constable, and approved of by herself.

The same preparations were made for her accommodation at every halting place which she had experienced upon her journey to Gloucester, and, as before, the purveyor was invisible, although she could be at little loss to guess his name. Yet it appeared as if the character of these preparations was in some degree altered. All the realities of convenience and accommodation, with the most perfect assurances of safety, accompanied her every where on the route; but they were no longer mingled with that display of tender gallantry and taste, which marked that the attentions were paid to a young and beautiful female. The clearest fountain-head, and the most shady grove, were no longer selected for the noontide repast; but the house of some franklin, or a small abbey, afforded the necessary hospitality. All seemed to be ordered with the most severe attention to rank and decorum—it seemed as if a nun of some strict order, rather than a young maiden of high quality and a rich inheritance, had been journeying through the land, and Eveline, though pleased with the delicacy which seemed thus to respect her unprotected and peculiar condition, would sometimes think it unnecessary, that, by so many indirect hints, it should be forced on her recollection.

She thought it strange also, that Damian, to whose care she had been so solemnly committed, did not even pay his respects to her on the road.

Something there was which whispered to her, that close and frequent intercourse might be unbecoming—even dangerous; but surely the ordinary duties of a knight and gentleman enjoined him some personal communication with the maiden under his escort, were it only to ask if her accommodations had been made to her satisfaction, or if she had any special wish which was ungratified. The only intercourse, however, which took place betwixt them, was through means of Amelot, Damian de Lacy's youthful page, who came at morning and evening to receive Eveline's commands concerning their route, and the hours of journey and repose.

These formalities rendered the solitude of Eveline's return less endurable; and had it not been for the society of Rose, she would have found herself under an intolerably irksome degree of constraint. She even hazarded to her attendant some remarks upon the singularity of De Lacy's conduct, who, authorized as he was by his situation, seemed yet as much afraid to approach her as if she had been a basilisk.

Rose let the first observation of this nature pass as if it had been unheard; but when her mistress made a second remark to the same purpose, she answered, with the truth and freedom of her character, though perhaps with less of her usual prudence, "Damian de Lacy judges well, noble lady. He to whom the safe keeping of a royal treasure is intrusted, should not indulge himself too often by gazing upon it."

Eveline blushed, wrapt herself closer in her veil, nor did she again during their journey mention the name of Damian de Lacy.

When the gray turrets of the Garde Doloureuse greeted her sight on the evening of the second day, and she once more beheld her father's banner floating from its highest watch-tower in honour of her approach, her sensations were mingled with pain; but, upon the whole, she looked towards that ancient home as a place of refuge, where she might indulge the new train of thoughts which circumstances had opened to her, amid the same scenes which had sheltered her infancy and childhood.

She pressed forward her palfrey, to reach the ancient portal as soon as possible, bowed hastily to the well-known faces which showed themselves on all sides, but spoke to no one, until, dismounting at the chapel door, she had penetrated to the crypt, in which was preserved the miraculous painting. There, prostrate on the ground, she implored the guidance and protection of the Holy Virgin through those intricacies in which she had involved herself, by the fulfilment of the vow which she had made in her anguish before the same shrine. If the prayer was misdirected, its purport was virtuous and sincere; nor are we disposed to doubt that it attained that Heaven towards which it was devoutly addressed.

CHAPTER THE TWENTY-SECOND

The Virgin's image falls—yet some, I ween,
Not unforgiven the suppliant knee might bend,
As to a visible power, in which might blend
All that was mix'd, and reconciled in her,
Of mother's love, with maiden's purity,
Of high with low, celestial with terrene.
   WORDSWORTH.

The household of the Lady Eveline, though of an establishment becoming her present and future rank, was of a solemn and sequestered character, corresponding to her place of residence, and the privacy connected with her situation, retired as she was from the class of maidens who are yet unengaged, and yet not united with that of matrons, who enjoy the protection of a married name. Her immediate female attendants, with whom the reader is already acquainted, constituted almost her whole society. The garrison of the castle, besides household servants, consisted of veterans of tried faith, the followers of Berenger and of De Lacy in many a bloody field, to whom the duties of watching and warding were as familiar as any of their more ordinary occupations, and whose courage, nevertheless, tempered by age and experience, was not likely to engage in any rash adventure or accidental quarrel. These men maintained a constant and watchful guard, commanded by the steward, but under the eye of Father Aldrovand, who, besides discharging his ecclesiastical functions, was at times pleased to show some sparkles of his ancient military education.

Whilst this garrison afforded security against any sudden attempt on the part of the Welsh to surprise the castle, a strong body of forces were disposed within a few miles of the Garde Doloureuse, ready, on the least alarm, to advance to defend the place against any more numerous body of invaders, who, undeterred by the fate of Gwenwyn, might have the hardihood to form a regular siege. To this band, which, under the eye of Damian de Lacy himself, was kept in constant readiness for action, could be added on occasion all the military force of the Marches, comprising numerous bodies of Flemings, and other foreigners, who held their establishments by military tenure.

While the fortress was thus secure from hostile violence, the life of its inmates was so unvaried and simple, as might have excused youth and beauty for wishing for variety, even at the expense of some danger. The labours of the needle were only relieved by a walk round the battlements, where Eveline, as she passed arm in arm with Rose, received a military salute from each sentinel in turn, or in the court-yard, where the caps and bonnets of the domestics paid her the same respect which she received above from the pikes and javelins of the warders. Did they wish to extend their airing beyond the castle gate, it was not sufficient that doors and bridges were to be opened and lowered; there was, besides, an escort to get under arms, who, on foot or horseback as the case might require, attended for the security of the Lady Eveline's person. Without this military attendance they could not in safety move even so far as the mills, where honest Wilkln Flammock, his warlike deeds forgotten, was occupied with his mechanical labours. But if a farther disport was intended, and the Lady of the Garde Doloureuse proposed to hunt or hawk for a few hours, her safety was not confided to a guard so feeble as the garrison of the castle might afford. It was necessary that Raoul should announce her purpose to Damian by a special messenger despatched the evening before, that there might be time before daybreak to scour, with a body of light cavalry, the region in which she intended to take her pleasure; and sentinels were placed in all suspicious places while she continued in the field. In truth, she tried, upon one or two occasions, to make an excursion, without any formal annunciation of her intention; but all her purposes seemed to be known to Damian as soon as they were formed, and she was no sooner abroad than parties of archers and spearmen from his camp were seen scouring the valleys, and guarding the mountain-pass, and Damian's own, plume was usually beheld conspicuous among the distant soldiers.

The formality of these preparations so much allayed the pleasure derived from the sport, that Eveline seldom resorted to amusement which was attended with such bustle, and put in motion so many persons.

The day being worn out as it best might, in the evening Father Aldrovand was wont to read out of some holy legend, or from the homilies of some departed saint, such passages as he deemed fit for the hearing of his little congregation. Sometimes also he read and expounded a chapter of the Holy Scripture; but in such cases, the good man's attention was so strangely turned to the military part of the Jewish history, that he was never able to quit the books of Judges and of Kings, together with the triumphs of Judas Maccabeus; although the manner in which he illustrated the victories of the children of Israel was much more amusing to himself than edifying to his female audience.

Sometimes, but rarely, Rose obtained permission for a strolling minstrel to entertain an hour with his ditty of love and chivalry; sometimes a pilgrim from a distant shrine, repaid by long tales of the wonders which he had seen in other lands, the hospitality which the Garde Doloureuse afforded; and sometimes also it happened, that the interest and intercession of the tiring-woman obtained admission for travelling merchants, or pedlars, who, at the risk of their lives, found profit by carrying from castle to castle the materials of rich dresses and female ornaments.

The usual visits of mendicants, of jugglers, of travelling jesters, are not to be forgotten in this list of amusements; and though his nation subjected him to close watch and observation, even the Welsh bard, with his huge harp strung with horse-hair, was sometimes admitted to vary the uniformity of their secluded life. But, saving such amusements, and saving also the regular attendance upon the religious duties at the chapel, it was impossible for life to glide away in more wearisome monotony than at the castle of the Garde Doloureuse. Since the death of its brave owner, to whom feasting and hospitality seemed as natural as thoughts of honour and deeds of chivalry, the gloom of a convent might be said to have enveloped the ancient mansion of Raymond Berenger, were it not that the presence of so many armed warders, stalking in solemn state on the battlements, gave it rather the aspect of a state-prison; and the temper of the inhabitants gradually became infected by the character of their dwelling.

The spirits of Eveline in particular felt a depression, which her naturally lively temper was quite inadequate to resist; and as her ruminations became graver, had caught that calm and contemplative manner, which is so often united with an ardent and enthusiastical temperament. She meditated deeply upon the former accidents of her life; nor can it be wondered that her thoughts repeatedly wandered back to the two several periods on which she had witnessed, or supposed that she had witnessed, a supernatural appearance. Then it was that it often seemed to her, as if a good and evil power strove for mastery over her destiny.

Solitude is favourable to feelings of self-importance; and it is when alone, and occupied only with their own thoughts, that fanatics have reveries, and imagined saints lose themselves in imaginary ecstasies. With Eveline the influence of enthusiasm went not such a length, yet it seemed to her as if in the vision of the night she saw sometimes the aspect of the Lady of the Garde Doloureuse, bending upon her glances of pity, comfort, and protection; sometimes the ominous form of the Saxon castle of Baldringbam, holding up the bloody hand as witness of the injuries with which she had been treated while in life, and menacing with revenge the descendant of her murderer.

On awaking from such dreams, Eveline would reflect that she was the last branch of her house—a house to which the tutelage and protection of the miraculous Image, and the enmity and evil influence of the revengeful Vanda, had been peculiarly attached for ages. It seemed to her as if she were the prize, for the disposal of which the benign saint and vindictive fiend were now to play their last and keenest game.

Thus thinking, and experiencing little interruption of her meditations from any external circumstance of interest and amusement, she became pensive, absent, wrapt herself up in contemplations which withdrew her attention from the conversation around her, and walked in the world of reality like one who is still in a dream. When she thought of her engagement with the Constable of Chester, it was with resignation, but without a wish, and almost without an expectation, that she would be called upon to fulfil it. She had accomplished her vow by accepting the faith of her deliverer in exchange for her own; and although she held herself willing to redeem the pledge—nay, would scarce confess to herself the reluctance with which she thought of doing so—yet it is certain that she entertained unavowed hopes that Our Lady of the Garde Doloureuse would not be a severe creditor; but, satisfied with the readiness she had shown to accomplish her vow, would not insist upon her claim in its full rigour. It would have been the blackest ingratitude, to have wished that her gallant deliverer, whom she had so much cause to pray for, should experience any of those fatalities which in the Holy Land so often changed the laurel-wreath into cypress; but other accidents chanced, when men had been long abroad, to alter those purposes with which they had left home.

A strolling minstrel, who sought the Garde Doloureuse, had recited, for the amusement of the lady and household, the celebrated lay of the Count of Gleichen, who, already married in his own country, laid himself under so many obligations in the East to a Saracen princess, through whose means he achieved his freedom, that he married her also. The Pope and his conclave were pleased to approve of the double wedlock, in a case so extraordinary; and the good Count of Gleichen shared his nuptial bed between two wives of equal rank, and now sleeps between them under the same monument. The commentaries of the inmates of the castle had been various and discrepant upon this legend. Father Aldrovand considered it as altogether false, and an unworthy calumny on the head of the church, in affirming his Holiness would countenance such irregularity. Old Margery, with the tender- heartedness of an ancient nurse, wept bitterly for pity during the tale, and, never questioning either the power of the Pope or the propriety of his decision, was pleased that a mode of extrication was found for a complication of love distresses which seemed almost inextricable. Dame Gillian declared it unreasonable, that, since a woman was only allowed one husband, a man should, under any circumstances, be permitted to have two wives; while Raoul, glancing towards her a look of verjuice, pitied the deplorable idiocy of the man who could be fool enough to avail himself of such a privilege.

"Peace, all the rest of you," said the Lady Eveline; "and do you, my dear Rose, tell me your judgment upon the Count of Gleichen and his two wives."

Rose blushed, and replied, "She was not much accustomed to think of such matters; but that, in her apprehension, the wife who could be contented with but one half of her husband's affections, had never deserved to engage the slightest share of them."

"Thou art partly right, Rose," said Eveline; "and methinks the European lady, when she found herself outshone by the young and beautiful foreign princess, would have best consulted her own dignity in resigning the place, and giving the Holy Father no more trouble than in annulling the marriage, as has been done in cases of more frequent occurrence."

This she said with an air of indifference and even gaiety, which intimated to her faithful attendant with how little effort she herself could have made such a sacrifice, and served to indicate the state of her affections towards the Constable. But there was another than the Constable on whom her thoughts turned more frequently, though involuntarily, than perhaps in prudence they should have done.

The recollections of Damian de Lacy had not been erased from Eveline's mind. They were, indeed, renewed by hearing his name so often mentioned, and by knowing that he was almost constantly in the neighbourhood, with his whole attention fixed upon her convenience, interest, and safety; whilst, on the other hand, so far from waiting on her in person, he never even attempted, by a direct communication with herself, to consult her pleasure, even upon what most concerned her.

The messages conveyed by Father Aldrovand, or by Rose, to Amelot, Damian's page, while they gave an air of formality to their intercourse, which Eveline thought unnecessary, and even unkind, yet served to fix her attention upon the connection between them, and to keep it ever present to her memory. The remark by which Rose had vindicated the distance observed by her youthful guardian, sometimes arose to her recollection; and while her soul repelled with scorn the suspicion, that, in any case, his presence, whether at intervals or constantly, could be prejudicial to his uncle's interest, she conjured up various arguments for giving him a frequent place in her memory.—Was it not her duty to think of Damian often and kindly, as the Constable's nearest, best beloved, and most trusted relative?—Was he not her former deliverer and her present guardian?—And might he not be considered as an instrument specially employed by her divine patroness, in rendering effectual the protection with which she had graced her in more than one emergency?

Eveline's mind mutinied against the restrictions which were laid on their intercourse, as against something which inferred suspicion and degradation, like the compelled seclusion to which she had heard the Paynim infidels of the East subjected their females. Why should she see her guardian only in the benefits which he conferred upon her, and the cares he took for her safety, and hear his sentiments only by the mouth of others, as if one of them had been infected with the plague, or some other fatal or infectious disorder, which might render their meeting dangerous to the other?—And if they did meet occasionally, what else could be the consequence, save that the care of a brother towards a sister —of a trusty and kind guardian to the betrothed bride of his near relative and honoured patron, might render the melancholy seclusion of the Garde Doloureuse more easy to be endured by one so young in years, and, though dejected by present circumstances, naturally so gay in temper?

Yet, though this train of reasoning appeared to Eveline, when tracing it in her own mind, so conclusive, that she several times resolved to communicate her view of the case to Rose Flammock, it so chanced that, whenever she looked on the calm steady blue eye of the Flemish maiden, and remembered that her unblemished faith was mixed with a sincerity and plain dealing proof against every consideration, she feared lest she might be subjected in the opinion of her attendant to suspicions from which her own mind freed her; and her proud Norman spirit revolted at the idea of being obliged to justify herself to another, when she stood self- acquitted to her own mind. "Let things be as they are," she said; "and let us endure all the weariness of a life which might be so easily rendered more cheerful, rather than that this zealous but punctilious friend should, in the strictness and nicety of her feelings on my account, conceive me capable of encouraging an intercourse which could lead to a less worthy thought of me in the mind of the most scrupulous of man—or of womankind." But even this vacillation of opinion and resolution tended to bring the image of the handsome young Damian more frequently before the Lady Eveline's fancy, than perhaps his uncle, had he known it, would altogether have approved of. In such reflections, however, she never indulged long, ere a sense of the singular destiny which had hitherto attended her, led her back into the more melancholy contemplations from which the buoyancy of her youthful fancy had for a short time emancipated her.

CHAPTER THE TWENTY-THIRD

—-Ours is the skie,
Where at what fowl we please our hawk shall flie.
  RANDOLPH.

One bright September morning, old Raoul was busy in the mews where he kept his hawks, grumbling all the while to himself as he surveyed the condition of each bird, and blaming alternately the carelessness of the under-falconer, and the situation of the building, and the weather, and the wind, and all things around him, for the dilapidation which time and disease had made in the neglected hawking establishment of the Garde Douloureuse. While in these unpleasing meditations, he was surprised by the voice of his beloved Dame Gillian, who seldom was an early riser, and yet more rarely visited him when he was in his sphere of peculiar authority. "Raoul, Raoul! where art thou, man?—Ever to seek for, when thou canst make aught of advantage for thyself or me!"

"And what want'st thou, dame?" said Raoul, "what means thy screaming worse than the seagull before wet weather? A murrain on thy voice! it is enough to fray every hawk from the perch."

"Hawk!" answered Dame Gillian; "it is time to be looking for hawks, when here is a cast of the bravest falcons come hither for sale, that ever flew by lake, brook, or meadow!"

"Kites! like her that brings the news," said Raoul.

"No, nor kestrils like him that hears it," replied Gillian; "but brave jerfalcons, with large nares, strongly armed, and beaks short and something bluish—"

"Pshaw, with thy jargon!—Where came they from?" said Raoul, interested in the tidings, but unwilling to give his wife the satisfaction of seeing that he was so.

"From the Isle of Man," replied Gillian.

"They must be good, then, though it was a woman brought tidings of them," said Raoul, smiling grimly at his own wit; then, leaving the mews, he demanded to know where this famous falcon-merchant was to be met withal.

"Why, between the barriers and the inner gate," replied Gillian, "where other men are admitted that have wares to utter—Where should he be?"

"And who let him in?" demanded the suspicious Raoul.

"Why, Master Steward, thou owl!" said Gillian; "he came but now to my chamber, and sent me hither to call you."

"Oh, the steward—the steward—I might have guessed as much. And he came to thy chamber, doubtless, because he could not have as easily come hither to me himself.—Was it not so, sweetheart?"

"I do not know why he chose to come to me rather than to you, Raoul," said Gillian; "and if I did know, perhaps I would not tell you. Go to—miss your bargain, or make your bargain, I care not which—the man will not wait for you—he has good proffers from the Seneschal of Malpas, and the Welsh Lord of Dinevawr."

"I come—I come," said Raoul, who felt the necessity of embracing this opportunity of improving his hawking establishment, and hastened to the gate, where he met the merchant, attended by a servant, who kept in separate cages the three falcons which he offered for sale.

The first glance satisfied Raoul that they were of the best breed in Europe, and that, if their education were in correspondence to their race, there could scarce be a more valuable addition even to a royal mews. The merchant did not fail to enlarge upon all their points of excellence; the breadth of their shoulders, the strength of their train, their full and fierce dark eyes, the boldness with which they endured the approach of strangers, and the lively spirit and vigour with which they pruned their plumes, and shook, or, as it was technically termed, roused themselves. He expatiated on the difficulty and danger with which they were obtained from the rock of Ramsey, on which they were bred, and which was an every unrivalled even on the coast of Norway.

Raoul turned apparently a deaf ear to all these commendations. "Friend merchant," said he, "I know a falcon as well as thou dost, and I will not deny that thine are fine ones; but if they be not carefully trained and reclaimed, I would rather have a goss-hawk on my perch than the fairest falcon that ever stretched wing to weather."

"I grant ye," said the merchant; "but if we agree on the price, for that is the main matter, thou shalt see the birds fly if thou wilt, and then buy them or not as thou likest. I am no true merchant if thou ever saw'st birds beat them, whether at the mount or the stoop."

"That I call fair," said Raoul, "if the price be equally so."

"It shall be corresponding," said the hawk-merchant; "for I have brought six casts from the island, by the good favour of good King Reginald of Man, and I have sold every feather of them save these; and so, having emptied my cages and filled my purse, I desire not to be troubled longer with the residue; and if a good fellow and a judge, as thou seemest to be, should like the hawks when he has seen them fly, he shall have the price of his own making."

"Go to," said Raoul, "we will have no blind bargains; my lady, if the hawks be suitable, is more able to pay for them than thou to give them away. Will a bezant be a conformable price for the cast?"

"A bezant, Master Falconer!—By my faith, you are no bold bodesman! nevertheless, double your offer, and I will consider it."

"If the hawks are well reclaimed," said Raoul, "I will give you a bezant and a half; but I will see them strike a heron ere I will be so rash as to deal with you."

"It is well," said the merchant, "and I had better take your offer than be longer cumbered with them; for were I to carry them into Wales, I might get paid in a worse fashion by some of their long knives.—Will you to horse presently?"

"Assuredly," said Raoul; "and, though March be the fitter month for hawking at the heron, yet I will show you one of these frogpeckers for the trouble of riding the matter of a mile by the water-side."

"Content, Sir Falconer," said the merchant. "But are we to go alone, or is there no lord or lady in the castle who would take pleasure to see a piece of game gallantly struck? I am not afraid to show these hawks to a countess." "My lady used to love the sport well enough," said Raoul; "but, I wot not why, she is moped and mazed ever since her father's death, and lives in her fair castle like a nun in a cloister, without disport or revelry of any kind. Nevertheless, Gillian, thou canst do something with her— good now, do a kind deed for once, and move her to come out and look on this morning's sport—the poor heart hath seen no pastime this summer."

"That I will do," quoth Gillian; "and, moreover, I will show her such a new riding-tire for the head, that no woman born could ever look at without the wish to toss it a little in the wind."

As Gillian spoke, it appeared to her jealous-pated husband that he surprised a glance of more intelligence exchanged betwixt her and the trader than brief acquaintance seemed to warrant, even when allowance was made for the extreme frankness of Dame Gillian's disposition. He thought also, that, on looking more closely at the merchant, his lineaments were not totally unknown to him; and proceeded to say to him dryly, "We have met before, friend, but I cannot call to remembrance where."

"Like enough," said the merchant; "I have used this country often, and may have taken money of you in the way of trade. If I were in fitting place, I would gladly bestow a bottle of wine to our better acquaintance."

"Not so fast, friend," said the old huntsman; "ere I drink to better acquaintance with any one, I must be well pleased with what I already know of him. We will see thy hawks fly, and if their breeding match thy bragging, we may perhaps crush a cup together. —And here come grooms and equerries, in faith—my lady has consented to come forth."

The opportunity of seeing this rural pastime had offered itself to Eveline, at a time when the delightful brilliancy of the day, the temperance of the air, and the joyous work of harvest, proceeding in every direction around, made the temptation to exercise almost irresistible.

As they proposed to go no farther than the side of the neighbouring river, near the fatal bridge, over which a small guard of infantry was constantly maintained, Eveline dispensed with any farther escort, and, contrary to the custom of the castle, took no one in her train save Rose and Gillian, and one or two servants, who led spaniels, or carried appurtenances of the chase. Raoul, the merchant, and an equerry, attended her of course, each holding a hawk on his wrist, and anxiously adjusting the mode in which they should throw them off, so as best to ascertain the extent of their powers and training.

When these important points had been adjusted, the party rode down the river, carefully looking on every side for the object of their game; but no heron was seen stalking on the usual haunts of the bird, although there was a heronry at no great distance.

Few disappointments of a small nature are more teasing than that of a sportsman, who, having set out with all means and appliances for destruction of game, finds that there is none to be met with; because he conceives himself, with his full shooting trim, and his empty game-pouch, to be subjected to the sneer of every passing rustic. The party of the Lady Eveline felt all the degradation of such disappointment.

"A fair country this," said the merchant, "where, on two miles of river, you cannot find one poor heron!"

"It is the clatter those d—d Flemings make with their water-mills and fulling-mills," said Raoul; "they destroy good sport and good company wherever they come. But were my lady willing to ride a mile or so farther to the Red Pool, I could show you a long- shanked fellow who would make your hawks cancelier till their brains were giddy."

"The Red Pool!" said Rose; "thou knowest it is more than three miles beyond the bridge, and lies up towards the hills."

"Ay, ay," said Raoul, "another Flemish freak to spoil pastime! They are not so scarce on the Marches these Flemish wenches, that they should fear being hawked at by Welsh haggards."

"Raoul is right, Rose," answered Eveline; "it is absurd to be cooped uplike birds in a cage, when all around us has been so uniformly quiet. I am determined to break out of bounds for once, and see sport in our old fashion, without being surrounded with armed men like prisoners of state. We will merrily to the Red Pool, wench, and kill a heron like free maids of the Marches."

"Let me but tell my father, at least, to mount and follow us," said Rose—for they were now near the re-established manufacturing houses of the stout

Fleming.

"I care not if thou dost, Rose," said Eveline; "yet credit me, girl, we will be at the Red Pool, and thus far on our way home again, ere thy father has donned his best doublet, girded on his two-handed sword, and accoutred his strong Flanderkin elephant of a horse, which he judiciously names Sloth—nay, frown not, and lose not, in justifying thy father, the time that may be better spent in calling him out."

Rose rode to the mills accordingly, when Wilkin Flammock, at the command of his liege mistress, readily hastened to get his steel cap and habergeon, and ordered half-a-dozen of his kinsmen and servants to get on horseback. Rose remained with him, to urge him to more despatch than his methodical disposition rendered natural to him; but in spite of all her efforts to stimulate him, the Lady Eveline had passed the bridge more than half an hour ere her escort was prepared to follow her.

Meanwhile, apprehensive of no evil, and riding gaily on, with the sensation of one escaped from confinement, Eveline moved forward on her lively jennet, as light as a lark; the plumes with which Dame Gillian had decked her riding-bonnet dancing in the wind, and her attendants galloping behind her, with dogs, pouches, lines, and all other appurtenances of the royal sport of hawking. After passing the river, the wild green-sward path which they pursued began to wind upward among small eminences, some-times bare and craggy, sometimes overgrown with hazel, sloethorn, and other dwarf shrubs, and at length suddenly descending, brought them to the verge of a mountain rivulet, that, like a lamb at play, leapt merrily from rock to rock, seemingly uncertain which way to run.

"This little stream was always my favourite, Dame Gillian," said Eveline, "and now methinks it leaps the lighter that it sees me again."

"Ah! lady," said Dame Gillian, whose turn for conversation never ex-tended in such cases beyond a few phrases of gross flattery, "many a fair knight would leap shoulder-height for leave to look on you as free as the brook may! more especially now that you have donned that riding-cap, which, in exquisite delicacy of invention, methinks, is a bow-shot before aught that I ever invented—What thinkest thou, Raoul?"

"I think," answered her well-natured helpmate, "that women's tongues were contrived to drive all the game out of the country.— Here we come near to the spot where we hope to speed, or no where; wherefore, pray, my sweet lady, be silent yourself, and keep your followers as much so as their natures will permit, while we steal along the bank of the pool, under the wind, with our hawks' hoods cast loose, all ready for a flight."

As he spoke, they advanced about a hundred yards up the brawling stream, until the little vale through which it flowed, making a very sudden turn to one side, showed them the Red Pool, the superfluous water of which formed the rivulet itself.

This mountain-lake, or tarn, as it is called in some countries, was a deep basin of about a mile in circumference, but rather oblong than circular. On the side next to our falconers arose a ridge of rock, of a dark red hue, giving name to the pool, which, reflecting this massive and dusky barrier, appeared to partake of its colour. On the opposite side was a heathy hill, whose autumnal bloom had not yet faded from purple to russet; its surface was varied by the dark green furze and the fern, and in many places gray cliffs, or loose stones of the same colour, formed a contrast to the ruddy precipice to which they lay opposed. A natural road of beautiful sand was formed by a beach, which, extending all the way around the lake, separated its waters from the precipitous rock on the one hand, and on the other from the steep and broken hill; and being no where less than five or six yards in breadth, and in most places greatly more, offered around its whole circuit a tempting opportunity to the rider, who desired to exercise and breathe the horse on which he was mounted. The verge of the pool on the rocky side was here and there strewed with fragments of large size, detached from the precipice above, but not in such quantity as to encumber this pleasant horse-course. Many of these rocky masses, having passed the margin of the water in their fall, lay immersed there like small islets; and, placed amongst a little archipelago, the quick eye of Raoul detected the heron which they were in search of.

A moment's consultation was held to consider in what manner they should approach the sad and solitary bird, which, unconscious that itself was the object of a formidable ambuscade, stood motionless on a stone, by the brink of the lake, watching for such small fish or water-reptiles as might chance to pass by its lonely station. A brief debate took place betwixt Raoul and the hawk-merchant on the best mode of starting the quarry, so as to allow Lady Eveline and her attendants the most perfect view of the flight. The facility of killing the heron at the *far jettee* or at the *jettee ferre*—that is, upon the hither or farther sid of the pool— was anxiously debated in language of breathless importance, as if some great and perilous enterprise was about to be executed.

At length the arrangements were fixed, and the party began to advance towards the aquatic hermit, who, by this time aware of their approach, drew himself up to his full height, erected his long lean neck, spread his broad fan-like wings, uttered his usual clanging cry, and, projecting his length of thin legs far behind him, rose upon the gentle breeze. It was then, with a loud whoop of encouragement, that the merchant threw off the noble hawk he bore, having first unhooded her to give her a view of her quarry.

Eager as a frigate in chase of some rich galleon, darted the falcon towards the enemy, which she had been taught to pursue; while, preparing for defence, if he should be unable to escape by flight, the heron exerted all his powers of speed to escape from an enemy so formidable. Plying his almost unequalled strength of wing, he ascended high and higher in the air, by short gyrations, that the hawk might gain no vantage ground for pouncing at him; while his spiked beak, at the extremity of so long a neck as enabled him to strike an object at a yard's distance in every direction, possessed for any less spirited assailant all the terrors of a Moorish javelin.

Another hawk was now thrown off, and encouraged by the halloos of the falconer to join her companion. Both kept mounting, or scaling the air, as it were, by a succession of small circles, endeavoring to gain that superior height which the heron on his part was bent to preserve; and to the exquisite delight of the spectators, the contest was continued until all three were well-nigh mingled with the fleecy clouds, from which was occasionally heard the harsh and plaintive cry of the quarry, appealing as it were to the heaven which he was approaching, against the wanton cruelty of those by whom he was persecuted.

At length on of the falcons had reached a pitch from which she ventured to stoop at the heron; but so judiciously did the quarry maintain his defence, as to receive on his beak the stroke which the falcon, shooting down at full descent, had made against his right wing; so that one of his enemies, spiked through the body by his own weight, fell fluttering into the lake, very near the land, on the side farthest from the falconers, and perished there.

"There goes a gallant falcon to the fishes," said Raoul. "Merchant, thy cake is dough."

Even as he spoke, however, the remaining bird had avenged the fate of her sister; for the success which the heron met with on one side, did not prevent his being assailed on the other wing; and the falcon stooping boldly, and grappling with, or, as it is called in falconry, *binding* his prey, both came tumbling down together, from a great height in the air. It was then no small object on the part of the falconers to come in as soon as possible, lest the falcon should receive hurt from the beak or talons of the heron; and the whole party, the men setting spurs, and the females switching their palfreys, went off like the wind, sweeping along the fair and smooth beach betwixt the rock and the water.

Lady Eveline, far better mounted than any of her train, her spirits elated by the sport, and by the speed at which she moved, was much sooner than any of her attendants at the spot where the falcon and heron, still engaged in their mortal struggle, lay fighting upon the moss; the wing of the latter having been broken by the stoop of the former. The duty of a falconer in such a crisis was to run in and assist the hawk, by thrusting the heron's bill into the earth, and breaking his legs, and thus permitting the falcon to dispatch him on easy terms.

Neither would the sex nor quality of the Lady Eveline have excused her becoming second to the falcon in this cruel manner; but, just as she had dismounted for that purpose, she was surprised to find herself seized on by wild form, who exclaimed in Welsh, that he seized her as a *waif*, for hawking on the demesnes of Dawfyd with the one eye. At the same time many other Welshmen, to the number of more than a score, showed them-selves from behind crags and bushes, all armed at point with the axes called Welsh hooks, long knives, darts, and bows and arrows.

Eveline screamed to her attendants for assistance, and at the same time made use of what Welsh phrases she possessed, to move the fears or excite the compassion of the outlawed mountaineers, for she doubted not that she had fallen under the power of such a party. When she found her requests were unheeded, and she perceived it was their purpose to detain her prisoner, she disdained to use farther entreaties, but demanded at their peril that they should treat her with respect, promising in that case that she would pay them a large ransom, and threatening them with the vengeance of the Lords Marchers, and particularly of Sir Damian de Lacy, if they ventured to use her otherwise.

The men seemed to understand her, and although they proceeded to tie a bandage over her eyes, and to bind her arms with her own veil, yet they observed in these acts of violence a certain delicacy and attention both to her feelings and her safety, which led her to hope that her request had had some effect on them. They secured her to the saddle of her palfrey, and led her away with them through the recesses of the hills; while she had the additional distress to hear behind her the noise of a conflict, occasioned by the fruitless efforts of her retinue to procure her rescue.

Astonishment had at first seized the hawking party, when they saw from some distance their sport interrupted by a violent assault on their mistress. Old Raoul valiantly put spurs to his horse, and calling on the rest to follow him to the rescue, rode furiously towards the banditti; but, having no other arms save a hawking- pole and short sword, he and those who followed him in his meritorious but ineffectual attempt were easily foiled, and Raoul and one or two of the foremost severely beaten; the banditti exercising upon them their own poles till they were broken to splinters, but generously abstaining from the use of more dangerous weapons. The rest of the retinue, completely discouraged, dispersed to give the alarm, and the merchant and Dame Gillian remained by the lake, filling the air with shrieks of useless fear and sorrow. The outlaws, meanwhile, drawing together in a body, shot a few arrows at the fugitives, but more to alarm than to injure them, and then marched off in a body, as if to cover their companions who had gone before, with the Lady Eveline in their custody.

CHAPTER THE TWENTY-FOURTH.

Four ruffians seized me yester morn—
Alas! a maiden most forlorn!
They choked my cries with wicked might,
And bound me on a palfrey white. COLERIDGE.

Such adventures as are now only recorded in works of mere fiction, were not uncommon in the feudal ages, when might was so universally superior to right; and it followed that those whose conditions exposed them to frequent violence, were more prompt in repelling, and more patient in enduring it, than could otherwise have been expected from their sex and age.

The Lady Eveline felt that she was a prisoner, nor was she devoid of fears concerning the purposes of this assault; but she suffered neither her alarm, nor the violence with which she was hurried along, to deprive her of the power of observing and reflecting. From the noise of hoofs which now increased around, she concluded that the greater part of the ruffians by whom she had been seized had betaken themselves to their horses. This she knew was consonant to the practice of the Welsh marauders, who, although the small size and slightness of their nags made them totally unfit for service in battle, availed themselves of their activity and sureness of foot to transport them with the necessary celerity to and from the scenes of their rapine; ensuring thus a rapid and unperceived approach, and a secure and speedy retreat. These animals traversed without difficulty, and beneath the load of a heavy soldier, the wild mountain paths by which the country was intersected, and in one of which Lady Eveline Berenger concluded she was now engaged, from the manner in which her own palfrey, supported by a man on foot at either rein, seemed now to labour up some precipice, and anon to descend with still greater risk on the other side.

At one of those moments, a voice which she had not yet distinguished addressed her in the Anglo-Norman language, and asked, with apparent interest, if she sat safely on her saddle, offering at the same time to have her accoutrements altered at her pleasure and convenience.

"Insult not my condition with the mention of safety," said Eveline; "you may well believe that I hold my safety altogether irreconcilable with these deeds of violence. If I or my vassals have done injury to any of the *Gymry*, let me know, and it shall be amended—If it is ransom which you desire, name the sum, and I will send an order to treat for it; but detain me not prisoner, for that can but injure me, and will avail you nothing."

"The Lady Eveline," answered the voice, still in a tone of courtesy inconsistent with the violence which she sustained, "will speedily find that our actions are more rough than purposes."

"If you know who I am," said Eveline, "you cannot doubt that this atrocity will be avenged—you must know by whose banner my lands are at present protected."

"Under De Lacy's," answered the voice, with a tone of indifference
"Be it so—falcons fear not falcons."

At this moment there was a halt, and a confused murmur arose amongst those around her, who had hitherto been silent, unless when muttering to each other in Welsh, and as briefly as possible, directions which way to hold, or encouragement to use haste.

These murmurs ceased, and there was a pause of several minutes; at length Eveline again heard the voice which formerly addressed her, giving directions which she could not understand. He then spoke to herself, "You will presently see," he said, "whether I have spoken truly, when I said I scorned the ties by which you are fettered. But you are at once the cause of strife and the reward of victory— your safety must be cared for as time will admit; and, strange as the mode of protection is to which we are to intrust you, I trust the victor in the approaching struggle will find you uninjured."

"Do not, for the sake of the blessed Virgin, let there be strife and bloodshed!" said Eveline; "rather unbind my eyes, and let me speak to those whose approach you dread. If friends, as it would seem to me, I will be the means of peace between you."

"I despise peace," replied the speaker. "I have not undertaken a resolute and daring adventure, to resign it as a child doth his plaything, at the first frown of fortune. Please to alight, noble lady; or rather be not offended that I thus lift you from thy seat, and place you on the greensward."

As he spoke, Eveline felt herself lifted from her palfrey, and placed carefully and safely on the ground, in a sitting posture. A moment after, the same peremptory valet who had aided her to dismount, disrobed her of her cap, the masterpiece of Dame Gillian, and of her upper mantle. "I must yet farther require you," said the bandit leader, "to creep on hands and knees into this narrow aperture. Believe me, I regret the nature of the singular fortification to which I commit your person for safety."

Eveline crept forwards as directed, conceiving resistance to be of no avail, and thinking that compliance with the request of one who spoke like a person of consequence, might find her protection against the unbridled fury of the Welsh, to whom she was obnoxious, as being the cause of Gwenwyn's death, and the defeat of the Britons under the walls of the Garde Doloureuse.

She crept then forwards through a narrow and damp passage, built on either side with rough stones, and so low that she could not have entered it in any other posture. When she had proceeded about two or three yards, the passage opened into a concavity or apartment, high enough to permit her to sit at her ease, and of irregular, but narrow, dimensions. At the same time she became sensible, from the noise which she heard behind her, that the ruffians were stopping up the passage by which she had been thus introduced into the bowels of the earth. She could distinctly hear the clattering of stone with which they closed the entrance, and she became sensible that the current of fresh air, which had rushed through the opening, was gradually failing, and that the atmosphere of the subterranean apartment became yet more damp, earthy, and oppressive than at first.

At this moment came a distant sound from without, in which Eveline thought she could distinguish cries, blows, the trampling of horse, the oaths, shouts, and screams of the combatants, but all deadened by the rude walls of her prison, into a confused hollow murmur, conveying such intelligence to her ears as we may suppose the dead to hear from the world they have quitted.

Influenced by desperation, under circumstances so dreadful, Eveline struggled for liberty with such frantic energy, that she partly effected her purpose by forcing her arms from the bonds which confined them. But this only convinced her of the impossibility to escape; for, rending off the veil which wrapped her head, she found herself in total darkness, and flinging her arms hastily around her, she discovered she was cooped up in a subterranean cavern, of very narrow dimensions. Her hands, which groped around, encountered only pieces of decayed metal, and a substance which, at another moment, would have made her shudder, being, in truth, the mouldering bones of the dead. At present, not even this circumstance could add to her fears, immured as she seemed to be, to perish by a strange and subterranean death, while her friends and deliverers were probably within a few yards of her. She flung her arms wildly around in search of some avenue of escape, but every effort she made for liberating herself from the ponderous circumvallation, was as ineffectual as if directed against the dome of a cathedral.

The noise by which her ears were at first assailed increased rapidly, and at one moment it seemed as if the covering of the vault under which she lay sounded repeatedly to blows, or the shock of substances which had fallen, or been thrown, against it. It was impossible that a human brain could have withstood these terrors, operating upon it so immediately; but happily this extremity lasted not long. Sounds, more hollow, and dying away in distance, argued that one or other of the parties had retreated; and at length all was silent.

Eveline was now left to the undisturbed contemplation of her own disastrous situation. The fight was over, and, as circumstances led her to infer, her own friends were conquerors; for otherwise the victor would have relieved her from her place of confinement, and carried her away captive with him, as his words had menaced. But what could the success of her faithful friends and followers avail Eveline, who, pent up under a place of concealment which, whatever was its character, must have escaped their observation, was left on the field of battle, to become again the prize of the enemy, should their band venture to return, or die in darkness and privation, a death as horrid as ever tyrant invented, or martyr underwent, and which the unfortunate young lady could not even bear to think of without a prayer that her agony might at least be shortened.

In this hour of dread she recollected the poniard which she wore, and the dark thought crossed her mind, that, when life became hopeless, a speedy death was at least within her reach. As her soul shuddered at so dreadful an alternative, the question suddenly occurred, might not this weapon be put to a more hallowed use, and aid her emancipation, instead of abridging her sufferings?

This hope once adopted, the daughter of Raymond Berenger hastened to prove the experiment, and by repeated efforts succeeded, though with difficulty, in changing her posture, so as to admit of her inspecting her place of confinement all around, but particularly the passage by which she had entered, and by which she now attempted again to return to the light of day. She crept to the extremity, and found it, as she expected, strongly blocked up with large stones and earth, rammed together in such a manner as nearly to extinguish all hope of escape. The work, however, had been hastily performed, and life and liberty were prizes to stimulate exertion. With her poniard she cleared away the earth and sods— with her hands, little accustomed to such labour, she removed several stones, and advanced in her task so far as to obtain a glimmering of light, and, what was scarce less precious, a supply of purer air. But, at the same time, she had the misfortune to ascertain, that, from the size and massiveness of a huge stone which closed the extremity of the passage, there was no hope that her unassisted strength could effect her extrication. Yet her condition was improved by the admission of air and light, as well as by the opportunity afforded of calling out for assistance.

Such cries, indeed, were for some time uttered in vain—the field had probably been left to the dead and the dying; for low and indistinct groans were the only answer which she received for several minutes. At length, as she repeated her exclamation, a voice, faint as that of one just awakened from a swoon, pronounced these words in answer:—"Edris of the Earthen House, dost thou call from thy tomb to the wretch who just hastens to his own?—Are the boundaries broken down which connect me with the living?—And do I already hear, with fleshly ears, the faint and screaming accents of the dead?"

"It is no spirit who speaks," replied Eveline, overjoyed at finding she could at least communicate her existence to a living person—"no spirit, but a most unhappy maiden, Eveline Berenger by name, immured beneath this dark vault, and in danger to perish horribly, unless God send me rescue!"

"Eveline Berenger!" exclaimed he whom she addressed, in the accents of wonder. "It is impossible!—I watched her green mantle —I watched her plumy bonnet as I saw her hurried from the field, and felt my own inability to follow to the rescue; nor did force or exertion altogether leave me till the waving of the robe and the dancing of the feathers were lost to my eyes, and all hope of rescuing her abandoned my heart."

"Faithful vassal, or right true friend, or courteous stranger, whichsoever I may name thee," answered Eveline, "know thou hast been abused by the artifices of these Welsh banditti—the mantle and head-gear of Eveline Berenger they have indeed with them, and may have used them to mislead those true friends, who, like thee, are anxious for my fate. Wherefore, brave sir, devise some succour, if thou canst, for thyself and me; since I dread that these ruffians, when they shall have escaped immediate pursuit, will return hither, like the robber to the hoard where he has deposited his stolen booty."

"Now, the Holy Virgin be praised," said the wounded man, "that I can spend the last breath of my life in thy just and honourable service! I would not before blow my bugle, lest I recalled from the pursuit to the aid of my worthless self some of those who might be effectually engaged in thy rescue; may Heaven grant that the recall may now be heard, that my eyes may yet see the Lady Eveline in safety and liberty!"

The words, though spoken in a feeble tone, breathed a spirit of enthusiasm, and were followed by the blast of a horn, faintly winded, to which no answer was made save the echoing of the dell. A sharper and louder blast was then sent forth, but sunk so suddenly, that it seemed the breath of him who sounded the instrument had failed in the effort.—A strange thought crossed Eveline's mind even in that moment of uncertainty and terror. "That," she said, "was the note of a De Lacy—surely you cannot be my gentle kinsman, Sir Damian?"

"I am that unhappy wretch, deserving of death for the evil care which I have taken of the treasure intrusted to me.—What was my business to trust to reports and messengers? I should have worshipped the saint who was committed to my keeping, with such vigilance as avarice bestows on the dross which he calls treasure —I should have rested no where, save at your gate; outwatched the brightest stars in the horizon; unseen and unknown myself, I should never have parted from your neighbourhood; then had you not been in the present danger, and—much less important consequence— thou, Damian de Lacy, had not filled the grave of a forsworn and negligent caitiff!"

"Alas! noble Damian," said Eveline, "break not my heart by blaming yourself for an imprudence which is altogether my own. Thy succour was ever near when I intimated the least want of it; and it imbitters my own misfortune to know that my rashness has been the cause of your disaster. Answer me, gentle kinsman, and give me to hope that the wounds you have suffered are such as may be cured.— Alas! how much of your blood have I seen spilled, and what a fate is mine, that I should ever bring distress on all for whom I would most willingly sacrifice my own happiness!—But do not let us imbitter the moments given us in mercy, by fruitless repinings— Try what you can to stop thine ebbing blood, which is so dear to England—to Eveline—and to thine uncle."

Damian groaned as she spoke, and was silent; while, maddened with the idea that he might be perishing for want of aid, Eveline repeated her efforts to extricate herself for her kinsman's assistance as well as her own. It was all in vain, and she had ceased the attempt in despair; and, passing from one hideous subject of terror to another, she sat listening, with sharpened ear, for the dying groan of Damian, when—feeling of ecstasy!—the ground was shaken with horses' feet advancing rapidly. Yet this joyful sound, if decisive of life, did not assure her of liberty— It might be the banditti of the mountains returning to seek their captive. Even then they would surely allow her leave to look upon and bind up the wounds of Damian de Lacy; for to keep him as a captive might vantage them more in many degrees, than could his death. A horseman came up—Eveline invoked his assistance, and the first word she heard was an exclamation in Flemish from the faithful Wilkin Flammock, which nothing save some spectacle of the most unusual kind was ever known to compel from that phlegmatic person.

His presence, indeed, was particularly useful on this occasion; for, being informed by the Lady Eveline in what condition she was placed, and implored at the same time to look to the situation of Sir Damian de Lacy, he began, with admirable composure and some skill, to stop the wounds of the one, while his attendants collected levers, left by the Welsh as they retreated, and were soon ready to attempt the liberation of Eveline. With much caution, and under the experienced direction of Flammock, the stone was at length so much raised, that the Lady Eveline was visible, to the delight of all, and especially of the faithful Rose, who, regardless of the risk of personal harm, fluttered around her mistress's place of confinement, like a bird robbed of her nestlings around the cage in which the truant urchin has imprisoned them. Precaution was necessary to remove the stone, lest falling inwards it might do the lady injury.

At length the rocky fragment was so much displaced that she could issue forth; while her people, as in hatred of the coercion which she had sustained, ceased not to heave, with bar and lever, till, totally destroying the balance of the heavy mass, it turned over from the little flat on which it had been placed at the mouth of the subterranean entrance, and, acquiring force as it revolved down a steep declivity, was at length put into rapid motion, and rolled, crashed, and thundered, down the hill, amid flashes of fire which it forced from the rocks, and clouds of smoke and dust, until it alighted in the channel of a brook, where it broke into several massive fragments, with a noise that might have been heard some miles off.

With garments rent and soiled through the violence which she had sustained; with dishevelled hair, and disordered dress; faint from the stifling effect of her confinement, and exhausted by the efforts she had made to relieve herself, Eveline did not, nevertheless, waste a single minute in considering her own condition; but with the eagerness of a sister hastening to the assistance of her only brother, betook herself to examine the several severe wounds of Damian de Lacy, and to use proper means to stanch the blood and recall him from his swoon. We have said elsewhere, that, like other ladies of the time, Eveline was not altogether unacquainted with the surgical art, and she now displayed a greater share of knowledge than she had been thought capable of exerting. There was prudence, foresight, and tenderness, in every direction which she gave, and the softness of the female sex, with their officious humanity, ever ready to assist in alleviating human misery, seemed in her enhanced, and rendered dignified, by the sagacity of a strong and powerful understanding. After hearing with wonder for a minute or two the prudent and ready-witted directions of her mistress, Rose seemed at once to recollect that the patient should not be left to the exclusive care of the Lady Eveline, and joining, therefore, in the task, she rendered what assistance she could, while the attendants were employed in forming a litter, on which the wounded knight was to be conveyed to the castle of the Garde Doloureuse.

CHAPTER THE TWENTY-FIFTH.

A merry place, 'tis said, in times of yore,

But something ails it now—the place is cursed.
WORDSWORTH.

The place on which the skirmish had occurred, and the deliverance of the Lady Eveline had been effected, was a wild and singular spot, being a small level plain, forming a sort of stage, or resting-place, between two very rough paths, one of which winded up the rivulet from below, and another continued the ascent above. Being surrounded by hills and woods, it was a celebrated spot for finding game, and, in former days, a Welsh prince, renowned for his universal hospitality, his love of *crw* and of the chase, had erected a forest-lodge, where he used to feast his friends and followers with a profusion unexampled in Cambria. The fancy of the bards, always captivated with magnificence, and having no objections to the peculiar species of profusion practised by this potentate, gave him the surname of Edris of the Goblets; and celebrated him in their odes in terms as high as those which exalt the heroes of the famous Hirlas Horn. The subject of their praises, however, fell finally a victim to his propensities, having been stabbed to the heart in one of those scenes of confusion and drunkenness which were frequently the conclusion of his renowned banquets. Shocked at this catastrophe, the assembled Britons interred the relics of the Prince on the place where he had died, within the narrow vault where Eveline had been confined, and having barricaded the entrance of the sepulchre with fragments of rock, heaped over it an immense*cairn*, or pile of stones, on the summit of which they put the assassin to death. Superstition guarded the spot; and for many a year this memorial of Edris remained unviolated, although the lodge had gone to ruin, and its vestiges had totally decayed.

In latter years, some prowling band of Welsh robbers had discovered the secret entrance, and opened it with the view of ransacking the tomb for arms and treasures, which were in ancient times often buried with the dead. These marauders were disappointed, and obtained nothing by the violation of the grave of Edris, excepting the knowledge of a secret place, which might be used for depositing their booty, or even as a place of retreat for one of their number in a case of emergency.

When the followers of Damian, five or six in number, explained their part of the history of the day to Wilkin Flammock, it appeared that Damian had ordered them to horse at break of day, with a more considerable body, to act, as they understood, against a party of insurgent peasants, when of a sudden he had altered his mind, and, dividing his force into small bands, employed himself and them in reconnoitring more than one mountain-pass betwixt Wales and the Marches of the English country, in the neighbourhood of the Garde Douloureuse.

This was an occupation so ordinary for him, that it excited no particular notice. These manoeuvres were frequently undertaken by the warlike marchers, for the purpose of intimidating the Welsh, in general, more especially the bands of outlaws, who, independent of any regular government, infested these wild frontiers. Yet it escaped not comment, that, in undertaking such service at this moment, Damian seemed to abandon that of dispersing the insurgents, which had been considered as the chief object of the day.

It was about noon, when, falling in, as good fortune would have it, with one of the fugitive grooms, Damian and his immediate attendants received information of the violence committed on the Lady Eveline, and, by their perfect knowledge of the country, wore able to intercept the ruffians at the Pass of Edris, as it was called, by which the Welsh rovers ordinarily returned to their strongholds in the interior. It is probable that the banditti were not aware of the small force which Damian headed in person, and at the same time knew that there would be an immediate and hot pursuit in their rear; and these circumstances led their leader to adopt the singular expedient of hiding Eveline in the tomb, while one of their own number, dressed in her clothes, might serve as a decoy to deceive their assailants, and lead them, from the spot where she was really concealed, to which it was no doubt the purpose of the banditti to return, when they had eluded their pursuers.

Accordingly, the robbers had already drawn up before the tomb for the purpose of regularly retreating, until they should find some suitable place either for making a stand, or where, if overmatched, they might, by abandoning their horses, and dispersing among the rocks, evade the attack of the Norman cavalry. Their plan had been defeated by the precipitation of Damian, who, beholding as he thought the plumes and mantle of the Lady Eveline in the rear of the party, charged them without considering either the odds of numbers, or the lightness of his own armour, which, consisting only of a headpiece and a buff surcoat, offered but imperfect resistance to the Welsh knives and glaives. He was accordingly wounded severely at the onset, and would have been slain, but for the exertions of his few followers, and the fears of the Welsh, that, while thus continuing the battle in front, they might be assaulted in the rear by the followers of Eveline, whom they must now suppose were all in arms and motion. They retreated, therefore, or rather fled, and the attendants of Damian were despatched after them by their fallen master, with directions to let no consideration induce them to leave off the chase, until the captive Lady of the Garde Doloureuse was delivered from her ravishers.

The outlaws, secure in their knowledge of the paths, and the activity of their small Welsh horses, made an orderly retreat, with the exception of two or three of their rear-guard, cut down by Damian in his furious onset. They shot arrows, from time to time, at the men-at-arms, and laughed at the ineffectual efforts which these heavy-armed warriors, with their barbed horses, made to overtake them. But the scene was changed by the appearance of Wilkin Flammock, on his puissant war-horse, who was beginning to ascend the pass, leading a party consisting both of foot and horse. The fear of being intercepted caused the outlaws to have recourse to their last stratagem, and, abandoning their Welsh nags, they betook themselves to the cliffs, and, by superior activity and dexterity, baffled, generally speaking, the attempts of their pursuers on either hand. All of them, however, were not equally fortunate, for two or three fell into the hands of Flammock's party; amongst others, the person upon whom Eveline's clothes had been placed, and who now, to the great disappointment of those who had attached themselves to his pursuit, proved to be, not the lady whom they were emulous to deliver, but a fair-haired young Welshman, whose wild looks, and incoherent speech, seemed to argue a disturbed imagination. This would not have saved him from immediate death, the usual doom of captives taken in such skirmishes, had not the faint blast of Damian's horn, sounding from above, recalled his own party, and summoned that of Wilkin Flammock to the spot; while, in the confusion and hurry of their obeying the signal, the pity or the contempt of his guards suffered the prisoner to escape. They had, indeed, little to learn from him, even had he been disposed to give intelligence, or capable of communicating it. All were well assured that their lady had fallen into an ambuscade, formed by Dawfyd the one-eyed, a redoubted freebooter of the period, who had ventured upon this hardy enterprise in the hope of obtaining a large ransom for the captive Eveline, and all, incensed at his extreme insolence and audacity, devoted his head and limbs to the eagles and the ravens.

These were the particulars which the followers of Flammock and of Damian learned by comparing notes with each other, on the incidents of the day. As they returned by the Red Pool they were joined by Dame Gillian, who, after many exclamations of joy at the unexpected liberation of her lady, and as many of sorrow at the unexpected disaster of Damian, proceeded to inform the men-at- arms, that the merchant, whose hawks had been the original cause of these adventures, had been taken prisoner by two or three of the Welsh in their retreat, and that she herself and the wounded Raoul would have shared the same fate, but that they had no horse left to mount her upon, and did not consider old Raoul as worth either ransom or the trouble of killing. One had, indeed, flung a stone at him as he lay on the hill-side, but happily, as his dame said, it fell something short of him—"It was but a little fellow who threw it," she said—"there was a big man amongst them—if he had tried, it's like, by our Lady's grace, he had cast it a thought farther." So saying, the dame gathered herself up, and adjusted her dress for again mounting on horseback.

The wounded Damian was placed on a litter, hastily constructed of boughs, and, with the females, was placed in the centre of the little troop, augmented by the rest of the young knight's followers, who began to rejoin his standard. The united body now marched with military order and precaution, and winded through the passes with the attention of men prepared to meet and to repel injury.

CHAPTER THE TWENTY-SIXTH.

What! fair and young-, and faithful too?
A miracle if this be true.
  WALLER.

Rose, by nature one of the most disinterested and affectionate maidens that ever breathed, was the first who, hastily considering the peculiar condition in which her lady was placed, and the marked degree of restraint which had hitherto characterized her intercourse with her youthful guardian, became anxious to know how the wounded knight was to be disposed of; and when she came to Eveline's side for the purpose of asking this important question, her resolution well-nigh failed her.

The appearance of Eveline was indeed such as might have made it almost cruelty to intrude upon her any other subject of anxious consideration than those with which her mind had been so lately assailed, and was still occupied. Her countenance was as pale as death could have made it, unless where it was specked with drops of blood; her veil, torn and disordered, was soiled with dust and with gore; her hair, wildly dishevelled, fell in, elf-locks on her brow and shoulders, and a single broken and ragged feather, which was all that remained of her headgear, had been twisted among her tresses and still flowed there, as if in mockery, rather than ornament. Her eyes were fixed on the litter where Damian was deposited, and she rode close beside it, without apparently wasting a thought on any thing, save the danger of him who was extended there.

Rose plainly saw that her lady was under feelings of excitation, which might render it difficult for her to take a wise and prudent view of her own situation. She endeavoured gradually to awaken her to a sense of it. "Dearest lady," said Rose, "will it please you to take my mantle?"

"Torment me not," answered Eveline, with some sharpness in her accent.

"Indeed, my lady," said Dame Gillian, bustling up as one who feared her functions as mistress of the robes might be interfered with—"indeed, my lady,

Rose Flammock speaks truth; and neither your kirtle nor your gown are sitting as they should do; and, to speak truth, they are but barely decent. And so, if Rose will turn herself, and put her horse out of my way," continued the tire-woman, "I will put your dress in better order in the sticking in of a bodkin, than any Fleming of them all could do in twelve hours."

"I care not for my dress," replied Eveline, in the same manner as before.

"Care then for your honour—for your fame," said Rose, riding close to her mistress, and whispering in her ear; "think, and that hastily, how you are to dispose of this wounded young man."

"To the castle," answered Eveline aloud, as if scorning the affectation of secrecy; "lead to the castle, and that straight as you can."

"Why not rather to his own camp, or to Malpas?" said Rose— "dearest lady, believe, it will be for the best."

"Wherefore not—wherefore not?—wherefore not leave him on the way-side at once, to the knife of the Welshman, and the teeth of the wolf?-Once—twice—three times has he been my preserver. Where I go, he shall go; nor will I be in safety myself a moment sooner than I know that he is so."

Rose saw that she could make no impression on her mistress, and her own reflection told her that the wounded man's life might be endangered by a longer transportation than was absolutely necessary. An expedient occurred to her, by which she imagined this objection might be obviated; but it was necessary she should consult her father. She struck her palfrey with her riding-rod, and in a moment her diminutive, though beautiful figure, and her spirited little jennet, were by the side of the gigantic Fleming and his tall black horse, and riding, as it were, in their vast shadow. "My dearest father," said Rose, "the lady intends that Sir Damian be transported to the castle, where it is like he may be a long sojourner;—what think you?-is that wholesome counsel?"

"Wholesome for the youth, surely, Roschen," answered the Fleming, "because he will escape the better risk of a fever."

"True; but is it wise for my lady?" continued Rose.

"Wise enough, if she deal wisely. But wherefore shouldst thou doubt her, Roschen?"

"I know not," said Rose, unwilling to breathe even to her father the fears and doubts which she herself entertained; "but where there are evil tongues, there may be evil rehearsing. Sir Damian and my lady are both very young-Methinks it were better, dearest father, would you offer the shelter of your roof to the wounded knight, in the stead of his being carried to the castle."

"That I shall not, wench," answered the Fleming, hastily—"that I shall not, if I may help. Norman shall not cross my quiet threshold, nor Englishman neither, to mock my quiet thrift, and consume my substance. Thou dost not know them, because thou art ever with thy lady, and hast her good favour; but I know them well; and the best I can get from them is Lazy Flanderkin, and Greedy Flanderkin, and Flemish, sot—-I thank the saints they cannot say Coward Flanderkin, since Gwenwyn's Welsh uproar."

"I had ever thought, my father," answered Rose, "that your spirit was too calm to regard these base calumnies. Bethink you we are under this lady's banner, and that she has been my loving mistress, and her father was your good lord; to the Constable, too, are you beholden, for enlarged privileges. Money may pay debt, but kindness only can requite kindness; and I forebode that you will never have such an opportunity to do kindness to the houses of Berenger and De Lacy, as by opening the doors of your house to this wounded knight."

"The doors of my house!" answered the Fleming—"do I know how long I may call that, or any house upon earth, my own? Alas, my daughter, we came hither to fly from the rage of the elements, but who knows how soon we may perish by the wrath of men!"

"You speak strangely, my father," said Rose; "it holds not with your solid wisdom to augur such general evil from the rash enterprise of a Welsh outlaw."

"I think not of the One-eyed robber," said Wilkin; "although the increase and audacity of such robbers as Dawfyd is no good sign of a quiet country. But thou, who livest within yonder walls, hearest but little of what passes without, and your estate is less anxious;—you had known nothing of the news from me, unless in case I had found it necessary to remove to another country."

"To remove, my dearest father, from the land where your thrift and industry have gained you an honourable competency?"

"Ay, and where the hunger of wicked men, who envy me the produce of my thrift, may likely bring me to a dishonourable death. There have been tumults among the English rabble in more than one county, and their wrath is directed against those of our nation, as if we were Jews or heathens, and not better Christians and better men than themselves. They have, at York, Bristol, and elsewhere, sacked the houses of the Flemings, spoiled their goods, misused their families, and murdered themselves.—And why?—except that we have brought among them the skill and industry which they possessed not; and because wealth, which they would never else have seen in Britain, was the reward of our art and our toil. Roschen, this evil spirit is spreading wider daily. Here we are more safe than elsewhere, because we form a colony of some numbers and strength. But I confide not in our neighbours; and hadst not thou,

Rose, been in security, I would long ere this have given up all, and left Britain."

"Given up all, and left Britain!"—The words sounded prodigious in the ears of his daughter, who knew better than any one how successful her father had been in his industry, and how unlikely one of his firm and sedate temper was to abandon known and present advantages for the dread of distant or contingent peril. At length she replied, "If such be your peril, my father, methinks your house and goods cannot have a better protection than, the presence of this noble knight. Where lives the man who dare aught of violence against the house which harbours Damian de Lacy?"

"I know not that," said the Fleming, in the same composed and steady, but ominous tone—"May Heaven forgive it me, if it be sin! but I see little save folly in these Crusades, which the priesthood have preached up so successfully. Here has the Constable been absent for nearly three years, and no certain tidings of his life or death, victory or defeat. He marched from hence, as if he meant not to draw bridle or sheathe sword until the Holy Sepulchre was won from the Saracens, yet we can hear with no certainty whether even a hamlet has been taken from the Saracens. In the mean-while, the people that are at home grow discontented; their lords, with the better part of their followers, are in Palestine—dead or alive we scarcely know; the people themselves are oppressed and flayed by stewards and deputies, whose yoke is neither so light nor so lightly endured as that of the actual lord. The commons, who naturally hate the knights and gentry, think it no bad time to make some head against them—ay, and there be some of noble blood who would not care to be their leaders, that they may have their share in the spoil; for foreign expeditions and profligate habits have made many poor; and he that is poor will murder his father for money. I hate poor people; and I would the devil had every man who cannot keep himself by the work of his own hand!"

The Fleming concluded, with this characteristic imprecation, a speech which gave Rose a more frightful view of the state of England, than, shut up as she was within the Garde Doloureuse, she had before had an opportunity of learning. "Surely," she said— "surely these violences of which you speak are not to be dreaded by those who live under the banner of De Lacy and of Berenger?"

"Berenger subsists but in name," answered Wilkin Flammock, "and Damian, though a brave youth, hath not his uncle's ascendency of character, and authority. His men also complain that they are harassed with the duty of watching for protection of a castle, in itself impregnable, and sufficiently garrisoned, and that they lose all opportunity of honourable enterprise, as they call it— that is, of fight and spoil—in this inactive and inglorious manner of life. They say that Damian the beardless was a man, but that Damian with the mustache is no better than a woman; and that age, which has darkened his upper lip, hath at the same time blenched his courage.—And they say more, which were but wearisome to tell."

"Nay, but, let me know what they say; let me know it, for Heaven's sake!" answered Rose, "if it concern, as it must concern, my dear lady."

"Even so, Roschen," answered Wilkin. "There are many among the Norman men-at-arms who talk, over their wine-cups, how that Damian de Lacy is in love with his uncle's betrothed bride; ay, and that they correspond together by art magic."

"By art magic, indeed, it must be," said Rose, smiling scornfully, "for by no earthly means do they correspond, as I, for one, can bear witness."

"To art magic, accordingly, they impute it," quoth Wilkin Flammock, "that so soon as ever my lady stirs beyond the portal of her castle, De Lacy is in the saddle with a party of his cavalry, though they are positively certain that he has received no messenger, letter, or other ordinary notice of her purpose; nor have they ever, on such occasions, scoured the passes long, ere they have seen or heard of my Lady Eveline's being abroad."

"This has not escaped me," said Rose; "and my lady has expressed herself even displeased at the accuracy which Damian displayed in procuring a knowledge of her motions, as well as at the officious punctuality with which he has attended and guarded them. To-day has, however, shown," she continued, "that his vigilance may serve a good purpose; and as they never met upon these occasions, but continued at such distance as excluded even the possibility of intercourse, methinks they might have escaped the censure of the most suspicious."

"Ay, my daughter Roschen," replied Wilkin; "but it is possible to drive caution so far as to excite suspicion. Why, say the men-at- arms, should these two observe such constant, yet such guarded intelligence with one another? Why should their approach be so near, and why, yet, should they never meet? If they had been merely the nephew, and the uncle's bride, they must have had interviews avowedly and frankly; and, on the other hand, if they be two secret lovers, there is reason to believe that they do find their own private places of meeting, though they have art sufficient to conceal them."

"Every word that you speak, my father," replied the generous Rose, "increases the absolute necessity that you receive this wounded youth into your house. Be the evils you dread ever so great, yet, may you rely upon it, that they cannot be augmented by admitting him, with a few of his faithful followers."

"Not one follower," said the Fleming, hastily, "not one beef-fed knave of them, save the page that is to tend him, and the doctor that is to attempt his cure."

"But I may offer the shelter of your roof to these three, at least?" answered Rose.

"Do as thou wilt, do as thou wilt," said the doating father. "By my faith, Roschen, it is well for thee thou hast sense and moderation in asking, since I am so foolishly prompt in granting. This is one of your freaks, now, of honour or generosity—but commend me to prudence and honesty.—Ah! Rose, Rose, those who would do what is better than good, sometimes bring about what is worse than bad!—But I think I shall be quit of the trouble for the fear; and that thy mistress, who is, with reverence, something of a damsel errant, will stand stoutly for the chivalrous privilege of lodging her knight in her own bower, and tending him in person."

The Fleming prophesied true. Rose had no sooner made the proposal to Eveline, that the wounded Damian should be left at her father's house for his recovery, than her mistress briefly and positively rejected the proposal. "He has been my preserver," she said, "and if there be one being left for whom the gates of the Garde Doloureuse should of themselves fly open, it is to Damian de Lacy. Nay, damsel, look not upon me with that suspicious and yet sorrowful countenance—they that are beyond disguise, my girl, contemn suspicion—It is to God and Our Lady that I must answer, and to them my bosom lies open!"

They proceeded in silence to the castle gate, when the Lady Eveline issued her orders that her Guardian, as she emphatically termed Damian, should be lodged in her father's apartment; and, with the prudence of more advanced age, she gave the necessary direction for the reception and accommodation of his followers, and the arrangements which such an accession of guests required in the fortress. All this she did with the utmost composure and presence of mind, even before she altered or arranged her own disordered dress.

Another step still remained to be taken. She, hastened to the Chapel of the Virgin, and prostrating herself before her divine protectress, returned thanks for her second deliverance, and implored her guidance and direction, and, through her intercession, that of Almighty God, for the disposal and regulation of her conduct. "Thou knowest," she said, "that from no confidence in my own strength, have I thrust myself into danger. Oh, make me strong where I am most weak—Let not my gratitude and my compassion be a snare to me; and while I strive to discharge the duties which thankfulness imposes on me, save me from the evil tongues of men—and save—oh, save me from the insidious devices of my own heart!"

She then told her rosary with devout fervour, and retiring from the chapel to her own apartment, summoned her women to adjust her dress, and remove the external appearance of the violence to which she had been so lately subjected.

CHAPTER THE TWENTY-SEVENTH

Julia.——Gentle sir,

> You are our captive—but we'll use you so,
> That you shall think your prison joys may match
> Whate'er your liberty hath known of pleasure.

Roderick.
No, fairest, we have trifled here too long;
And, lingering to see your roses blossom,
I've let my laurels wither.

OLD PLAY.

Arrayed in garments of a mourning colour, and of a fashion more matronly than perhaps altogether befitted her youth—plain to an extremity, and devoid of all ornament, save her rosary—Eveline now performed the duty of waiting upon her wounded deliverer; a duty which the etiquette of the time not only permitted, but peremptorily enjoined. She was attended by Rose and Dame Gillian. Margery, whose element was a sick-chamber, had been already despatched to that of the young knight, to attend to whatever his condition might require.

Eveline entered the room with a light step, as if unwilling to disturb the patient. She paused at the door, and cast her eyes around her. It had been her father's chamber; nor had she entered it since his violent death. Around the walls hung a part of his armour and weapons, with hawking gloves, hunting-poles, and other instruments of silvan sport. These relics brought as it were in living form before her the stately presence of old Sir Raymond. "Frown not, my father,"—her lips formed the words, though her voice did not utter them —"Frown not—Eveline will never be unworthy of thee."

Father Aldrovand, and Amelot, the page of Damian, were seated by the bedside. They rose as Lady Eveline entered; and the first, who meddled a little with the healing art, said to Eveline "that the knight had slumbered for some time, and was now about to awake."

Amelot at the same time came forward, and in a hasty and low voice, begged that the chamber might be kept quiet, and the spectators requested to retire.

"My lord," he said, "ever since his illness at Gloucester, is apt to speak something wildly as he awakes from sleep, and will be displeased with me should I permit any one to be near him."

Eveline accordingly caused her women and the monk to retire into the anteroom, while she herself remained standing by the door- communication which connected the apartments, and heard Damian mention her name as he turned himself painfully on his couch. "Is she safe and unharmed?" was his first question, and it was asked with an eagerness which intimated how far it preceded all other considerations. When Amelot replied in the affirmative, he sighed, as one whose bosom is relieved from some weighty load, and in a less animated voice, asked of the page where they were. "This apartment," he said, "with its furniture, are all strange to me."

"My dear master," said Amelot, "you are at present too weak to ask questions and receive explanations."

"Be I where I will," said Damian, as if recovering his recollection, "I am not in the place where my duty calls me. Tell my trumpets to sound to horse—to horse, and let Ralph Genvil carry my banner. To horse—to horse! we have not a moment to lose!"

The wounded knight made some effort to rise, which, in his state of weakness, Amelot was easily able to frustrate. "Thou art right," he said, as he sunk back into his reclining posture—"thou art right—I am weak—but why should strength remain when honour is lost?" The unhappy young man covered his face with his hands, and groaned in agony, which seemed more that of the mind than of the body. Lady Eveline approached his bedside with unassured steps, fearing she knew not what, yet earnest to testify the interest she felt in the distresses of the sufferer. Damian looked up and beheld her, and again hid his face with his hands.

"What means this strange passion, Sir Knight?" said Eveline, with a voice which, at first weak and trembling, gradually obtained steadiness and composure. "Ought it to grieve you so much, sworn as you are to the duties of chivalry, that Heaven hath twice made you its instrument to save the unfortunate Eveline Berenger?"

"Oh no, no!" he exclaimed with rapidity; "since you are saved, all is well—but time presses—it is necessary I should presently depart—no-where ought I now to tarry—least of all, within this castle—Once more, Amelot, let them get to horse!"

"Nay, my good lord." said the damsel, "this must not be. As your ward, I cannot let my guardian part thus suddenly—as a physician, I cannot allow my patient to destroy himself—It is impossible that you can brook the saddle."

"A litter—a bier—a cart, to drag forth the dishonoured knight and traitor—all were too good for me—a coffin were best of all! —But see, Amelot, that it be framed like that of the meanest churl—no spurs displayed on the pall—no shield with the ancient coat of the De Lacys—no helmet with their knightly crest must deck the hearse of him whose name is dishonoured!"

"Is his brain unsettled?" said Eveline, looking with terror from the wounded man to his attendant; "or is there some dreadful mystery in these broken words?—If so, speak it forth; and if it may be amended by life or goods, my deliverer will sustain no wrong."

Amelot regarded her with a dejected and melancholy air, shook his head, and looked down on his master with a countenance which seemed to express, that the questions which she asked could not be prudently answered in Sir Damian's presence. The Lady Eveline, observing this gesture, stepped back into the outer apartment, and made Amelot a sign to follow her. He obeyed, after a glance at his master, who remained in the same disconsolate posture as formerly, with his hands crossed over his eyes, like one who wished to exclude the light, and all which the light made visible.

When Amelot was in the wardrobe, Eveline, making signs to her attendants to keep at such distance as the room permitted, questioned him closely on the cause of his master's desperate expression of terror and remorse. "Thou knowest," she said, "that I am bound to succour thy lord, if I may, both from gratitude, as one whom he hath served to the peril of his life—and also from kinsmanship. Tell me, therefore, in what case he stands, that I may help him if I can—that is," she added, her pale cheeks deeply colouring, "if the cause of the distress be fitting for me to hear."

The page bowed low, yet showed such embarrassment when he began to speak, as produced a corresponding degree of confusion in the Lady Eveline, who, nevertheless, urged him as before "to speak without scruple or delay—so that the tenor of his discourse was fitting for her ears."

"Believe me, noble lady," said Amelot, "your commands had been instantly obeyed, but that I fear my master's displeasure if I talk of his affairs without his warrant; nevertheless, on your command, whom I know he honours above all earthly beings, I will speak thus far, that if his life be safe from the wounds he has received, his honour and worship may be in great danger, if it please not Heaven to send a remedy."

"Speak on," said Eveline; "and be assured you will do Sir Damian de Lacy no prejudice by the confidence you may rest in me."

"I well believe it, lady," said the page. "Know, then, if it be not already known to you, that the clowns and rabble, who have taken arms against the nobles in the west, pretend to be favoured in their insurrection, not only by Randal Lacy, but by my master, Sir Damian."

"They lie that dare charge him with such foul treason to his own blood, as well as to his sovereign!" replied Eveline.

"Well do I believe they lie," said Amelot; "but this hinders not their falsehoods from being believed by those who know him less inwardly. More than one runaway from our troop have joined this rabblement, and that gives some credit to the scandal. And then they say—they say—that—in short, that my master longs to possess the lands in his proper right which he occupies as his uncle's administrator; and that if the old Constable—I crave your pardon, madam—should return from Palestine, he should find it difficult to obtain possession of his own again."

"The sordid wretches judge of others by their own base minds, and conceive those temptations too powerful for men of worth, which they are themselves conscious they would be unable to resist. But are the insurgents then so insolent and so powerful? We have heard of their violences, but only as if it had been some popular tumult."

"We had notice last night that they have drawn together in great force, and besieged or blockaded Wild Wenlock, with his men-at-arms, in a village about ten miles hence. He hath sent to my master, as his kinsman and companion-at-arms, to come to his assistance. We were on horseback this morning to march to the rescue—when—"

He paused, and seemed unwilling to proceed. Eveline caught at the word. "When you heard of my danger?" she said. "I would ye had rather heard of my death!"

"Surely, noble lady," said the page, with his eyes fixed on the ground, "nothing but so strong a cause could have made my master halt his troop, and carry the better part of them to the Welsh mountains, when his countryman's distress, and the commands of the King's Lieutenant, so peremptorily demanded his presence elsewhere."

"I knew it," she said—"I knew I was born to be his destruction! yet methinks this is worse than I dreamed of, when the worst was in my thoughts. I feared to occasion his death, not his loss of fame. For God's sake, young Amelot, do what thou canst, and that without loss of time! Get thee straightway to horse, and join to thy own men as many as thou canst gather of mine—Go—ride, my brave youth—show thy master's banner, and let them see that his forces and his heart are with them, though his person be absent. Haste, haste, for the time is precious."

"But the safety of this castle—But your own safety?" said the page. "God knows how willingly I would do aught to save his fame! But I know my master's mood; and were you to suffer by my leaving the Garde Doloureuse, even although I were to save him lands, life, and honour, by my doing so, I should be more like to taste of his dagger, than of his thanks or bounty."

"Go, nevertheless, dear Amelot," said she; "gather what force thou canst make, and begone."

"You spur a willing horse, madam," said the page, springing to his feet; "and in the condition of my master, I see nothing better than that his banner should be displayed against these churls."

"To arms, then," said Eveline, hastily; "to arms, and win thy spurs. Bring me assurance that thy master's honour is safe, and I will myself buckle them on thy heels. Here—take this blessed rosary—bind it on thy crest, and be the thought of the Virgin of the Garde Doloureuse, that never failed a votary, strong with thee in the hour of conflict."

She had scarcely ended, ere Amelot flew from her presence, and summoning together such horse as he could assemble, both of his master's, and of those belonging to the castle, there were soon forty cavaliers mounted in the court-yard.

But although the page was thus far readily obeyed, yet when the soldiers heard they were to go forth on a dangerous expedition, with no more experienced general than a youth of fifteen, they showed a decided reluctance to move from the castle. The old soldiers of De Lacy said, Damian himself was almost too youthful to command them, and had no right to delegate his authority to a mere boy; while the followers of Berenger said, their mistress might be satisfied with her deliverance of the morning, without trying farther dangerous conclusions by diminishing the garrison of her castle—"The times," they said, "were stormy, and it was wisest to keep a stone roof over their heads."

The more the soldiers communicated their ideas and apprehensions to each other, the stronger their disinclination to the undertaking became; and when Amelot, who, page-like, had gone to see that his own horse was accoutred and brought forth, returned to the castle-yard, he found them standing confusedly together, some mounted, some on foot, all men speaking loud, and all in a state of disorder. Ralph Genvil, a veteran whose face had been seamed with many a scar, and who had long followed the trade of a soldier of fortune, stood apart from the rest, holding his horse's bridle in one hand, and in the other the banner-spear, around which the banner of De Lacy was still folded.

"What means this, Genvil?" said the page, angrily. "Why do you not mount your horse and display the banner? and what occasions all this confusion?"

"Truly, Sir Page," said Genvil, composedly, "I am not in my saddle, because I have some regard for this old silken rag, which I have borne to honour in my time, and I will not willingly carry it where men are unwilling to follow and defend it."

"No march—no sally—no lifting of banner to-day" cried the soldiers, by way of burden to the banner-man's discourse. "How now, cowards! do you mutiny?" said Amelot, laying his hand upon his sword.

"Menace not me, Sir Boy," said Genvil; "nor shake your sword my way. I tell thee, Amelot, were my weapon to cross with yours, never flail sent abroad more chaff than I would make splinters of your hatched and gilded toasting-iron. Look you, there are gray- bearded men here that care not to be led about on any boy's humour. For me, I stand little upon that; and I care not whether one boy or another commands me. But I am the Lacy's man for the time; and I am not sure that, in marching to the aid of this Wild Wenlock, we shall do an errand the Lacy will thank us for. Why led he us not thither in the morning when we were commanded off into the mountains?"

"You well know the cause," said the page.

"Yes, we do know the cause; or, if we do not, we can guess it," answered the banner-man, with a horse laugh, which was echoed by several of his companions.

"I will cram the calumny down thy false throat, Genvil!" said the page; and, drawing his sword, threw himself headlong on the banner-man, without considering their great difference of strength.

Genvil was contented to foil his attack by one, and, as it seemed, a slight movement of his gigantic arm, with which he forced the page aside, parrying, at the same time, his blow with the standard-spear.

There was another loud laugh, and Amelot, feeling all his efforts baffled, threw his sword from him, and weeping in pride and indignation, hastened back to tell the Lady Eveline of his bad success. "All," he said, "is lost—the cowardly villains have mutinied, and will not move; and the blame of their sloth and faintheartedness will be laid on my dear master."

"That shall never be," said Eveline, "should I die to prevent it. —Follow me, Amelot."

She hastily threw a scarlet scarf over her dark garments, and hastened down to the court-yard, followed by Gillian, assuming, as she went, various attitudes and actions expressing astonishment and pity, and by Rose, carefully suppressing all appearance of— the feelings which she really entertained.

Eveline entered the castle-court, with the kindling eye and glowing brow which her ancestors were wont to bear in danger and extremity, when their soul was arming to meet the storm, and displayed in their mien and looks high command and contempt of danger. She seemed at the moment taller than her usual size; and it was with a voice distinct and clearly heard, though not exceeding the delicacy of feminine tone, that the mutineers heard her address them. "How is this, my masters?" she said; and as she spoke, the bulky forms of the armed soldiers seemed to draw closer together, as if to escape her individual censure. It was like a group of heavy water-fowl, when they close to avoid the stoop of the slight and beautiful merlin, dreading the superiority of its nature and breeding over their own inert physical strength.—"How now?" again she demanded of them; "is it a time, think ye, to mutiny, when your lord is absent, and his nephew and lieutenant lies stretched on a bed of sickness?— Is it thus you keep your oaths?—Thus ye merit your leader's bounty?—Shame on ye, craven hounds, that quail and give back the instant you lose sight of the huntsman!"

There was a pause—the soldiers looked on each other, and then again on Eveline, as if ashamed alike to hold out in their mutiny, or to return to their usual discipline.

"I see how it is, my brave friends—ye lack a leader here; but stay not for that —I will guide you myself, and, woman as I am, there need not a man of you fear disgrace where a Berenger commands.—Trap my palfrey with a steel saddle," she said, "and that instantly." She snatched from the ground the page's light head-piece, and threw it over her hair, caught up his drawn sword, and went on. "Here I promise you my countenance and guidance— this gentleman," she pointed to Genvil, "shall supply my lack of military skill. He looks like a man that hath seen many a day of battle, and can well teach a young leader her devoir."

"Certes," said the old soldier, smiling in spite of himself, and shaking his head at the same time, "many a battle have I seen, but never under such a commander."

"Nevertheless," said Eveline, seeing how the eyes of the rest turned on Genvil, "you do not—cannot—will not—refuse to follow me? You do not as a soldier, for my weak voice supplies your captain's orders—you cannot as a gentleman, for a lady, a forlorn and distressed female, asks you a boon—you will not as an Englishman, for your country requires your sword, and your comrades are in danger. Unfurl your banner, then, and march."

"I would do so, upon my soul, fair lady," answered Genvil, as if preparing to unfold the banner—"And Amelot might lead us well enough, with advantage of some lessons from me, But I wot not whether you are sending us on the right road."

"Surely, surely," said Eveline, earnestly, "it must be the right road which conducts you to the relief of Wenlock and his followers, besieged by the insurgent boors."

"I know not," said Genvil, still hesitating. "Our leader here, Sir Damian de Lacy, protects the commons—men say he befriends them— and I know he quarrelled with Wild Wenlock once for some petty wrong he did to the miller's wife at Twyford. We should be finely off, when our fiery young leader is on foot again, if he should find we had been fighting against the side he favoured."

"Assure yourself," said the maiden, anxiously, "the more he would protect the commons against oppression, the more he would put them down when oppressing others. Mount and ride—save Wenlock and his men—there is life and death in every moment. I will warrant, with my life and lands, that whatsoever you do will be held good service to De Lacy. Come, then, follow me."

"None surely can know Sir Damian's purpose better than you, fair damsel," answered Genvil; "nay, for that matter, you can make him change as ye list,— And so I will march with the men, and we will aid Wenlock, if it is yet time, as I trust it may; for he is a rugged wolf, and when he turns to bay, will cost the boors blood enough ere they sound a mort. But do you remain within the castle, fair lady, and trust to Amelot and me.—Come, Sir Page, assume the command, since so it must be; though, by my faith, it is pity to take the headpiece from that pretty head, and the sword from that pretty hand—By Saint George! to see them there is a credit to the soldier's profession."

The Lady accordingly surrendered the weapons to Amelot, exhorting him in few words to forget the offence he had received, and do his devoir manfully. Meanwhile Genvil slowly unrolled the pennon—then shook it abroad, and without putting his foot in the stirrup, aided himself a little with resting on the spear, and threw himself into the saddle, heavily armed as he was. "We are ready now, an it like your juvenility," said he to Amelot; and then, while the page was putting the band into order, he whispered to his nearest comrade, "Methinks, instead of this old swallow's tail, we should muster rarely under a broidered petticoat—a furbelowed petticoat has no fellow in my mind.—Look you, Stephen Pontoys—I can forgive Damian now for forgetting his uncle and his own credit, about this wench; for, by my faith, she is one I could have doated to death upon *par amours.*Ah! evil luck be the women's portion!—they govern us at every turn, Stephen," and at every age. When they are young, they bribe us with fair looks, and sugared words, sweet kisses and love tokens; and when they are of middle age, they work us to their will by presents and courtesies, red wine and red gold; and when they are old, we are fain to run their errands to get out of sight of their old leathern visages. Well, old De Lacy should have staid at home and watched his falcon. But it is all one to us, Stephen, and we may make some vantage to-day, for these boors have plundered more than one castle."

"Ay, ay," answered Pontoys, "the boor to the booty, and the banner-man to the boor, a right pithy proverb. But, prithee, canst thou say why his pageship leads us not forward yet?"

"Pshaw!" answered Genvil, "the shake I gave him has addled his brains—or perchance he has not swallowed all his tears yet; sloth it is not, for 'tis a forward cockeril for his years, wherever honour is to be won.—See, they now begin to move.—Well, it is a singular thing this gentle blood, Stephen; for here is a child whom I but now baffled like a schoolboy, must lead us gray beards where we may get our heads broken, and that at the command of a light lady."

"I warrant Sir Damian is secretary to my pretty lady," answered Stephen Pontoys, "as this springald Amelot is to Sir Damian; and so we poor men must obey and keep our mouths shut."

"But our eyes open, Stephen Pontoys—forget not that."

They were by this time out of the gates of the castle, and upon the road leading to the village, in which, as they understood by the intelligence of the morning, Wenlock was besieged or blockaded by a greatly superior number of the insurgent commons. Amelot rode at the head of the troop, still embarrassed at the affront which he had received in presence of the soldiers, and lost in meditating how he was to eke out that deficiency of experience, which on former occasions had been supplied by the counsels of the banner-man, with whom he was ashamed to seek a reconciliation. But Genvil was not of a nature absolutely sullen, though a habitual grumbler. He rode up to the page, and having made his obeisance, respectfully asked him whether it were not well that some one or two of their number pricked forward upon good horses to learn how it stood with Wenlock, and whether they should be able to come up in time to his assistance.

"Methinks, banner-man," answered Amelot, "you should take the ruling of the troop, since you know so fittingly what should be done. You may be the fitter to command, because—But I will not upbraid you."

"Because I know so ill how to obey," replied Genvil; "that is what you would say; and, by my faith, I cannot deny but there may be some truth in it. But is it not peevish in thee to let a fair expedition be unwisely conducted, because of a foolish word or a sudden action?—Come, let it be peace with us."

"With all my heart," answered Amelot; "and I will send out an advanced party upon the adventure, as thou hast advised me."

"Let it be old Stephen Pontoys and two of the Chester spears—he is as wily as an old fox, and neither hope nor fear will draw him a hairbreadth farther than judgment warrants."

Amelot eagerly embraced the hint, and, at his command, Pontoys and two lances started forward to reconnoitre the road before them, and inquire into the condition of those whom they were advancing to succour. "And now that we are on the old terms, Sir Page," said the banner-man, "tell me, if thou canst, doth not yonder fair lady love our handsome knight *par amours?*"

"It is a false calumny," said Amelot, indignantly; "betrothed as she is to his uncle, I am convinced she would rather die than have such a thought, and so would our master. I have noted this heretical belief in thee before now, Genvil, and I have prayed thee to check it. You know the thing cannot be, for you know they have scarce ever met."

"How should I know that," said Genvil, "or thou either? Watch them ever so close—much water slides past the mill that Hob Miller never wots of. They do correspond; that, at least, thou canst not deny?"

"I do deny it," said Amelot, "as I deny all that can touch their honour."

"Then how, in Heaven's name, comes he by such perfect knowledge of her motions, as he has displayed no longer since than the morning?"

"How should I tell?" answered the page; "there be such things, surely, as saints and good angels, and if there be one on earth deserves their protection, it is Dame Eveline Berenger."

"Well said, Master Counsel-keeper," replied Genvil, laughing; "but that will hardly pass on an old trooper.—Saint and angels, quotha? most saint-like doings, I warrant you."

The page was about to continue his angry vindication, when Stephen Pontoys and his followers returned upon the spur. "Wenlock holds out bravely," he exclaimed, "though he is felly girded in with these boors. The large crossbows are doing good service; and I little doubt his making his place good till we come up, if it please you to ride something sharply. They have assailed the barriers, and were close up to them even now, but were driven back with small success."

The party were now put in as rapid motion as might consist with order, and soon reached the top of a small eminence, beneath which lay the village where Wenlock was making his defence. The air rung with the cries and shouts of the insurgents, who, numerous as bees, and possessed of that dogged spirit of courage so peculiar to the English, thronged like ants to the barriers, and endeavoured to break down the palisades, or to climb over them, in despite of the showers of stones and arrows from within, by which they suffered great loss, as well as by the swords and battle-axes of the men-at-arms, whenever they came to hand-blows.

"We are in time, we are in time," said Amelot, dropping the reins of his bridle, and joyfully clapping his hands; "shake thy banner abroad, Genvil—give Wenlock and his fellows a fair view of it.— Comrades, halt—breathe your horses for a moment.—Hark hither, Genvil—If we descend by yonder broad pathway into the meadow where the cattle are—" "Bravo, my young falcon" replied Genvil, whose love of battle, like that of the war-horse of Job, kindled at the sight of the spears, and at the sound of the trumpet; "we shall have then an easy field for a charge on yonder knaves."

"What a thick black cloud the villains make" said Amelot; "but we will let daylight through it with our lances—See, Genvil, the defenders hoist a signal to show they have seen us."

"A signal to us?" exclaimed Genvil. "By Heaven, it is a white flag—a signal of surrender!"

"Surrender! they cannot dream of it, when we are advancing to their succour," replied Amelot; when two or three melancholy notes from the trumpets of the besieged, with a thundering and tumultuous acclamation from the besiegers, rendered the fact indisputable.

"Down goes Wenlock's pennon," said Genvil, "and the churls enter the barricades on all points.—Here has been cowardice or treachery—What is to be done?"

"Advance on them," said Amelot, "retake the place, and deliver the prisoners."

"Advance, indeed!" answered the banner-man—"Not a horse's length by my counsel—we should have every nail in our corslets counted with arrow-shot, before we got down the hill in the face of such a multitude and the place to storm afterwards—it were mere insanity."

"Yet come a little forward along with me," said the page; "perhaps we may find some path by which we could descend unperceived."

Accordingly they rode forward a little way to reconnoitre the face of the hill, the page still urging the possibility of descending it unperceived amid the confusion, when Genvil answered impatiently, "Unperceived!-you are already perceived—here comes a fellow, pricking towards us as fast as his beast may trot."

As he spoke, the rider came up to them. He was a short, thick-set peasant, in an ordinary frieze jacket and hose, with a blue cap on his head, which he had been scarcely able to pull over a shock head of red hair, that seemed in arms to repel the covering. The man's hands were bloody, and he carried at his saddlebow a linen bag, which was also stained with blood. "Ye be of Damian de Lacy's company, be ye not?" said this rude messenger; and, when they answered in the affirmative, he proceeded with the same blunt courtesy, "Hob Miller of Twyford commends him to Damian de Lacy, and knowing his purpose to amend disorders in the commonwealth, Hob Miller sends him toll of the grist which he has grinded;" and with that he took from the bag a human head, and tendered it to Amelot.

"It is Wenlock's head," said Genvil—"how his eyes stare!"

"They will stare after no more wenches now," said the boor—"I have cured him of caterwauling."

"Thou!" said Amelot, stepping back in disgust and indignation.

"Yes, I myself," replied the peasant; "I am Grand Justiciary of the Commons, for lack of a better."

"Grand hangman, thou wouldst say," replied Genvil.

"Call it what thou list," replied the peasant. "Truly, it behoves men in state to give good example. I'll bid no man do that I am not ready to do myself. It is as easy to hang a man, as to say hang him; we will have no splitting of offices in this new world, which is happily set up in old England."

"Wretch!" said Amelot, "take back thy bloody token to them that sent thee! Hadst thou not come upon assurance, I had pinned thee to the earth with my lance—But, be assured, your cruelty shall be fearfully avenged.—Come, Genvil, let us to our men; there is no farther use in abiding here."

The fellow, who had expected a very different reception, stood staring after them for a few moments, then replaced his bloody trophy in the wallet, and rode back to those who sent him.

"This comes of meddling with men's *amourettes*," said Genvil; "Sir Damian would needs brawl with Wenlock about his dealings with this miller's daughter, and you see they account him a favourer of their enterprise; it will be well if others do not take up the same opinion.—I wish we were rid of the trouble which such suspicions may bring upon us—ay, were it at the price of my best horse—I am like to lose him at any rate with the day's hard service, and I would it were the worst it is to cost us."

The party returned, wearied and discomforted, to the castle of the Garde

Doloureuse, and not without losing several of their number by the way, some straggling owing to the weariness of their horses, and others taking the opportunity of desertion, in order to join the bands of insurgents and plunderers, who had now gathered together in different quarters, and were augmented by recruits from the dissolute soldiery.

Amelot, on his return to the castle, found that the state of his master was still very precarious, and that the Lady Eveline, though much exhausted, had not yet retired to rest, but was awaiting his return with impatience. He was introduced to her accordingly, and, with a heavy heart, mentioned the ineffectual event of his expedition.

"Now the saints have pity upon us!" said the Lady Eveline; "for it seems as if a plague or pest attached to me, and extended itself to all who interest themselves in my welfare. From the moment they do so, their very virtues become snares to them; and what would, in every other case, recommend them to honour, is turned to destruction to the friends of Eveline Berenger."

"Fear not, fair lady," said Amelot; "there are still men enough in my master's camp to put down these disturbers of the public peace. I will but abide to receive his instructions, and will hence to- morrow, and draw out a force to restore quiet in this part of the country."

"Alas! you know not yet the worst of it," replied Eveline. "Since you went hence, we have received certain notice, that when the soldiers at Sir Damian's camp heard of the accident which he this morning met with, already discontented with the inactive life which they had of late led, and dispirited by the hurts and reported death of their leader, they have altogether broken up and dispersed their forces. Yet be of good courage, Amelot," she said; "this house is strong enough to bear out a worse tempest than any that is likely to be poured on it; and if all men desert your master in wounds and affliction, it becomes yet more the part of Eveline Berenger to shelter and protect her deliverer."

CHAPTER THE TWENTY-EIGHTH

Let our proud trumpet shako their castle wall,
  Menacing death and ruin.
   OTWAY

The evil news with which the last chapter concluded were necessarily told to Damian de Lacy, as the person whom they chiefly concerned; and Lady Eveline herself undertook the task of communicating them, mingling what she said with tears, and again interrupting those tears to suggest topics of hope and comfort, which carried no consolation to her own bosom.

The wounded knight continued with his face turned towards her, listening to the disastrous tidings, as one who was not otherwise affected by them, than as they regarded her who told the story. When she had done speaking, he continued as in a reverie, with his eyes so intently fixed upon her, that she rose up, with the purpose of withdrawing from looks by which she felt herself embarrassed. He hastened to speak, that he might prevent her departure. "All that you have said, fair lady," he replied, "had been enough, if told by another, to have broken my heart; for it tells me that the power and honour of my house, so solemnly committed to my charge, have been blasted in my misfortunes. But when I look upon you, and hear your voice, I forget every thing, saving that you have been rescued, and are here in honour and safety. Let me therefore pray of your goodness that I may be removed from the castle which holds you, and sent elsewhere. I am in no shape worthy of your farther care, since I have no longer the swords of others at my disposal, and am totally unable for the present to draw my own."

"And if you are generous enough to think of me in your own misfortunes, noble knight," answered Eveline, "can you suppose that I forget wherefore, and in whose rescue, these wounds were incurred? No, Damian, speak not of removal—while there is a turret of the Garde Doloureuse standing, within that turret shall you find shelter and protection. Such, I am well assured, would be the pleasure of your uncle, were he here in person."

It seemed as if a sudden pang of his wound had seized upon Damian; for, repeating the words "My. uncle!" he writhed himself round, and averted his face from Eveline; then again composing himself, replied, "Alas! knew my uncle how ill I have obeyed his precepts, instead of sheltering me within this house, he would command me to be flung from the battlements!"

"Fear not his displeasure," said Eveline, again preparing to withdraw; "but endeavour, by the composure of your spirit, to aid the healing of your wounds; when, I doubt not, you will be able again to establish good order in the Constable's jurisdiction, long before his return."

She coloured as she pronounced the last words, and hastily left the apartment. When she was in her own chamber, she dismissed her other attendants and retained Rose. "What dost thou think of these things, my wise maiden and monitress?" said she.

"I would," replied Rose, "either that this young knight had never entered this castle—or that, being here, he could presently leave it—or, that he could honourably remain here for ever."

"What dost thou mean by remaining here for ever?" said Eveline sharply and hastily. "Let me answer that question with another— How long has the Constable of Chester been absent from England?"

"Three years come Saint Clement's day," said Eveline; "and what of that?"

"Nay, nothing; but——"

"But what?—I command you to speak out."

"A few weeks will place your hand at your own disposal."

"And think you, Rose," said Eveline, rising with dignity, "that there are no bonds save those which are drawn by the scribe's pen?—We know little of the Constable's adventures; but we know enough to show that his towering hopes have fallen, and his sword and courage proved too weak to change the fortunes of the Sultan Saladin. Suppose him returning some brief time hence, as we have seen so many crusaders regain their homes, poor and broken in health— suppose that he finds his lands laid waste, and his followers dispersed, by the consequence of their late misfortunes, how would it sound should he also find that his betrothed bride had wedded and endowed with her substance the nephew whom he most trusted?—Dost thou think such an engagement is like a Lombard's mortgage, which must be redeemed on the very day, else forfeiture is sure to be awarded?"

"I cannot tell, madam," replied Rose; "but they that keep their covenant to the letter, are, in my country, held bound to no more."

"That is a Flemish fashion, Rose," said her mistress; "but the honour of a Norman is not satisfied with an observance so limited. What! wouldst thou have my honour, my affections, my duty, all that is most valuable to a woman, depend on the same progress of the kalendar which an usurer watches for the purpose of seizing on a forfeited pledge?—Am I such a mere commodity, that I must belong to one man if he claims me before Michaelmas, to another if he comes afterwards?—No, Rose; I did not thus interpret my engagement, sanctioned as it was by the special providence of Our Lady of the Garde Doloureuse."

"It is a feeling worthy of you, my dearest lady," answered the attendant; "yet you are so young—so beset with perils—so much exposed to calumny—that I, at least, looking forward to the time when you may have a legal companion and protector, see it as an extrication from much doubt and danger." "Do not think of it, Rose," answered Eveline; "do not liken your mistress to those provident dames, who, while one husband yet lives, though in old age or weak health, are prudently engaged in plotting for another."

"Enough, my dearest lady," said Rose;——"yet not so. Permit me one word more. Since you are determined not to avail yourself of your freedom, even when the fatal period of your engagement is expired, why suffer this young man to share our solitude?—He is surely well enough to be removed to some other place of security. Let us resume our former sequestered mode of life, until Providence send us some better or more certain prospects."

Eveline sighed—looked down—then looking upwards, once more had opened her lips to express her willingness to enforce so reasonable an arrangement, but for Damian's recent wounds, and the distracted state of the country, when she was interrupted by the shrill sound of trumpets, blown before the gate of the castle; and Raoul, with anxiety on his brow, came limping to inform his lady, that a knight, attended by a pursuivant-at-arms, in the royal livery, with a strong guard, was in front of the castle, and demanded admittance in the name of the King.

Eveline paused a moment ere she replied, "Not even to the King's order shall the castle of my ancestors be opened, until we are well assured of the person by whom, and the purpose for which, it is demanded. We will ourself to the gate, and learn the meaning of this summons—My veil, Rose; and call my women.—Again that trumpet sounds! Alas! it rings like a signal to death and ruin."

The prophetic apprehensions of Eveline were not false; for scarce had she reached the door of the apartment, when she was met by the page Amelot, in a state of such disordered apprehension as an eleve of chivalry was scarce on any occasion permitted to display. "Lady, noble lady," he said, hastily bending his knee to Eveline, "save my dearest master!—You, and you alone, can save him at this extremity."

"I!" said Eveline, in astonishment—"I save him?—And from what danger?—God knows how willingly!"

There she stopped short, as if afraid to trust herself with expressing what rose to her lips.

"Guy Monthermer, lady, is at the gate, with a pursuivant and the royal banner. The hereditary enemy of the House of Lacy, thus accompanied, comes hither for no good—the extent of the evil I know not, but for evil he comes. My master slew his nephew at the field of Malpas, and therefore"——He was here interrupted by another flourish of trumpets, which rung, as if in shrill impatience, through the vaults of the ancient fortress.

The Lady Eveline hasted to the gate, and found that the wardens, and others who attended there, were looking on each other with doubtful and alarmed countenances, which they turned upon her at her arrival, as if to seek from, their mistress the comfort and the courage which they could not communicate to each other. Without the gate, mounted, and in complete armour, was an elderly and stately knight, whose raised visor and beaver depressed, showed a beard already grizzled. Beside him appeared the pursuivant on horseback, the royal arms embroidered on his heraldic dress of office, and all the importance of offended consequence on his countenance, which was shaded by his barret-cap and triple plume. They were attended by a body of about fifty soldiers, arranged under the guidon of England.

When the Lady Eveline appeared at the barrier, the knight, after a slight reverence, which seemed more informal courtesy than in kindness, demanded if he saw the daughter of Raymond Berenger. "And is it," he continued, when he had received an answer in the affirmative, "before the castle of that approved and favoured servant of the House of Anjou, that King Henry's trumpets have thrice sounded, without obtaining an entrance for those who are honoured with their Sovereign's command?"

"My condition," answered Eveline, "must excuse my caution. I am a lone maiden, residing in a frontier fortress. I may admit no one without inquiring his purpose, and being assured that his entrance consists with the safety of the place, and mine own honour."

"Since you are so punctilious, lady," replied Monthermer, "know, that in the present distracted state of the country, it is his Grace the King's pleasure to place within your walls a body of men-at-arms, sufficient to guard this important castle, both from the insurgent peasants, who burn and slay, and from the Welsh, who, it must be expected, will, according to their wont in time of disturbance, make incursions on the frontiers. Undo your gates, then, Lady of Berenger, and suffer his Grace's forces to enter the castle."

"Sir Knight," answered the lady, "this castle, like every other fortress in England, is the King's by law; but by law also I am the keeper and defender of it; and it is the tenure by which my ancestors held these lands. I have men enough to maintain the Garde Doloureuse in my time, as my father, and my grandfather before him, defended it in theirs. The King is gracious to send me succours, but I need not the aid of hirelings; neither do I think it safe to admit such into my castle, who may, in this lawless time, make themselves master of it for other than its lawful mistress."

"Lady," replied the old warrior, "his Grace is not ignorant of the motives which produce a contumacy like this. It is not any apprehension for the royal forces which influences you, a royal vassal, in this refractory conduct. I might proceed upon your refusal to proclaim you a traitor to the Crown, but the King remembers the services of your father. Know, then, we are not ignorant that Damian de Lacy, accused of instigating and heading this insurrection, and of deserting his duty in the field, and abandoning a noble comrade to the swords of the brutal peasants, has found shelter under this roof, with little credit to your loyalty as vassal, or your conduct as a high-born maiden. Deliver him up to us, and I will draw off these men-at-arms, and dispense, though I may scarce answer doing so, with the occupation of the castle."

"Guy de Monthermer," answered Eveline, "he that throws a stain on my name, speaks falsely and unworthily; as for Damian de Lacy, he knows how to defend his own fame. This only let me say, that, while he takes his abode in the castle of the betrothed of his kinsman, she delivers him to no one, least of all to his well- known feudal enemy—Drop the portcullis, wardens, and let it not be raised without my special order."

The portcullis, as she spoke, fell rattling and clanging to the ground, and Monthermer, in baffled spite, remained excluded from the castle. "Un-worthy lady"—he began in passion, then, checking himself, said calmly to the pursuivant, "Ye are witness that she hath admitted that the traitor is within that castle,—ye are witness that, lawfully summoned, this Eveline Berenger refuses to deliver him up. Do your duty, Sir Pursuivant, as is usual in such cases."

The pursuivant then advanced and proclaimed, in the formal and fatal phrase befitting the occasion, that Eveline Berenger, lawfully summoned, refusing to admit the King's forces into her castle, and to deliver up the body of a false traitor, called Damian de Lacy, had herself incurred the penalty of high treason, and had involved within the same doom all who aided, abetted, or maintained her in holding out the said castle against their allegiance to Henry of Anjou. The trumpets, so soon as the voice of the herald had ceased, confirmed the doom he had pronounced, by a long and ominous peal, startling from their nests the owl and the raven, who replied to it by their ill-boding screams.

The defenders of the castle looked on each other with blank and dejected countenances, while Monthermer, raising aloft his lance, exclaimed, as he turned his horse from the castle gate, "When I next approach the Garde Doloureuse, it will be not merely to intimate, but to execute, the mandate of my Sovereign."

As Eveline stood pensively to behold the retreat of Monthermer and his associates, and to consider what was to be done in this emergency, she heard one of the Flemings, in a low tone, ask an Englishman, who stood beside him, what was the meaning of a traitor.

"One who betrayeth a trust reposed—a betrayer," said the interpreter. The phrase which he used recalled to Eveline's memory her boding vision or dream. "Alas!" she said, "the vengeance of the fiend is about to be accomplished. Widow'd wife and wedded maid—these epithets have long been mine. Betrothed!—wo's me! it is the key-stone of my destiny. Betrayer I am now denounced, though, thank God, I am clear from the guilt! It only follows that I should be betrayed, and the evil prophecy will be fulfilled to the very letter." fir?

CHAPTER THE TWENTY-NINTH

Out on ye, owls;
Nothing but songs of death?
  RICHARD III.

More than three months had elapsed since the event narrated in the last chapter, and it had been the precursor of others of still greater importance, which will evolve themselves in the course of our narrative. But, profess to present to the reader not a precise detail of circumstances, according to their order and date, but a series of pictures, endeavouring to exhibit the most striking incidents before the eye or imagination of those whom it may concern, we therefore open a new scene, and bring other actors upon the stage.

Along a wasted tract of country, more than twelve miles distant from the Garde Doloureuse, in the heat of a summer noon, which shed a burning lustre on the silent valley, and the blackened ruins of the cottages with which it had been once graced, two travellers walked slowly, whose palmer cloaks, pilgrims' staves, large slouched hats, with a scallop shell bound on the front of each, above all, the cross, cut in red cloth upon their shoulders, marked them as pilgrims who had accomplished their vow, and had returned from that fatal bourne, from which, in those days, returned so few of the thousands who visited it, whether in the love of enterprise, or in the ardour of devotion.

The pilgrims had passed, that morning, through a scene of devastation similar to, and scarce surpassed in misery by, those which they had often trod during the wars of the Cross. They had seen hamlets which appeared to have suffered all the fury of military execution, the houses being burned to the ground; and in many cases the carcasses of the miserable inhabitants, or rather relics of such objects, were suspended on temporary gibbets, or on the trees, which had been allowed to remain standing, only, it would seem, to serve the convenience of the executioners. Living creatures they saw none, excepting those wild denizens of nature who seemed silently resuming the now wasted district, from which they might have been formerly expelled by the course of civilization. Their ears were no less disagreeably occupied than their eyes. The pensive travellers might indeed hear the screams of the raven, as if lamenting the decay of the carnage on which he had been gorged; and now and then the plaintive howl of some dog, deprived of his home and master; but no sounds which argued either labour or domestication of any kind.

The sable figures, who, with wearied steps, as it appeared, travelled through these scenes of desolation and ravage, seemed assimilated to them in appearance. They spoke not with each other —they looked not to each other— but one, the shorter of the pair, keeping about half a pace in front of his companion, they moved slowly, as priests returning from a sinner's death-bed, or rather as spectres flitting along the precincts of a church-yard.

At length they reached a grassy mound, on the top of which was placed one of those receptacles for the dead of the ancient British chiefs of distinction, called Kist-vaen, which are composed of upright fragments of granite, so placed as to form a stone coffin, or something bearing that resemblance. The sepulchre had been long violated by the victorious Saxons, either in scorn or in idle curiosity, or because treasures were supposed to be sometimes concealed in such spots. The huge flat stone which had once been the cover of the coffin, if so it might be termed, lay broken in two pieces at some distance from the sepulchre; and, overgrown as the fragments were with grass and lichens, showed plainly that the lid had been removed to its present situation many years before. A stunted and doddered oak still spread its branches over the open and rude mausoleum, as if the Druid's badge and emblem, shattered and storm-broken, was still bending to offer its protection to the last remnants of their worship.

"This, then, is the Kist-vaen," said the shorter pilgrim; "and here we must abide tidings of our scout. But what, Philip Guarine, have we to expect as an explanation of the devastation which we have traversed?"

"Some incursion of the Welsh wolves, my lord," replied Guarine; "and, by Our Lady, here lies a poor Saxon sheep whom they have snapped up."

The Constable (for he was the pilgrim who had walked foremost) as he heard his squire speak, and saw the corpse of a man amongst the long grass; by which, indeed, it was so hidden, that he himself had passed without notice, what the esquire, in less abstracted mood, had not failed to observe. The leathern doublet of the slain bespoke him an English peasant—the body lay on its face, and the arrow which had caused his death still stuck in his back.

Philip Guarine, with the cool indifference of one accustomed to such scenes, drew the shaft from the man's back, as composedly as he would have removed it from the body of a deer. With similar indifference the Constable signed to his esquire to give him the arrow—looked at it with indolent curiosity, and then said, "Thou hast forgotten thy old craft, Guarine, when thou callest that a Welsh shaft. Trust me, it flew from a Norman bow; but why it should be found in the body of that English churl, I can ill guess."

"Some runaway serf, I would warrant—some mongrel cur, who had joined the Welsh pack of hounds," answered the esquire.

"It may be so," said the Constable; "but I rather augur some civil war among the Lords Marchers themselves. The Welsh, indeed, sweep the villages, and leave nothing behind them but blood and ashes, but here even castles seem to have been stormed and taken. May God send us good news of the Garde Doloureuse!"

"Amen!" replied his squire; "but if Renault Vidal brings it, 'twill be the first time he has proved a bird of good omen."

"Philip," said the Constable, "I have already told thee thou art a jealous-pated fool. How many times has Vidal shown his faith in doubt—his address in difficulty-his courage in battle-his patience under suffering?"

"It may be all very true, my lord," replied Guarine; "yet—but what avails to speak?—I own he has done you sometimes good service; but loath were I that your life or honour were at the mercy of Renault Vidal."

"In the name of all the saints, thou peevish and suspicious fool, what is it thou canst found upon to his prejudice?"

"Nothing, my lord," replied Guarine, "but instinctive suspicion and aversion. The child that, for the first time, sees a snake, knows nothing of its evil properties, yet he will not chase it and take it up as he would a butterfly. Such is my dislike of Vidal—I cannot help it. I could pardon the man his malicious and gloomy sidelong looks, when he thinks no one observes him; but his sneering laugh I cannot forgive—it is like the beast we heard of in Judea, who laughs, they say, before he tears and destroys."

"Philip," said De Lacy, "I am sorry for thee—sorry, from my soul, to see such a predominating and causeless jealousy occupy the brain of a gallant old soldier. Here, in this last misfortune, to recall no more ancient proofs of his fidelity, could he mean otherwise than well with us, when, thrown by shipwreck upon the coast of Wales, we would have been doomed to instant death, had the Cymri recognized in me the Constable of Chester, and in thee his trusty esquire, the executioner of his commands against the Welsh in so many instances?"

"I acknowledge," said Philip Guarine, "death had surely been our fortune, had not that man's ingenuity represented us as pilgrims, and, under that character, acted as our interpreter—and in that character he entirely precluded us from getting information from any one respecting the state of things here, which it behoved your lordship much to know, and which I must needs say looks gloomy and suspicious enough."

"Still art thou a fool, Guarine," said the Constable; "for, look you, had Vidal meant ill by us, why should he not have betrayed us to the Welsh, or suffered us, by showing such knowledge as thou and I may have of their gibberish, to betray ourselves?'

"Well, my lord," said Guarine, "I may be silenced, but not satisfied. All the fair words he can speak—all the fine tunes he can play—Renault Vidal will be to my eyes ever a dark and suspicious man, with features always ready to mould themselves into the fittest form to attract confidence; with a tongue framed to utter the most flattering and agreeable words at one time, and at another to play shrewd plainness or blunt honesty; and an eye which, when he thinks himself unobserved, contradicts every assumed expression of features, every protestation of honesty, and every word of courtesy or cordiality to which his tongue has given utterance. But I speak not more on the subject; only I am an old mastiff, of the true breed—I love my master, but cannot endure some of those whom he favours; and yonder, as I judge, comes Vidal, to give us such an account of our situation as it shall please him."

A horseman was indeed seen advancing in the path towards the Kist-vaen, with a hasty pace; and his dress, in which something of the Eastern fashion was manifest, with the fantastic attire usually worn by men of his profession, made the Constable aware that the minstrel, of whom they were speaking, was rapidly approaching them.

Although Hugo de Lacy rendered this attendant no more than what in justice he supposed his services demanded, when he vindicated him from the suspicions thrown out by Guarine, yet at the bottom of his heart he had sometimes shared those suspicions, and was often angry at himself, as a just and honest man, for censuring, on the slight testimony of looks, and sometimes casual expressions, a fidelity which seemed to be proved by many acts of zeal and integrity.

When Vidal approached and dismounted to make his obeisance, his master hasted to speak to him in words of favour, as if conscious he had been partly sharing Guarine's unjust judgment upon him, by even listening to it. "Welcome, my trusty Vidal," he said; "thou hast been the raven that fed us on the mountains of Wales, be now the dove that brings us good tidings from the Marches.—Thou art silent. What mean these downcast looks—that embarrassed carriage—that cap plucked down o'er thine eyes?—In God's name, man, speak!—Fear not for me—I can bear worse than tongue of man may tell. Thou hast seen me in the wars of Palestine, when my brave followers fell, man by man, around me, and when I was left well-nigh alone—and did I blench then?—Thou hast seen me when the ship's keel lay grating on the rock, and the billows flew in foam over her deck—did I blench then?—No—nor will I now."

"Boast not," said the minstrel, looking fixedly upon the Constable, as the former assumed the port and countenance of one who sets Fortune and her utmost malice at defiance—"boast not, lest thy bands be made strong." There was a pause of a minute, during which the group formed at this instant a singular picture.

Afraid to ask, yet ashamed to _seem to fear the ill tidings which impended, the Constable confronted his messenger with person erect, arms folded, and brow expanded with resolution: while the minstrel, carried beyond his usual and guarded apathy by the interest of the moment, bent on his master a keen fixed glance, as if to observe whether his courage was real or assumed.

Philip Guarine, on the other hand, to whom Heaven, in assigning him a rough exterior, had denied neither sense nor observation, kept his eye in turn, firmly fixed on Vidal, as if endeavouring to determine what was the character of that deep interest which gleamed in the minstrel's looks apparently, and was unable to ascertain whether it was that of a faithful domestic sympathetically agitated by the bad news with which he was about to afflict his master, or that of an executioner standing with his knife suspended over his victim, deferring his blow until he should discover where it would be most sensibly felt. In Guarine's mind, prejudiced, perhaps, by the previous opinion he had entertained, the latter sentiment so decidedly predominated, that he longed to raise his staff, and strike down to the earth the servant, who seemed thus to enjoy the protracted sufferings of their common master.

At length a convulsive movement crossed the brow of the Constable, and Guarine, when he beheld a sardonic smile begin to curl Vidal's lip, could keep silence no longer. "Vidal," he said, "thou art a—"

"A bearer of bad tidings," said Vidal, interrupting him, "therefore subject to the misconstruction of every fool who cannot distinguish between the author of harm, and him who unwillingly reports it."

"To what purpose this delay?" said the Constable. "Come, Sir Minstrel, I will spare you a pang—Eveline has forsaken and forgotten me?" The minstrel assented by a low inclination.

Hugo de Lacy paced a short turn before the stone monument, endeavouring to conquer the deep emotion which he felt. "I forgive her," he said. "Forgive, did I say—Alas! I have nothing to forgive. She used but the right I left in her hand —yes—our date of engagement was out—she had heard of my losses—my defeats—the destruction of my hopes—the expenditure of my wealth; and has taken the first opportunity which strict law afforded to break off her engagement with one bankrupt in fortune and fame. Many a maiden would have done—perhaps in prudence should have done— this;—but that woman's name should not have been Eveline Berenger."

He leaned on his esquire's arm, and for an instant laid his head on his shoulder with a depth of emotion which Guarine had never before seen him betray, and which, in awkward kindness, he could only attempt to console, by bidding his master "be of good courage—he had lost but a woman."

"This is no selfish emotion, Philip," said the Constable, resuming self-command. "I grieve less that she has left me, than that she has misjudged me —that she has treated me as the pawnbroker does his wretched creditor, who arrests the pledge as the very moment elapses within which it might have been relieved. Did she then think that I in my turn would have been a creditor so rigid?—that I, who, since I knew her, scarce deemed myself worthy of her when I had wealth and fame, should insist on her sharing my diminished and degraded fortunes? How little she ever knew me, or how selfish must she have supposed my misfortunes to have made me! But be it so—she is gone, and may she be happy. The thought that she disturbed me shall pass from my mind; and I will think she has done that which I myself, as her best friend, must in honour have advised."

So saying, his countenance, to the surprise of his attendants, resumed its usual firm composure.

"I give you joy," said the esquire, in a whisper to the minstrel; "your evil news have wounded less deeply than, doubtless, you believed was possible."

"Alas!" replied the minstrel, "I have others and worse behind." This answer was made in an equivocal tone of voice, corresponding to the peculiarity of his manner, and like that seeming emotion of a deep but very doubtful character.

"Eveline Berenger is then married," said the Constable; "and, let me make a wild guess,—she has not abandoned the family, though she has forsaken the individual—she is still a Lacy? ha?—Dolt that thou art, wilt thou not understand me? She is married to Damian de Lacy—to my nephew?"

The effort with which the Constable gave breath to this supposition formed a strange contrast to the constrained smile to which he compelled his features while he uttered it. With such a smile a man about to drink poison might name a health, as he put the fatal beverage to his lips. "No, my lord—not married," answered the minstrel, with an emphasis on the word, which the Constable knew how to interpret.

"No, no," he replied quickly, "not married, perhaps, but engaged- troth-plighted. Wherefore not? The date of her old alliance was out, why not enter into a new engagement?"

"The Lady Eveline and Sir Damian de Lacy are not affianced that I know of," answered his attendant.

This reply drove De Lacy's patience to extremity.

"Dog! dost thou trifle with me?" he exclaimed: "Vile wire-pincher, thou torturest me! Speak the worst at once, or I will presently make thee minstrel to the household of Satan."

Calm and collected did the minstrel reply,—"The Lady Eveline and Sir Damian are neither married nor affianced, my lord. They have loved and lived together—*par amours*."

"Dog, and son of a dog," said De Lacy, "thou liest!" And, seizing the minstrel by the breast, the exasperated baron shook him with his whole strength. But great as that strength was, it was unable to stagger Vidal, a practised wrestler, in the firm posture which he had assumed, any more than his master's wrath could disturb the composure of the minstrel's bearing.

"Confess thou hast lied," said the Constable, releasing him, after having effected by his violence no greater degree of agitation than the exertion of human force produces upon the Rocking Stones of the Druids, which may be shaken, indeed, but not displaced.

"Were a lie to buy my own life, yea, the lives of all my tribe," said the minstrel, "I would not tell one. But truth itself is ever termed falsehood when it counteracts the train of our passions."

"Hear him, Philip Guarine, hear him!" exclaimed the Constable, turning hastily to his squire: "He tells me of my disgrace—of the dishonour of my house—of the depravity of those whom I have loved the best in the world—he tells me of it with a calm look, an eye composed, an unfaltering tongue.—Is this—can it be natural? Is De Lacy sunk so low, that his dishonour shall be told by a common strolling minstrel, as calmly as if it were a theme for a vain ballad? Perhaps thou wilt make it one, ha!" as he concluded, darting a furious glance at the minstrel.

"Perhaps I might, my lord," replied the minstrel, "were it not that I must record therein the disgrace of Renault Vidal, who served a lord without either patience to bear insults and wrongs, or spirit to revenge them on the authors of his shame."

"Thou art right, thou art right, good fellow," said the Constable, hastily; "it is vengeance now alone which is left us—And yet upon whom?"

As he spoke he walked shortly and hastily to and fro; and, becoming suddenly silent, stood still and wrung his hands with deep emotion.

"I told thee," said the minstrel to Guarine, "that my muse would find a tender part at last. Dost thou remember the bull-fight we saw in Spain? A thousand little darts perplexed and annoyed the noble animal, ere he received the last deadly thrust from the lance of the Moorish Cavalier."

"Man, or fiend, be which thou wilt," replied Guarine, "that can thus drink in with pleasure, and contemplate at your ease, the misery of another, I bid thee beware of me! Utter thy cold-blooded taunts in some other ear; for if my tongue be blunt, I wear a sword that is sharp enough."

"Thou hast seen me amongst swords," answered the minstrel, "and knowest how little terror they have for such as I am." Yet as he spoke he drew off from the esquire. He had, in fact, only addressed him in that sort of fulness of heart, which would have vented itself in soliloquy if alone, and now poured itself out on the nearest auditor, without the speaker being entirely conscious of the sentiments which his speech excited.

Few minutes had elapsed before the Constable of Chester had regained the calm external semblance with which, until this last dreadful wound, he had borne all the inflictions of fortune. He turned towards his followers, and addressed the minstrel with his usual calmness, "Thou art right, good fellow," he said, "in what thou saidst to me but now, and I forgive thee the taunt which accompanied thy good counsel. Speak out, in God's name! and speak to one prepared to endure the evil which God hath sent him. Certes, a good knight is best known in battle, and a Christian in the time of trouble and adversity."

The tone in which the Constable spoke, seemed to produce a corresponding effect upon the deportment of his followers. The minstrel dropped at once the cynical and audacious tone in which he had hitherto seemed to tamper with the passions of his master; and in language simple and respectful, and which even approached to sympathy, informed him of the evil news which he had collected during his absence. It was indeed disastrous.

The refusal of the Lady Eveline Berengor to admit Monthermer and his forces into her castle, had of course given circulation and credence to all the calumnies which had been circulated to her prejudice, and that of Damian de Lacy; and there were many who, for various causes, were interested in spreading and supporting these slanders. A large force had been sent into the country to subdue the insurgent peasants; and the knights and nobles despatched for that purpose, failed not to avenge to the utter- most, upon the wretched plebeians, the noble blood which they had spilled during their temporary triumph.

The followers of the unfortunate Wenlock were infected with the same persuasion. Blamed by many for a hasty and cowardly surrender of a post which might have been defended, they endeavoured to vindicate themselves by alleging the hostile demonstrations of De Lacy's cavalry as the sole cause of their premature submission.

These rumours, supported by such interested testimony, spread wide and far through the land; and, joined to the undeniable fact that Damian had sought refuge in the strong castle of Garde Doloureuse, which was now defending itself against the royal arms, animated the numerous enemies of the house of De Lacy, and drove its vassals and friends almost to despair, as men reduced either to disown their feudal allegiance, or renounce that still more sacred fealty which they owed to their sovereign.

At this crisis they received intelligence that the wise and active monarch by whom the sceptre of England was then swayed, was moving towards that part of England, at the head of a large body of soldiers, for the purpose at once of pressing the siege of the Garde Doloureuse, and completing the suppression of the insurrection of the peasantry, which Guy Monthermer had nearly accomplished.

In this emergency, and when the friends and dependents of the House of Lacy scarcely knew which hand to turn to, Randal, the Constable's kinsman, and, after Damian, his heir, suddenly appeared amongst them, with a royal commission to raise and command such followers of the family as might not desire to be involved in the supposed treason of the Constable's delegate. In troublesome times, men's vices are forgotten, provided they display activity, courage, and prudence, the virtues then most required; and the appearance of Randal, who was by no means deficient in any of these attributes, was received as a good omen by the followers of his cousin. They quickly gathered around him, surrendered to the royal mandate such strongholds as they possessed, and, to vindicate themselves from any participation in the alleged crimes of Damian, they distinguished themselves, under Randal's command, against such scattered bodies of peasantry as still kept the field, or lurked in the mountains and passes; and conducted themselves with such severity after success, as made the troops even of Monthermer appear gentle and clement in comparison with those of De Lacy. Finally, with the banner of his ancient house displayed, and five hundred good men assembled under it, Randal appeared before the Garde Poloureuse, and joined Henry's camp there.

The castle was already hardly pressed, and the few defenders, disabled by wounds, watching, and privation, had now the additional discouragement to see displayed against their walls the only banner in England under which they had hoped forces might be mustered for their aid.

The high-spirited entreaties of Eveline, unbent by adversity and want, gradually lost effect on the defenders of the castle; and proposals for surrender were urged and discussed by a tumultuary council, into which not only the inferior officers, but many of the common men, had thrust themselves, as in a period of such general distress as unlooses all the bonds of discipline, and leaves each man at liberty to speak and act for himself. To their surprise, in the midst of their discussions, Damian de Lacy, arisen from the sick-bed to which he had been so long confined, appeared among them, pale and feeble, his cheek tinged with the ghastly look which is left by long illness—he leaned on his page Amelot. "Gentlemen," he said, "and soldiers—yet why should I call you either?—Gentlemen are ever ready to die in behalf of a lady— soldiers hold life in scorn compared to their honour."

"Out upon him! out upon him!" exclaimed some of the soldiers, interrupting him; "he would have us, who are innocent, die the death of traitors, and be hanged in our armour over the walls, rather than part with his leman."

"Peace, irreverent slave!" said Damian, in a voice like thunder, "or my last blow shall be a mean one, aimed against such a caitiff as thou art.—And you," he continued, addressing the rest,—"you, who are shrinking from the toils of your profession, because if you persist in a course of honour, death may close them a few years sooner than it needs must—you, who are scared like children at the sight of a death's-head, do not suppose that Damian de Lacy would desire to shelter himself at the expense of those lives which you hold so dear. Make your bargain with King Henry. Deliver me up to his justice, or his severity; or, if you like it better, strike my head from my body, and hurl it, as a peace- offering, from the walls of the castle. To God, in his good time, will I trust for the clearance of mine honour. In a word, surrender me, dead or alive, or open the gates and permit me to surrender myself. Only, as ye are men, since I may not say better of ye, care at least for the safety of your mistress, and make such terms as may secure HER safety, and save yourselves from the dishonour of being held cowardly and perjured caitiffs in your graves."

"Methinks the youth speaks well and reasonably," said William Flammock. "Let us e'en make a grace of surrendering his body up to the King, and assure thereby such terms as we can for ourselves and the lady, ere the last morsel of our provision is consumed."

"I would hardly have proposed this measure," said, or rather mumbled, Father Aldrovand, who had recently lost four of his front teeth by a stone from a sling,—"yet, being so generously offered by the party principally concerned, I hold with the learned scholiast, *Volenti non fit injuria*."

"Priest and Fleming," said the old banner-man, Ralph Genvil, "I see how the wind stirreth you; but you deceive yourselves if you think to make our young master, Sir Damian, a scape-goat for your light lady.—Nay, never frown nor fume, Sir Damian; if you know not your safest course, we know it for you.—Followers of De Lacy, throw yourselves on your horses, and two men on one, if it be necessary—we will take this stubborn boy in the midst of us, and the dainty squire Amelot shall be prisoner too, if he trouble us with his peevish opposition. Then, let us make a fair sally upon the siegers. Those who can cut their way through will shift well enough; those who fall, will be provided for."

A shout from the troopers of Lacy's band approved this proposal. Whilst the followers of Berenger expostulated in loud and angry tone, Eveline, summoned by the tumult, in vain endeavoured to appease it; and the anger and entreaties of Damian were equally lost on his followers. To each and either the answer was the same.

"Have you no care of it—Because you love *par amours*, is it reasonable you should throw away your life and ours?" So exclaimed Genvil to De Lacy; and in softer language, but with equal obstinacy, the followers of Raymond Berenger refused on the present occasion to listen, to the commands or prayers of his daughter.

Wilkin Flammock had retreated from the tumult, when he saw the turn which matters had taken. He left the castle by a sally-port, of which he had been intrusted with the key, and proceeded without observation or opposition to the royal camp, where he requested access to the Sovereign. This was easily obtained, and Wilkin speedily found himself in the presence of King Henry. The monarch was in his royal pavilion, attended by two of his sons, Richard and John, who afterwards swayed the sceptre of England with very different auspices.

"How now?—What art thou?" was the royal question.

"An honest man, from the castle of the Garde Doloureuse."

"Thou may'st be honest," replied the Sovereign, "but thou comest from a nest of traitors."

"Such as they are, my lord, it is my purpose to put them at your royal disposal; for they have no longer the wisdom to guide themselves, and lack alike prudence to hold out, and grace to submit. But I would first know of your grace to what terms you will admit the defenders of yonder garrison?"

"To such as kings give to traitors," said Henry, sternly—"sharp knives and tough cords."

"Nay, my gracious lord, you must be kinder than that amounts to, if the castle is to be rendered by my means; else will your cords and knives have only my poor body to work upon, and you will be as far as ever from the inside of the Garde Doloureuse."

The King looked at him fixedly. "Thou knowest," he said, "the law of arms. Here, provost-marshal, stands a traitor, and yonder stands a tree."

"And here is a throat," said the stout-hearted Fleming, unbuttoning the collar of his doublet.

"By mine honour," said Prince Richard, "a sturdy and faithful yeoman! It were better send such fellows their dinners, and then buffet it out with them for the castle, than to starve them as the beggarly Frenchmen famish their hounds."

"Peace, Richard," said his father; "thy wit is over green, and thy blood over hot, to make thee my counsellor here.—And you, knave, speak you some reasonable terms, and we will not be over strict with thee."

"First, then," said the Fleming, "I stipulate full and free pardon for life, limb, body, and goods, to me, Wilkin Flammock, and my daughter Rose."

"A true Fleming," said Prince John; "he takes care of himself in the first instance."

"His request," said the King, "is reasonable. What next?"

"Safety in life, honour, and land, for the demoiselle Eveline Berenger."

"How, sir knave!" said the King, angrily, "is it for such as thou to dictate to our judgment or clemency in the case of a noble Norman Lady? Confine thy mediation to such as thyself; or rather render us this castle without farther delay; and be assured thy doing so will be of more service to the traitors within, than weeks more of resistance, which must and shall be bootless."

The Fleming stood silent, unwilling to surrender without some specific terms, yet half convinced, from the situation in which he had left the garrison of the Garde Doloureuse, that his admitting the King's forces would be, perhaps, the best he could do for Lady Eveline.

"I like thy fidelity, fellow," said the King, whose acute eye perceived the struggle in the Fleming's bosom; "but carry not thy stubbornness too far. Have we not said we will be gracious to yonder offenders, as far as our royal duty will permit?"

"And, royal father," said Prince John, interposing, "I pray you let me have the grace to take first possession, of the Garde Doloureuse, and the wardship or forfeiture of the offending lady."

"*I* pray you also, my royal father, to grant John's boon," said his brother Richard, in a tone of mockery. "Consider, royal father, it is the first desire he hath shown to approach the barriers of the castle, though we have attacked them forty times at least. Marry, crossbow and mangonel were busy on the former occasions, and it is like they will be silent now."

"Peace, Richard," said the King; "your words, aimed at thy brother's honour, pierce my heart.—John, thou hast thy boon as concerns the castle; for the unhappy young lady, we will take her in our own charge.—Fleming, how many men wilt thou undertake to admit?"

Ere Flammock could answer, a squire approached Prince Richard, and whispered in his ear, yet so as to be heard by all present, "We have discovered that some internal disturbance, or other cause unknown, has withdrawn many of the warders from the castle walls, and that a sudden attack might—"

"Dost thou hear that, John?" exclaimed Richard. "Ladders, man—get ladders, and to the wall. How I should delight to see thee on the highest round—thy knees shaking—thy hands grasping convulsively, like those of one in an ague fit—all air around thee, save a baton or two of wood—the moat below—half-a-dozen pikes at thy throat—"

"Peace, Richard, for shame, if not for charity!" said his father, in a tone of anger, mingled with grief. "And thou, John, get ready for the assault."

"As soon as I have put on my armour, father," answered the Prince; and withdrew slowly, with a visage so blank as to promise no speed in his preparations.

His brother laughed as he retired, and said to his squire, "It were no bad jest, Alberick, to carry the place ere John can change his silk doublet for a steel one."

So saying, he hastily withdrew, and his father exclaimed in paternal distress, "Out, alas! as much too hot as his brother is too cold; but it is the manlier fault. —Gloucester," said he to that celebrated earl, "take sufficient strength, and follow Prince Richard to guard and sustain him. If any one can rule him, it must be a knight of thy established fame. Alas, alas! for what sin have I deserved the affliction of these cruel family feuds!"

"Be comforted, my lord," said the chancellor, who was also in attendance.

"Speak not of comfort to a father, whose sons are at discord with each other, and agree only in their disobedience to him!"

Thus spoke Henry the Second, than whom no wiser, or, generally speaking, more fortunate monarch ever sat upon the throne of England; yet whose life is a striking illustration, how family dissensions can tarnish the most brilliant lot to which Heaven permits humanity to aspire; and how little gratified ambition, extended power, and the highest reputation in war and in peace, can do towards curing the wounds of domestic affliction.

The sudden and fiery attack of Richard, who hastened to the escalade at the head of a score of followers, collected at random, had the complete effect of surprise; and having surmounted the walls with their ladders, before the contending parties within were almost aware of the assault, the assailants burst open the gates, and admitted Gloucester, who had hastily followed with a strong body of men-at-arms. The garrison, in their state of surprise, confusion, and disunion, offered but little resistance, and would have been put to the sword, and the place plundered, had not Henry himself entered it, and by his personal exertions and authority, restrained the excesses of the dissolute soldiery.

The King conducted himself, considering the times and the provocation, with laudable moderation. He contented himself with disarming and dismissing the common soldiers, giving them some trifle to carry them out of the country, lest want should lead them to form themselves into bands of robbers. The officers were more severely treated, being for the greater part thrown into dungeons, to abide the course of the law. In particular, imprisonment was the lot of Damian de Lacy, against whom, believing the various charges with which he was loaded, Henry was so highly incensed, that he purposed to make him an example to all false knights and disloyal subjects. To the Lady Eveline Berenger he assigned her own apartment as a prison, in which she was honourably attended by Rose and Alice, but guarded with the utmost strictness. It was generally reported that her demesnes would be declared a forfeiture to the crown, and bestowed, at least in part, upon Randal de Lacy, who had done good service during the siege. Her person, it was thought, was destined to the seclusion of some distant French nunnery, where she might at leisure repent her of her follies and her rashness.

Father Aldrovand was delivered up to the discipline of the convent, long experience having very effectually taught Henry the imprudence of infringing on the privileges of the church; although, when the King first beheld him with a rusty corslet clasped over his frock, he with difficulty repressed the desire to cause him to hanged over the battlements, to preach to the ravens.

With Wilkin Flammock, Henry held much conference, particularly on his subject of manufactures and commerce; on which the sound- headed, though blunt-spoken Fleming, was well qualified to instruct an intelligent monarch. "Thy intentions," he said, "shall not be forgotten, good fellow, though they have been anticipated by the headlong valour of my son Richard, which has cost some poor caitiffs their lives—Richard loves not to sheathe a bloodless weapon. But thou and thy countrymen shall return to thy mills yonder, with a full pardon for past offences, so that you meddle no more with such treasonable matters."

"And our privileges and duties, my liege?" said Flammock. "Your Majesty knows well we are vassals to the lord of this castle, and must follow him in battle."

"It shall no longer be so," said Henry; "I will form a community of Flemings here, and thou, Flammock, shalt be Mayor, that thou may'st not plead feudal obedience for a relapse into treason."

"Treason, my liege!" said Flammock, longing, yet scarce venturing, to 'interpose a word in behalf of Lady Eveline, for whom, despite the constitutional coolness of his temperament, he really felt much interest—"I would that your Grace but justly knew how many threads went to that woof."

"Peace, sirrah!—meddle with your loom," said Henry; "and if we deign to speak to thee concerning the mechanical arts which thou dost profess, take it for no warrant to intrude farther on our privacy."

The Fleming retired, rebuked, and in silence; and the fate of the unhappy prisoners remained in the King's bosom. He himself took up his lodging in the castle of the Garde Doloureuse, as a convenient station for sending abroad parties to suppress and extinguish all the embers of rebellion; and so active was Randal de Lacy on these occasions, that he appeared daily to rise in the King's grace, and was gratified with considerable grants out of the domains of Berenger and Lacy, which the King seemed already to treat as forfeited property. Most men considered this growing favour of Randal as a perilous omen, both far the life of young De Lacy, and for the fate of the unfortunate Eveline.

CHAPTER THE THIRTIETH

A vow, a vow—I have a vow in Heaven.
Shall I bring perjury upon my soul?
No, not for Venice.
  MERCHANT OF VENICE.

The conclusion of the last chapter contains the tidings with which the minstrel greeted his unhappy master, Hugo de Lacy; not indeed with the same detail of circumstances with which we have been able to invest the narrative, but so as to infer the general and appalling facts, that his betrothed bride, and beloved and trusted kinsman, had leagued together for his dishonour—had raised the banner of rebellion against their lawful sovereign, and, failing in their audacious attempt, had brought the life of one of them, at least, into the most imminent danger, and the fortunes of the House of Lacy, unless some instant remedy could be found, to the very verge of ruin.

Vidal marked the countenance of his master as he spoke, with the same keen observation which the chirurgeon gives to the progress of his dissecting-knife. There was grief on the Constable's features—deep grief—but without the expression of abasement or prostration which usually accompanies it; anger and shame were there—but they were both of a noble character, seemingly excited by his bride and nephew's transgressing the laws of allegiance, honour, and virtue, rather than by the disgrace and damage which he himself sustained through their crime.

The minstrel was so much astonished at this change of deportment, from the sensitive acuteness of agony which attended the beginning of his narrative, that he stepped back two paces, and gazing on the Constable with wonder, mixed with admiration, exclaimed, "We have heard of martyrs in. Palestine, but this exceeds them!"

"Wonder not so much, good friend," said the Constable, patiently; "it is the first blow of the lance or mace which pierces or stuns —those which follow are little felt."

"Think, my lord," said Vidal, "all is lost—love, dominion, high office, and bright fame—so late a chief among nobles, now a poor palmer!"

"Wouldst thou make sport with my misery?" said Hugo, sternly; "but even that comes of course behind my back, and why should it not be endured when said to my face?—Know, then, minstrel, and put it in song if you list, that Hugo de Lacy, having lost all he carried to Palestine, and all which he left at home, is still lord of his own mind; and adversity can no more shake him, than the breeze which strips the oak of its leaves can tear up the trunk by the roots."

"Now, by the tomb of my father," said the minstrel, rapturously, "this man's nobleness is too much for my resolve!" and stepping hastily to the Constable, he kneeled on one knee, and caught his hand more freely than the state maintained by men of De Lacy's rank usually permitted. "Here," said Vidal, "on this hand—this noble hand—I renounce—" But ere he could utter another word, Hugo de Lacy, who, perhaps, felt the freedom of the action as an intrusion on his fallen condition, pulled back his hand, and bid the minstrel, with as stern frown, arise, and remember that misfortune made not De Lacy a fit personage for a mummery.

Renault Vidal rose rebuked. "I had forgot," he said, "the distance between an Armorican violer and a high Norman baron. I thought that the same depth of sorrow, the same burst of joy, levelled, for a moment at least, those artificial barriers by which men are divided. But it is well as it is. Live within the limits of your rank, as heretofore within your donjon tower and your fosses, my lord, undisturbed by the sympathy of any mean man like me. I, too, have my duties to discharge."

"And now to the Garde Doloureuse," said the baron, turning to Philip Guarine —"God knoweth how well it deserveth the name!— there to learn, with our own eyes and ears, the truth of these woful tidings. Dismount, minstrel, and give me thy palfrey—I would, Guarine, that I had one for thee—as for Vidal, his attendance is less necessary. I will face my foes, or my misfortunes, like a man—that be assured of, violer; and look not so sullen, knave—I will not forget old adherents."

"One of them, at least, will not forget you, my lord," replied the minstrel, with his usual dubious tone of look and emphasis.

But just as the Constable was about to prick forwards, two persons appeared on the path, mounted on one horse, who, hidden by some dwarf-wood, had come very near them without being perceived. They were male and female; and the man, who rode foremost, was such a picture of famine, as the eyes of the pilgrims had scarce witnessed in all the wasted land through which they had travelled. His features, naturally sharp and thin, had disappeared almost entirely among the uncombed gray beard and hairs with which they were overshadowed; and it was but the glimpse of a long nose, that seemed as sharp as the edge of a knife, and the twinkling glimpse of his gray eyes, which gave any intimation of his lineaments. His leg, in the wide old boot which enclosed it, looked like the handle of a mop left by chance in a pail—his arms were about the thickness of riding-rods—and such parts of his person as were not concealed by the tatters of a huntsman's cassock, seemed rather the appendages of a mummy than a live man.

The female who sat behind this spectre exhibited also some symptoms of extenuation; but being a brave jolly dame naturally, famine had not been able to render her a spectacle so rueful as the anatomy behind which she rode. Dame Gillian's cheek (for it was the reader's old acquaintance) had indeed lost the rosy hue of good cheer, and the smoothness of complexion which art and easy living had formerly substituted for the more delicate bloom of youth; her eyes were sunken, and had lost much of their bold and roguish lustre; but she was still in some measure herself, and the remnants of former finery, together with the tight-drawn scarlet hose, though sorely faded, showed still a remnant of coquettish pretension.

So soon as she came within sight of the pilgrims, she began to punch Raoul with the end of her riding-rod. "Try thy new trade, man, since thou art unfit for any other—to the good man—to them —crave their charity."

"Beg from beggars?" muttered Raoul; "that were hawking at sparrows, dame."

"It will bring our hand in use though," said Gillian; and commenced, in a whining tone, "God love you, holy men, who have had the grace to go to the Holy Land, and, what is more, have had the grace to come back again; I pray, bestow some of your alms upon my poor old husband, who is a miserable object, as you see, and upon one who has the bad luck to be his wife—Heaven help me!"

"Peace, woman, and hear what I have to say," said the Constable, laying his hand upon the bridle of the horse—"I have present occasion for that horse, and ____"

"By the hunting-horn of St. Hubert, but thou gettest him not without blows!" answered the old huntsman "A fine world it is, when palmers turn horse-stealers."

"Peace, fellow" said the Constable, sternly,—"I say I have occasion presently for the service of thy horse. Here be two gold bezants for a day's use of the brute; it is well worth the fee-simple of him, were he never returned."

"But the palfrey is an old acquaintance, master," said Raoul; "and if perchance —"

"Out upon *if* and *perchance* both," said the dame, giving her husband so determined a thrust as well-nigh pushed him out of the saddle. "Off the horse! and thank God and this worthy man for the help he hath sent us in this extremity. What signifies the palfrey, when we have not enough to get food either for the brute or ourselves? not though we would eat grass and corn with him, like King Somebody, whom the good father used to read us to sleep about."

"A truce with your prating, dame," said Raoul, offering his assistance to help her from the croupe; but she preferred that of Guarine, who, though advanced in years, retained the advantage of his stout soldierly figure. "I humbly thank your goodness," said she, as, (having first kissed her,) the squire set her on the ground. "And, pray, sir, are ye come from the Holy Land?—Heard ye any tidings there of him that was Constable of Chester?"

De Lacy, who was engaged in removing the pillion from behind the saddle, stopped short in his task, and said, "Ha, dame! what would you with him?"

"A great deal, good palmer, an I could light on him; for his lands and offices are all to be given, it's like, to that false thief, his kinsman."

"What!—to Damian, his nephew?" exclaimed the Constable, in a harsh and hasty tone.

"Lord, how you startle me, sir!" said Gillian; then continued, turning to Philip

Guarine, "Your friend is a hasty man, belike.";

"It is the fault of the sun he has lived under so long," said the squire; "but look you answer his questions truly, and he will make it the better for you."

Gillian instantly took the hint. "Was it Damian de Lacy you asked after?—Alas I poor young gentleman! no offices or lands for him— more likely to have a gallows-cast, poor lad—and all for nought, as I am a true dame. Damian!—no, no, it is not Damian, or damson neither—but Randal Lacy, that must rule the roast, and have all the old man's lands, and livings, and lordships."

"What?" said the Constable—"before they know whether the old man. is dead or no?-Methinks that were against law and reason both."

"Ay, but Randal Lacy has brought about less likely matters. Look you, he hath sworn to the King that they have true tidings of the Constable's death—ay, and let him alone to make them soothfast enough, if the Constable were once within his danger."

"Indeed!" said the Constable. "But you are forging tales on a noble gentleman. Come, come, dame, you say this because you like not Randal Lacy."

"Like him not!—And what reason have I to like him, I trow?" answered Gillian. "Is it because he seduced my simplicity to let him into the castle of the Garde Doloureuse-ay, oftener than once or twice either,-when he was disguised as a pedlar, and told him all the secrets of the family, and how the boy Damian, and the girl Eveline, were dying of love with each other, but had not courage to say a word of it, for fear of the Constable, though he were a thousand miles off?-You seem concerned, worthy sir—may I offer your reverend worship a trifling sup from my bottle, which is sovereign for *tremor cordis*, and fits of the spleen?"

"No, no," ejaculated De Lacy—"I was but grieved with the shooting of an old wound. But, dame, I warrant me this Damian and Eveline, as you call them, became better, closer friends, in time?"

"They?—not they indeed, poor simpletons!" answered the dame; "they wanted some wise counsellor to go between and advise them. For, look you, sir, if old Hugo be dead, as is most like, it were more natural that his bride and his nephew should inherit his lands, than this same Randal who is but a distant kinsman, and a foresworn caitiff to boot.—Would you think it, reverend pilgrim, after the mountains of gold he promised me?—when the castle was taken, and he saw I could serve him no more, he called me old beldame, and spoke of the beadle and the cucking-stool.—Yes, reverend sir, old beldame and cucking-stool were his best words, when he knew I had no one to take my part, save old Raoul, who cannot take his own. But if grim old Hugh bring back his weatherbeaten carcass from Palestine, and have but half the devil in him which he had when he was fool enough to go away, Saint Mary, but I will do his kinsman's office to him!"

There was a pause when she had done speaking.

"Thou say'st," at length exclaimed the Constable, "that Damian de Lacy and Eveline love each other, yet are unconscious of guilt or falsehood, or ingratitude to me—I would say, to their relative in Palestine!"

"Love, sir!—in troth and so it is—they do love each other," said Gillian; "but it is like angels—or like lambs—or like fools, if you will; for they would never so much as have spoken together, but for a prank of that same Randal Lacy's."

"How!" demanded the Constable—"a prank of Randal's?—What motive had he that these two should meet?"

"Nay, their meeting was none of his seeking; but he had formed a plan to carry off the Lady Eveline himself, for he was a wild rover, this same Randal; and so he came disguised as a merchant of falcons, and trained out my old stupid Raoul, and the Lady Eveline, and all of us, as if to have an hour's mirth in hawking at the heron. But he had a band of Welsh kites in readiness to pounce upon us; and but for the sudden making in of Damian to our rescue, it is undescribable to think what might have come of us; and Damian being hurt in the onslaught, was carried to the Garde Doloureuse in mere necessity; and but to save his life, it is my belief my lady would never have asked him to cross the drawbridge, even if he had offered."

"Woman," said the Constable, "think what thou say'st! If thou hast done evil in these matters heretofore, as I suspect from thine own story, think not to put it right by a train of new falsehoods, merely from spite at missing thy reward."

"Palmer," said old Raoul, with his broken-toned voice, cracked by many a hollo, "I am wont to leave the business of tale-bearing to my wife Gillian, who will tongue-pad it with any shrew in Christendom. But thou speak'st like one having some interest in these matters, and therefore I will tell thee plainly, that although this woman has published her own shame in avowing her correspondence with that same Randal Lacy, yet what she has said is true as the gospel; and, were it my last word, I would say that Damian and the Lady Eveline are innocent of all treason and all dishonesty, as is the babe unborn.— But what avails what the like of us say, who are even driven to the very begging for mere support, after having lived at a good house, and in a good lord's service-blessing be with him!"

"But hark you," continued the Constable, "are there left no ancient servants of the House, that could speak out as well as you?" "Humph!" answered the huntsman—"men are not willing to babble when Randal Lacy is cracking his thong above their heads. Many are slain, or starved to death—some disposed of—some spirited away. But there are the weaver Flammock and his daughter Rose, who know as much of the matter as we do."

"What!—Wilkin Flammock the stout Netherlander?" said the Constable; "he and his blunt but true daughter Rose?—I will venture my life on their faith. Where dwell they?—What has been their lot amidst these changes?" "And in God's name who are you that ask these questions?" said Dame Gillian. "Husband, husband— we have been too free; there is something in that look and that tone which I should remember."

"Yes, look at me more fixedly," said the Constable, throwing "back the hood which had hitherto in some degree obscured his features.

"On your knees—on your knees, Raoul!" exclaimed Gillian, dropping on her own at the same time; "it is the Constable himself, and he has heard me call him old Hugh!"

"It is all that is left of him who was the Constable, at least," replied De Lacy; "and old Hugh willingly forgives your freedom, in consideration of your good news. Where are Flammock and his daughter?"

"Rose is with the Lady Eveline," said Dame Gillian; "her ladyship, belike, chose her for bower-woman in place of me, although Rose was never fit to attire so much as a Dutch doll."

"The faithful girl!" said the Constable. "And where is Flammock?"

"Oh, for him, he has pardon and favour from the King," said Raoul; "and is at his own house, with his rabble of weavers, close beside the Battle-bridge, as they now call the place where your lordship quelled the Welsh."

"Thither will I then," said the Constable; "and will then see what welcome King Henry of Anjou has for an old servant. You two must accompany me."

"My lord," said Gillian, with hesitation, "you know poor folk are little thanked for interference with great men's affairs. I trust your lordship will be able to protect us if we speak the truth; and that you will not look back with displeasure on what I did, acting for the best."

"Peace, dame, with a wanion to ye!" said Raoul. "Will you think of your own old sinful carcass, when you should be saving your sweet young mistress from shame and oppression?—And for thy ill tongue, and worse practices, his lordship knows they are bred in the bone of thee."

"Peace, good fellow!" said the Constable; "we will not look back on thy wife's errors, and your fidelity shall be rewarded.—For you, my faithful followers," he said, turning towards Guarine and Vidal, "when De Lacy shall receive his rights, of which he doubts nothing, his first wish shall be to reward your fidelity."

"Mine, such as it is, has been and shall be its own reward," said Vidal. "I will not accept favours from him in prosperity, who, in adversity, refused me his hand—our account stands yet open."

"Go to, thou art a fool; but thy profession hath a privilege to be humorous," said the Constable, whose weatherbeaten and homely features looked even handsome, when animated by gratitude to Heaven and benevolence towards mankind. "We will meet," he said, "at Battle-bridge, an hour before vespers—I shall have much achieved before that time."

"The space is short," said his esquire.

"I have won a battle in yet shorter," replied the Constable.

"In which," said the minstrel, "many a man has died that thought himself well assured of life and victory."

"Even so shall my dangerous cousin Randal find his schemes of ambition blighted," answered the Constable; and rode forwards, accompanied by Raoul and his wife, who had remounted their palfrey, while the minstrel and squire followed a-foot, and, of course, much more slowly.

CHAPTER THE THIRTY-FIRST

"Oh, fear not, fear not, good Lord John,
That I would you betray,
Or sue requital for a debt,
Which nature cannot pay.
Bear witness, all ye sacred powers—
Ye lights that 'gin to shine—
This night shall prove the sacred tie
That binds your faith and mine."
　　ANCIENT SCOTTISH BALLAD.

Left behind by their master, the two dependants of Hugh de Lacy marched on in sullen silence, like men who dislike and distrust each other, though bound to one common service, and partners, therefore, in the same hopes and fears. The dislike, indeed, was chiefly upon Guarine's side; for nothing could be more indifferent to Renault Vidal than was his companion, farther than as he was conscious that Philip loved him not, and was not unlikely, so far as lay in his power, to thwart some plans which he had nearly at heart. He took little notice of his companion, but hummed over to himself, as for the exercise of his memory, romances and songs, many of which were composed in languages which Guarine, who had only an ear for his native Norman, did not understand.

They had proceeded together in this sullen manner for nearly two hours, when they were met by a groom on horseback, leading a saddled palfrey. "Pilgrims," said the man, after looking at them with some attention, "which of you is called Philip Guarine?"

"I, for fault of a better," said the esquire, "reply to that name."

"Thy lord, in that case, commends him to you," said the groom; "and sends you this token, by which you shall know that I am his true messenger."

He showed the esquire a rosary, which Philip instantly recognized as that used by the Constable.

"I acknowledge the token," he said; "speak my master's pleasure."

"He bids me say," replied the rider, "that his visit thrives as well as is possible, and that this very evening, by time that the sun sets, he will be possessed of his own. He desires, therefore, you will mount this palfrey, and come with me to the Garde Doloureuse, as your presence would be wanted there."

"It is well, and I obey him," said the esquire, much pleased with the Import of the message, and not dissatisfied at being separated from his travelling companion.

"And what charge for me?" said the minstrel, addressing the messenger.

"If you, as I guess, are the minstrel, Renault Vidal, you are to abide your master at the Battle-bridge, according to the charge formerly given."

"I will meet him, as in duty bound," was Vidal's answer; and scarce was it uttered, ere the two horsemen, turning their backs on him, rode briskly forward, and were speedily out of sight.

It was now four hours past noon, and the sun was declining, yet there was more than three hours' space to the time of rendezvous, and the distance from the place did not now exceed four miles. Vidal, therefore, either for the sake of rest or reflection, withdrew from the path into a thicket on the left hand, from which gushed the waters of a streamlet, fed by a small fountain that bubbled up amongst the trees. Here the traveller sat himself down, and with an air which seemed unconscious of what he was doing, bent his eye on the little sparkling font for more than half an hour, without change of posture; so that he might, in Pagan times, have represented the statue of a water-god bending over his urn, and attentive only to the supplies which it was pouring forth. At length, however, he seemed to recall himself from this state of deep abstraction, drew himself up, and took some coarse food from his pilgrim's scrip, as if suddenly reminded that life is not supported without means. But he had probably something at his heart which affected his throat or appetite. After a vain attempt to swallow a morsel, he threw it from him in disgust, and applied him to a small flask, in which he had some wine or other liquor. But seemingly this also turned distasteful, for he threw from him both scrip and bottle, and, bending down to the spring, drank deeply of the pure element, bathed in it his hands and face, and arising from the fountain apparently refreshed, moved slowly on his way, singing as he went, but in a low and saddened tone, wild fragments of ancient poetry, in a tongue equally ancient.

Journeying on in this melancholy manner, he at length came in sight of the Battle-bridge; near to which arose, in proud and gloomy strength, the celebrated castle of the Garde Doloureuse. "Here, then," he said—"here, then, I am to await the proud De Lacy. Be it so, in God's name!—he shall know me better ere we part."

So saying, he strode, with long and resolved steps, across the bridge, and ascending a mound which arose on the opposite side at some distance, he gazed for a time upon the scene beneath—the beautiful river, rich with the reflected tints of the western sky— the trees, which were already brightened to the eye, and saddened to the fancy, with the hue of autumn—and the darksome walls and towers of the feudal castle, from which, at times, flashed a glimpse of splendour, as some sentinel's arms caught and gave back a transient ray of the setting sun.

The countenance of the minstrel, which had hitherto been dark and troubled, seemed softened by the quiet of the scene. He threw loose his pilgrim's dress, yet suffering part of its dark folds to hang around him mantle-wise; under which appeared his minstrel's tabard. He took from his side a *rote*, and striking, from time to time, a "Welsh descant, sung at others a lay, of which we can offer only a few fragments, literally translated from the ancient language in which they were chanted, premising that they are in that excursive symbolical style of poetry, which Taliessin, Llewarch Hen, and other bards, had derived perhaps from the time of the Druids.

"I asked of my harp, 'Who hath injured thy chords?'
And she replied, 'The crooked finger, which I mocked in my tune.'
A blade of silver may be bended—a blade of steel abideth—
Kindness fadeth away, but vengeance endureth.

"The sweet taste of mead passeth from the lips,
But they are long corroded by the juice of wormwood;
The lamb is brought to the shambles, but the wolf rangeth the mountain;
Kindness fadeth away, but vengeance endureth.

"I asked the red-hot iron, when it glimmered on the anvil,
'Wherefore glowest thou longer than the firebrand?'—
'I was born in the dark mine, and the brand in the pleasant greenwood.'
Kindness fadeth away, but vengeance endureth.

"I asked the green oak of the assembly, wherefore its boughs
  were dry and seared like the horns of the stag?
And it showed me that a small worm had gnawed its roots.
The boy who remembered the scourge, undid the wicket of the
  castle at midnight.
Kindness fadeth away, but vengeance endureth.

"Lightning destroyeth temples, though their spires pierce the clouds;
Storms destroy armadas, though their sails intercept the gale.
He that is in his glory falleth, and that by a contemptible enemy.
Kindness fadeth away, but vengeance endureth."

More of the same wild images were thrown out, each bearing some analogy, however fanciful and remote, to the theme, which occurred like a chorus at the close of each stanza; so that the poetry resembled a piece of music, which, after repeated excursions through fanciful variations, returns ever and anon to the simple melody which is the subject of ornament.

As the minstrel sung, his eyes were fixed on the bridge and its vicinity; but when, near the close of his chant, he raised up his eyes towards the distant towers of the Garde Doloureuse, he saw that the gates were opened, and that there was a mustering of guards and attendants without the barriers, as if some expedition were about to set forth, or some person of importance to appear on the scene. At the same time, glancing his eyes around, he discovered that the landscape, so solitary when he first took his seat on the gray stone from which he overlooked it, was now becoming filled with figures.

During his reverie, several persons, solitary and in groups, men, women, and children, had begun to assemble themselves on both sides of the river, and were loitering there, as if expecting some spectacle. There was also much bustling at the Fleming's mills, which, though at some distance, were also completely under his eye. A procession seemed to be arranging itself there, which soon began to move forward, with pipe and tabor, and various other instruments of music, and soon approached, in regular order, the place where Vidal was seated.

It appeared the business in hand was of a pacific character; for the gray-bearded old men of the little settlement, in their decent russet gowns, came first after the rustic band of music, walking in ranks of three and three, supported by their staves, and regulating the motion of the whole procession by their sober and staid pace. After these fathers of the settlement came Wilkin Flammock, mounted on his mighty war-horse, and in complete armor, save his head, like a vassal prepared to do military service for his lord. After him followed, and in battle rank, the flower of the little colony, consisting of thirty men, well armed and appointed, whose steady march, as well as their clean and glittering armour, showed steadiness and discipline, although they lacked alike the fiery glance of the French soldiery, or the look of dogged defiance which characterized the English, or the wild ecstatic impetuosity of eye which then distinguished the Welsh. The mothers and the maidens of the colony came next; then followed the children, with faces as chubby, and features as serious, and steps as grave as their parents; and last, as a rear-guard, came the youths from fourteen to twenty, armed with light lances, bows, and similar weapons becoming their age.

This procession wheeled around the base of the mound or embankment on which the minstrel was seated; crossed the bridge with the same slow and regular pace, and formed themselves into a double line, facing inwards, as if to receive some person of consequence, or witness some ceremonial. Flammock remained at the extremity of the avenue thus formed by his countrymen, and quietly, yet earnestly, engaged in making arrangements and preparations.

In the meanwhile, stragglers of different countries began to draw together, apparently brought there by mere curiosity, and formed a motley assemblage at the farther end of the bridge, which was that nearest to the castle. Two English peasants passed very near the stone on which Vidal sat—"Wilt thou sing us a song, minstrel," said one of them, "and here is a tester for thee?" throwing into his hat a small silver coin.

"I am under a vow," answered the minstrel, "and may not practise the gay science at present."

"Or you are too proud to play to English churls," said the elder peasant, "for thy tongue smacks of the Norman."

"Keep the coin, nevertheless," said the younger man. "Let the palmer have what the minstrel refuses to earn."

"I pray you reserve your bounty, kind friend," said Vidal, "I need it not;—and tell me of your kindness, instead, what matters are going forward here."

"Why, know you not that we have got our Constable de Lacy again, and that he is to grant solemn investiture to the Flemish weavers of all these fine things

Harry of Anjou has given?—Had Edward the Confessor been alive, to give the Netherland knaves their guerdon, it would have been a cast of the gallows-tree. But come, neighbour, we shall lose the show."

So saying, they pressed down the hill. Vidal fixed his eyes on the gates of the distant castle; and the distant waving of banners, and mustering of men on horseback, though imperfectly seen at such a distance, apprized him that one of note was about to set forth at the head of a considerable train of military attendants. Distant flourishes of trumpets, which came faintly yet distinctly on his ear, seemed to attest the same. Presently he perceived, by the dust which began to arise in columns betwixt the castle and the bridge, as well as by the nearer sound of the clarions, that the troop was advancing towards him in procession.

Vidal, on his own part, seemed as if irresolute whether to retain his present position, where he commanded a full but remote view of the whole scene, or to obtain a nearer but more partial one, by involving himself in the crowd which now closed around on either hand of the bridge, unless where the avenue was kept open by the armed and arrayed Flemings.

A monk next hurried past Vidal, and on his enquiring as formerly the cause of the assembly, answered, in a muttering tone, from beneath his hood, that it was the Constable de Lacy, who, as the first act of his authority, was then and there to deliver to the Flemings a royal charter of their immunities. "He is in haste to exercise his authority, methinks," said the minstrel.

"He that has just gotten a sword is impatient to draw it," replied the monk, who added more which the minstrel understood imperfectly; for Father Aldrovand had not recovered the injury which he had received during the siege.

Vidal, however, understood him to say, that he was to meet the Constable there, to beg his favourable intercession.

"I also will meet him," said Renault Vidal, rising suddenly from the stone which he occupied.

"Follow me, then," mumbled the priest; "the Flemings know me, and will let me forward."

But Father Aldrovand being in disgrace, his influence was not so potent as he had flattered himself; and both he and the minstrel were jostled to and fro in the crowd, and separated from each other.

Vidal, however, was recognized by the English peasants who had before spoke to him. "Canst thou do any jugglers' feats, minstrel?" said one. "Thou may'st earn a fair largess, for our Norman masters love *jonglerie*."

"I know but one," said Vidal, "and I will show it, if you will yield me some room."

They crowded a little off from him, and gave him time to throw aside his oonnet, bare his legs and knees, by stripping off the leathern buskins which swathed them, and retaining only his sandals. He then tied a parti-coloured handkerchief around his swarthy and sunburnt hair, and casting off his upper doublet, showed his brawny and nervous arms naked to the shoulder.

But while he amused those immediately about him with these preparations, a commotion and rush among the crowd, together with the close sound of trumpets, answered by all the Flemish instruments of music, as well as the shouts in Norman and English, of "Long live the gallant Constable!—Our Lady for the bold De Lacy!" announced that the Constable was close at hand.

Vidal made incredible exertions to approach the leader of the procession, whose morion, distinguished by its lofty plumes, and right hand holding his truncheon, or leading-staff, was all he could see, on account of the crowd of officers and armed men around him. At length his exertions prevailed, and he came within three yards of the Constable, who was then in a small circle which had been with difficulty kept clear for the purpose of the ceremonial of the day. His back was towards the minstrel, and he was in the act of bending from his horse to deliver the royal charter to Wilkin Flammock, who had knelt on one knee to receive it the more reverentially. His discharge of this duty occasioned the Constable to stoop so low that his plume seemed in the act of mixing with the flowing mane of his noble charger.

At this moment, Vidal threw himself, with singular agility, over the heads of the Flemings who guarded the circle; and, ere an eye could twinkle, his right knee was on the croupe of the Constable's horse—the grasp of his left hand on the collar of De Lacy's buff- coat; then, clinging to its prey like a tiger after its leap, he drew, in the same instant of time, a short, sharp dagger—and buried it in the back of the neck, just where the spine, which was severed by the stroke, serves to convey to the trunk of the human body the mysterious influences of the brain. The blow was struck with the utmost accuracy of aim and strength of arm. The unhappy horseman dropped from his saddle, without groan or struggle, like a bull in the amphitheatre, under the steel of the tauridor; and in the same saddle sat his murderer, brandishing the bloody poniard, and urging the horse to speed.

There was indeed a possibility of his having achieved his escape, so much were those around paralyzed for the moment by the suddenness and audacity of the enterprise; but Flammock's presence of mind did not forsake him—he seized the horse by the bridle, and, aided by those who wanted but an example, made the rider prisoner, bound his arms, and called aloud that he must be carried before King Henry. This proposal, uttered in Flammock's strong and decided tone of voice, silenced a thousand wild cries of murder and treason, which had arisen while the different and hostile natives, of which the crowd was composed, threw upon each other reciprocally the charge of treachery.

All the streams, however, now assembled in one channel, and poured with unanimous assent towards the Garde Doloureuse, excepting a few of the murdered nobleman's train, who remained to transport their master's body, in decent solemnity of mourning, from the spot which he had sought with so much pomp and triumph.

When Flammock reached the Garde Doloureuse, he was readily admitted with his prisoner, and with such witnesses as he had selected to prove the execution of the crime. To his request of an audience, he was answered, that the King had commanded that none should be admitted to him for some time; yet so singular were the tidings of the Constable's slaughter, that the captain of the guard ventured to interrupt Henry's privacy, in order to communicate that event; and returned with orders that Flammock and his prisoner should be instantly admitted to the royal apartment. Here they found Henry, attended by several persons, who stood respectfully behind the royal seat, in a darkened part of the room.

When Flammock entered, his large bulk and massive limbs were strangely contrasted with cheeks pale with horror at what he had just witnessed, and with awe at finding himself in the royal presence-chamber. Beside him stood his prisoner, undaunted by the situation in which he was placed. The blood of his victim, which had spirited from the wound, was visible on his bare limbs and his scanty garments; but particularly upon his brow and the handkerchief with which it was bound.

Henry gazed on him with a stern look, which the other not only endured without dismay, but seemed to return with a frown of defiance.

"Does no one know this caitiff?" said Henry, looking around him.

There was no immediate answer, until Philip Guarine, stepping from the group which stood behind the royal chair, said, though with hesitation, "So please you, my liege, but for the strange guise in which he is now arrayed, I should say there was a household minstrel of my master, by name Renault Vidal."

"Thou art deceived, Norman," replied the minstrel; "my menial place and base lineage were but assumed!—I am Cadwallon the Briton—Cadwallon of the Nine Lays—Cadwallon, the chief bard of Gwenwyn of Powys-land—and his avenger!"

As he uttered the last word, his looks encountered those of a palmer, who had gradually advanced from the recess in which the attendants were stationed, and now confronted him.

The Welshman's eyes looked eagerly ghastly, as if flying from their sockets, while he exclaimed, in a tone of surprise, mingled with horror, "Do the dead come before monarchs?—Or, if thou art alive, *whom* have I slain?—I dreamed not, surely, of that bound, and of that home-blow?—yet my victim, stands before me! Have I not slain the Constable of Chester?"

"Thou hast indeed slain the Constable," answered the King; "but know, Welshman, it was Randal de Lacy, on whom that charge was this morning conferred, by our belief of our loyal and faithful Hugh de Lacy's having been lost upon his return from the Holy Land, as the vessel in which ho had taken passage was reported to have suffered shipwreck. Thou hast cut short Randal's brief elevation but by a few hours; for to-morrow's sun would have again seen him without land or lordship."

The prisoner dropped his head on his bosom in evident despair. "I thought," he murmured, "that he had changed his slough, and come forth so glorious, all too soon. May the eyes drop out that were cheated with those baubles, a plumed cap and a lacquered baton!"

"I will take care, Welshman, thine eyes cheat thee not again," said the King, sternly; "before the night is an hour older, they shall be closed on all that is earthly."

"May I request of your nobleness," said the Constable, "that you will permit me to ask the unhappy man a few questions?"

"When I have demanded of him myself," said the King, "why he has dipt his hands in the blood of a noble Norman."

"Because he at whom I aimed my blow," said the Briton, his eye glancing fiercely from the King to De Lacy, and back, "had spilled the blood of the descendant of a thousand kings; to which his own gore, or thine, proud Count of Anjou, is but as the puddle of the highway to the silver fountain."

Henry's eye menaced the audacious speaker; but the King reined in his wrath when he beheld the imploring look of his servant.—"What wouldst thou ask of him?" he said; "be brief, for his time is short."

"So please you, my liege, I would but demand wherefore he has for years forborne to take the life he aimed at, when it was in his power—nay, when it must have been lost but for his seemingly faithful service?"

"Norman," said Cadwallon, "I will answer thee. When I first took upon me thy service, it was well my purpose to have slain thee that night. There stands the man," pointing to Philip Guarine, "to whose vigilance thou owedst thy safety."

"Indeed," said De Lacy, "I do remember some indications of such a purpose; but why didst thou forego it, when following opportunities put it in thy power?"

"When the slayer of my sovereign became God's soldier," answered Cadwallon, "and served his cause in Palestine, he was safe from my earthly vengeance."

"A wonderful forbearance on the part of a Welsh assassin!" said the King, scornfully.

"Ay," answered Cadwallon; "and which certain Christian princes have scarce attained to, who have never neglected the chance of pillage or conquest afforded by the absence of a rival in the Holy Crusade."

"Now, by the Holy Rood"—said Henry, on the point of bursting out, for the insult affected him peculiarly; but, suddenly stopping, he said, with an air of contempt, "To the gallows with the knave!"

"But one other question," said De Lacy, "Renault, or by whatever name thou art called. Ever since my return thou hast rendered me service inconsistent with thy stern resolution upon my life—thou didst aid me in my shipwreck— and didst guide me safely through Wales, where my name would have ensured my death; and all this after the crusade was accomplished?"

"I could explain thy doubt," said the bard, "but that it might be thought I was pleading for my life."

"Hesitate riot for that," said the King; "for were our Holy Father to Intercede for thee, his prayer were in vain."

"Well then," said the bard, "know the truth—I was too proud to permit either wave or Welshman to share in my revenge. Know also, what is perhaps Cadwallon's weakness—use and habit had divided my feelings towards De Lacy, between aversion and admiration. I still contemplated my revenge, but as something which I might never complete, and which seemed rather an image in the clouds, than an object to which I must one day draw near. And when I beheld thee," he said, turning to De Lacy, "this very day so determined, so sternly resolved, to bear thy impending fate like a man—that you seemed to me to resemble the last tower of a ruined palace, still holding its head to heaven, when its walls of splendour, and its bowers of delight, lay in desolation around—may I perish, I said to myself in secret, ere I perfect its ruin! Yes, De Lacy, then, even then—but some hours since—hadst thou accepted my proffered hand, I had served thee as never follower served master. You rejected it with scorn—and yet notwithstanding that insult, it required that I should have seen you, as I thought, trampling over the field in which you slew my master, in the full pride of Norman insolence, to animate my resolution to strike the blow, which, meant for you, has slain at least one of your usurping race.—I will answer no more questions—lead on to axe or gallows—it is indifferent to Cadwallon—my soul will soon be with my free and noble ancestry, and with my beloved and royal patron."

"My liege and prince," said De Lacy, bending his knee to Henry, "can you hear this, and refuse your ancient servant one request?— Spare this man!— Extinguish not such a light, because it is devious and wild."

"Rise, rise, De Lacy; and shame thee of thy petition," said the King "Thy kinsman's blood-the blood of a noble Norman, is on the Welshman's hands and brow. As I am crowned King, he shall die ere it is wiped off.—Here! have him to present execution!"

Cadwallon was instantly withdrawn under a guard. The Constable seemed, by action rather than words, to continue his intercession.

"Thou art mad, De Lacy—thou art mad, mine old and true friend, to urge me thus," said the King, compelling De Lacy to rise. "See'st thou not that my care in this matter is for thee?—This Randal, by largesses and promises, hath made many friends, who will not, perhaps, easily again be brought to your allegiance, returning as thou dost, diminished in power and wealth. Had he lived, we might have had hard work to deprive him entirely of the power which he had acquired. We thank the Welsh assassin who hath rid us of him; but his adherents would cry foul play were the murderer spared. When blood is paid for blood, all will be forgotten, and their loyalty will once more flow in its proper channel to thee, their lawful lord."

Hugo de Lacy arose from his knees, and endeavoured respectfully to combat the politic reasons of his wily sovereign, which he plainly saw were resorted to less for his sake than with the prudent purpose of effecting the change of feudal authority, with the |east possible trouble to the country or Sovereign.

Henry listened to De Lacy's arguments patiently, and combated them with temper, until the death-drum began—to beat, and the castle bell to toll. He then led De Lacy to the window; on which, for it was now dark, a strong ruddy light began to gleam from without. A body of men-at-arms, each holding in his hand a blazing torch, were returning along the terrace from the execution of the wild but high-soul'd Briton, with cries of "Long live King Henry! and so perish all enemies of the gentle Norman men!"

CONCLUSION

A sun hath set-a star hath risen,
O, Geraldine! since arms of thine
Have been the lovely lady's prison.
  COLERIDGE.

Popular fame had erred in assigning to Eveline Berenger, after the capture of her castle, any confinement more severe than that of her aunt the Lady Abbess of the Cistertians' convent afforded. Yet that was severe enough; for maiden aunts, whether abbesses or no, are not tolerant of the species of errors of which Eveline was accused; and the innocent damosel was brought in many ways to eat her bread in shame of countenance and bitterness of heart. Every day of her confinement was rendered less and less endurable by taunts, in the various forms of sympathy, consolation, and exhortation; but which, stript of their assumed forms, were undisguised anger and insult. The company of Rose was all which Eveline had to sustain her under these inflictions, and that was at length withdrawn on the very morning when so many important events took place at the Garde Doloureuse.

The unfortunate young lady inquired in vain of a grim-faced nun. who appeared in Rose's place to assist her to dress, why her companion and friend was debarred attendance. The nun observed on that score an obstinate silence, but threw out many hints on the importance attached to the vain ornaments of a frail child of clay, and on the hardship that even a spouse of Heaven was compelled to divert her thoughts from her higher duties, and condescend to fasten clasps and adjust veils.

The Lady Abbess, however, told her niece after matins, that her attendant had not been withdrawn from her for a space only, but was likely to be shut up in a house of the severest profession, for having afforded her mistress assistance in receiving Damian de Lacy into her sleeping apartment at the castle of Baldringham.

A soldier of De Lacy's band, who had hitherto kept what he had observed a secret, being off his post that night, had now in Damian's disgrace found he might benefit himself by telling the story. This new blow, so unexpected, so afflictive—this new charge, which it was so difficult to explain, and so impossible utterly to deny, seemed to Eveline to seal Damian's fate and her own; while the thought that she had involved in ruin her single- hearted and high-soul'd attendant, was all that had been wanting to produce a state which approached to the apathy of despair. "Think of me what you will," she said to her aunt, "I will no longer defend myself—say what you will, I will no longer reply— carry me where you will, I will no longer resist—God will, in his good time, clear my fame—may he forgive my persecutors!"

After this, and during several hours of that unhappy day, the Lady Eveline, pale, cold, silent, glided from chapel to refectory, from refectory to chapel again, at the slightest beck of the Abbess or her official sisters, and seemed to regard the various privations, penances, admonitions, and repreaches, of which she, in the course of that day, was subjected to an extraordinary share, no more than a marble statue minds the inclemency of the external air, or the rain-drops which fall upon it, though they must in time waste and consume it.

The Abbess, who loved her niece, although her affection showed itself often in a vexatious manner, became at length alarmed— countermanded her orders for removing Eveline to an inferior cell— attended herself to see her laid in bed, (in which, as in every thing else, the young lady seemed entirely passive,) and, with something like reviving tenderness, kissed and blessed her on leaving the apartment. Slight as the mark of kindness was, it was unexpected, and, like the rod of Moses, opened the hidden fountains of waters. Eveline wept, a resource which had been that day denied to her—she prayed—and, finally, sobbed herself to sleep, like an infant, with a mind somewhat tranquillized by having given way to this tide of natural emotion.

She awoke more than once in the night to recall mingled and gloomy dreams of cells and of castles, of funerals and of bridals, of coronets and of racks and gibbets; but towards morning she fell into sleep more sound than she had hitherto enjoyed, and her visions partook of its soothing character. The Lady of the Garde Doloureuse seemed to smile on her amid her dreams, and to promise her votaress protection. The shade of her father was there also; and with the boldness of a dreamer, she saw the paternal resemblance with awe, but without fear: his lips moved, and she heard words-their import she did not fully comprehend, save that they spoke of hope, consolation, and approaching happiness. There also glided in, with bright blue eyes fixed upon hers, dressed in a tunic of saffron-coloured silk, with a mantle of cerulean blue of antique fashion, the form of a female, resplendent in that delicate species of beauty which attends the fairest complexion. It was, she thought, the Britoness Vanda; but her countenance was no longer resentful—her long yellow hair flew not loose on her shoulders, but was mysteriously braided with oak and mistletoe; above all, her right hand was gracefully disposed of under her mantle; and it was an unmutilated, unspotted, and beautifully formed hand which crossed the brow of Eveline. Yet, under these assurances of favour, a thrill of fear passed over her as the vision seemed to repeat, or chant,

"Widow'd wife and wedded maid,
Betrothed, betrayer, and betray'd,
All is done that has been said;

Vanda's wrong has been wroken—
Take her pardon by this token."

She bent down, as if to kiss Eveline, who started at that instant, and then awoke. Her hand was indeed gently pressed, by one as pure and white as her own. The blue eyes and fair hair of a lovely female face, with half-veiled bosom and dishevelled locks, flitted through her vision, and indeed its lips approached to those of the lovely sleeper at the moment of her awakening; but it was Rose in whose arms her mistress found herself pressed, and who moistened her face with tears, as in a passion of affection she covered it with kisses.

"What means this, Rose?" said Eveline; "thank God, you are restored to me!— But what mean these bursts of weeping?"

"Let me weep—let me weep," said Rose; "it is long since I have wept for joy, and long, I trust, it will be ere I again weep for sorrow. News are come on the spur from the Garde Doloureuse— Amelot has brought them—he is at liberty —so is his master, and in high favour with Henry. Hear yet more, but let me not tell it too hastily—You grow pale."

"No, no," said Eveline; "go on—go on—I think I understand you—I think I do."

"The villain Randal de Lacy, the master-mover of all our sorrows, will plague you no more; he was slain by an honest Welshman, and grieved am I that they have hanged the poor man for his good service. Above all, the stout old Constable is himself returned from Palestine, as worthy, and somewhat wiser, than he was; for it is thought he will renounce his con-tract with your ladyship."

"Silly girl," said Eveline, crimsoning as high as she had been before pale, "jest not amidst such a tale.—But can this be reality?—Is Randal indeed slain?— and the Constable returned?"

These were hasty and hurried questions, answered as hastily and confusedly, and broken with ejaculations of surprise and thanks to Heaven, and to Our Lady, until the ecstasy of delight sobered down into a sort of tranquil wonder.

Meanwhile Damian Lacy also had his explanations to receive, and the mode in which they were conveyed had something remarkable. Damian had for some time been the inhabitant of what our age would have termed a dungeon, but which, in the ancient days, they called a prison. We are perhaps censurable in making the dwelling and the food of acknowledged and convicted guilt more comfortable and palatable than what the parties could have gained by any exertions when at large, and supporting themselves by honest labour; but this is a venial error compared to that of our ancestors, who, considering a charge and a conviction as synonymous, treated the accused before sentence in a manner which would have been of itself a severe punishment after he was found guilty. Damian, therefore, notwithstanding his high birth and distinguished rank, was confined after the manner of the most atrocious criminal, was heavily fettered, fed on the coarsest food, and experienced only this alleviation, that he was permitted to indulge his misery in a solitary and separate cell, the wretched furniture of which was a mean bedstead, and a broken table and chair. A coffin—and his own arms and initials were painted upon it—stood in one corner, to remind him of his approaching fate; and a crucifix was placed in another, to intimate to him that there was a world beyond that which must soon close upon him. No noise could penetrate into the iron silence of his prison—no rumour, either touching his own fate or that of his friends. Charged with being taken in open arms against the King, he was subject to military law, and to be put to death even without the formality of a hearing; and he foresaw no milder conclusion to his imprisonment.

This melancholy dwelling had been the abode of Damian for nearly a month, when, strange as it may seem, his health, which had suffered much from his wounds, began gradually to improve, either benefited by the abstemious diet to which he was reduced, or that certainty, however melancholy, is an evil better endured by many constitutions than the feverish contrast betwixt passion and duty. But the term of his imprisonment seemed drawing speedily to a close; his jailer, a sullen Saxon of the lowest order, in more words than he had yet used to him, warned him to look to a speedy change of dwelling; and the tone in which he spoke convinced the prisoner there was no time to be lost. He demanded a confessor, and the jailer, though he withdrew without reply, seemed to intimate by his manner that the boon would be granted.

Next morning, at an unusually early hour, the chains and bolts of the cell were heard to clash and groan, and Damian was startled from a broken sleep, which he had not enjoyed for above two hours. His eyes were bent on the slowly opening door, as if he had expected the headsman and his assistants; but the jailer ushered in a stout man in a pilgrim's habit. "Is it a priest whom you bring me, warden?" said the unhappy prisoner.

"He can best answer the question himself," said the surly official, and presently withdrew.

The pilgrim remained standing on the floor, with his back to the small window, or rather loophole, by which the cell was imperfectly lighted, and gazed intently upon. Damian, who was seated oil the side of his bed; his pale cheek and dishevelled hair bearing a melancholy correspondence to his heavy irons. He returned the pilgrim's gaze, but the imperfect light only showed him that his visiter was a stout old man, who wore the scallop- shell on his bonnet, as a token that he had passed the sea, and carried a palm branch in his hand, to show he had visited the Holy Land.

"Benedictine, reverend father," said the unhappy young man; "are you a priest come to unburden my conscience?"

"I am not a priest," replied the Palmer, "but one who brings you news of discomfort."

"You bring them to one to whom comfort has been long a stranger, and to a place which perchance never knew it," replied Damian.

"I may be the bolder in my communication," said the Palmer; "those in sorrow will better hear ill news than those whom they surprise in the possession of content and happiness."

"Yet even the situation of the wretched," said Damian, "can be rendered more wretched by suspense. I pray you, reverend sir, to speak the worst at once—if you come to announce the doom of this poor frame, may God be gracious to the spirit which must be violently dismissed from it!"

"I have no such charge," said the Palmer. "I come from the Holy Laud, and have the more grief in finding you thus, because my message to you was one addressed to a free man, and a wealthy one."

"For my freedom," said Damian, "let these fetters speak, and this apartment for my wealth.—But speak out thy news—should my uncle —for I fear thy tale regards him—want either my arm or my fortune, this dungeon and my degradation have farther pangs than I had yet supposed, as they render me unable to aid him."

"Your uncle, young man," said the Palmer, "is prisoner, I should rather say slave, to the great Soldan, taken in a battle in which he did his duty, though unable to avert the defeat of the Christians, with which it was concluded. He was made prisoner while covering the retreat, but not until he had slain with his own hand, for his misfortune as it has proved, Hassan Ali, a favourite of the Soldan. The cruel pagan has caused the worthy knight to be loaded with irons heavier than those you wear, and the dungeon to which he is confined would make this seem a palace. The infidel's first resolution was to put the valiant Constable to the most dreadful death which his tormentors could devise. But fame told him that Hugo de Lacy was a man of great power and wealth; and he has demanded a ransom of ten thousand bezants of gold. Your uncle replied that the payment would totally impoverish him, and oblige him to dispose of his whole estates; even then he pleaded, time must be allowed him to convert them into money. The Soldan replied, that it imported little to him whether a hound like the Constable were fat or lean, and that he therefore insisted upon the full amount of the ransom. But he so far relaxed as to make it payable in three portions, on condition that, along with the first portion of the price, the nearest of kin and heir of De Lacy must be placed in his hands as a hostage for what remained due. On these conditions he consented your uncle should be put at liberty so soon as you arrive in Palestine with the gold."

"Now may I indeed call myself unhappy," said Damian, "that I cannot show my love and duty to my noble uncle, who hath ever been a father to me in my orphan state."

"It will be a heavy disappointment, doubtless, to the Constable," said the Palmer, "because he was eager to return to this happy country, to fulfil a contract of marriage which he had formed with a lady of great beauty and fortune."

Damian shrunk together in such sort that his fetters clashed, but he made no answer.

"Were he not your uncle," continued the Pilgrim, "and well known as a wise man, I should think he is not quite prudent in this matter. Whatever he was before he left England, two summers spent in the wars of Palestine, and another amid the tortures and restraints of a heathen prison, have made him a sorry bridegroom."

"Peace, pilgrim," said De Lacy, with a commanding tone. "It is not thy part to censure such a noble knight as my uncle, nor is it meet that I should listen to your strictures."

"I crave your pardon, young man," said the Palmer. "I spoke not without some view to your interest, which, methinks, does not so well consort with thine uncle having an heir of his body."

"Peace, base man!" said Damian. "By Heaven, I think worse of my cell than I did before, since its doors opened to such a counsellor, and of my chains, since they restrain me from chastising him.—Depart, I pray thee."

"Not till I have your answer for your uncle," answered the Palmer. "My age scorns the anger of thy youth, as the rock despises the foam of the rivulet dashed against it."

"Then, say to my uncle," answered Damian, "I am a prisoner, or I would have come to him—I am a confiscated beggar, or I would have sent him my all."

"Such virtuous purposes are easily and boldly announced," said the Palmer, "when he who speaks them knows that he cannot be called upon, to make good the boast of his tongue. But could I tell thee of thy restoration to freedom and wealth, I trow thou wouldst consider twice ere thy act confirmed the sacrifice thou hast in thy present state promised so glibly."

"Leave me, I prithee, old man," said Damian; "thy thought cannot comprehend the tenor of mine—go, and add not to my distress insults which I have not the means to avenge."

"But what if I had it in my power to place thee in the situation of a free and wealthy man, would it please thee then to be reminded of thy present boast? for if not, thou may'st rely on my discretion never to mention the difference of sentiment between Damian bound and Damian at liberty."

"How meanest thou?-or hast thou any meaning, save to torment me?" said the youth.

"Not so," replied the old Palmer, plucking from his bosom, a parchment scroll to which a heavy seal was attached.—"Know that thy cousin Randal hath been strangely slain, and his treacheries towards the Constable and thee as strangely discovered. The King, in requital of thy sufferings, hath sent thee this full pardon, and endowed thee with a third part of those ample estates, which, by his death, revert to the crown."

"And hath the King also restored my freedom and my right of blood?" exclaimed Damian.

"From this moment, forthwith," said the Palmer—"look upon the parchment—behold the royal hand and seal."

"I must have better proof.—Here," he exclaimed, loudly clashing his irons at the same time, "Here, thou Dogget-warder, son of a Saxon wolfhound!"

The Palmer, striking on the door, seconded the previous exertions for summoning the jailer, who entered accordingly.

"Warder," said Damian de Lacy, in a stern tone, "am I yet thy prisoner, or no?"

The sullen jailer consulted the Palmer by a look, and then answered to Damian that he was a free man.

"Then, death of thy heart, slave," said Damian, impatiently, "why hang these fetters on the free limbs of a Norman noble? each moment they con-fine him are worth a lifetime of bondage to such a serf as thou!"

"They are soon rid of, Sir Damian," said the man; "and I pray you to take some patience, when you remember that ten minutes since you had little right to think these bracelets would have been removed for any other purpose than your progress to the scaffold."

"Peace, ban-dog," said Damian, "and be speedy;—And thou, who hast brought me these good tidings, I forgive thy former bearing—thou thoughtest, doubtless, that it was prudent to extort from me professions during my bondage which might in honour decide my conduct when at large. The suspicion inferred in it was somewhat offensive, but thy motive was to ensure my uncle's liberty."

"And it is really your purpose," said the Palmer, "to employ your newly-gained freedom in a voyage to Syria, and to exchange your English prison for the dungeon of the Soldan?"

"If thou thyself wilt act as my guide," answered the undaunted youth, "you shall not say I dally by the way."

"And the ransom," said the Palmer, "how is that to be provided?"

"How, but from the estates, which, nominally restored to me, remain in truth and justice my uncle's, and must be applied to his use in the first instance? If I mistake not greatly, there is not a Jew or Lombard who would not advance the necessary sums on such security.—Therefore, dog," he continued, addressing the jailer, "hasten thy unclenching and undoing of rivets, and be not dainty of giving me a little pain, so thou break no limb, for I cannot afford to be stayed on my journey."

The Palmer looked on a little while, as if surprised at Damian's determination, then exclaimed, "I can keep the old man's secret no longer—such high-souled generosity must not be sacrificed.—Hark thee, brave Sir Damian, I have a mighty secret still to impart, and as this Saxon churl understands no French, this is no unfit opportunity to communicate it. Know that thine uncle is a changed man in mind, as he is debilitated and broken down in body. Peevishness and jealousy have possessed themselves of a heart which was once strong and generous; his life is now on the dregs, and I grieve to speak it, these dregs are foul and bitter."

"Is this thy mighty secret?" said Damian. "That men grow old, I know; and if with infirmity of body comes infirmity of temper and mind, their case the more strongly claims the dutiful observance of those who are bound to them in blood or affection."

"Ay," replied the Pilgrim, "but the Constable's mind has been poisoned against thee by rumours which have reached his ear from England, that there have been thoughts of affection betwixt thee and his betrothed bride, Eveline Berenger.—Ha! have I touched you now?"

"Not a whit," said Damian, putting on the strongest resolution with which his virtue could supply him—"it was but this fellow who struck my shin-bone somewhat sharply with his hammer. Proceed. My uncle heard such a report, and believed it?"

"He did," said the Palmer—"I can well aver it, since he concealed no thought from me. But he prayed me carefully to hide his suspicions from you, 'otherwise,' said he, 'the young wolf-cub will never thrust himself into the trap for the deliverance of the old he-wolf. Were he once in my prison-house,' your uncle continued to speak of you, 'he should rot and die ere I sent one penny of ransom to set at liberty the lover of my betrothed bride.'"

"Could this be my uncle's sincere purpose?" said Damian, all aghast. "Could he plan so much treachery towards me as to leave me in the captivity into which I threw myself for his redemption?— Tush! it cannot be."

"Flatter not yourself with such a vain opinion," said the Palmer— "if you go to Syria, you go to eternal captivity, while your uncle returns to possession of wealth little diminished—and of Eveline Berenger."

"Ha!" ejaculated Damian; and looking down for an instant, demanded of the Palmer, in a subdued voice, what he would have him do in such an extremity.

"The case is plain, according to my poor judgment," replied the Palmer. "No one is bound to faith with those who mean to observe none with him. Anticipate this treachery of your uncle, and let his now short and infirm existence moulder out in the pestiferous cell to which he would condemn your youthful strength. The royal grant has assigned you lands enough for your honourable support; and wherefore not unite with them those of the Garde Doloureuse?— Eveline Berenger, if I do not greatly mistake, will scarcely say nay. Ay, more—I vouch it on my soul that she will say yes, for I have sure information of her mind; and for her precontract, a word from Henry to his Holiness, now that they are in the heyday of their reconciliation, will obliterate the name Hugh from the parchment, and insert Damian in its stead."

"Now, by my faith," said Damian, arising and placing his foot upon the stool, that the warder might more easily strike off the last ring by which he was encumbered,—"I have heard of such things as this—I have heard of beings who, with seeming gravity of word and aspect—with subtle counsels, artfully applied to the frailties of human nature—have haunted the cells of despairing men, and made them many a fair promise, if they would but exchange for their by-ways the paths of salvation. Such are the fiend's dearest agents, and in such a guise hath the fiend himself been known to appear. In the name of God, old man, if human thou art, begone!—I like not thy words or thy presence—I spit at thy counsels. And mark me," he added, with a menacing gesture, "Look to thine own safety —I shall presently be at liberty!"

"Boy," replied the Palmer, folding his arms contemptuously in his cloak, "I scorn thy menaces—I leave thee not till we know each other better!"

"I too," said Damian, "would fain know whether thou be'st man or fiend; and now for the trial!" As he spoke, the last shackle fell from his leg, and clashed on the pavement, and at the same moment he sprung on the Palmer, caught him by the waist, and exclaimed, as he made three distinct and separate attempts to lift him up, and dash him headlong to the earth, "This for maligning a nobleman—this for doubting the honour of a knight—and this (with a yet more violent exertion) for belying a lady!"

Each effort of Damian seemed equal to have rooted up a tree; yet though they staggered the old man, they overthrew him not; and while Damian panted with his last exertion, he replied, "And take this, for so roughly entreating thy father's brother."

As he spoke, Damian de Lacy, the best youthful wrestler in Cheshire, received no soft fall on the floor of the dungeon. He arose slowly and astounded; but the Palmer had now thrown back both hood and dalmatique, and the features, though bearing marks of age and climate, were those of his uncle the Constable, who calmly observed, "I think, Damian, thou art become stronger, or I weaker, since my breast was last pressed against yours in our country's celebrated sport. Thou hadst nigh had me down in that last turn, but that I knew the old De Lacy's back-trip as well as thou.—But wherefore kneel, man?" He raised him with much kindness, kissed his cheek, and proceeded; "Think not, my dearest nephew, that I meant in my late disguise to try your faith, which I myself never doubted. But evil tongues had been busy, and it was this which made me resolve on an experiment, the result of which has been, as I expected, most honourable for you. And know, (for these walls have sometimes ears, even according to the letter,) there are ears and eyes not far distant which have heard and seen the whole. Marry, I wish though, thy last hug had not been so severe a one. My ribs still feel the impression of thy knuckles."

"Dearest and honoured uncle," said Damian—"excuse——"

"There is nothing to excuse," replied his uncle, interrupting him. "Have we not wrestled a turn before now?—But there remains yet one trial for thee to go through—Get thee out of this hole speedily—don thy best array to accompany me to the Church at noon; for, Damian, thou must be present at the marriage of the Lady Eveline Berenger."

This proposal at once struck to the earth the unhappy young man. "For mercy's sake," he exclaimed, "hold me excused in this, my gracious uncle!—I have been of late severely wounded, and am very weak."

"As my bones can testify," said his uncle. "Why, man, thou hast the strength of a Norway bear."

"Passion," answered Damian, "might give me strength for a moment; but, dearest uncle, ask any thing of me rather than this. Methinks, if I have been faulty, some other punishment might suffice."

"I tell thee," said the Constable, "thy presence is necessary— indispensably necessary. Strange reports have been abroad, which thy absence on this occasion would go far to confirm, Eveline's character and mine own are concerned in this."

"If so," said Damian, "if it be indeed so, no task will be too hard for me. But I trust, when the ceremony is over, you will not refuse me your consent to take the cross, unless you should prefer my joining the troops destined, as I heard, for the conquest of Ireland."

"Ay, ay," said the Constable; "if Eveline grant you permission, I will not withhold mine."

"Uncle," said Damian, somewhat sternly, "you do not know the feelings which you jest with."

"Nay," said the Constable, "I compel nothing; for if thou goest to the church, and likest not the match, thou may'st put a stop to it if thou wilt—the sacrament cannot proceed without the bridegroom's consent."

"I understand you not, uncle," said Damian; "you have already consented."

"Yes, Damian," he said, "I have—to withdraw my claim, and to relinquish it in thy favour; for if Eveline Berenger is wedded to-day, thou art her bridegroom! The Church has given her sanction— the King his approbation—the lady says not nay—and the question only now remains, whether the bridegroom will say yes."

The nature of the answer may be easily conceived; nor is it necessary to dwell upon the splendour of the ceremonial, which, to atone for his late unmerited severity, Henry honoured with his own presence. Amelot and Rose were shortly afterwards united, old Flammock having been previously created a gentleman of coat armour, that the gentle Norman blood might without utter derogation, mingle with the meaner stream that coloured the cheek with crimson, and meandered in azure over the lovely neck and bosom of the fair Fleming. There was nothing in the manner of the Constable towards his nephew and his bride, which could infer a regret of the generous self-denial which he had exercised in favour of their youthful passion. But he soon after accepted a high command in the troops destined to invade Ireland; and his name is found amongst the highest in the roll of the chivalrous Normans who first united that fair island to the English crown.

Eveline, restored to her own fair castle and domains, failed not to provide for her Confessor, as well as for her old soldiers, servants, and retainers, forgetting their errors, and remembering their fidelity. The Confessor was restored to the flesh-pots of Egypt, more congenial to his habits than the meagre fare of his convent. Even Gillian had the means of subsistence, since to punish her would have been to distress the faithful Raoul. They quarrelled for the future part of their lives in plenty, just as they had formerly quarrelled in poverty; for wrangling curs will fight over a banquet as fiercely as over a bare bone. Raoul died first, and Gillian having lost her whetstone, found that as her youthful looks decayed her wit turned somewhat blunt. She therefore prudently commenced devotee, and spent hours in long panegyrics on her departed husband.

The only serious cause of vexation which I can trace the Lady Eveline having been tried with, arose from a visit of her Saxon relative, made with much form, but, unfortunately, at the very time which the Lady Abbess had selected for that same purpose. The discord which arose between these honoured personages was of a double character, for they were Norman and Saxon, and, moreover, differed in opinion concerning the time of holding Easter. This, however, was but a slight gale to disturb the general serenity of Eveline; for with her unhoped-for union with Damian, ended the trials and sorrows of THE BETROTHED.

Milton Keynes UK
Ingram Content Group UK Ltd.
UKHW051600260524
443160UK00012B/524

9 781835 527573